JULI

Dear Reader,

Writing my first novel, *Marlena,* meant submerging myself in a lot of unprocessed grief. Writing *Famous Men* meant submerging myself in a lot of unprocessed anger.

I grew up with many siblings in small-town Michigan, a conservative-leaning area where we did things like save extra breakfast sausage for the boys, even the youngest ones. There, I learned all the lessons of a 1990s/2000s American girlhood: If your skirt's too short you're asking for it, your physical flaws are personal failings, boys can't help the things they do. I thought I'd left all that behind when I left home, but it turns out the old patterns were so baked into my way of being I couldn't tell where they ended and I began.

I started this book—about a young woman who falls into a boundary-blurring entanglement with an older, famous writer—fresh off the first phase of #MeToo's anger, as I began to unpack so many of the complicated experiences from my early adulthood. Laughing about having to leave the door open in certain professors' offices. Not being sure whether the dream was to become one of the Jonathans happily ruling the literary world or get them to pat me on the head. The time, on tour overseas for my first book, a photographer suggested we do the photos in my hotel room for a change of scene, and I mutely followed him up the stairs. I wanted to trace all the ways the male gaze can warp a young woman's sense of self from her very earliest memories.

At every turn, I tried to write into what I couldn't make sense of, steering toward sticky questions about consent and coercion, and how the answers might change from person to person, or generation to generation. What do we make of women who participate, with seeming free will, in dynamics with men that limit or harm them? What is the line between victimhood and agency, especially when a very young woman is concerned? When does a woman stop being "very young"? What if she's poor? Smart? Wants it and then changes her mind? Doesn't recognize that she's allowed to want something different, or something more? What if she's a fan?

My favorite books are the ones that provoke and unsettle—that force me to challenge my assumptions, that submerge me in the lives of characters who feel like they exist beyond the boundaries of the page, who fill me with rage and sympathy, grief and hope. My greatest ambition for *Famous Men* is that it sparks conversation, exchanges of real stories; that it looks out at the world and offers readers a nuanced truth. I am so grateful to you for reading it, and I can't wait to hear what you think.

Thank you for all you do for books and readers.

Yours,
Julie

BY JULIE BUNTIN

Famous Men

Marlena

FAMOUS MEN

FAMOUS MEN

A NOVEL

JULIE BUNTIN

RANDOM HOUSE
NEW YORK

Random House
An imprint and division of Penguin Random House LLC
1745 Broadway, New York, NY 10019
randomhousebooks.com
penguinrandomhouse.com

["Dedication" by Czeslaw Milosz permission TK]

Hardcover ISBN 9780593229958
Ebook ISBN 9780593229965

Printed in the United States of America on acid-free paper

2 4 6 8 9 7 5 3 1

$PrintCode

First Edition

BOOK TEAM: Production editor: Evan Camfield • Managing editor: Rebecca Berlant • Production manager: Sandra Sjursen • Copy editor: [Name] • Proofreaders: [Names]

Book design by Susan Turner

The authorized representative in the EU for product safety and compliance is Penguin Random House Ireland, Morrison Chambers, 32 Nassau Street, Dublin D02 YH68, Ireland. https://eu-contact.penguin.ie

[dedication TK]

Fathers are like blocks of marble—giant cubes, highly polished, with veins and seams, placed squarely in your path. They block your path. They cannot be climbed over, neither can they be slithered past. . . .

Donald Barthelme, "Manual for Sons"

Do you feel ashamed when you hear my name?

Phoebe Bridgers, "Scott Street"

FAMOUS MEN

I

A FACT

He doesn't remember me, but I know who he is. I met the biographer at a party Nathaniel took me to about a year after I arrived in New York, a literary fundraiser at one of those apartments where the elevator opens right into the living room. "Wilhelmina, this good man wants to write about me," Nathaniel said. "Your assignment tonight is to persuade him of a better idea."

A tray of miniature hamburgers floated by, and the biographer grabbed one and ate it looking down at my feet. He was squarely middle-aged, with a saddish face and damp-looking skin that suggested an indoor life. He followed us from the bar to the bookshelves and back again as Nathaniel drifted through the crowd greeting people. Nathaniel, as I recall, was kind but distracted, and probably irritated by how I hovered at his elbow, laughing a beat late at every joke. I was too new to that scene to talk to anyone without them addressing me first. And who would? I was, what, twenty-four, conspicuously younger than every other guest. For months, I'd wanted Nathaniel to bring me along to one of his obligations, as he called them—but when I got there, I found it sterile and frightening. All those long-haired women with their stylish glasses, the men, like the biographer, looking at me in that furtive, knowing way, like I was something—a dollar bill, or a pen—Nathaniel might drop for them to pick up.

"I'm going to do it, you know," the biographer said, grabbing another tiny hamburger. "Write that book." On the mantel above the fireplace—a fireplace, in a penthouse!—the hosts grinned from a photo, bookended by Bill and Hillary Clinton.

"The definitive biography! Get in line," I said, taking a sip of wine. I'd never heard anything from anyone about a biography, but amplifying Nathaniel's importance seemed a key task in my vague job description, along with maintaining the orderliness of his sock drawer and always being available for a daytime trip to the movie theater.

"To think he wanted to be an actor," the biographer said. "Can you imagine?" Nathaniel was already a few steps away, making a quarter he kept in his suit pocket for this purpose appear and disappear behind an elderly woman's ear.

"Nathaniel as an actor?" I said. "Of course I can."

"I mean a world where he never wrote his books."

In those early days I could be disarmed by the performative fandom of Nathaniel's readers. They were contributing to a different conversation, a secret one about influence and loyalty and status that underpinned the one happening on the surface. I hadn't learned to hear it yet. "No, I can't," I agreed. And wasn't it true? Nathaniel's books had made this world for me. They'd been the doorway, and now here I was, on the inside.

At the time of the party, the biographer had not yet written a single biography. I had written many poems, but not yet anything Nathaniel liked. Nathaniel had written six collections of poetry, two screenplays, four literary novels, one essay collection. A book of food writing; a pocket-sized collection of aphoristic wisdoms about the weather that sold better than all the poetry books combined. A bestselling memoir that had been adapted into a movie; a gritty, out-of-character romance that had been adapted into an even more famous movie.

Lili had not yet written the piece that would change all our lives.

I took a hamburger, too, and ate it looking into the biographer's eyes. A piece of bun fell straight out of my mouth. The biographer watched it fall and then stepped on it, as if to hide my bad manners from both of us. In those days, especially in Nathaniel's settings, I was mostly quiet and accommodating. But sometimes an urge to be distasteful would overtake me. I didn't know how to explain these urges to myself—or to Nathaniel, when he noticed—and they were always followed by an effervescent, almost pleasurable burst of shame. After I finished the burger, I wiped my fingers on my thigh, blushing.

The biographer got to talking about his apartment in Williamsburg, a neighborhood being gentrified into oblivion. In five, six years, he said, living on Graham Avenue would be like living in a juice bar. 2017 seemed as far away to me as Michigan. When he asked, I said I was living in Manhattan, and then I changed the subject. I was living in Nathaniel's spare room. I was Nathaniel's spare girl. Assistant, I told him, in response to the biographer's precisely executed question about my relationship to Nathaniel. Literary assistant.

The sun had set. The cityscape through the windows was like a starry night from the future, galactic and buzzing. Over by the bar, Nathaniel gave me the signal for let's split, the one we'd planned on the walk over—a finger gun raised to his head. But then a woman in a long dress grabbed his arm and he turned toward her, taking the drink she offered. I tried not to look disappointed.

"Stop touching your hair," the biographer said. We'd been trapped together all evening, two shy losers.

"What?"

"When you talk, you touch your hair over and over." He made an effeminate swooping motion; it took a beat to recognize he was showing me myself. "It makes you seem insecure about your face." He reached out and paused my hand. I was startled to find he was right—his hand and mine were in my hair now, almost cupping my face. There was something funny about this intimacy and I laughed without meaning to, but when the biographer didn't join, I stopped, a bit afraid. He brought my hand down slowly, as if I couldn't be trusted to do it myself. When my arm was safely by my side, he wrapped his fingers around my wrist, measuring its perimeter, and then squeezed my hand.

"That's it," he said. "Relax." I tried not to move my arm. Adjusting my hair would prove a point, but I couldn't guarantee he would interpret the action as rebellion, instead of more involuntary female idiocy. So I pretended I had no arm, no hand at all. When my hair drifted into my face, I blew it away like a horse, wishing I were a different sort of woman.

Oh, the relief when Nathaniel appeared beside the biographer with my purse. The thing about living in New York City was that no matter how bad an event was, when you left, you were still in New York City. Down on the street, I skipped, I was so happy, and that made Nathaniel laugh. "Never take me to another party again," I said, and we shook on it.

"Shall we run back?" he asked. I didn't think he was serious, but he took off, his jacket winging as he weaved between clusters of people on the sidewalk. They cursed at him, jumped aside, stared in wonder at the gray-haired man galloping in his dress shoes. Within a minute he had a block on me, but then—I was just drunk enough for this—I kicked my kitten heels off and held them in one hand as I ran. The city under my feet had an animal's warm, breathing give, scaled with glass and bottle caps and still-burning cigarettes. I caught Nathaniel by the coat and only then did he slow. I was sweating; he was not. We got dollar slices a block from Nathaniel's apartment, licking oil off our fingers as we made fun of the way the biographer stuck to my side, afraid to be seen in that room standing alone. "I can only imagine the questions he'd ask," Nathaniel said. "What was your mother like?" He started in on his crust. My heels were bleeding, but I couldn't feel it yet. I loved him very much.

Now, the first line of the biographer's email: *I don't think we've met.* Outside the window of my temporary office, everything is gray—gray leaves, gray sky, gray sidewalk, the students walking in pairs and trios toward the cafeteria, which hulks grayly on the horizon. It's been almost five years since that awful party; Nathaniel is due to arrive in Rosendale in a matter of days, for a reading I couldn't manage to get canceled. *I am writing the authorized biography of Nathaniel Fellow,* writes the biographer. Authorized! Was it possible Nathaniel had agreed? Worry churns in my gut at the thought, and I try to ignore it. Not my problem anymore. *I was told you knew him well,* the biographer writes. *Would you be open to a brief interview?*

Maybe he's just being polite, but the email is worded stiffly, a modification of a form. This happens to me often. I was a pretty girl in a city full of pretty girls. Easy to forget.

If you want to write fiction, Nathaniel said, start with as many real details as possible. His women were mostly based on women he'd known. His men were mostly based on him. Versions of him, he said. One can sort of throw one's voice. The writer's job, first and foremost, is to make what they are lying about feel true. We were on a blanket in Sheep Meadow when he told me this, finding shapes in the clouds, a game I'd never played, not even in childhood. And then, once the thing is written, change it up just enough so the person you've stolen from doesn't recognize themselves. Elephant, he said. The Mackinac Bridge! The clouds floated into new shapes. A strawberry burst in my mouth.

The biographer probably wouldn't think to ask me about Nathaniel as a teacher—he'd ask his verifiable former students, if he could get any of them to answer.

Another one of Nathaniel's rules: If you need the past to tell a story, you're telling the wrong story. When I started writing fiction, he handed all my stories back with the first three or four pages cut. I learned he did this to most of his students. He'd skim the first few pages, scanning for something interesting, and then write: *Start here.* Almost always, the second drafts were improvements.

I know where he'd start our story. His office, late August, New York City. A woman, opening the door. I'd read scenes like it so many times; when he called for me to come in, looked up from his desk, it wasn't him I saw, not exactly, but him seeing *me.* The moment, as I lived it, played through his eyes: the girl with her long hair down, lipstick an endearing bid to look older, bare legs shiny with lotion. A heavy bag of books, the pretense for this meeting, slipping off her shoulder, tugging the strap of her cheap dress with it.

I'll begin our story much earlier than he would, and with a fact. Nathaniel didn't know I existed until I made him learn my name.

II

GRIST

1

My mother, three months pregnant and not yet showing, follows the director of facilities around on his tour of Rosendale Academy's cafeteria. Warren, he calls it, as if it's a restaurant, a destination. And for my mother, twenty-two years old, it is. They stand in a walk-in freezer, the ceiling bristling with frost. When she hears the salary, she says that'll work for me, no, I don't need any time to think about it, shakes his hand. She knows about Rosendale's six weeks of maternity leave, the pension plan offered to even the lowliest workers. When my mother talks about her past, she starts it in that freezer, as if she emerged blinking into the world in the middle of Rosendale's campus and on the cusp of her second trimester. Me already, secretly there, but otherwise alone.

Rosendale Academy is a kind of finishing school for teenagers from around the world who show exceptional early talent in the arts. The annual tuition is shocking. Campus is on the outskirts of a northern Michigan resort town called Quincy, full of boutique hotels and stuffy restaurants that cater to visiting parents and tourists. Our house was in Greening, forty minutes away in good weather. Sometimes parents of scholarship kids would stay in Greening's Super 8; you could tell them by their bumper stickers supporting liberal causes and candidates and, during parents' weekend, by their insufficient coats. Otherwise, Greening, an hour's drive from Lake Michigan, wasn't much of an attraction, except for the occasional eccentric interested in the birthplace of Nathaniel Fellow, Pulitzer winner, "genius grant" recipient, great American writer. Nathaniel considers himself, above all, a poet, though it's the prose you'll know, the memoir or the novels. Or maybe the poorly reviewed movie, its first bleary hour shot in a replica of his childhood home, located in real life less than a mile from my own. The movie star transformed into Janet Fellow, face roughened with makeup until she bore a squinting resemblance to the stooped woman dragging her cart through the aisles of Save A Lot. Every Greening kid knew Nathaniel's story. There was a framed photo of him at Greening Public Library, right behind the checkout desk, and in the high school library, too—the one from a two-page spread in *Vanity Fair,* Nathaniel forty-two and in a navy suit, staring wryly at the field of text on the lefthand page. It meant something, that one of our own sons had alchemized the unceasing snow and unemployed hours, the skinned deer hoof-strung in the garage, the raw-eyed fathers and their identical boys, all the messy, shameful stuff of our lives, into art, into beauty. He'd shared our secrets, sure, but in doing so he'd demanded the world acknowledge us, and for that, in Greening, he was legend.

The two of us share a birth month, October, and maybe even an exact location (Munson Health, the only hospital for sixty miles). I was born too late for us to be classmates, friends, whatever. For me to influence him, instead of the other way around. A town like ours, population 1,943 and dwindling every year, only gets one success story per generation; that's what my ninth-grade English teacher said when he taught an excerpt from Nathaniel's memoir, looking around at our yawning faces as if one of us might have that special thing, a fire in our belly that would turn us to history.

To travel from Greening, through Quincy, and into Rosendale is an act of magic. In summer, I go to work with my mother—money too tight for a weekday babysitter, no older siblings to help, my grandparents long dead. My dad our household's unsolved mystery. From our dire, weedy street we wind through downtown (pie shop, bar, video store, hunting supplier, bar), across the rusted bridge, and into a sea of trees that thins as I swivel the radio dial, slices of blue appearing between the trunks. And then the sparkling lake, crowned by the soaring bronze dome of the amphitheater. Rosendale. When I'm little, four, five, Mom tells me to sit in the dry pantry while she sautés onions for the industrial-sized vat of chili and gives me a bag of brand-new coloring books. When I'm tall enough, I stand cutely on a bucket and tong brownies onto administrators' plates. They ask indulgent questions, tell me they like my braid. At ten, eleven, twelve, I break down boxes and stack them by the dumpsters, check quantities of canned tomatoes and canola oil, tidy the mess people make of the salad bar. No one clucks over me; I'm lumpy those years, with scabbed knees and greasy hair. The phrase *thank you* makes me blush. On the drive home, the magic of Rosendale undoes itself, the coach turned back into a pumpkin, life reduced and returned to me as my own. By the time we reach our front door, it's always night.

As a teenager, I take so long emptying the silverware bins, cutting lemons, Mom tells me to buzz off. Then I'm free to roam the golden campus, empty except for the twelve-month staff my mother cooks for. Most of the buildings are unlocked for maintenance. I bang the practice room pianos, tease "Twinkle, Twinkle, Little Star" from an out-of-tune guitar. From the catwalk in the black box theater, I look down at the tape left on the stage where the stars stood, waiting for the curtain to rise. In the upper girls' residence, I doze on bottom bunks, the plastic mattress sticking to my legs, pretending I'm a soprano destined for Juilliard. I trace the initials hacked into the bed frame, follow the curve of heart after heart with my fingertip. I know this place better than any of them, the ones who left their marks. Brilliant teenagers from around the world with their violin hickeys and perfect turnout and award-winning poems. Nathaniel Fellow himself was once a student. They only belong to Rosendale nine months a year, for four years, tops—they know it when the paint is fresh, when the doors open without creaking, the cobwebs swept from the eaves of the dorm rooms wherever they dream whatever kids like them dream. What's that compared to an entire life of secret summers? Nobody sees a place more clearly than someone who isn't supposed to be there.

Rosendale was the best part of my life, the thing that made me special to myself, but I didn't know how to explain it. When my closest friend—Theresa, with her milky smell and that gray front tooth—asked what I did there all summer, I said activities. Arts stuff.

"So, it's like camp?"

I had no idea what people at camp did, but I told her yes. It might have been like camp for the real Rosendale students, those kids I entirely imagined, and I felt closer to them, somehow, than to the students at my own school, a low, pigeon-colored building surrounded by cornfields. On warm days, the air reeked of manure, and the shop boys, who'd walked sleepily through the halls all winter, sprang to life, competing to unclip the most bras. One would hold a girl by the shoulders as she shrieked, laughing, while the other got to work behind her back. They undid mine a lot. The other girls looked on with nervous envy as my breasts spilled dolefully from my bra. I covered my nipples with my hands, lifting my breasts up and together on instinct. I didn't shriek, but I did laugh. What else was I supposed to do? It was treated as a kind of embarrassing honor to be picked—even the teachers grinned as they shook their heads, told the boys to knock it off.

Well before I found Nathaniel, I was loyal to my Rosendale summers, ignored the invites on the answering machine, Theresa's suggestions of a girls' day at the lake. I'd had the tiniest, loneliest taste, those days soaking up Rosendale's offseason pleasures, but it was proof something better was out there, if only I could figure out how to reach it.

2

I remember everything about the day I found him.

Not Nathaniel Fellow, commemorated on the Greening town water fountain, author of the only books in my house that weren't the Bible; son of Janet Fellow, the scowling lady who sat in the front row at church. I'm talking about Nathaniel the poet. The voice that would tell me where to go, the person who got me, as they say, into all this mess.

The school year had just ended. I was fourteen, a summer away from starting at Greening High, drifting around Rosendale as the staff cleaned up the fingerprints the students had left all over campus. That day, for no reason I can remember, I was shooting small branches with a lighter gun in a clearing behind the chapel, arranging them, lit up, into shapes on the packed dirt.

"I smelled burning," said Tray, one of the groundskeepers, new that year and always *around*. "The heck you doing?" He said it with a kind of mock aggression, as if he were trying to scare me, but only a little.

"Nothing," I said. "Just playing."

Tray was a confusing person, not just because he seemed to appear wherever I was, but also because he was younger than the rest of the staff, early twenties, maybe. Big veiny muscles, blond hair on the edge of brown. A hottie, to use Theresa's word; good-looking, to use my mother's. His T-shirt and jeans made him seem like he wasn't a real employee. He carried nothing, no tool or workbag, but was covered in sweat, his smell something you could pick up and hold. "Play somewhere else," he said, scuffing out my tiny fire. "You're gonna burn down the whole friggin' school."

"Is this, like, hide-and-seek? I go somewhere, you find me, tell me to go away, just so you can find me again?" He seemed closer in spirit to the boys at my school than to a real adult, so I talked to him the way I would a male peer: sarcasm to make me seem older, performative indifference to communicate I did not care about his attention or his hotness.

"You wish, little girl," he said, stepping toward me and yanking the lighter gun from my hand. "Should I go show this to your mama?" He pointed it at my chest, pulling the trigger. An orange flame licked out.

"Whatever," I said, and left, leaving the lighter with him. I passed the boys' dorms, the auditorium, and then the textile arts building, a triangle of moldering planks that looked condemned. That was basically the end of campus except for a grassy open space where students kicked around a soccer ball, a barn perched at its northernmost corner. The woods bordering the field were littered with empty liquor bottles and condom wrappers and lost winter hats. Here and there you'd stumble across a brick shoe box of a house—residences for visiting artists, dark and spiderwebby, with hotplates and single beds, not even half as nice as the dorms.

Mom hadn't mentioned construction during the school year, but even from a distance, I could tell the barn had changed. All my childhood it had seemed of a piece with the landscape, weathered red paint, as natural there as a tree. Now it vibrated with purpose, sunlight reflecting off the new second-floor windows. A sign near the front path read: THE GRYCE WRITING LODGE. Creative writing had long been an afterthought at Rosendale, a catchall for kids whose parents could pay full tuition. Later, I'd learn an alum had left the writing program so much money it suddenly had the highest endowment of any department. I could taste the new white paint as I approached the glass doors. I expected them to be locked—the building looked too special to be left unattended like the rest of campus. But they opened easily into the cool, cavernous atrium, columns of sun shooting down from the skylights, the refinished wide-planked floors the only remnant of the old building. That teenagers should be the beneficiaries of such a place, creatures who were, technically, the same species as the shop boys, as Theresa, as me—envy clawed at my heart, and with it, the arrival of a hot little question: Why them? Why couldn't I have this, too?

In the main room hung large portraits of writers, all with some connection to Rosendale. Men, except for an old woman holding a gardening spade, and all of them white. I recognized one. I'd seen it a million times before—it was the photo from the checkout at Greening Public Library. Nathaniel Fellow. I stepped closer. The image was blown up, half my size, so my eyes were nearly parallel to Nathaniel's feet. Between pant hem and sock lip, a flash of ankle, obscured by the faintest thatch of hair—a detail that made him suddenly human to me, this hometown boy. There, in that beautiful, quiet place, was someone I already felt I knew—seeing him was like a welcome.

On the second floor I found a small library with an ugly plaid couch and the same side tables as all over campus—scratched blond wood, with wide grains that perfectly accommodated the tip of a pen. The shelves held only periodicals—literary magazines and journals with names like *Blazer* and *Pine* and *So Much Depends.* Five shelves were dedicated to *The Rosendale Literary Review,* which had been published twice a year since the school's founding. I'd never had a particular interest in writing. I was a regular at the Greening library because I liked comics and fantasy, and because you could also take out movies. But Mom's shift wouldn't be over for hours.

Watery sunlight fell across the spines, landing in a warmish puddle on the floor where I sat, cross-legged, to begin at the beginning. What might they tell me about Rosendale? What secrets would they hold?

The inaugural issue was shoddily bound, page after page of poems in verse so constrained I could hardly make sense of it; a dozen sonnets about trees and/or love, about time and/or growing up and/or God; a very long poem about whales, I think; a brief ode to Rosendale Lake and/or the sky above it? Underneath each poem, the author's name was typed in bold, followed by their age and grade. WALLARD TRASK, AGE 16, JUNIOR. RALPH POMEROY, AGE 18, SENIOR. One poem seemed to sympathize with the Nazis; another praised the style and rigor of Mussolini. I didn't quite know who Mussolini was, but I knew he was bad. An uncountable number about the glory of war. I didn't find a girl's name until 1959. NAN HOOVER, AGE 18, SENIOR. Her poem was a snappy, unrhyming description of a pollen-drunk bumblebee, which may or may not have been a metaphor for—I read it again, sweat springing to my temples—sex.

The majority wrote about love: first love, eternal love, lost love. Hundreds of teenagers, old now, maybe even dead, had left these earnest little smears of themselves here for anyone to find. Now and then, between stanzas or after an overlabored metaphor, it was as though I'd caught a glimpse of a wild animal, a flash of eyes, the snowy spot on the tail, just before it disappeared into the trees ahead. There, gone: the unformed thing, sheer potential, they had aspired to say. Had one of the authors walked into the library, I would have slammed the covers shut, as if, instead of poems, I'd been looking at their naked pictures. Even their pretension and posturing—perhaps those most of all—were intimate.

The sunlight had moved off me and up the wall; I'd missed lunch. In the bathroom, I peed as fast as I could. Always, in Rosendale's tiled stalls, even in that unused building, I felt the whispering presence of students reminding me I did not belong. I envied them for Rosendale, but also—and this was a new feeling—for the ambition that had brought them there, where their words could speak to each other forever in a book. Rain clouds darkened the windows. In the library, I switched on the overhead lamp, pulled a selection from the sixties to take with me to the couch.

The poem wasn't like the others. NATHANIEL FELLOW, AGE 14, FRESHMAN. Fourteen lines, one tight little block, a heart-seizing image of Greening River at the height of noon, the sun above all fat and glittery. To read it was to enter a room I'd known my whole life, been defined by without ever having seen the walls or understanding a thing about how it was built and why I was trapped there. Or maybe the poem made a room in me? I was teenager, the age art can change a person—I still believe that much, at least, about poetry. Our first true point of contact, Nathaniel's fourteen-year-old soul calling out to mine. What shape would my life have taken if our relationship had stayed in this realm, two children who felt stuck in Michigan, a glance exchanged across time and ink?

I pulled the issues from three subsequent years. In each of them, more work by Nathaniel Fellow, more language I didn't read so much as absorb at the base of my spine, a cellular vibration, an activation of some long-buried way of feeling. I stood, paced, read one out loud. The last issue was almost entirely devoted to Nathaniel, poem after poem after poem, and then—I made a noise of pleasure, seeing so many of his words on a page—the closing piece, a long story told from the perspective of a precocious five-year-old named Jim about the day his father had broken Jim's nose by pushing him off a swing. The story was set in Greening. I had never read anything that felt so *true.*

I didn't need the rest of the issues. I put them all back and read Nathaniel's words over and over until the room was dim and my legs were stiff and my mother was calling my name.

Tray had told her where to look.

Fourteen. What had my life been like up until then? I had few friends besides Theresa, a couple of other forgettable girls who liked me until they didn't, or vice versa. I'd never been kissed, never held a boy's hand. My mother was probably my best friend, but I wouldn't have called us close. I watched a lot of TV, but I have no memory, now, of the shows I loved or hated. Sometimes I babysat, tricking the toddlers into playing a game called "sleep" so I could do nothing. Dads who'd been silent in the house with their wives and children turned chatty as soon as I hopped into their cars—attention that flattered and scared me. What's your strongest subject, they'd ask, or how's your mother doing, right as we pulled into the driveway, so I had to stay an extra beat or two to answer. Most of them were too young to be *my* dad; I did the math without thinking.

I was open, is what I'm trying to say. I was bored. I was a teenage girl from a small town, desperate for something to happen to me.

"Mom," I asked as we turned out of campus, the poems buzzing in my mind. "Do you know Nathaniel Fellow?"

"The writer? Of course." Her bun strained against her scalp, strands unraveling along her neck; above her ears, her hairnet had left an imprint.

"No, I mean, did you know him, growing up?"

"Ha. I know I seem old to you, but I'm not that old. He was long gone by the time I was in school." We drove in silence for a while. "I do remember," she said, meeting my eyes in the rearview, "hearing him read. I was maybe twenty-two? A girlfriend twisted my arm. It was in St. Joe's, the reading, and to tell you the truth it was embarrassing, how he stood there shouting at the altar. Weird, that they let him read those poems in a church, all the profanity and drugs. Some pretty lines, I guess. I didn't really understand it. Depressing stuff." We were turning into our neighborhood. A few blocks ahead, our five-room house, smelling of stale coffee and cinnamon potpourri, was waiting for us to begin our evening routine: reheated cafeteria leftovers, three hours of TV. "After, we went to the pub, and he was there," she added. And then, with something like pride: "He bought me a drink."

"He did? What was he like?"

"Arrogant. Handsome."

"What else?"

"Dear lord, Will, we barely talked. You know he went to Rosendale, right?"

"Yeah."

"I just don't know where he gets off, making out like he's the blue-collar truth-teller of Greening. He was a boarder there. Nathaniel's uncle—his mom's oldest brother, kind of a mean guy—was some hot-shot on the board."

Was it my imagination, or did she sound defensive, even angry? As I opened the trunk, carried the aluminum trays from Rosendale into the kitchen, I filled out the scene, my mother and Nathaniel at the pub, peanut shells crackling under their shoes, a glass slid her way. He was wearing the navy suit from the *Vanity Fair* spread, as he always would be in my imagination, even after we met. I'd seen pictures—she was a beauty, long legs, ropes of black hair down to her waist, a little gap between her front teeth that must have been adorable when she was young, though the older I got the more it bothered me she'd never gotten it fixed, didn't seem to care that it made her look poor. Sometimes, when I was in a bad mood, she'd wedge straws, coffee stirrers, even french fries into that tiny space so they stuck out of her mouth like antennae. Willie, she'd say in a goofy voice, then stroke me with whatever it was until I couldn't help it and laughed. What had they talked about? Maybe she'd challenged him, *where do you get off,* maybe he'd put his hands up, bought another drink as a peace offering, the two of them tucked away in one of the corner booths. What if she and Nathaniel had sat in the pub until last call, slotting quarters into the jukebox, what if it had been August, still warm out, and they'd crossed the bridge to one of their two houses and, well, I didn't quite know what would happen next—my first kiss was still on the horizon—but thanks to movies I could at least draw the outline, the swooning embrace, the bedroom curtain sucked in by the wind, then released. On my birth certificate, where the father's name should have been, it said: *Unknown.* It was a fact of life, something I'd taken so for granted throughout my childhood that asking about it would have been like asking why people lived in houses, or whether my mom saw any point in shoes. And then, around nine, ten, when I started to wonder out loud why most other kids had dads, my mother got either so angry or so sad, I knew the question of my father was something I'd have to deal with alone.

Nathaniel would have been older than her, but not impossibly older. *Maybe* twenty-two, she'd said. I was born when my mother was twenty-three. The math worked. And there was no way she'd call some one-night stand and ask him for help, money, a name for a birth certificate. She never talked about her childhood, but I knew my mother was proud of having built her life without help from anybody. She often reminded me of not just how much we had, but how little we needed. I pushed a piece of breaded whitefish—Rosendale leftovers—around my plate. My mother was laughing, open-mouthed, at the TV, where Bill Cosby was trying to explain something. Then my eye stopped at the glass case in the dining alcove off the kitchen, where we kept the holiday crystal, a gilt-edged King James Bible, and on the top shelf, a row of hardcovers. I put my plate on the floor and walked toward it.

"Miss Wilhelmina Miles," my mother called. "If you think for one second I'm cleaning up these plates."

"Roger that," I said, but my heart slammed, I swallowed the words. There, inside the cover of *Copper Harbor: Poems,* was a message, written big and bold above the title. He'd drawn a line through his printed name and signed underneath, the N and F filling the bottom half of the page. My mother wasn't much of a reader. For what other reason would we have so many of his books?

In narrow, right-leaning cursive, he'd written:

For my Northern Star—

3

Every day that summer, I headed straight for the writing house, Nathaniel's poems. I'm sure this sounds obsessive. Probably it was.

I worked my way through the archives of *The Rosendale Literary Review,* reading all the way up to the present, then tackled the rest of the library—a shrine, built by rugged white men, to the glory of nature. What sort of talent was writing? Were you born with it? Was it learned? Did you find it in the woods? I had a pen and paper, a chance it was in my genes. I liked to read. What if talent was, simply, a path one chose?

I sat on the floor when I tried to write. *Poem,* I'd write on the top of the page, and then I'd follow it with a subject that seemed poetic, something to guide me forward. Poem about morning. Poem about the taste of spoiled milk. Poem about the first worms after rain. The only appropriate reaction to the way Nathaniel's teenage writing agitated my soul was to try to speak back. Poem about loneliness. But every word died the instant it was pinned in place. I spent hours like that, trying different combinations. It wasn't pleasant, and it did something odd to time, both stretching and collapsing it; often I didn't notice how many hours had passed and would be frustrated by how little I had to show for all that thinking. And yet I had the sensation of having lived, in those hours, more deeply than usual, as if the writing itself, or the act of trying, was a portal to a plane of existence outside of time altogether. Had teenage Nathaniel used it like this, too? As a way out?

On a rainy day in June during one of these sessions, Tray appeared in the doorway. "Some mad scientist shit going on in here," he said, referring to the books tented open on the floor.

"Go away." I was furious at having been torn from my own mind. He stepped back. I hurled my pen and it bounced off his chest.

"You are not a normal girl," he told me, and then he was gone, but everything I did after that felt stupid. The next day, I opened my notebook, and instead of trying to write something beautiful, I focused on how to ask the question I couldn't stop thinking about.

In a way, that letter to Nathaniel was my first real poem. I wrote and rewrote it. My first attempts were pages long, a paragraph of pleasantries—it took several drafts to cut out questions about the weather, a Greeningism if there ever was one—followed by an outline of my mother's history from birth to the present. In later drafts, I cut every digression. One letter asked, simply: *Are you my father?*

My mother and Nathaniel meeting, the positive pregnancy test, her contractions dialing up while she waited at a red light a mile from the hospital, her conviction, as she exhaled slowly through her nose, that she could do this by herself, on the side of the road if she had to. It was all very easy to imagine. The story unspooled into the future: me stepping off a bus in the rain, carrying only a backpack, watching a family through a window before taking a deep breath, striding to the front door, and ringing the bell. Nathaniel and I looking at each other, the proof all over our faces. Come in, he'd say. We're just about to eat. Welcome to your real life. The scene ended there. I had no idea what families with fathers were like in the privacy of their own homes.

Sometimes it seems like everything I ever wrote, will ever write, was in those drafts, that my destiny is to send the same question to the wrong person until I'm out of words. After countless tries, I settled on a polite three-paragraph note outlining the facts—Greening, his reading at St. Joe's Church, drinks with my mother at the pub, my fatherless birth less than a year later—and nothing more. I wrote the note by hand on thick off-white paper, creased once in the center and sent in an envelope addressed to his literary agency, along with a photograph of my mother in her twenties. Two stamps, because it had to make it to New York City, and that seemed very far.

The photo of my mother is overexposed, three by five, probably from a disposable. She's sitting on a picnic table, wearing a bikini, cowboy boots, and a long, crocheted robe, her two braided pigtails hanging so long the tips catch in a fold of her belly. A few wisps flutter around her ears. She's eating a vanilla ice cream cone—a fat dollop of cream seconds from dropping to her wrist—and looking at the camera a little sideways. When I found the photo again in New York, almost a decade after dropping it in the mail, its sexiness shocked me. You can almost see what comes next. Why had I chosen *that* picture? Had I recognized it, or was I just naïve? Maybe I assumed it had been taken by him. Looking at it, you can tell whoever's watching through the camera is her lover.

High school started. Over the summer, some kids had grown a foot, or sprouted a thousand pimples, or gotten braces off and turned beautiful; the social order redefined itself, and Theresa and I caught the attention of the sophomore boys on the basketball team. They invited us to sit with them at lunch, and then, after a late September football game, to a party.

There weren't many other girls, Theresa and I the only freshmen. "This is for you guys," Jerry Kowalski said, pulling a bottle of Apple Pucker from his backpack. The party was in a barn far enough behind his house his parents, he swore, couldn't hear a thing. It was set up like a living room, rafters strung with Christmas lights, seating of various types pushed against the walls.

"Yuck," Theresa said, sniffing her drink. I thought it was good.

The next morning, I woke up in the corner, one shoe off, all five toes blue with cold. Theresa was gone, but a few basketball guys, including Jerry, were asleep nearby—Ralphie a few feet away on the floor, snoring lightly, Matty B on the couch, Blake cross-legged on a dirty recliner. My mouth tasted so bad I rolled over and vomited, which is when I realized my bra wasn't on. "Did she just puke and leave?" one of the boys said as I slipped through the side door. Outside, the grass was tipped with frost. My breasts jounced coldly under my sweatshirt. Where was Theresa? Was she okay? I had a fuzzy memory of her trying to balance on a rocking horse, her arms spread like wings—after that, nothing. What had I said? Go home without me?

On Monday, I learned what I had done. No one told me straight; I seemed to hear it from the walls of the school itself. At lunch, Theresa was sitting with some other girls from our grade, not the basketball boys. When I tried to join them, Carrie Branson held up her hand. "You can't sit here until you say sorry to Theresa," she said. Theresa stared at her Pop-Tart. I had no idea what Carrie was talking about, but I took my lunch to an empty table, where I ate alone as I would for much of high school, the freshman girl who'd tried to make out with Jerry Kowalski after having sex with Ralphie under the ping-pong table, in plain sight of the entire party. Jerry had gone along with it, even though Ralphie was his best friend—he was just a guy, after all—and now, because of me, the two weren't talking. Bros before hos. I'd undone the sacred tenant. Was I the biggest slut in the history of the school? It was possible, people said, casting glances my way as if I were a celebrity.

Had I really fucked Ralphie? The morning I left the party barn, I squatted behind a stand of pines just before the turnoff to my street. It took a very long time for urine to come out, a weak, steaming dribble that stung on its way to the ground. But the next day, my pee was normal. Nothing hurt. I didn't quite believe what everyone was saying—even annihilated by alcohol, wouldn't my mind retain some imprint of being kissed, touched, for the very first time? The word gonged—fucked, fucked, fucked. I had no hickeys, no marks. I felt for a memory and came up with nothing, again and again.

A few weeks later, around the time of my fifteenth birthday, a rumor started that my breasts were oddly shaped: "wild ass," "freaky," "pancake titties with pepperoni nipples." A girl named Ginny passed this along in the bathroom, as if she were telling me, kindly but with great urgency, that my car was on fire. I spent a lot of time that year standing naked in front of my bedroom mirror. I'd lift each breast, pulling the skin on top and trying to pin it near my collarbone, imagining a stitch that would hold my breasts there, an inch or so off my ribcage. Were the bumps on my nipples normal, or were they extra, somehow? My right side had a nipple-like protrusion beside what was definitely my actual nipple—but it was smaller, more like the glandular bumps around my areola. Did other women have those? One night, after applying some Scotch tape to make my breasts more pleasingly U-shaped, the phone rang. My mother knocked. "Someone for you," she called, as I pulled a shirt over my head. "Boy," she mouthed, when I opened the door.

"Hi?" I said, bracing myself. I'd been expecting Theresa. On the other line, heavy breathing followed by a long moan, and then a dial tone.

After the party barn, shame was with me always, a kind of sidekick. Sometimes it got very close, wrapped its arms around me, breathed hot and wet into my ear, and I felt myself dissolve completely into it, disappearing, almost wanting it to eat me whole. And sometimes I felt that skulking companion had nothing to do with me at all—it was an invention from the outside, the product of whispers and smoke, a million times less concrete, even, than a written word. Our relationship could change several times over the course of a single day.

I developed the skill of reading while walking the halls, holding a book slightly up and in front of my face so I didn't have to see anyone. For Christmas I asked for *The Norton Anthology of Modern and Contemporary Poetry.* I began in winter with volume one and Walt Whitman. Here was beauty and meaning: everything missing from my life in cruel, stupid Greening. In those pages I found writing I liked as much as Nathaniel's early poems. Wallace Stevens, E. E. Cummings, Hart

Crane, Theodore Roethke. All day at school I read, and when I got home, I checked the mailbox: nothing but bills, bills, bills.

I developed a reputation for being trampy *and* aloof. During a moment of renewed semi-closeness with Theresa—we'd apologized to each other, without ever addressing what happened—I pointed out the improbability of this. It was said, I knew, that I let boys climb through my window at night, that I begged for it, sex, a penis in my mouth. The cross-country girls, the artsy girls, the druggie girls—whenever any group passed me in the halls, they'd tilt their chins up in an exaggerated way, laughing. The boys slipped notes into my locker, called my house at all hours and left their numbers with my mother, who seemed almost flattered by their attention to me.

Sylvia Plath, Pablo Neruda, Robert Lowell, Rita Dove. In June, I finished volume two, which ended with Sherman Alexie. Months had gone by and my letter to New York City remained unanswered. But I never stopped checking.

4

Something was happening to my body, and without my consent: I was trying to see if I could catch it, a firefly in my palm, and stub it out. The process seemed to accelerate after Jerry Kowalski's party barn, as if whatever I had or hadn't done with the boys had caused my cells to mature at a faster rate.

My mother kept a plug-in vanity mirror on a short wooden table at the foot of her bed. It was the kind with two sides: one normal, the other a magnifying glass. Spotlights lined the frame. When you turned the knob at its base, a tinted lens slid over the glowing circles—bright, soft, day, disco—and changed your perspective on your face. It was an expensive mirror; since childhood, the rule was it stayed in her room. A shallow drawer in the table held her makeup, tiles of eyeshadow and blush in shades like dusky rose, a handful of brushes and black pencils. My mother didn't really wear makeup except for lipstick or mascara on a special occasion, so the mirror was mostly used by me, for picking at the pimples along my hairline, and for gazing into as I revolved through the casts of light and watched my blue eyes brighten and dim.

Occasionally, I'd find a springy blond hair in the tweezers, too coarse to be mine or my mother's, and I'd drown the pincers in the sink, squeezing soap into the scalding water. The hairs belonged to Tray.

A couple months after the party barn, he started showing up at our house, the same way he so often appeared wherever I was on

Rosendale's campus. "He's closer to my age than yours," I hissed at my mother when she told me he'd be staying with us for a while. "Aren't you ashamed?"

"Nope," she said. "Are you?"

"Yes," I told her, dropping my plate into the sink with a clatter. "I am horrified. I'm disgusted. Honestly, Mom, it's revolting."

"Would you find it disgusting if our ages were reversed? I don't remember you saying it was disgusting when I was dating Adam Kismer. You know he was seventeen years older than me?"

"Adam Kismer was an adult with an actual job, he was nice, and he didn't give me the creeps." White froth accumulated at the corners of Adam Kismer's mouth when he spoke with excitement, which he could do about almost anything (snowfall, dogs, varieties of cinnamon cereal), and I'd seen my mother cringe when he reached for her hand. But he was a reporter for the local radio station and did things like shovel our walk and drop off radishes from the farm stand. He was distractedly polite to me; he seemed like someone's dad. I was disappointed when my mother stopped seeing him, though she acted lighter for months afterward.

"Don't be such a prude," my mother said, all dressed up to meet Tray for dinner. "I'm not going to marry the guy." Her hair was brushed straight and glossy down to the middle of her back, a lightless black without a single strand of gray. Her eyelids sparkled, her nails shone apple red.

"I would literally kill myself," I said. "I would stab myself in the face." Reading so much poetry had made me prone to hyperbole. My mother and I were at the beginning of our cold period. She was thirty-seven. She didn't look old and she didn't look young. Around that time, she'd started dreaming out loud about making some big change—quitting Rosendale, going back to Quincy Community College. There was a new restlessness to her, a yearning. How odd it must have been to share her home with *me,* a teenage girl on the brink of it all, the one who'd stopped her life short when she actually was so very, very young. I fogged up her bathroom, pawed through her clothes, applied her makeup to a younger version of her face. Now I see what I couldn't then: Tray didn't seem to realize she was edging closer to the middle point of her life. He treated her like a girl.

Tray's job at Rosendale was seasonal, summer months only. I'm not sure he had a high school degree. He started spending most nights at our house, except Fridays and Saturdays, when he drove all over Michigan, even into the Upper Peninsula, picking things up and dropping them off. Radios, extension cords, cocaine, prescription painkillers, oil paint he must have stolen from Rosendale, hunting rifles and handguns, chickens, tires, copper piping, gold and silver coins. He kept most of it in our garage, a moving-in process that spanned months, so much stuff it was hard to wedge open the door. The guns were stored in an old refrigerator—unplugged, the inside shelves taken out—barrels pointing up at the freezer, where a few labeled baggies contained different kinds of ammunition. When you pulled the refrigerator handle, a couple would clatter out onto the floor.

"What does he even do with all that crap?" I asked my mother one Saturday. "Does he own it, or is he, like, a delivery boy?"

"It's just sales," she said.

"Sales? That sounds made up."

"Well, he helps pay this mortgage, so it's real enough for me." She slammed a handful of popcorn into her mouth. Her jaw bunched. The TV light glanced off the creases around her eyes, the sunspot on her temple. I thought she was stupid, that he was using her, and she knew I did.

When he got back from wherever he was, Tray would throw open the door. "What are my girlies doing?" he'd shout, a suitcase banging behind him full of high-tech alarm clocks or dog leashes still in their plastic wrapping or sometimes, to my mother's delight, a piece of blown glass for her to keep. "I missed you," he'd say, hugging my mother so hard he picked her up off the ground. They'd kiss, tongues and all, right in front of me. My mother was her own person, allowed to kiss, have sex, whatever—I told myself I wasn't objecting to that—but something about Tray's awareness of me during those kisses, even when his eyes were closed, drove me from the room. Eventually, Tray would find me to say hello, dropping his hands on my shoulders, digging his thumbs into my muscles until they released, and I sighed despite myself.

When Tray was in it, our house—already small—shrank. He took up no less than three-quarters of every room, even when he was asleep. When he sat on the couch, he sank so deep into the cushions you tipped his way. I tried to hook myself over the armrest, but somehow we'd wind up arm to arm, thigh to thigh. It was the same at the kitchen table—to stretch out, cross or uncross your legs, move at all, meant clunking into his knees, his shins, his feet. If you did this, he might reach his hand under the table and squeeze whatever part of you made contact. The smell changed, too, from whatever it was when it was just me and my mother, some odor I could barely perceive, laced with Yankee candle and old potpourri, to *Tray,* sweat and smoke and the astringent, artificial pine of the air freshener he kept in his car.

A few months after Tray moved in, my mother bought me two sets of real pajamas with pants and matching long-sleeved shirts. "No more T-shirt nightgowns, and no more tank tops without bras," she said, pulling them out of the Walmart bag. She'd driven all the way to Quincy. "You're too old to wander around the house with your breasts out." I have my mother's tiny ears and long toes, her double-jointedness; other than my height, the only physical trait I must have, by process of elimination, inherited from my father was breasts—no help in my search at all.

Most nights, Tray watched sports on the TV in my mother's bedroom, propped up on her pillows like an invalid, a beer cracked open on the bedside table. She often treated him more like a child than a partner—favored, yes, but ultimately subject to her rule. She wouldn't relinquish her setup in the living room, her nighttime shows and routine, not for me, and not for him. Greening gets dark early in the winter, and sometimes he'd be in her room from dinner until we all went to bed. This created a problem for me. The makeup mirror was a powerful lure. I'd push open the bedroom door, the room sunk in blue, the TV casting a flickering light onto the bed. Sometimes Tray talked, usually that "whattayadoing" that made every muscle in my body tighten. Mostly he'd just nod when I entered and then act like I wasn't there at all. I don't know which bothered me more.

This was the era when eyebrows were kept thin, angry worms plucked into submission above our eyes. Body hair of any kind on women was a special sin. Though I mostly neglected my appearance, wearing oversized clothes, leaving my hair up and unwashed, I was vain about my face. If I had a pretty face, it would make my slutty reputation less depressing. I'd tried plucking and picking in the bathroom mirror, sticking my nose as close as possible to the glass, but my breath clouded my view. I had to go into my mother's room. Zoomed in, I couldn't see Tray's reflection in the mirror behind me, only the dozens of wispy hairs between my eyebrows, the translucent fuzz on my upper lip. As soon as I sat down, I began to lose track of what I was doing there, picking at nothing, taking out too many hairs. When I flipped the mirror back to the normal side, to review my work as it would be seen by others, I'd confirm what I could feel all along: He'd been watching.

A couple of weeks before Halloween, Tray met me at the foot of the driveway where the bus dropped me off after school. "You've been up to something," he said, and draped his arm over my shoulder. I dug my hands into my coat pockets as far as they would go. My mother wasn't back from Rosendale yet—three nights a week she worked dinners and didn't get home until close to nine P.M. I saw the chalk on the front door before anything else, big blue capital letters scrawled on the white paint. WILHEMINA MILES, I THINK YOU LOST SOMETHING? They'd spelled my first name wrong.

"What's this?" Tray asked, almost giddy, shuffling me toward the house. Below the chalk, on our concrete front step, were what looked like a few shreds of plastic. I stepped closer. Not plastic—three unwrapped condoms, each dribbling milky fluid.

"Looks like three used condoms," I said. It was easy to sound like I didn't care; I was still in the numb, nothing zone I lived in during the school day.

"I got home around lunchtime, and I just walked right into these here. You have something to explain?"

"Why would I? I didn't put them there."

Tray's attention moved from my crusty work boots, laces tied loose, up my baggy jeans, and across my thigh-length corduroy parka. So quick I almost missed it, confusion creased his face. He reached for my chin, pinching it between an oily thumb and index finger. My breath snared in my throat. "I'm not going to tell your mom. You get rid of this, and I don't see it's something we need to talk about. Your life is your life. Just tell your boyfriends to keep their shit to themselves. Or, I don't know, stop fucking with them." His fingers moved from my chin to my braid, gave it a quick tug.

The chalk didn't really come off. Something about how cold it was outside, the powder ground too deep into the wood—or maybe I'd made a mistake, spraying it with cleaner and rubbing with a paper towel instead of just wetting a washcloth. I covered my hand with a plastic baggie and scooped up the rubbery tubes, as if I were gathering dog shit from the sidewalk. When I turned the bag inside out, taking care not to touch anything, I smelled sugar. I took a cautious sniff. White icing, mixed, perhaps, with a little water.

That night, after I showered, I pushed open the door to my mother's room. I settled in front of the mirror and picked up the tweezers, Tray measuring every shift and fidget, clocking the wet trail left by my braid as it dried against my pajamas. I tried to sit as still as I could. I flipped the mirror from the normal view—Tray's face in blue outline just beyond my reflection, mouth a deeper shadow—to magnified, erasing him, and took the tweezers to my eyebrows, plucking all but a narrow chain of hairs. I did the same thing to my pimples, biting the white tops off with the tweezers until I bled. I didn't stop until I knew was I ugly. I left the mirror on and turned my face toward Tray on the way out, hoping there was enough light for him to see what I'd done.

"You gotta stop that picking," he said, turning back to the TV. I stayed a beat and looked at him, just to see what it felt like, watching him while he refused to look back.

He never touched-me touched me, beyond the constant fluttering of his hands at my hips or shoulders or ass or waist, my hair, the inner skin of my arms, the pinchable spots on my thighs, my toes if my feet were bare and propped up on the armrest, the backs of my knees in a swirl of fingers if we happened to be sitting by each other. But. Tray was context, not foreground. He was the disturbance outside the bathroom door, the reflection trapped in the blank TV, the person already in the room when you turned on the light.

I stopped talking at home, too. I tried to disappear, my face and body the enemy, the source of an attention I did not want. To write was a magic trick, an escape route to my thoughts, the part of me nobody seemed to care about at all. Back then, it was as close as I got to freedom.

Nathaniel hates context in fiction. Cut this, he wrote, cut this and this and this. Goodbye, back story, transitions, explication—death to setup. Imagine what you wrote, but with only the good stuff, a book made up of snapshots, each one a perfect bullet to the heart.

"What does that mean?" I asked him once. "The good stuff?" He looked at me from across the couch.

"You know," he said. "And if you don't, not even I can help you."

5

I did try to escape. Winter of my sophomore year, I applied to Rosendale. I didn't tell my mother. How could I admit I wanted to be one of the kids we rolled our eyes at, who called each other "darling" and submitted multipage charts about their food preferences, who either treated my mother like she was invisible or like she was their personal maid?

I couldn't tell her how I hated being in our house.

Or about the night I'd heard a sound outside my window, right after stripping down to my underwear. When I squinted, I could see Tray, staring up weirdly at a backyard tree in the dark, as if he'd come out to bird-watch. I closed the thin curtains and took my book into the closet, where I read it by the light that fell through the slats.

I couldn't tell her that what she'd given me—everything—wasn't enough. A single year's tuition and board cost a few thousand more than my mother's annual salary. Tuition discounts were only for faculty kids. My poems had to get me in and win me a scholarship, too.

On the night of the application deadline, I crept to the shared desktop tucked in a corner of the dining room and waited the years it took to dial up to the internet. Minutes before the portal closed, I clicked submit and paid the fee using a credit card I slipped from my mother's wallet, hoping she wouldn't notice the charge. When I got in, it wouldn't be possible to avoid her entirely, but I knew her schedule well—I'd time meals so I arrived fifteen minutes after start, when she'd be too busy to look for me. I could already see myself wandering the footpaths while fall leaves swirled through the sky, or curled up in one of the library carrels, working my way through a list of books I hadn't even known existed. And best of all, every single person I met would know nothing about Jerry Kowalski's party barn.

I'd chosen my most Nathaniel-esque poems for the portfolio—the confirmation email, my first ever correspondence from the place I'd spent so much of my life, felt as official as an acceptance. I clicked unread, just so I could open it again.

My mother stood behind me, working mayonnaise into my hair. Sunday night mayo hair masks had been a ritual since I was ten or so, our hair rinsed at the end in cold water and combed to a sheet of black silk reflective as a mirror. That eggy tang, one of the smells of home. She scooped the mayo from a wholesale jar pilfered from Rosendale, drew it from my scalp to ends, her fingers cold and strong in her rubber gloves.

"I saw a strange charge on my card," she said, and I stiffened. "Forty bucks. Rosendale Academy."

"Did you buy something at Rosendale?" I said, trying to sound like I was barely paying attention.

"What would I buy at Rosendale, Wilhelmina?"

"I don't know, maybe something at the gift shop? Maybe you forgot?"

"Forty dollars' worth of something?" Her fingers hit a tangle and my head jerked back.

"Mom!"

"Tray told me you'd do this."

"Do what?"

"Lie."

"I'm not lying!"

She pulled off her gloves, grabbed a Walgreens bag, and tucked my hair up into it, twist-tying it at the base of my neck. "The choices you make, they matter. The secrecy and the lying, they add up to something. You're sixteen years old. You're not child. I'm asking you a direct question, and you're going to lie to my face?"

"I can't actually see your face."

My mother made an exasperated noise.

"I thought I'd tell you if I got in. I probably won't," I continued, lying again, because I believed my acceptance was days away.

"Is this about the poetry?"

It was the way she said the word. "This is exactly why I didn't tell you." I was shouting, and we didn't shout, but I didn't care. I stood up, stomped to the sink, tore the plastic bag off my head, my hair falling in greasy snakes around my shoulders. I was crying, but it didn't feel bad—it felt perfectly appropriate. "I'm the one who keeps secrets? I'm the one who tells lies? Who do you think I learned it from?"

"What the hell is that supposed to mean? Don't you dare turn this back around on me."

"Who is he, Mom?" I'd asked where he was, why he wasn't there, but never this vast and simple question. We both looked surprised.

"Oh, Will," she said. Her face was gray under the yellow kitchen light, and with her hair tied up in the plastic bag on her head I felt I was seeing her as she would be one day, an old woman. "He was just a guy. I don't even remember his last name. Too many drinks. It was a one-night thing. He never even knew I was pregnant. Don't you get it, honey? He doesn't matter. He's not a part of our story."

There was no way she was telling the truth—she wouldn't forget something as important as the last name of the person who brought me into her life. "It's not fair. You don't get to decide if I care about this." A glop of mayonnaise slipped down my neck. I wanted to throw it at her. "You're lying." She didn't deny it. I hadn't yelled since I was a tiny child and it felt insane and delicious and I didn't want to stop. I almost asked her about the inscription—*For my Northern Star*—but then Tray shuffled in. "That's enough," he told me, playacting dad. That night I think he'd been drinking, because for a long second, he just stood there, blinking slowly.

"You need to quiet," he said. "You're didn't. Didn't get in."

"What the hell, Tray?" I pushed past him, hurling myself into the bathroom, where I sobbed under the shower spray. I don't know what he was talking about, or how he knew it—I wouldn't hear from Rosendale for another six weeks—but anyway, he was right.

I didn't get in.

Right on the heels of my rejection from Rosendale, almost two years after mailing the letter, I received a response. There was no return address on the envelope, but when I saw it addressed to me, I knew what it was. I opened it, hands trembling.

Dear Wilhelmina,

Thank you for your interest in Nathaniel Fellow's life and work. He wishes you the best of luck with your quest!

Geraldine Keene
Literary Assistant

Quest. A word for a child. I felt a flash of anger at her, Geraldine Keene, whoever she was. It was unlikely that Nathaniel was my father; I'd always known that. But the letter didn't offer enough evidence to outweigh the points that had driven me to write it in the first place. Who inscribed a book to a random stranger with a possessive like *my*? Why had my mother mentioned, so pointedly, that Nathaniel had bought her a drink? Geraldine's letter was evasive, a sidestep. I tucked it under my desk lamp. My mother rarely came in my room, but if she did, the letter would be in plain view. I think I wanted her to find it.

A few weeks later, on the first truly warm day of spring, a senior boy I knew only by first name left a message on our home phone. It was eleven at night; my mother and Tray were already upstairs, in bed. "I'm, uh, calling for Wilhelmina," he said. "This is Brian B. I heard you might like to go out sometime and eat some . . . pizza supreme." Muffled laughter in the background—a girl's. He left his number. I'd gotten so many messages like that since Jerry's party barn; they came in waves, months where I'd get one every couple of days, and then long periods of silence before someone remembered the game. I had a habit of checking the voice mailbox as soon as I got home, so I could delete any messages before they were noticed by my mother or Tray. That night, though, I replayed the message. I picked up the cordless and took it into my room.

I waited to call him back until just after midnight. Brian answered right away. He was alone now—I could tell by how different his voice sounded. Formal, like he was talking to an adult. "Oh, hi!" he said. "Thank you so much for calling me back."

"It's no problem," I said, doodling circles on the back of Geraldine's envelope. "The thing is, I do like pizza." I didn't exactly know what I was doing. I'd called him back on impulse, but hearing his gasp of surprise made me feel powerful. I was stuck in Greening. Nothing was going to change. It wasn't supposed to matter, what people said, if you knew the truth about yourself—wasn't that the cliché? But how could that be right? I'd never kissed a boy, as far as I could remember, and yet my reality in Greening was defined by the story people told about me. I might as well see what hooking up was like.

Brian arrived thirty minutes after I hung up. I'd never seen him up close; he had the dramatic cheekbones of a runway model, dozens of blackheads on his nose. I didn't know what to do next, so I pretended I was someone who did. His shampoo smelled good. Kissing was wetter than I'd imagined. After a couple of minutes my chin was slimy. We rolled around in my bed in the dark. My mother and Tray's room was upstairs, and mine was off the kitchen; I didn't really worry they'd wake up. Brian didn't try for more than making out, and whenever I saw him at school after that, he'd say hi, which did make my days slightly more bearable.

I want to see you, the boys would say into the phone. They used a different voice when they said this, not one you ever heard at school. I didn't invite as many as people said, and stuck to seniors, or townies who'd recently graduated. Jacob Annala came over every month or so for most of my junior year, a relationship of sorts that unfolded between the hours of one A.M. and four A.M. in my bedroom. He was from Quincy, a basketball star who lived in one of the rambling Victorians, both of his parents admin at Rosendale—he'd called out of the blue, said he'd heard I liked Dashboard Confessional. Word of my sluttiness had traveled towns. That Jacob had to drive so far to get to me made me feel special. We listened to music quietly. Sometimes we just cuddled. The week before he left for Notre Dame, we had sex—my first time. I knew I should be ashamed about our relationship unfolding only in this secret way, but there was nothing traumatic about how he unrolled the condom, asking me every step of the way if it hurt, if I needed a break. Thank you, he said, when it was done, his head against my chest.

I liked the feeling of being picked, even if I knew it wouldn't carry over to daylight, the halls of school. I liked how the boys looked outside the window, the tentative sound of their secret knock. And most of all, I liked that it was me who slid up the glass, that I stood there warm in my pajamas while they tipped themselves headfirst over the windowsill, snow in their hair. The boys had to almost crawl in—the window didn't open wide and was low to the ground, so they had to brace themselves with their hands against the floor. Most of them fell. Some of them laughed when I laughed; some of them looked angry.

"Come here," I'd say. And every single one of them would.

6

My senior year, Nathaniel and his wife of a decade, the novelist Vilma Wise, officially filed for divorce. I tried to read one of her books when I heard of their split, which was reported in the tabloids alongside the news of Nathaniel's new relationship with a thirty-something television actress whose previous husband had died when his private jet spiraled into the Gulf of Mexico, but I stopped before finishing the opening.

My mother saw the book on the coffee table. "Oh, I love her," she said, picking the novel up and rubbing her hand over its face, as if it were a friend. Usually, she didn't comment on the things I read. When I returned to the novel—*Baby's Breath,* it was called, Vilma's third—its faded blue cover splashed with birds seemed alarmingly unliterary. Vilma had been Nathaniel's wife—that was the only reason I'd checked out the book—but she wasn't serious. How could she be, if my mother liked her?

I fed it through the library drop-off slot that same afternoon. I told myself Vilma just wasn't my thing. Nathaniel was still my favorite writer, a loyalty I didn't question, even when he published a novel about a sailing trip so dense with binnacles and bimmies and anchor cables the sentences swam right out of my brain. The truth is, I still hadn't let go of that vision of myself on his doorstep in the rain, the implicit question in the dumb letter I'd hurled through space. The secret thrummed in me whenever I picked up one of his books. I tended to it, in the private part of my imagination, where wishes and anxiety and dreams took root. I let it grow.

Novels—the ones I was reading at least, checked out from the tiny literature corner at Greening Public Library—were never about promiscuous high school girls who hadn't bothered to apply to college; that's how I knew the novel that would be my life hadn't started yet. From those same novels, I also knew it took only a sudden swerve (picnic, lightning, et cetera) for one's destiny to take shape. Sometimes, in the secret dark of my bedroom, it occurred to me perhaps everyone felt as I did—maybe even my mother, drifting off on the other side of the wall, was wondering when the plot was finally going to twist and rescue her from me.

Even though we hadn't spoken in months, Theresa invited me to the senior party, a bonfire out by Elbow Lake, and somehow I worked up the courage to go. She could drive me back, but I needed a ride there. My mother wasn't up for it, but Tray offered—and so, with no better choice, I climbed into the passenger seat of his car.

"Woods are full of bucks out here," he said when we were far from town, pines whisking by the windows. Tray liked to drive down country roads after dark, flashing deer into stillness. "Brights are good for nothing." Tray pulled over, glancing my way. I was wearing low-rise jeans, and my belly poked over the waistband. I pulled them up, sucking my stomach in. I hated when Tray looked at me, but still felt obligated to make myself presentable when he did.

"Tray," I said. "Can't you do this on the way back? I gotta get there." But I was grateful for the delay. The last real party I'd gone to, I'd woken up in the corner of Jerry's barn without my bra. Theresa said I'd regret missing this one, high school's last hurrah, and a bit of preemptive nostalgia, my idea of what my adult self might think years from now, allowed her to convince me.

"It'll just be a minute." And then Tray was at the back of the car, pulling something from the trunk. He slid back into the driver's seat and plugged a handheld spotlight into the cigarette lighter, letting it charge up. When it switched on, he turned it toward the woods. "Yup," he said, unplugging it. "There they are. I'm going to take a quick look."

I groaned. He left his door hanging open and headed into the trees. It was early June, a warm night, and the crickets drowned out the sound of Tray stomping through the brush. I knew he'd be a while. I opened his glove compartment, looking for something to eat. I didn't really smoke, but maybe I'd sneak a couple of his cigarettes, offer them to people at the party as an excuse for making conversation. The drugstore photo sleeve fell right out, its contents spilling onto the floor. I picked the photos up, shuffling them back together. It wouldn't have occurred to me to look at any image Tray felt moved to capture with a disposable—I was aggressively disinterested in his interior life, a kind of protective mechanism that had only increased with time. But his left-open door had activated one of the car's overheads, and in the dim glow, I saw something that made me look.

It was my room.

I'd never seen my room like that before, from the outside, the window a kind of frame within the frame. But I recognized it instinctively, as if I were hearing my favorite song played backward. There were no blinds, which meant the photo must have been at least a year old—as a kid I'd had curtains, but my junior year my mother had outfitted the whole house with new blinds. Inside the window—the curtains were closed only partway—a girl in shorts and a T-shirt was bending over, scooping something off the floor. I shuffled through the others—my room, my room, my room. Some of the photos were duplicates. Some were taken later, from so close to the glass that the curtains bisected the image of the girl, me, sitting on the floor with my back against my twin bed, bare legs pulled up to my chest, chin between my knees. I couldn't remember doing any of the things in the photos, but there I was. Reading, reading, staring at nothing, asleep on top of my comforter, sitting cross-legged on the floor with my left foot raised toward my face. I heard Tray's voice outside and I stuffed the photos back into the sleeve, slamming the glove compartment shut.

Tray loomed over the car and then he was partway inside, less than a foot away from me, breathing hard as he kept the spotlight trained on the woods. Fear had made me stupid. There was nothing in my head but wind. "Wait for it," he said, reaching awkwardly into the backseat with his free hand. He clunked me in the head with his bow as he pulled it over the seat. Between trees, a coin flash of light, and then a deer wobbled into the road ahead, froze with its face turned our way. Tray balanced the spotlight on the dashboard and edged himself back out of the car, raising his bow to aim first at the deer's chest, then its neck, then the tender spot between its loony, girlish eyes.

"Tray, quit," I said, as loud as I could without shouting.

"Shh," he hissed.

The deer's ears flicked and then she was bounding into the woods, and Tray and I were alone.

Back in the car, he asked, "Why'd you scare her? I wasn't going to shoot. I just wanted to look."

"Does the bow make it easier to see?" It felt very important to act exactly as I always did. It was amazing, how normal my voice sounded.

"Practice aim, dumbass." He gave me a look, to show he meant *dumbass* with affection. My hands were shaking, and I was very cold. I tucked them under my legs, pressing down, willing my body to still. I don't remember what I said to him when I got out of the car, or how I found my way to the fire, where a few dozen kids from my high school were already very, very drunk.

I pulled a Natty Ice from an open cooler and popped the tab. I couldn't taste the beer. I was in my room, watching the party through the window, my breath fogging the glass.

"You're beautiful and I love you," Theresa told me, wrapping her arms around me and lifting me off the ground. Her voice made me real to myself again, brought me into the actual scene, and with the help of the beer I pushed the photos out of my mind. My life had already trained me well for this specific trick. The photos rose up—had I been trying to bite a nail off my toe?—and coolly, as if I were flipping off the TV, my mind turned the images face down.

"No, you are," I said, and she hugged me harder.

Theresa and I were barely friends anymore; this was an eruption of long-dead feeling, sneaking up through her drunkenness from childhood. As she held me, swaying, I knew with a little kick of guilt that was my fault as much as hers. A few minutes later one of her real friends fluttered up to us and she let go of my waist, disappeared into a cluster of girls. A bunch of kids from yearbook were trying and failing do a synchronized dance. I watched them lift their arms at random, shout at each other. I'd known most of them since preschool but had no idea what moved them, what they hoped for, or feared. What songs they listened to in the car. Had it been a choice? Or had the distance been there all along?

I drank another beer, shouted back at the people who shouted at me. Jack Macon, a super senior who had once begged me to let him go "downtown," was making out with a freshman girl who seemed to be half asleep. He was the only boy there I'd invited into my room; I remembered his penis, which had lilted to the right side, almost as drunk-looking as he was right now. I took a cigarette out of a pack someone had left open on the ground and set off into the woods, fireflies blinking in my periphery, throat sore from campfire smoke. The sound of people dimmed. Behind me, a rustle in the brush turned distinctly humanlike. "Fuck," someone whispered. Instead of anxiety I felt the satisfaction of an intuition confirmed as true—I was never truly alone.

I wheeled toward the voice with my arms out.

"What?" said Ralphie, the boy I was supposed to have fucked in the party barn, stepping out of the shadows. "Jesus. Why is everything you do *weird*?"

The music down at the bonfire was loud, and we were far enough away that no one would hear us if I yelled. But I didn't think I was afraid of Ralphie. He took a few steps closer. A bobbling, idiotic daisy was pinned to his shirt. He hadn't gone away to college and was technically a townie now; a couple carloads of them had crashed the party.

"Do you need to take a piss or something?" I said. "Because it's a big woods."

"No. I wanted to talk to you."

"Ha." *Talk* must be a euphemism. The shame arrived all mixed up; I recognized it, could put it in its place, separate it from the core of myself. Or so I thought. "Go away," I said, but I was dimly flattered when Ralphie fell into step beside me.

He was tall—much taller now than he'd been my freshman year—and he'd grown into his big, girlish lips. A nice face, really, open and friendly. Outside of the occasional exchange in the halls, I couldn't think of a single time we'd talked, but it felt somehow fated to be alone with him now—we were bound together, for better or worse, by the sex everyone said we'd had. I love you, I imagined him saying. I always have. I love you. That was it, wasn't it? The only thing that could transform what did or didn't happen between us, make me, in Greening at least, a salvageable, normal kind of girl. Someone like Theresa, with a boyfriend, and a hundred forever friends. A firefly blinked in Ralphie's hair.

He took a deep breath. "Wilhelmina Miles, the part I played in all that crap people said about you—I'm really sorry. I gotta tell you that. I should have been like, no, but I didn't." The firefly blinked again up ahead, near where the path met the road. "I don't know how it even got started, like, oh, her clit is supersize, oh, she likes it in two holes at once, and I was just stone-faced, didn't affirm or deny. But Theresa says that added fuel to the fire and I get it now, how that shit is just not right. J-dog feels bad, too. What I really hope is you can forgive and forget, and we can be cool."

Laughter, instead. A relief, that Ralphie would not see me cry. The loose, uncontrollable kind you feel in your toes. Theresa wore her FEMINIST sweatpants almost every Friday, the word bold across her butt. She and Jerry had been dating on and off all year. It was something we simply never spoke about, but I could imagine her needing all sorts of retractions and apologies and pledges from him once they hooked up. Those would have extended, by the transitive property of best friendship, to Ralphie. "Sure," I told him.

"Okay? Yeah? Whew. I *do* feel lighter. Can you believe I practiced saying all that?" Ralphie beat a fist against his sternum. I was still laughing, and he snuck me an uneasy look. "I guess I'll just walk you to back to the fire?" His hand on my arm, hot and dry.

"So let me just—You're sorry for not speaking up when people talked about me."

"A real dick move, yeah. But I gotta say, you didn't help yourself, walking around all quiet all the time, with your nose up in the air."

"But what about what happened at Jerry's?"

"Jerry's?" he said. "Oh. When we?" He made a gesture I couldn't quite see, and my stomach flipped over.

"Never mind." My curiosity couldn't override my body—and my body didn't want to hear anything else he had to say. We reached the edge of the firelight, and I was grateful.

"Yeah, no. Because that was—" Ralphie said. Carrie Branson waved and he waved back. I expected Ralphie to walk away, but he stayed beside me, a short distance from the group. "You still do that writing stuff?"

"Yes."

"Cool, cool. I write poems sometimes."

His hands were in his pockets. He wanted me to ask about his writing. I knew from the way he said *sometimes,* drawing out the word; I'd said it that way myself.

"I'm actually writing something about you," I said.

"Me? A poem?"

I wasn't, but maybe I would someday. I waited for him to ask me why, or what about. "You want to say anything, for the record?"

"Huh. The record." Ralphie shifted, backed away, as if I'd released a bad smell. "I mean, no. Yeah, no. Okay, then! I guess I'll see you around, Miles."

On the way home, Theresa singing "Cowboy Take Me Away" in

the driver's seat, my mind kept skipping on the feeling of Ralphie's hand on my arm—warmth and then sudden cold, a normal touch. It told me nothing, dredged up zero from the blank depths of the night we'd—

"I love you," I said out loud, as involuntary as a sneeze, cringing in the dark. Theresa was so drunk she didn't notice. I couldn't bear the things my mind spat up. Of course I didn't love him, or want him to love me, or really believe that's what he'd followed me to say. I'd just liked, for one second, holding the possibility up to the light, playing with how it changed everything.

Back at home I couldn't pretend the photos didn't exist. Dread walloped me as soon as Theresa honked goodbye. Once I was certain the noise of her car hadn't woken up Tray or my mother, I took a black garbage bag from under the kitchen sink and duct-taped it to my window, over the blinds, until the wall looked bruised. I had to rip the bag in half, go back for another one to rig it so no light filtered through.

Did I think about telling? My mother? Theresa? Someone at school, from that office with the bulletin boards about sexual assault all over the walls?

No, not really. It was my window, and hadn't I often gotten a creeping feeling while alone in my room, as if someone were in there with me? Shouldn't I have figured it out? Listened more closely to my own bad feeling? And what, exactly, was Tray's crime? How he'd made me feel? The pictures themselves? That he'd looked in the first place? I'd never heard of a crime like that. Hadn't I left the curtains open, day after day after day, even after the time I'd heard the cough?

Every time I saw Tray's car, the pictures for all I knew still in the glove compartment, shame started to twist and ferment, slowly turning into something else. Not anger, not guilt, though those were there, too, but instead a conviction: If I didn't leave Greening, I would die. I'm not sure if I believed this literally—it wasn't a suicidal impulse—but I knew it to be true. I might remain, a teenager and then a young woman and then an adult, moving around the same bedroom in my mother's house, but myself as I knew her would be dead, turned into whomever Tray saw when he shuffled through those photos. I had no other choice; I had to go.

7

Four years. That's how long it took to gather the nerve and the money to leave, bags taped over my window even in the depths of summer, except when I unstuck the tape and unfolded the plastic to let someone I'd invited in. I told my mother I could only sleep in lightless dark; Tray put on a bored look as I talked, but the stillness of his body told me he was listening. He knew I knew, and the longer I went without saying anything, the more the power between us shifted. One Saturday morning about a year after I graduated, I knocked a carton of orange juice off the counter while reaching for a piece of toast. "Whoops," Tray said, from the kitchen table, where he was eating a chicken Hot Pocket. "That'll be a bitch to clean up." Juice waterfalled along the cabinets, pooling on the linoleum under the sink. My mother was at Rosendale, working alumni weekend.

I opened the drawer where we kept clean rags. Tray took a bite, and the dumb look on his face as he chewed made me stop what I was doing. I grabbed my toast and vanished into my room, leaving the carton glugging out.

"What the heck," Tray shouted, but after a few minutes his chair scraped across the floor and the faucet turned on. When I came out a couple of hours later, the kitchen was cleaner than before I'd spilled the juice.

Nathaniel was not an everyday thought, but I kept track of him loosely; sometimes on purpose, and sometimes because news of him found its way to me as it did to all of Greening. I hadn't quite let go of my question. Plus, he'd given me something no one else had: an idea of where I might go. It was not an unhappy time, that holding period. I lost whole days in books, and walked around with the edges of myself dissolved, already partway gone. I was an orphan, hiding in a misty field; I was a murderer, brushing pipe ashes onto the floor; I was a ghost, looking for my baby; I was Nathaniel himself, thumb out on the highway, headed for New York. Sometimes I rode my bike out to his mother's house, comparing it in real life to the descriptions from his memoir. It was funny how they didn't match at all.

I submitted a poem to a local writing contest and read it in the same church where my mother said Nathaniel had shouted his words from the altar; that same spring, Nathaniel's cowritten screenplay about a twenty-year-old pregnant pool hustler in backwoods Wisconsin received an Oscar nod. After two unspeakably dull years working on Rosendale's cleaning crew—riding silently to work with my mother, the car reeking of perfume in the morning, bleach on the way home—I enrolled at Quincy Community College. I majored in liberal studies because there were few requirements and signed up for classes that seemed likely to transfer. I had my eye on a few colleges in New York City, attainable-seeming ones. Barth College was a mediocre place, but I was still surprised when I got in, and even more surprised about the thirty-thousand-dollar renewable "merit" scholarship available only to transfer students above a certain GPA threshold who also qualified for Pell Grants. Best of all, the campus was one crosstown bus away from the famous university where Nathaniel Fellow taught in a small but prestigious MFA program.

When I got to New York, I decided, I would find him and ask if he would read my poems. He would like them so much, recognizing in them the same source material that had driven him to write, that he would let me take one of his classes. That was the whole plan. The last step was hardest to envision, but I had faith in its contours. I had once come across a story about Berryman and Lowell sitting in the back of the class at Iowa Writers' Workshop drunk as skunks, neither of them enrolled. Knowing not a single writer in real life, I believed they inhabited a world of limitless passion, arms always open for someone at the start of the line.

Not long after I accepted Barth's offer, I picked up *People* magazine and learned that Nathaniel's television actress girlfriend had been spotted in Cannes, canoodling with her director. On Memorial Day my mother and Tray blew through the front door, laughing, home a bit early from a long weekend in Tahquamenon Falls—on my mother's left ring finger, a gold band studded with chips of green. That same weekend, Nathaniel was hospitalized briefly for a tiny stroke. The news, which took the form of an overwrought wish for his good health—the editor in chief was a fan—made *The Greening Gazette*'s front page.

I was almost twenty-three. I mailed a check to the roommates I found on Craigslist and bought a Greyhound ticket to New York City's Port Authority, departure date July 30, 2010. My lease started on August 1, and I wanted to arrive in time for an event I'd found online, a reading Nathaniel was headlining for an anthology called *Best of the New*. The event was free, and refreshments would be served; I was as excited for it as I would be for a wedding. I would wear my mother's black shift dress, short on me but still long enough to be on the right side of professional, and I would bring, in my purse, three typed poems.

Oh, those days before I left! As leaving will do to a place, everything took on a sweetness. My mother was a hero, tragic and flawed and imprisoned here forever in her tulip-printed bathrobe, squinting at the paper as the birds shrieked outside the kitchen window. I loved the headband she used to keep her bangs off her face, a twist of stretchy fabric turned gray from washing. I loved the vinyl tablecloth with its garish yellow pinwheels, the creak in the dining room floor, the way the water spurted cold then burning hot out of the showerhead. And Greening, in July! Bushes dripping with early blackberries, hawks on the power lines, our across-the-street neighbor on her front porch shouting the exact number of minutes the mailman was late. I would miss it. I relished the big, complicated swirl of feelings, all so poetic and adult. The perfect kind of pain, softened by relief. I never expected for one second to come back.

I didn't take very much. A couple pairs of jeans, my old corduroy parka, a flimsy sundress of my mother's, a bit too short for me, and her black shift for the event. A pillowcase—Goofy's face smiling up at me—and a towel and some loose tampons. A Rosendale sweatshirt I'd stolen years before from the gift shop, two holes worn into wrist seams through which I poked my thumbs. The Nortons, of course. They went into the suitcase first, with a few of Nathaniel's novels. I packed a separate box with books to be sent in the mail. Nathaniel's poems were staying with me, for easy access while I traveled.

The next morning, my last full day in Greening, I drove my mother's car to the UPS office in the near-abandoned strip mall between Greening and Quincy. I had never mailed a box and felt as bumbling as I had during the many administrative steps of applying to college, registering for classes, getting transcripts sent and financial details hammered out.

"I'm so sorry," I told the man behind the counter. "I'm sending this box to New York City?"

The man made almost no impression. He was tall, with grayish-brown hair, somewhere in the second half of his life. Behind one of his hairy ears dangled an uncapped red pen. Media mail would be the cheapest way to send the box, he confirmed, and my bus was likely to arrive at my destination before the books. He grabbed a tape roll and deftly mummied the box a few extra times, "to keep all your goodies safe."

"Wilhelmina," he said, handing back my debit card. "Pretty name. You never hear it anymore. That's what my grandmom was called, makes me picture those doilies from cookie plates."

"Doilies," I said. "I like that." But I was thinking about New York City, about my books moving through the country in the dark back of a truck, whether they'd be lonely, somehow, without me. All those years casting every man I met as father, and would you believe I took the shipping receipt without saying thanks? Without meeting his eyes, the exact same shade of blue as mine?

"Don't leave me here," my mother said as I slid my suitcase into the luggage compartment. It was just before ten P.M., a Wednesday night; the Indian Trails bus I needed—Greyhound's regional line—only stopped in Greening once a week. "You're killing me." A joke, but the words came out with a desperate edge.

"Mom, stop." She'd always been a couple of inches shorter than me, but she seemed even smaller than usual, dressed in one of my old hoodies with her hands balled up in the front pouch.

"You are," she said. When I went for a hug, she stood there in the same position, her knuckles digging into my belly. I couldn't bear it and turned away without saying anything else. I took a window seat in the exact middle of the bus, the other seats empty except for a couple of snoring men in the very last row, a smell coming off them—sweat, or the crispy tang of urine—that inched toward me and away, as if in time with their exhales. I lifted a hand, unsure if my mother could see me from the curb, where she'd taken a seat under the party store's neon sign. I was the only passenger who boarded in Greening. Above the parking lot, the sky was an unsettled purple, the sun still pressing up against the edge of the horizon.

The same day I boarded the bus, Geraldine Keene, Nathaniel's longest-lasting assistant, gave her notice, though I wouldn't learn about that bit of synchronicity until much, much later, after snooping in his university inbox and noticing, with a start, the date. While she was deleting emails, checking her account balances, packing her things to return to her family's house in West Virginia, I was drifting in and out of sleep as strip malls and scrubby forests scrolled by, waking for a few minutes whenever the bus pulled over into a gravel parking lot and swallowed up another man.

It was a thirty-four-hour trip; much cheaper than the plane, and I needed all my money. My temple smacking against the cold glass of the bus window, legs zipped up to my chest and tipped against the wall, I thought not of New York, not of the poems I aspired to write, not even of Nathaniel, but instead, of my mother. I was already farther away from Greening than she'd been since I was born. I didn't think I'd ever understand it, how you could live your whole life burrowing only into what was right in front of you without wondering what you were missing. My mother never told me what I really wanted to know: whether there was something she hoped she'd grow up to be, why she married Tray, the hold Greening had on her, which seemed to come from the landscape itself. If there was more to her Nathaniel story, all those signed copies of his books. Who my father was, and why she'd kept the answer from me.

On weekend afternoons when I was little, we'd drive to Elbow Lake and park ourselves on a blanket for hours, my mother reading a mystery, me running between the blanket and the water, where I'd wade in up to my thighs, screaming from the cold, before turning back to her. At dusk we'd roam the corners of the beach where the shoreline turned from sand to rocks, casting our flashlights in wide circles until a stone winked under the beam, its mineral veins throwing back the light. Gray and plain in daylight, those rocks, but full of secret fire at night—you just had to look a certain way to find it. What did it mean for my mother, that I'd left her? What did it mean for me? Something we'd been able to ignore in Greening, at least most of the time, a fundamental difference between us, had been dragged out and exposed. There wasn't really a way to get back to before we'd seen it, and as the bus sped through the thickets of gas stations and Home Depots and Walmarts that made up the interstitial geography of every state in the Midwest, I knew that with every mile, I was losing my mother.

I'd traded her—look how easily!—for whatever my life was about to become.

There. The lessons I took with me on my quest to find Nathaniel, all the still-stuck thorns of my early life. Slut, poet, mother killer, girl. Grist, Nathaniel would call it. Feed it to the mill.

So that's what I did.

A BEDLAMITE SPEEDS TO THY PARAPETS

1

Two days after I watched my mother disappear on the curb, I saw New York City for the first time. It was late morning, and I was delirious with lack of sleep, desperate for a shower. The bus had entered the Lincoln Tunnel to deposit us on a new planet, where there was no soil, only concrete and brick and funny, stoic trees that seemed of a different genus than any I'd seen before, more animal than plant. I pressed my forehead to the window. Here it was, city nested in bays, the place I'd read so much about, its multitudes bent toward some flashing scene. New York was Greening's perfect inverse. Both places simply could not exist at once. Except for Nathaniel, I was the only proof of where I'd come from, and as I tripped over a hot dog boat filled with something soupy and opaque, our tie seemed stronger, and more important, than ever.

I was too dazed to be afraid. After heading the wrong way on two different trains, I took a cab to Ninety-fourth Street and First Avenue, biting into the seven hundred dollars that was supposed to last until I got my financial aid refund or found a job, whichever happened first. The building was a five-story walk-up wreathed by a black gate that mirrored the ones over the first-floor windows and kept about four hundred trash bags from spilling onto the sidewalk. The bags seemed to rustle as I climbed the stoop, the stench, foul as it was, a welcome interruption from my own bad smell. I sat down to wait for Dev, my new roommate, whom I'd texted from the cab—he was supposed to meet me there, with a key. I leaned hard against the buzzer. Nothing. I tried on and off for an hour, a fresh sunburn tightening across my nose.

I was half asleep, curled up against the graffitied door with a T-shirt over my head, when a person I presumed was Dev shouted, "The subway, the subway!" from about halfway down the block. It had been three hours since I'd texted. My forearms were giving off heat. When he reached the building he leaned, panting, against the rail of the stoop and raked a hand through his shoulder-length tangle of hair. "I'm so sorry, Wilhelmina—you are Wilhelmina, right? The fucking subway. First there was a signal problem, then someone died somewhere or something, and then the doors wouldn't close for ten entire minutes at Eighty-sixth street. They'd get, like, almost there, like an inch from shutting, and bam, they'd shoot back open. I swear, I was *vibrating* with stress. I hope you weren't just *waiting* here."

"It's okay. I, um, napped."

I shoved the T-shirt I'd been using as a sunshade into my backpack and stood up, Dev's glance moving from my slimy ponytail to my rumpled tank top to my sweatpants, so stretched out from my hours on the bus I'd rolled the waistband four times. "You're so tall and pretty!" he said, digging his keys out of his pocket. "You could make a fortune in this city if you wanted to. Tell me how on earth you got to New York." His face crinkled; he could smell me, too. "For some reason I don't think you flew."

"I took the bus."

"From Iowa! Wilhelmina!" He put his hand on his chest, as if I had struck him there. He was wearing a white T-shirt, the Hanes kind that came in packs, the most familiar thing I'd seen since leaving Greening. I knew almost nothing about Dev, except that he and my other roommate, Cody, were "open-minded professional twenty-somethings looking for a clean housemate with no pets," and so desperate to rent their spare room they were okay waiting for the security deposit until I got my financial aid refund.

Of course it felt unreal to me, like a cutscene from the chapter in

Nathaniel's memoir about his first days in New York, the grimy vestibule Dev and I couldn't fit into at the same time, the four flights of steep stairs, the long hallways tiled with mustardy checkerboard squares, interrupted here and there by an ominous-looking drain. "No air-conditioning," Dev said as he unlocked the door of the apartment. It was ten degrees hotter than in the stairwell. "Except for the window unit in Cody's room. But that bitch always keeps his door shut. Your room is here"—he gestured to a door on our left, kicking my rolling suitcase in—"but first let me give you the tour."

There wasn't much to see. The entry hallway led to Dev's room, and then the bathroom, a psychedelic chamber of loosening pieces of tile—red backsplash behind the blue sink, the same yellow checkerboard from the hallway in a bath-mat-shaped square at the foot of the tub, narrow teal planks inside the shower—because, Dev explained, the landlord made repairs with whatever he had lying around. No common space but the kitchen, sliced in half with a temporary wall partitioning off Cody's room and presumably the space's only window; through a glass panel on the top a band of daylight illuminated the stack of dishes in the sink.

My room had a block window that didn't open. Nothing inside but a stackable set of plastic drawers—three—coated with a layer of dust as sticky as sap. I couldn't quite tell where I'd fit a bed. At $550 a month, it had been one of the more affordable places on Craigslist. Now I understood why. "The last guy had a sort of folding mat thing," Dev said cheerfully. I peered through the window at an identical one across the alley—I couldn't make out anything behind it except a blurry dark shape. It could be anything, anyone; that I couldn't tell filled me with a tremendous buoyancy, a feeling I had no words for, something entirely new, gifted by the indifferent city. No one was watching. Here, in my room in New York City, no one could see me at all.

2

I thought I was in the wrong place. I'd imagined the *Best of the New* reading inside a theater like the one at Rosendale, that hill of red velvet chairs steep enough to sled down, but the event listing had led me to a room deep in a random building on the outskirts of the university where Nathaniel taught. It was barely the size of a tennis court and half full of folding metal chairs. On a platform against the far wall, a woman in black jeans and a black T-shirt crawled alongside a cord trailing off the microphone stand, affixing it in places with squares of electrical tape. "I'm here for the reading?" I said in her general direction.

"Are you one of the poets?" she asked. "The event doesn't start for thirty minutes."

"No," I answered, thrilled. "I'm just here to listen."

The woman stood, threading the roll of tape onto her forearm. "Ah, well. You have your pick of seats. People are always late for these things." I'd assumed there'd be a crowd. I put my bag on the chair closest to the table where the woman had begun setting up a tray of fruit and cheese. "Go on," she said. "Help yourself, before it's all diseased."

I filled a plate with cheddar cubes. An event with free food! On nights she worked Rosendale fundraisers, my mother would get home close to midnight. Some people eat the cheese, other people make the plates, she told me once, when I asked her why she never brought back the good appetizers from those parties. A few days in New York, and I'd already switched sides.

The woman's name was Tilda, like the movie star, and she was the program coordinator for the English department. In the time it took me to eat two plates of cheddar, she'd finished setting up the book table, opened several bottles of wine, unloaded and arranged an additional row of chairs, and sorted the cashbox. Sweat shimmered on her upper lip. She had my mother's way of doing several things at once.

"Can I help at all?" I asked. Tilda glanced up from the stack of programs she was folding down the middle.

"Are you an undergraduate here?"

"No, I go to Barth." School didn't start for a couple of weeks. I hadn't even been inside the main building. "I mean I will. In September."

"It's nice of you to offer," Tilda said. Her eyebrow ring gave her a cool skepticism. She didn't know what to make of me. "Are you sure?" The doors swung open, and a few people trickled in, heading straight for the food.

"It'll be better than sitting by myself."

"If you want to, I won't say no." She handed a program to a woman wearing a denim baseball hat. "Finish folding these and then you can pre-pour drinks—when people start to show up, the wine table will be a nightmare. And feel free to help yourself."

Ten minutes before the reading, all but a handful of chairs were empty. But just when I thought the whole thing might be canceled—no sign of Nathaniel, let alone any of the other readers—the doors whooshed open. Within minutes, the theater was full of people shrieking and hugging, sometimes when they were in the middle of trying to get wine from me, so I stood there, one arm outstretched, while I waited for them to notice. With my free arm, I poured new glasses. A few said thank you. Most did not, but I didn't begrudge them this—it seemed right somehow. I was as happy as I've ever been, almost levitating out of gratitude to be among them, on the periphery of their conversations about Lamar or Jesse or Rachel's new book and did you read that piece and how they loved it, just loved it, it was so fucking good. The whole time I'd been in Greening, reading my Norton anthology for the fortieth time, this world had existed. Rosendale had never been the answer—this was the place I'd been waiting for.

They were writers, I realized, watching them filter down the rows, tossing their jackets onto chairs to reserve a space or sitting down briefly before popping up to shout at someone across the room, triggering a conversation in affectionate gestures because who could hear anything in the swirl of voices and laughter. Could it be that they *all* were? I hadn't expected everyone to be so radiant and young. Their beauty was a side effect of their specificity; almost every single person was intentional in their appearance in a way people in Greening were not.

Tilda appeared at my side. "Five after seven and he's not even *here* yet. Extremely typical. How are we doing on wine?" *He* meant Nathaniel. Tilda knew him. There was no reverence in her voice; she seemed not to like him very much. Tilda picked up a cup and drank the entire thing, then knelt and groped around under the table, retrieving one of the few remaining bottles of wine. She filled her glass and took a polite-looking sip that somehow depleted half of her drink. "Don't serve this one. This one is ours," she said, topping herself off before stashing the bottle behind a table leg and rushing to do something else. As the minutes ticked by, people began to take their seats, a prickle of irritation in their collective voice.

I felt Nathaniel before I saw him—a change in the air, the buzz of something about to happen sharpened into an opening note. I almost couldn't bring myself to look. All the years I'd spent reading his poems, the dozens of times I'd parked my bike on the corner outside his mother's house, searching for some clue to what I wanted to know, who I was or might become—in that dingy reading room with all those actual writers, my decision to come seemed very, very silly, and more than a little crazy. Here he was, not a character I'd invented, but a man, a person I knew nothing about except for what he'd made publicly available. I felt, in a word, mortified, standing behind a folding table covered in plastic cups of wine, wearing my mother's best dress.

Tilda jogged toward Nathaniel, unsmiling. Two young people followed in his wake like beautiful, ineffectual bodyguards. Reg and Liliam, I'd learn; that year, they were his favorites. The room had gone quiet, as if someone had muffled everyone else with a towel. Or maybe it only went quiet for me.

"Right on time," Tilda said. The tape still bobbled around her wrist, and I felt oddly embarrassed for her, letting Nathaniel see her like that. They intersected just in front of the drinks table. He was slight, and not very tall—perhaps two inches shorter than me. I'd imagined him my height, taller, for so long that now the truth kept hitching in my brain: Was it really him? No navy suit. Instead, acid-washed jeans even I could tell were uncool, a sweat-stained button-down, pointy-toed gray cowboy boots that looked as though they'd been chewed by a bear. This illogical getup—it could have been assembled from Tray's closet—gave me a jolt of intimacy, and with it, a flicker of confidence. Anyone, New Yorker or not, could see Nathaniel wasn't from the city, but how many people would recognize his personal style as a fingerprint of Greening, where cowboys were still the masculine ideal and trends took so long to arrive they stuck around forever, eras blending into each other? Anything that had once been cool stayed that way forever. My ears were very, very hot. I had the strange thought that he might recognize *me*.

"Your forgiveness, Tilda, please," he said. When he spoke, you knew he was a good singer. His voice seemed the oldest thing about him, older even than his graying hair, which began high on his head, like a crown. "I was having such a wonderful meal."

I leaned across the table toward Nathaniel, mouth open, trying to figure out the most earth-shatteringly poetic way to say, excuse me, sir, would you like a glass of wine? But before I could arrive at a single word, before I could even take him all the way in, this man I'd traveled years of my life to meet, there was Liliam—not yet Lili to me, just a girl in the way.

"I'll take a wine?" Her hair was too red to be natural, parted deeply on the left and trailing down to the middle of her back. With her Disney eyes—lash extensions, I'd later learn, two hundred dollars a set—and lipsticked bow of a mouth, she looked like a sort of punk-rock Ariel, though whatever edge she might have gained from her leather leggings was undercut by the aggressive cuteness of her face. I gestured to the full cups on the table. "A fresh one if you can? Those have been *sitting*." She gave me a look of intimate disappointment, as if I were her child and I'd just handed her a report card full of D's. It was somehow winning. I reached under the table for Tilda's bottle, which I poured into a fresh glass. "A little more," Liliam said, smiling, when I reached the halfway mark. Nathaniel was already receding down the aisle. Liliam is short—five three in bare feet—but she has a way of blotting everything around her out. Like Reg, for example, who must have been right beside her, who surely took one of the lukewarm glasses without complaint, who probably smiled at me and said thank you, who told me, later, that when he saw me that night—*so eager to please*, he said, so obviously *new*—he immediately marked me as one of Nathaniel's.

Had I really even *seen* Reg, that night? He comes to me only as outline, the fact of him, not the feeling. Did he read? He must have. It was a party for Nathaniel's pets—and Reg, back then, was a pet, the rare male allowed into Nathaniel's regular orbit—the launch of an annual anthology featuring mostly current and former students, published by a small press helmed by one of Nathaniel's friends. *Best of the New* was a pocket-sized paperback with a dusty-feeling cover and smudgy paper, but Nathaniel's name was on the spine, and every poem inside had been steered toward profundity by the elegant, chastising mark of his pencil. As a title, *Best of the New* seemed incomplete, almost nonsensical, but probably I was missing some literary reference.

Tilda introduced the event and Nathaniel took the stage to "say a few words" about the anthology that expanded into a story about the time, as a young writer new to the city, he'd attempted to hand-deliver a manuscript to the then–poetry editor of *The New Yorker,* camping out on a bench beside the man's favorite coffee cart every morning for weeks, conspicuously reading library copies of books by writers the editor had championed, until one day the man turned to him, coughed politely, and said, "Son, I'll take a look at your work, but if it's bad I'm calling the police." Here, Nathaniel paused, and the room leaned forward. "He didn't publish me—never would—but he didn't send me to the clink either, and that was enough to keep me going." Everyone laughed, me included, because Nathaniel had been published in *The New Yorker* countless times. The story was endearing—a little pathetic, even as it underscored the inevitability of his great career—and it buoyed me to think of teenage Nathaniel trying to elbow his way into a place he didn't belong.

The readers were mostly women. If she was a great writer but not pretty, I was, unthinkingly, comforted. If she was pretty and bad, that too was a comfort. A very good poem could make a man look more attractive, but it had only minor effects on the perceived attractiveness of a woman. I rated prettiness in a limited way, informed by the media I'd consumed in Greening and with a cluster of actresses (including Nathaniel's former girlfriend) as aspirational points. I wish I could say my ear for the work was more sophisticated, but my "better" was determined by familiarity, the work's likeness to the poems I'd gorged on back home, Norton- and Nathaniel-approved.

Liliam, unfortunately, was brilliant and ravishing and weird, prettier than me, prettier than everyone, and a better poet, too. Onstage, her cuteness sharpened. She positioned herself in front of the microphone and sent a dead-eyed stare into the audience. The poem started with an orange. As she read, she seemed to grow, and the orange changed, too, losing its peel, falling apart into sections, each composed of cells that cordoned off a tiny star of juice, the juice not orange juice at all but an evocation of what the speaker had lost in the transition from girlhood to adolescence, a bright and vibrant and stinging essence that shocked you when you bit it. I couldn't believe how she got the orange, the thing itself, to hold that transformation. The poem was two pages long and when she reached the end of the first sheet she balled it up and threw it. When Liliam's paper flower ricocheted off those listening heads, goosebumps rose on my arms. After finishing, she let the second piece of paper drift to the floor. "Thank you," she said once it settled near the microphone's feet; she returned to her normal size and stepped off the stage, leaving the paper behind her. Every poet that followed would walk carefully around it, not stepping on it, but not picking it up either.

No one else really stood out, mumbling one after another into the microphone under a tent of yellow light, except for the only Black writer in the lineup, who recited her poem from memory, and a mousy brunette with tortoiseshell glasses who read for nearly ten minutes, pausing so long after each line that the anticipation of the ending became almost unbearable. When she finished, she looked as relieved as the audience. I watched Nathaniel—in an aisle seat, beside Reg—from a chair behind the drinks table. Sometimes he leaned forward, elbows on his knees and chin propped in his hands, like a teenager. After Liliam, he barked a laugh-like, incredulous sound, leaning across Reg's lap to tell her something as she sat back down. When the tortoiseshell woman passed him on her way back to her seat, Nathaniel told her bravo, loud enough for everyone to hear.

There was another mad dash for wine at the end—the stack of books ignored—glasses on the table disappearing even as people drifted away, to do whatever beautiful young people did in New York City on a weekday evening. I was grateful for the set of small, obvious tasks—the scattering of trampled cups on the floor, which would need to be thrown away, the rows of folding chairs waiting to be collapsed and stacked on their cart, the souring cheese tray, which had to be cleared—they gave me a reason to stay. Tilda gestured at me as if to say, please, don't do that, but I shook my head. I had no intention of trying to talk to him; the reality of it all had blown my plan from my brain. I just wasn't ready for it to be over.

I tackled the cups first, leaving the remaining bottles on the table for the small group of writers who'd gathered there to talk to Nathaniel, Tilda chatting aimlessly with the ones still waiting for his attention, Reg and Liliam a few feet away, as if to ensure his protection against a too-eager fan. Next, the chairs. I found if I slid two under each armpit and one a bit lower, squeezed between chair and forearm with my elbow as a hook, I could waddle to the cart with six on my person. On the other side of the room, the poets were laughing at something Reg said. Though I'd been painfully awake to Nathaniel's presence all evening, his voice in my periphery was as astonishing, and somehow predetermined, as if he'd shown up to meet me at Port Authority.

Nathaniel! I'd willed him to me. I almost dropped the chairs in relief and fear.

"You're overburdened," he said.

"A pack mule," I agreed, staring at his ugly boots, dizzy with panic.

"I will relieve you of a side bag!"

He stepped closer and tried to take the weight of three chairs onto his own arm, his hand coming underneath the seat edge of the lowest chair, very near where my curled and cramping fingers bumped up against my thigh. Then his fingers were between the chair and my body; his knuckles grazed my leg, first softly, and then—was I imagining it?—with more intention. It was the wrong kind of first contact. I gripped harder, startled, and pulled the chairs back into myself so that I almost lost my balance and clattered over. He looked at me with some alarm, and I looked slightly downward at him.

"It's your *party.*" The degree of emotion in my voice disturbed us both. His irises were brown, a touch lighter than his pupils. "You shouldn't be picking up the *chairs*!"

"It's no problem," he said, and backed away. He picked up the chair nearest to him and folded it, striding beside me to the cart with that single one held before him like a shield. I couldn't move very fast, and this bothered him, I could tell, that he had to match my pace to keep up the charade of honestly wanting to help. He rushed ahead, unable to take it any longer, and, looking over at the group he'd left by the drinks table, he stacked his chair onto the cart.

"Really," I said, struggling to lean mine against the wall without calamity. "You didn't need to!"

"I said no problem. Did you like the reading?"

"Oh yes. It was incredible. I don't think I've ever . . ." He glanced toward Liliam and Reg, not even pretending to listen, so I stopped.

"Well, good. Thank you for this." He waved his hand around the theater. "If you're sure?"

"I've got it. Thank you."

Nothing else. A few minutes later they were gone. It had been a terrific failure, and the most interesting night of my life. Tilda turned up the lights until the room was bright and horrible. "You're hired, you angel!" she said as I finished the chairs.

"Really?"

"I mean, no. There's no job. But yes, come back anytime, though I want to tell you that it is not right to do work without getting paid." She handed me a grocery bag—inside, two unopened bricks of cheddar, a bag of grapes, a bottle of wine, and a copy of *Best of the New.* I hadn't thought of any of it as work, and now I was getting a book and a bag of free food. Tilda asked for my email address, and I wrote it down for her on the back of a program.

I squeezed the handle of the grocery bag, paper melting into my sweaty palm. "Tilda? What should I do?" I hadn't meant to ask it out loud. It's just, I had no idea.

She laughed, and when I didn't, her face softened. "With your life? I can't help you with that one. But right now? If I didn't have a hundred emails, I'd head over to Noodle Fun on First Ave. and get the dumpling soup. Or, I don't know, kiddo, just walk around. It's the city." She put her free hand on my arm and gave it an awkward pat. "Everyone's first year in New York is hell. It does get easier, I promise." It was clear she wanted me to leave—her phone was in her hand, and she was actively trying not to look at the screen.

Eating at a sit-down restaurant alone! I'd never done it. Though my day had already been full of tests and newness—had I really met Nathaniel?—that seemed one trial too many.

I walked home, weaving into and around knots of people, stopping with them at crosswalks, shoulder to shoulder, temporary intimates before we dissolved into our separate lives. Lilac and shit and alcohol and garlic and body odors of various flavors and degrees, shaving cream and Lysol and wet dog, yeast and yogurt, Parmesan, hot coffee and—how strange, to find myself suddenly transported there—the precise, mossy exhalation of Rosendale's cafeteria dumpster after heaving a full bag over the side. Tickle of a stranger's hair against my bare shoulder, a broad, sweaty hip nudging me to the side, sourceless dusting of cigarette ash on my forearm, a splat of ooze against my cheekbone, just below my eye. Tattoos and handbags the size of wagons and curse words in languages I couldn't guess. Nathaniel, the poets, where had they gone? I kept expecting to see them, as if they were the entire city, the only real people in it, everyone else just actors in a play, cast to set the stars of the show in relief.

Near my apartment, the crowds thinned. I passed storefronts and restaurant windows, each one a frame for a story I couldn't begin to imagine. In one, a girl—a woman, I corrected myself, like me—at a table alone, a napkin unfolded on her knees, a steak in front of her, half covered by fries. A magazine upright and tilted against her water glass. Two more blocks, I noticed another, a little older than the first, eating sushi, her long hair pulled over one shoulder. And then another, a series of women eating alone, all of them sitting by the window, watching me, perhaps, just as I was watching them.

I sat on the stoop outside of my apartment building and took my shoes half off. The concrete still held the day's heat; someone was frying chicken. A little after ten P.M. My mother would be asleep, but I punched her number into my decrepit Razr anyway. She answered on the first ring.

"Is everything okay?" she said.

Maybe being on the phone made it easier. Maybe it was the wine, the adrenaline from the reading, the long walk to my apartment. Maybe it was the city itself, a place full of people who'd done impossible things, like get there in the first place. I was so far from home—

what did it matter if I broke one of its most important rules?

"I need to ask you a question."

"Okay." She sounded wary. Was Tray next to her?

"Why is your copy of *Copper Harbor* signed *For my Northern Star*?"

"*Copper Harbor*?"

"Yeah, Mom."

"I don't know what that is—"

"The book."

"Book?"

That should have been answer enough, but I wanted it to hear her say it. I wanted the story all the way dead. I needed it for everything that was going to come next. "Nathaniel Fellow's book. The poems. He crossed out his name, signed the book *For my Northern Star.* You said you met him. You *drank* with him. Why would he say that to you? Write *my*, like that?"

"I don't know, honey, I didn't even remember he did that. Why does—" She stopped. The silence unfolded and unfolded again. I heard her understand what I was asking, and I waited for her to comfort me, to tell me the truth, to explain. Instead, she laughed. "Oh my lord. You didn't really think?"

"I didn't," I said, but oh God, hadn't I? I didn't fully realize how much I'd needed it to be true until I knew for sure it wasn't. "Not really." She was still laughing; I was falling through space.

"Lordy, I'm sorry," she said. "I was not expecting that."

"It's so personal." I hated how upset I sounded. "The word *my*."

"He signed my friend's book the exact same way. We made fun of him for it. That man—I don't remember a word of his poems, but he was a wicked, wicked flirt. I bet every house in Greening has an inscription like that in one of his books."

There was another pause; an opportunity, I see now, to ask her, for only the second time in my life. Who he really was, my father. I didn't take it. Is anything harder than asking someone you love a question you know they don't want you to ask? She started talking about a problem with the roof that turned into a monologue about volunteering more at church, now that I was gone, and I let her go on like that for a while. A few of the windows in the sky went black; a few more filled with light. A child-sized shadow looked down from the sixth-floor apartment across the street. "Mom, I gotta go," I said. She asked me again if I was okay, the wariness back in her voice, and that was it.

He was short. Hadn't I known the instant I saw him? Yes. Short, with those dark eyes, no sign of me anywhere. Stupid, all of it. Of course no one was waiting to claim me. If I wanted to become someone—and didn't I, still? if only so I wouldn't have to go back to Greening?—I'd have to make it happen on my own.

At the reading, everyone seemed to know each other. What would it be like to walk into a place like that, one of them, and climb onto the stage? To learn to do what Liliam had done with little more than the word *orange*? A week ago, this world hadn't just been impossible, closed permanently to someone like me: It had been unimaginable.

But if I was going to last in New York long enough to figure out how to get Nathaniel to teach me how to write, I needed money.

3

A few days later, after much creative math involving the shrinking digits in my bank account, I wandered into an Italian place near my apartment and asked the girl at the hostess stand if they had any jobs. She returned with the manager, an indeterminately aged man in a gray suit, who took me to a table in the back and gave me a seltzer with bitters. "Good for the stomach," he said, using his thumbnail to wedge out something from between his bottom teeth. He asked about my experience, and I embroidered the work I'd done in the cafeteria at Rosendale. "So not much. Okay." His eyes ticked over my hair, lips, breasts, as if checking off items on a list. A professional look, not a sexual one. "What would you do if everything's seated, busy night, and a party of four came in?"

"I would tell them to come back in a little while?"

"Fifteen minutes." He held out a hand, flashing five three times fast. "You'd tell them, please, have a drink at the bar while you wait—your table will be ready soon. Right this way, pull the stools, get the bartender's attention. Menus, for the wait."

"What if it took longer than fifteen minutes?" And if there were no seats at the bar, I didn't ask.

"Bar time is different than regular time. But sure, maybe they ask about the table. No problem. We just dropped the check, we're getting the table ready for you. Beautiful table, best seat in the house."

"But wouldn't they want to know how long it would take?"

"Fifteen minutes," he said, enunciating each syllable. "Next, you get a woman, comes in alone. What do you say to her?"

"Um—first, I guess, hello? Is it, will it just be you dining with us this evening?"

"Never just, like it's a bad thing. No. You say, table for one? And then where do you seat her?"

"Wherever she wants? That's open?"

"A two-top at the window." He pointed at a table I'd seen on my way in, tucked between the bar and the street-facing window, where a cheerful yellow flower bobbed in a squat vase. "Always seat a woman dining alone at the window. It draws people in." If I could have picked anywhere to sit, I would have picked that seat—it seemed both private, safe, somehow, and in the center of things. I hadn't noticed it was the restaurant's point of contact with the outside world, though was that really true? Hadn't I stared at women eating in windows, evaluated their appearances, imagined what they went home to, or didn't, after paying the check? I thought I wanted to be invisible, but maybe only if someone really *was* secretly watching. "Unless, if she's old or . . ." He gestured vaguely. "Then back here is good."

I didn't get that job, but the next day I found an Irish pub—Genesis—that hired me on the spot, even after I admitted I'd only mixed drinks in "social settings." "Wear your hair down," Mack said, handing me a rumpled black apron. "But brush it before you get here. Last girl left hairs all over the place."

Nathaniel's email wasn't on the university website, or anywhere else on the internet. I'd looked many times. But a week after the *Best of the New* launch, Tilda sent a message to two people, and cc'd, for some reason, me. "N like a hundred of your unsold BoN issues are still in my office. Please send Gerry to get them ASAP. Or do it yourself."

The next email in the thread was just to me. "Crap, Will. I meant to write you to say thanks and I got my wires crossed. Working too fast! Ignore that email! Let's get coffee sometime. Hope NYC is treating you good."

I read the emails at an internet café a few blocks from my apartment, where I exchanged wads of cash for a plastic card that bought me time—eight dollars an hour, or two for fifteen dollars—at one of seven ancient desktop computers. I liked the one in the corner nearest the door, with a mountainscape on its mouse pad, the screen angled slightly away from the rest of the room. My first year in New York I killed a lot of time there before shifts, typing poems into WordPad. Net Café was open twenty-four hours and sold gritty coffee for a buck twenty-five and yogurt parfaits in saran-wrapped plastic cups and fluffy samosas studded with peas, one of the few vegetables I ate in those days. I was somewhere now—even this forgotten corner of the city elevated my life to a higher frequency. I thought things like that, wrote them into poem after poem, biting into my fourth samosa, a word I wouldn't learn to pronounce correctly until almost a year later, when Lili, cringing, corrected me. ("Sa as in *sauce,*" she said, "not *Sam.*") Happiness, I didn't know to call it then, but that's what it was, the pleasure of being mid-step, just before.

Usually, it was just me and Arjun, the owner, who always gave me free refills, and sometimes a handful of teenage girls who huddled around a single computer, arguing and elbowing each other. I always checked my Barth email, which never had anything in it except generic dispatches from various administrative offices reminding of things like preregistration deadlines and incentive programs for healthy eating. I read them all. Barth was a real college—with colors and a logo, unlike QCC, where every email seemed to come from a different computer program—and I was about to be a real college student, even if I was sort of old, and wouldn't be attending the Truman dorm welcome sleepover for new residents, or whatever Strawberry Fest was—you needed friends for that, I was sure, and besides, I worked Friday evenings.

Work had eaten my plan to find Nathaniel. The training shifts were brutal—I wasn't paid, and Genesis was an understaffed operation, where I was expected to be able to work the floor and the bar, depending on the number of customers. For days I'd thought of little except the thousand humiliations I experienced there an hour. But Tilda's unexpected message brought back the thrill of the event, the feeling of Nathaniel's fingers against my leg as he pretended to help with the chairs. Finally, his email address. Faced with it, I heard my mother laughing into the phone.

Gerry's reply came while I was fiddling with an open draft to Nathaniel, replacing *hi* with *hello,* then *dear,* then *greetings.*

Tilda, I don't work for Nathaniel anymore and do not want to be affiliated with his books or literary events. Please delete this address from your contacts.

Here, as if the universe had designed it, was an opening.

Gerry, whoever she was—a person who'd worked for him, who picked up his forgotten books and answered strange questions from teenagers—did not want to be affiliated with Nathaniel anymore. I registered her tone—annoyed, obviously—but I didn't worry about what she was saying between the lines. I was so eager for an opportunity that I could only read it as one. If Nathaniel needed a replacement, why not me?

The email took nearly as long as the letter I'd written as a teenager, draft upon draft upon draft over the course of a week or so, typed and revised in hour-long chunks at Net Café, buying time with cash from my shifts at Genesis, but this one was no poem. I wrote him a sales pitch.

Before making my requests, one nested inside the other, I described myself. Tall, I wrote, with longish black hair and dark blue eyes. Quiet—the men at Genesis loved that word, why are you so quiet, they said, when I passed them their pints, what are you thinking about?—but maybe you remember me serving wine, stacking up chairs. You were a very kind helper. I said, I'd do pretty much anything to audit one of your workshops. Of course, I didn't tell him I knew he might be looking for help—that would be weird—but I made sure to mention tasks I thought an assistant might take on. Errands, dog walking, proofreading, you name it, ha ha. I said, I've only been here a couple of weeks, and I'm free most mornings. The truth is, I'm from Greening, too, and I don't know if I ever would have considered trying to make it in New York if it weren't for you. I included a recent poem, written at Net Café at dawn after a few too many cups of coffee, a draft that contained the phrase: *Only here, only me.*

Your pack mule. That's how I signed it, thinking of "my Northern Star."

I doubt he even looked at the poem.

This time, he responded within hours. *Greening! Goodness. You must be out of your mind with terror. Let's talk. My office, Thursday at 11 a.m.?*

4

I've almost arrived, now, at where we began for Nathaniel. I woke early the morning of our meeting. My mother's black dress might have been right for a daughter, but I knew it wasn't right for whatever this was going to be, because I'd read everything Nathaniel Fellow had ever written.

His books are full of women. They're easy to imagine. There she is, opening the door. Thirteen, a sucker in her mouth, quick to swear. Often young, but not always—sometimes she's approaching forty, still beautiful, smart and sly, the kind of woman who has seen a lot but can still learn something new. She's a brunette, a blonde, her hair the texture of cornsilk/a dusty miller/your old dog Chance, shining in the starlight and the sunlight and the moonlight. She wasn't a cliché, she was unique. She had knock-knees, a scar on her neck from the rock thrown by her little brother, her belly wasn't even perfectly flat, it had a nice soft ledge for your hand. She was sixteen, itchy with virginity. She was twenty-two behind the wheel of a car she stole, looking at you through her sunglasses. She wanted something; you knew what it was, or you didn't, and that was going to drive you mad. If she was a mother she was angry but also kind of a saint. If she was a wife she smoked and stared out the window and couldn't really be trusted. Sometimes the lovers were brown, from an island climate, but the wives were always white. If she was a girl she hadn't had sex yet. She was a girl until she was a wife or a mother. Maybe that's why when I read those stories, fourteen, fifteen, sitting in my mom's lounger in the backyard, the weave unfurling under my calves, I always cast myself as hero, as him—there were so many more interesting ways a man's story could end.

I picked the ratty sundress that stopped a couple of inches above my knees. He would like that I worked in a bar—I would try to find a way to mention it.

Nathaniel's office was technically in the same building as the *Best of the New* reading, but a different quadrant, fused with the rest of the structure only on the upper floors. I roamed the fluorescent, dingy corridors, retracing my steps back to identical elevator banks and riding them up and down. It seemed a metaphor for something, my inability to decode the names and numbers on various tiny placards all over the walls, and a reminder of the wrongness of my being there—a student at a far inferior college, who'd never known anyone personally who'd gone to graduate school. By the time I got off the elevator on the right level and made the correct series of turns, I was sweating and ten minutes late.

I followed the numbers down a hallway with wooden planks that gleamed in the sunlight. A rounded entryway led to an atrium lined with books, and beyond it, a secret-feeling classroom-like space where, that day, the seminar table was awash with stained plastic cups. Just beyond that was Nathaniel's office, overlooking a brick courtyard with a little spitting fountain that I never found my way into. Sometimes, tidying his desk, I wondered if they'd built the courtyard just for him, so he'd have something nice to look at from his chair.

I dabbed my forehead with a tissue, adjusted the bag on my shoulder, and knocked gently on the door. It yawned open under the pressure of my hand until I could just see in—a sliver of bare and indifferent wall.

"It's you, is it?" Nathaniel called. "The girl from Greening!"

I hovered on the threshold as he told me to sit, sit down. He stood halfway, gestured to a short couch upholstered in green velvet. I chose the chair facing his desk. He gave me a look like, okay, grinning a little, and sat back down behind it.

"A Greening girl," he said. "I've never met one of those in this city." We blinked at each other.

"A Greening boy," I said. "I've known some."

"Boy!" I blushed, like the idiot I was. "Your"—he waved his hand around, feeling for the word in space—"coloring"—I tensed—"is quite unusual." I'd trimmed my hair the night before with scissors Dev had pulled from the silverware drawer. I swooped it to one side, trying to make it less black and straight and conspicuous, but it fell back in my face.

"What ethnicity are you?"

"White? My mother is white," I said.

"Your father?"

The word almost evaporated me in my seat. The letter I'd sent as a teenager—I'd been so convinced he wouldn't link that to me—if he'd even seen it—but maybe he had? How many letters could he have received from teenagers claiming he was their father? How many emails from girls begging to be let into his poetry workshop? Of course he'd put it together, drawn the line connecting one deranged note to another. Now he was going to tell me to get out, flash a restraining order, something like that.

"What?" And then, carefully, my voice rattling only a little: "I don't know him. She didn't really either." I could taste the sweat on my upper lip.

"Greening. God, I wonder if *I* know him. But no, you're very young." I searched for extra meaning in his words and came up with nothing. He had never seen it, probably. Gerry, that invisible, diligent girl who never wanted to attend a literary event again, had taken care of it all.

"You should do a little genealogy research. Just for fun. A writing prompt, even. I would guess there's something besides white lurking in your blood." Nathaniel leaned back in his chair and folded his arms behind his head. His eyes skated from me to the window, the clock, his office door. His neck cracked; his gingham shirt strained against its buttons. He should have known better, though maybe he felt free to do anything, say anything, in a conversation with an undergrad who was not his student, a pack mule from nowhere with no one, his biggest fan.

My arms tightened around the pile of books in my lap, the ones I'd brought for him to sign. On top was the audit form I'd found deep on the famous university's website, printed out at Net Café. A pressure welled up behind my eyes, hot and stinging. I'd expected—even counted on—appraisal, but not in this way, so verbal and overt, so completely unrelated to the poems I'd sent. Nathaniel was looking at his computer monitor now. The rope—so taut between us when I'd called him boy—slackened as he put his hand on his mouse.

"The great poet is an asshole," I said, pulling it. "I guess I'm not surprised."

He looked up. It wasn't enough, and a familiar kind of move, but he was back, at least. "Did I offend you? Writers don't get offended. At least not the real ones. It's not an interesting reaction. It closes, instead of opening." He smiled, revealing a very straight and white set of teeth. New veneers, I'd learn.

"Well then, maybe I'm not really a writer," I snapped, or tried to.

"But that's why you're here, isn't it? Wilhelmina Miles? With your permission slip and your handful of drafts? You want to *become* one."

How could he say it so easily, the thing I wanted? The stinging turned—horrible, horrible—to tears. "I do," I said, fisting my eyes as if to dislodge an errant piece of dust. "Yes." His collected poems, all three hundred pages of them, clattered to the floor, along with a pristine hardcover copy of his memoir, purchased for our meeting because I'd been too ashamed to show the dog-eared paperback stuffed with slips of paper, the corners of every page folded and refolded, the margins blue with pen. I'd spent all night doling out pints to twenty-four-hour drunks, the time between five and eight revising the poems buried in his email, and now, at eleven, the sun blaring through his office window, I was here, awaiting my judgment. I bent over to snake one of the fallen books from its resting place near my right foot, bare and dirty in its strappy sandal. Nathaniel's collected was just ahead, a bit closer to his untied leather tennis shoe. Did I dare? I grabbed the memoir and slipped it up onto his desk and then bent down again.

"I'm not being serious," he said. "But if you want to make it as a writer, you'll need to be able to withstand soul-withering humiliation, among other things. Questions are nothing." Instead of picking up the collected, I pushed it. The book slid a few inches, stopping almost at his shoe. To reach it now, I would have to leave my chair and crawl. Above me, a pen clicked, then swirled across paper. I inched toward the giant book. So it had been a test?

"Okay," I said, without any idea of what that had to do with my looking exotic to him. I was fully underneath his desk, face to face with his untied shoe. The laces were flopped over to the right side, the plastic end of one curled oddly up and over so it rested in the little hollow where the top of his foot—sockless—met the tongue. A mushroomy fog, not unpleasant, emanated from the seams between his shoe and skin. The laces were slick with dirt and coldly damp. I tied them into a loopy bow, pressing down hard on the toe when I finished, just as I had with all the sticky boys I babysat. Nathaniel made a startled grinning sound, the shoe shifting upward by just a fraction, toward my hand. His ankle, up close, was threaded with veins, pale green and purple, and my mind tried to reconcile the image with the ankle from the *Vanity Fair* photograph.

I backed up, taking the collected with me, and reemerged, blinking, to the world above the desk. My hands jittered on my lap.

"Why did you do that?" His mouth was twisted to one side, as if he were biting back a laugh, but he was looking at me now, for real, not just at my hair, my collarbones, the noisy, assertive shape of my breasts.

"It was untied," I managed, shoving my palms under my thighs. "And I was already down there." But no one asked me to do it. And then, a blurt: "Your feet smell." I sounded angry, and hearing myself,

I realized maybe I was.

Into Nathaniel's silence I backpedaled, taking on the tone of my email, repeating that though I was an undergrad, not even a student at this university, I hoped there might be a loophole, some way for me to audit his MFA workshop, only if, of course, he liked my work. The thing is, we were both from Greening and—dear lord (oh God, I'd used my mother's expression), forgive my presumption—he was the only real writer probably on earth from that forsaken, narrow place, born and raised there, and his work, I'd read every single book. Thanks to him, I'd realized something more than Greening was possible. Honestly? He'd saved my life. Now I was following in his footsteps, all the way to New York City. I placed the audit form on the desk between us, right on top of my poems. My eyes were damp, my chest heaved. I'd talked so much I was out of breath.

"I miss Michigan," he said. "All the stars, the space to think. I don't get back much anymore. I like to keep a few states between me and my mother." When I was sixteen, there'd been a big fuss in the paper over Janet's refusal to allow the town to put a plaque on her house commemorating the birthplace of Nathaniel Fellow. How odd to think of him that way: Janet Fellow's son.

Janet Fellow's son scribbled on the audit form, handed it back. "You know you're not allowed to audit an MFA workshop, even with one of those. They're closed to students outside the program, let alone the university. This isn't even how auditing works. Your request is so entitled it's long-jumped the line and come back around to naïve."

"Then why are you—Wait, are you letting me?"

How I hoped, how I prayed, he would say: *Your poems. They're rare. Brilliant.* I wanted that to be the reason so badly for years, that's how I remembered it, the self-protective narrative filter I applied to our origin story. It would take Lili's piece to bring the truth back to me: He'd never, that day in his office, mentioned my poems directly at all. I'd thought of myself as brave, as willful. But naïve was the best word for my hubris. It was also my primary credential.

Nathaniel leaned forward. "It must have taken a lot for you to get here, to this office, to this very moment." His voice was different, kinder now, as if he knew the busboys made fun of my walk and pretended to jerk off in my shift meal, or about how I ate lunch most days alone in my room, or about my bed, a video game chair unfolded all the way and covered with a top sheet. I almost cried again. "You'll be my first exception."

"Thank you," I said, believing him completely, because I didn't yet have a reason not to. "I'm so grateful—" Irritation flashed across his face. He didn't like to be thanked, flattered—at least not in an obvious way. I made note of it and stopped talking.

"Now. What will we tell them?"

"Who?"

Nathaniel swung his chair around so it faced the broad, cloudy window, the secret fountain in the courtyard below. "Hmm. What are your skills? I know you can't proofread."

Could it really be this easy? But what did a writer's assistant *do*? What did a *writer* do? And how did he know I couldn't proofread? Was Gerry the one who'd arranged his books in mostly alphabetical order, who'd hung the giant black-and-white photograph of an open field, stocked the mini fridge plugged in by the door?

He still wasn't looking at me, which made it easier to talk. "Skills? I'm good at cleaning. Enthusiastic. I see things other people don't." During my months on the cleaning crew, I'd wiped Rosendale's toilets and sinks with the same gray rag, but I tried to make sure all the tiny hairs were gone, so it only felt like half a lie. "I read fast." This seemed relevant, something a famous autodidact might like—and like a bigger lie. What was a normal reading speed? "But I guess, if I really boil it down, my main skill is that I'll do anything. When it comes to work." The last part was pretty much true.

"Shoelaces."

"Yes," I said.

"A workhorse, with a keen eye for the askew," Nathaniel said, facing me again. "Sounds useful. I've been without support for some personal tasks and my home has reached a staggering level of disarray.

Yesterday I found a soup can in the dishwasher."

That didn't seem like staggering disarray to me—my mother often repurposed soup cans.

Liliam didn't knock—she never did, I'd learn. She just stepped in, bringing with her a warm, nutty smell. "N, am I interrupting?" she said. Her long red ponytail was draped expressively over her right shoulder, like a mink. "I thought we had a meeting now."

"No, no. Sit," he said, so she did, right in the middle of the green couch. She pulled her legs up and to the side and stared at me. "Wilhelmina, drop in tomorrow morning, please, and we can finish up."

"When?" I asked. I could track every tiny movement of Lili's legs by the crushed velvet on the couch. She passed Nathaniel a piece of paper.

"First thing," he said. "Whenever." He was reading, and I was dismissed.

On the audit form, where his signature should have been, he'd written: *Trenor Hall, room 624, Thursdays at 6:30. Let's see what you can do, Greening girl.*

I framed the scrap of paper and kept it, for a very long time, above my writing table.

5

The first credit card was a Visa from Chase Bank. Chipper, scratched blue, NATHANIEL FELLOW in that raised typewriter font. In exchange for helping with general tasks—"a grab bag," Nathaniel told me, "will vary somewhat by the week"—I could charge up to five hundred dollars a month on the Visa for my own purchases, in addition to using the card for whatever he needed. It would be easier this way. Better for my taxes—"you're on significant financial aid," he said, confirming instead of asking—and better for his. Nathaniel unscrewed the cap from his thermos, and then tipped it upside down, pouring a stream of coffee into it. He slid the makeshift cup to me. We'd start with two mornings a week, Mondays and Fridays, four-hour shifts, which worked out to roughly fifteen dollars an hour. "A smidge more, really," he said. The coffee was sweeter than I expected, and still steaming. The hours I'd be in his poetry class—not as a student, but as his assistant, distributing handouts, taking notes, but encouraged to listen, contribute even, and he'd see what he could do about a workshop—did not count toward the total.

"It's important that we're both clear on the details. Does this all sound fair and proper?" He tucked a curl behind his ears almost primly. I often looked at his hair when we spoke; eye contact seemed too bold. It was a ruddy mixture of brown and gold and white, grayest at his temples. His shirtsleeves were folded above his elbows, and the muscles of his forearms were noticeable, as if he spent time exercising them.

"Perfectly," I said, raising his thermos cap in a kind of salute. In response, the Visa skittered across the table. I shoved it deep into my purse.

My task that Friday—I'd shown up at nine-fifty, correctly guessing that "first thing" for a poet meant after ten—was to gather all the items of clothing in his office and take them to Lucky 999 Laundromat on Second Avenue. I'd pick them up Monday, on my way in. I was to remind them to add a hole to his customer punch card—they kept it onsite for him, because otherwise he'd misplace it. Nathaniel was always losing cards and other kinds of identification—a minor annoyance mostly dealt with by others.

He climbed onto his office couch and felt around behind it, retrieving a laundry bag with a drawstring. "I have an appointment," he said, handing it over. "You'll be done before I'm back. When in haste, I have been known to toss a garment or two in the big file drawers. And thank you. Next time, I'll think of something fun." He didn't seem embarrassed to be asking me to do these things, nor was I to receive his requests. We were both familiar with this sort of transaction.

By clothes, he mostly meant socks. Aside from a sweater I found behind the garbage can, the bottom drawers of both filing cabinets were full of socks, the plain white kind everyone owns at some point or another. His felt expensive, soft and thick, and most were a bit stretched, as if they'd been worn in a relaxed way, perhaps just around the office as Nathaniel padded back and forth from door to desk, thinking up voltas. Gingerly, I smelled one, to get a baseline for "dirty" versus "clean." Degrees of vinegar. I couldn't tell. I decided to wash them all, even the balled-up, obviously unused pairs. I took one of the cleaner socks and wiped the dust off his books until the spines shone. It felt good to do a little more than he'd asked of me. And what a relief, tasks so clear and finite, instead of my work at the bar, where I was forever slicing lemons the wrong way, overflowing pints with head, coming up short when I cashed out. I would have done Nathaniel's tasks for free. His students were scheduling office hours, polishing drafts for workshop, which would start in a little over a week. I swung the bag of laundry over my shoulder. This was my apprenticeship. It wasn't ideal, but I would take what I could get.

At eleven in the morning, New York was full of people in perpetual conflict with the city itself. It released endless specific, personal obstacles—slow-walking tourists goggling at a breakdancer, a fire hydrant spewing greenish water, a blond coil of excrement in the middle of the sidewalk, a teenager urgently handing out froyo samples—as well as the occasional general, apocalyptic one, as when, midway through a crosswalk, a thunderous crash came from everywhere at once. A few people looked up with alarm and then kept moving. When you finally reached your destination, blood tingling with adrenaline, it was as if you'd defeated the big boss. It was hard *not* to feel important, even carrying dirty clothes. Lucky 999 was a closet between a bodega and a pawnshop, with only a few churning machines. When I handed over Nathaniel's bag, confirming his name and pickup date, a woman beside a pile of unfolded T-shirts nodded without a word. A week earlier, I would have left terrified I'd made mistake; but now I understood. She was conserving energy. There was a lot of day to go.

Back at Nathaniel's office, someone was inside—a male voice, agitated. I slid the laundry drop-off receipt under the door. The voices did not register its arrival. The errands had taken under two hours, but I knew what *you'll be done before I'm back* meant. The head of cleaning crew at Rosendale used to say things like that when task managing had become tiresome, and I was to occupy myself. This suited me just fine, because on Fridays I had to be at the bar by four. That left only a couple of hours, tops, for Net Café, to work on the poems Nathaniel might—he'd see what he could do!—let me workshop.

On the way out, there they were again—Liliam and Reg, walking down the hallway deep in some brilliant conversation. Liliam's dress was a tissuey pink that did not go with her hair; she looked a bit dowdy, drowning under all that fabric. Recognition crackled when we passed each other. I imagined dropping my purse, the credit card skipping across the floor and into Liliam's path. What would she think when she picked it up and saw Nathaniel's name?

At Net Café, I used Nathaniel's Visa to buy twenty-five dollars of printing credits, ten hours of computer access, two samosas, and a large coffee. The total came to $58.74; two dollars less than he owed me for a four-hour shift. In the beginning, I was careful with his money like that. When Arjun swiped the card, I held my breath, waiting for REJECTED to flash across the screen. But nothing happened. "Appa," shouted one of the teenage girls clustered around the oldest desktop. "The bouncing wheelie ball is on the screen again!"

"Ditya, I am with a customer," he said.

"A customer," I heard her repeat, and then all the girls laughed in unison.

Arjun looked at me apologetically. "I don't know why they laugh at everything. I say, looks like rain, they laugh. I tell Ditya, we're having soup for lunch, she laughs. It makes me crazy. Is there nothing in her head?"

The girls were already laughing about something else. One wearing a skort was giggling so hard she collapsed onto the keyboard in front of her, which set the rest of them off again. I grinned; it was hard not to.

"Ah, but you're just a girl, too," Arjun said. "Your father probably sings the same song."

How this pleased me, Arjun's assumption that someone loved me as much as he did Ditya. "Oh, he does," I said. "He's always telling me to take things more seriously."

I'd never had so much computer credit. Just weeks later I'd cringe at the waste, when I learned I could have used Barth's lab at any point prior to the start of the semester without paying a cent, about the forty dollars in printing credit automatically added to my student account, courtesy of my merit scholarship. But that day, I felt abundant and grateful. I printed a draft just to see it, and then another, after changing only a few words.

At Genesis, halfway up the basement steps with a full crate of Jose Cuervo, I was thinking about how I would like to try to write a poem that began and ended with the same word, the way Liliam had, when my head began to spin. I slid the Cuervo onto the bar as the ground and the ceiling traded places. Oh good, I won't have to pay for any broken bottles, I thought. And then, with the strangest sensation, as if a bird had gotten trapped, fluttering, in my rib cage, I fainted, just like a princess in a storybook.

Robby, the younger of the two guys who served as a cross between a busboy and a barback, was crouched next to me. "Man," he said, his breath very minty, razor burn on his chin. "You went down. Hungover?"

"No," I told him, sitting up. "Maybe hungry." My heart was hitching between beats. "I'm sorry." It pulsed in my throat so fast I wanted to gag.

"You want, like, some bread?"

"I guess you're going to want to go home," said Mack, his expression unreadable. He didn't say it meanly. "Can you stand?" He extended both hands. It wasn't a very nice bar, but Mack always wore a shirt and jacket on Friday and Saturday. Upright, my pulse settled, all at once, into a rhythm I could no longer feel.

"I'm fine. I just need to eat." Two samosas were more than I usually ate before a shift. But why else would I have passed out?

Robby and Mack exchanged a look. "I don't want to have to scrape her up off the floor all night," Robby said.

"I'm fine, really. I'll eat a lot of shift meal." How much would it set me back if I lost the cash I'd expected to take home tonight? Maybe I could ask Dev to spot me some rent money, and pay him back with Nathaniel's Visa until I got my financial aid refund? But what if Dev wanted to buy something extravagant or embarrassing, like a million peonies or edible lube or seven pizzas from Domino's? He was always coming home with things that made no sense. "Guys—please," I said. "I need the money."

"If you feel weird, any floaties, you get Robby, and he gets me, okay?"

"Definitely," I said. When my heart revved and I got the spins again a few hours later, I kept my mouth shut. In the dip between happy hour and the after-dinner rush, Robby slipped me a few chicken tenders. Mack was on me as if nothing had happened, barking orders, snapping when I took too long to print a check, but when a giant party swarmed the bar, all the women ordering cocktails with names like Sex on the Beach, he stepped in without making me ask for help.

After close, he poured me a beer. "Stop being so nice to people," he said.

"I thought that was part of my job."

"Your job is to serve. Being nice slows you down."

"It helps my tips."

"You think it helps your tips, but you get trapped in this cycle, where you have to be nice to make up for being slow, and so on. You don't owe anyone anything but a drink."

I sipped my beer, considering this.

"I don't have an emergency contact for you," he said abruptly. I had filled out no paperwork, signed nothing. I wasn't sure Mack even knew my last name. On top of my tips, I got paid a twenty per shift—at the end of the week, three twenties in a plain white envelope with my name on it under the cashbox in the register.

"I guess I don't really have one."

"Boyfriend? Parents? Grandma?"

"My mom's in Michigan."

"Roommate or something? Friend?"

I imagined Mack calling Dev to tell him I was knocked out cold under a crate of tequila. Be there in ten, Dev would say, and then show up two days later. For some reason Liliam came to my mind next, dressed in her ugly pink chiffon.

"You?" I joked, but Mack didn't smile.

At least three shifts a week at Genesis: Friday, Saturday, Sunday. Sometimes, when asked, a double on a weekend day. Monday and Friday mornings were Nathaniel's; Thursday nights were his workshop. I squeezed my Barth classes into the leftover space. Four classes equaled a full schedule, but there was no extra charge to take a fifth, so I did. One hundred twenty credits to graduate; sixty of the sixty-three I'd taken at QCC had transferred. I didn't know all students had advisers, and so I didn't think to initiate a meeting. Besides, it was simple enough to check the course listings and figure out what counted for my major, communications, which I'd chosen because it lined up best with my credits from QCC. My first semester I signed up for baroque art (three hours on Monday nights, a good time slot), anthropology (I thought it might help my poetry), yoga (it was at eight on Tuesday mornings and three whole credits, even though it met just once a week for ninety minutes), public speaking because it was required, and a mandatory course for all new Barth students called City Seminar, which seemed to be mostly a series of tours around New York and very light on any real academic work. It proved easy to skip. I didn't register for any creative writing courses. Everything but Intro to Poetry was application only, and I had no idea how to apply. Intro was 100-level, for freshmen, or so I thought, and I was an incoming junior; wasn't I too old? And hadn't I already been introduced to poetry?

On Monday, Nathaniel wasn't in his office. It was the first official week of the semester, and I'd expected to be stopped, but it seemed the famous university didn't care who wandered in and out of the buildings. I sat at the seminar table in the room outside his door, waiting, his bag of clean laundry in the big chair at the head. Sunlight everywhere, scalded, milky coffee in my paper cup. Reading Milosz, whom I only knew a little, because I'd found *The Collected Poems* tented open and waiting.

What is poetry which does not save

Nations or people?
A connivance with official lies,
A song of drunkards whose throats will be cut in a moment,
Readings for sophomore girls.

I read "Dedication" once, then a second time, because Nathaniel had said in a *Belvedere* interview that all poems must be read at least twice. The first time through was for feeling, and to prep the heart and mind for meaning, which a poem delivered only to those in the right frame of mind. The poem's closing stanza made me ache, the image of mourners scattering millet over the graves to feed the dead who appeared as birds, the poet's words a warning to stay gone, not to come back to this world, where the living suffered so. There, for the briefest second, that illumination I was always seeking and could never express—the vast, rippling truth of what it meant to be human, the inexplicable, in words. It was like glimpsing a vital organ. I read the poem again, skin prickling when I hit the last lines:

I put this book here for you, who once lived
So that you visit us no more.

A miracle, and I didn't even know what millet was. But. Why was it that sophomore girls were and had always been a synonym for silly? And why did I have to make everything, even Nobel Prize–winning poetry by a man who'd survived multiple wars, the German occupation, about *me*? Surely there were more interesting questions to ask. Maybe we would discuss them in workshop.

Liliam swung open the door, dressed very much for college: white button-down shirt, pleated gray skirt, a leather shoulder bag crossing her chest. "You again," she said. "What are you, like an independent study?"

"I'm Nathaniel's assistant," I said, trying not to stare at the zit on her chin. Red liquid had seeped through a dab of concealer. Her plaid headband was the most stylish thing I'd ever seen. Nathaniel's assistant. The first time I'd said it out loud. I liked the person it suggested I was—someone with a place in this room.

"Me too," she said, and my pride faded. "Kind of. I'm his research fellow." She chose the chair next to mine, plopping her bag on the table and rooting around inside.

"Fellow's fellow," I said. What was a fellow? Did she have a credit card, too?

"An esteemed occupation," she said, unwrapping a bowling ball of foil to reveal a bagel sandwich, stuffed with egg and cheese. "Last week he had me send him forty pages of notes about the invention and eventual ubiquity of the microwave. For a project he will probably never even begin."

"Why not?"

"Because he doesn't write anymore." She opened her mouth very wide, to fit the bagel in. "Dang," she said, chewing. "You know when you're on your period and all you want to eat is cheese?"

"Didn't he write the screenplay for *Beauty and Mud*?"

"I mean, yeah, he writes some schlocky crap. But not the real stuff. It's been years."

"How do you know that?"

"He told me," Liliam said. "Hold up—I think I hear him." Within seconds, she'd disappeared her bagel and her zit. She was capping a stick of concealer when he entered, but when I looked her way again, it was gone. "You're early," she said.

"Is today your day, Lil? I can't remember."

"According to the schedule we made together, indeed it is."

Nathaniel rubbed his face. "I don't have anything for you."

"Nothing for class? You don't need me to print the syllabus or something?"

"I received a very stern email from Tilda a few days ago telling me I am not to use my fellow for administrative tasks. Research purposes only, or else, and so forth. Which I think you know."

"Ah yes, your research," Liliam said. "Except you don't have anything for me."

"Walk around. Write a poem. Figure out how to do one thing without bothering me about it. That's your assignment."

"Sounds glorious." She heaved her bag over her shoulder. "Maybe I'll write about taking the subway during rush hour for no reason at all." She looked down at me for a moment and removed her headband, sliding it over my forehead so it lifted my hair from my eyes. Her fingers smelled like butter. I could feel my ears sticking out, and knew I looked worse. It was a performance for Nathaniel, not me. Why had I just sat there and let her do it? "There we go," she said as I reeled. "Less plain, and now you'll stop fussing with your hair. Nice to meet you, Will."

Then she was gone, and I was alone with him. I followed Nathaniel into his office, pulling the headband off, certain that if Lili had it her way, I'd never graduate from laundry to research. "I've been doing this for a long time," Nathaniel said, shutting his door. "And still, I don't know what it is everyone wants from me."

The curtain rod looked like a pipe. Instead of brackets on either side, a bar you could easily remove, each end was screwed into the wall. It appeared to have segments you might be able to twist apart, but Nathaniel assured me they did not twist. The rod was coming loose from the drywall on one side, so the whole bar dipped heavily to the right. Nathaniel wanted me to fix it. "Really, it's a job for facilities. But they never come when I call."

"Okay," I said. "I'll need to go to the hardware store."

"I have a toolbox," he said, pointing at a case wedged between books on an upper shelf. "And somewhere, a drill."

"You have a drill in your office?"

"When I moved in here two decades ago, I hung these pictures," he said.

"Surely you don't have spackling?"

"Spackling! I don't think I know what spackling is, used as a noun. I was half joking—this rod has been threatening to behead me for a decade. And look, I'm still here. But by all means, go, acquire the materials. I'll also need nine copies of this packet for workshop. The printer is in English."

When I came back with the spackling, Nathaniel was still in his office. I waited in the doorway, holding the large plastic bag, which also contained a small collapsible laundry basket I'd purchased to pay myself, at least partially, for the work I was about to do. "Yes?" Nathaniel said.

"I'm back to fix it."

"Okay," he said, making no move to get up. He stared at his computer screen without typing. Was it true, what Liliam said? That he didn't write anymore?

The curtain rod spanned a wall kitty-corner from his desk, above the velvet couch—I could stand there to patch the hole, and then drill it back in. But it wasn't really a one-person job—I'd have to remove the rod to patch the hole, which would take a solid thirty minutes to dry, and how would I drill without someone helping me? I climbed onto the couch and looked up. I could do it if I kept the left side attached and loosened the screw just enough for the rod to swivel down—it was long enough to rest the right end on the couch. Once the hole was patched, I could hold the rod in place with one arm as I drilled. I could feel Nathaniel watching me think. I loosened the attached side, nearly losing my balance. I tucked one of the curtains, a heavy swath of beige fabric, behind a box stacked on the bookshelf so it wouldn't pull at the rod. The other slid onto my feet with a whoosh of ancient cigarette smoke and I balled it on the bookshelf, too, with the first one. Nathaniel did not offer to help.

I hopped off the couch to make his copies. "Not only does that not look done," he said, "it looks worse."

"Oh. Well. It's not. The spackling is drying."

"Ah yes. The spackling." Had he never patched a wall? He did have a toolbox and a drill in his office. Why did he keep saying *spackling* like that? I couldn't tell if he was savoring the word or mocking me.

The printer was harder to figure out than the curtain rod. First, I had to find it—when he'd said it was in English, I thought he'd meant its *instructions.* But after a couple of circles around the seminar room, I understood. I found it hulking in a walk-in closet in the English department office across the hall from Nathaniel's annex, a beige walrus that smelled, when it ejected patchy copies, like a ham sandwich. It took me a long time to make a single copy. Then every third sheet printed half blank. The ink was on its last dribble, but where did they keep extra cartridges? And where would they be inserted, even if I could find them?

By the time I managed to get nine readable copies of each of the ten poems in the packet, a lump bobbed in my throat. I'd taken the staple out of Nathaniel's packet to make the copies, scanning each of them in turn—clearer than running it through the belly of the machine—and had lost track of the order, even after breathlessly reading the Hughes (familiar), the "Dream Songs" 1 and 29 (familiar and glorious), Arnold's "Dover Beach" (high school stuff, I was surprised to see it there), and Louise Bogan (*This is a dead scene forever now,* yes!), and skimming the excerpts from Shakespeare, the Wallace Stevens, the Antonio Machado poem that was effective but (wasn't it?) a little corny (life, garden, I got it). Milosz, too, and a crisp, odd poem by a writer named Tomas Tranströmer. But what order had he put them in? Which had been *first?*

I spread the nine piles across the back of the printer and the file cabinet. I was flitting between them, rereading, when Reg pushed the door open, holding his own pile of papers.

"Let me guess," he said. "Independent study."

"Why does everyone keep saying that?"

"You're not in the first-year cohort. But you're always around. What else could you be?"

"Nathaniel Fellow's assistant."

"Very experienced, I see. You forgot to collate."

"That's what I am doing right now!" I sounded upset, and it made me dislike him, that he was hearing one of my private voices.

"I meant, to have the *printer* collate. It staples, too." He nudged some of my piles closer together, pressed a few buttons on the panel, and fed one of his packets into the machine. The machine released a whiff of ham, and then there it was, another packet, stapled and, presumably, in the correct order. Reg held it up and then rustled around in a box in the corner I hadn't even noticed. Within ten seconds, he'd replaced the ink, and a few minutes later the machine was whirring again. "Ah, love, let us be true to one another!" he declared, glancing around the room at the poems. "These must be for Nathaniel. Looks like his packet of random mostly dead guys."

"'Dover Beach,'" I said, hoping to impress. "Where ignorant armies clash by night."

"Nathaniel loves it. How can you not, though."

"Are you new?" I asked, even though I knew he was not.

"A first-year? No. I'm a second. Scrambling to get all my printing done for my class. Intro to Poetry. I teach tomorrow."

At QCC, I'd had versions of the same teacher, no matter the subject: a gray-haired person with spotted hands, who shared their landline for emergency use and stood by the whiteboard, swallowing little froggy burps you could smell if you sat in the front row. I had trouble squaring that with the person in front of me—my height exactly, with a petulant mouth and owlish eyes, blue and so long-lashed I thought for a moment he was wearing eyeliner. Pale, oily skin, lots of dark curly hair. A few years my senior, but with a delicate, untested look, as if adults had been slipping him treats his whole life. Seeing him with Lili, I hadn't been able to tell if he was straight or gay, or if they were somehow *involved,* but now that we were alone in a room together, I clocked the subtle awareness of my body I'd been getting from straight men my whole life. I wanted very much to read the poems he was photocopying.

"Do you need some help?" He smiled; good teeth. More Rosendale than Greening. I could already tell.

"I can't remember the order they were in. I took them all apart to print and—"

"He did the exact same poems first day first semester last year,"

Reg said, looking over the copies on the printer. "He always does. He goes loosely chronological—so Shakespeare first, though I think he ends with Bogan, for some reason I can't remember now. It's like an exam for the returning students, to see whether we're brainwashed yet, and trial by fire for the new ones. Or maybe he likes teaching the same thing." Reg began assembling a packet. "What are you? His private assistant?"

"Private? What's that supposed to mean?"

To his credit, I suppose, a red circle appeared on each of his cheeks, as if he'd been slapped. "I mean, are you with the college, or?"

"I'm an undergrad." I left off that I was an undergrad at Barth, another college entirely. It seemed too much to explain. One small lie of omission, the first of so many between us.

"Ha!" Reg said uncomfortably. "Maybe I'll have you in class." He handed me the poems, restored to their Nathaniel-approved order, or something close to it. "But if you're with Nathaniel, you're probably beyond intro."

"I think I might see you in his—in the workshop."

"Workshop?" Reg looked almost hurt. "But it's only for MFAs." He turned away from me to put another packet together. It was impossible for Reg to convey anything but exactly what he was feeling.

"Not as a student," I said, and he brightened. "Just to help Nathaniel. With notes and, um, keeping track."

"He never had a helper before."

I'd already surpassed Geraldine Keene, whoever she'd been. "Well, he is getting older." Reg seemed to accept this. Maybe Nathaniel really did need me there—maybe it wasn't just for my benefit, or because he'd seen something in my work.

We were interrupted by a distant, papery explosion, as if a grapefruit had met, midair, an unbound copy of *Infinite Jest* or Nathaniel's collected. "Weird," Reg said. "Wonder what that was." And even though I knew the answer, I peeked with him into the main office. One of the administrative doors popped open; a tiny woman in a wizardy dress stared with us in the direction of Nathaniel's annex. I grabbed the stacks of poems and rushed across the hall. "Uh," Reg said, already far behind me.

Nathaniel stood in a maelstrom of documents. Torn notebook pages, photocopies, fancy stationery, an uncountable number of receipts. The curtain rod had pulled out of the wall. I must have loosened it too much, and the weight of the curtains bunched up at its end had, somehow, caused not just one but two boxes of paper to tip off the bookshelf. It was a horrible mess, but the patched hole, at least, looked dry. I was afraid to look at him.

"I'm so sorry," I told the papers.

"All that talk of spackling lulled me into thinking you knew what you were doing."

"I—misjudged."

Nathaniel laughed, picking up a thank-you card and frisbeeing it at my head. Not the laugh I'd heard at the reading, that tight-knit chuckle that was a cue for the audience—this was the real thing. It was joyful and infectious and I laughed, too. I'd learn it was rare for Nathaniel to laugh like that. "I'm sorry I don't have time to help you with this," he said. "I have to finish a few things and then I have a lunch."

Again, he didn't leave. He filled his arms with paper and stuffed it into one of the boxes, but once I began to help, he sat back down at his desk. His typing gained speed until the sound of it filled the room. Whatever he was writing wasn't a poem—even a famous poet couldn't write one so fast—but he was writing *something*. He didn't seem to notice when I filled in the new hole, or when I began moving the furniture—first the couch, so I could slide the bookshelf under the window, and then a wobbly chair I'd use, along with the backrest of the couch, as a makeshift stepstool. The end of my four-hour shift came and went; lunchtime passed as well, at least what I thought of as lunchtime, and still Nathaniel remained at his computer. I dropped the rod twice, swallowed a thousand curses, drilled, rehung the curtains—through it all, only his fingers moved.

I was pushing back the furniture. There, in a gap between the bookshelf and the couch, was a scatter of paper I'd missed. I'd barely looked at the other documents for fear Nathaniel would see me salivating over his private correspondence, but he was still battering his keyboard. I turned my back to him and sifted through what was on the floor. Flyers for readings, countless thank-you cards from former students, stickers I now know to call bookplates, a receipt from Café Loup for $567 (he'd left a 30 percent tip). A photo of four men smiling in a field, eyes red from the camera flash, Nathaniel near the middle and the rest of them vaguely familiar. A handwritten poem—it looked like a draft of "Oh, Lark." I folded it up and wedged it into the waistband of my jeans. From Vilma, a letter that began: *Tundra, ice miles deep. I'm buried in it. Choking on it. Can't sleep, can't work*—Nathaniel's typing slowed, and without finishing the rest, I stuffed it into my front pocket. Near the baseboard, another photo. I reached for it.

Me, I thought at first. But when had I sat on a picnic table eating an ice cream cone, mostly naked and in *those* boots? Slowly, the image resolved. Not me, of course. My mother, in her life before. The photo I'd sent all those years ago, banished to a random box, probably by Gerry. If he'd ever seen it, wouldn't Nathaniel have recognized me the day I walked through his door?

I'd been so focused on catching glimpses of my father I'd missed how alike my mother and I were, a process of replication still underway, as if I'd sprung from her body alone. I put the photo back in the box, flipping it over to hide my face from Nathaniel and myself.

"I'm done," I said, and Nathaniel mumbled thanks. On my way to Net Café, I felt an urge to look at the photo again. Why had I left it and taken the draft, Vilma's letter, things he might miss? Of all the documents, my mother's picture seemed indisputably his. Maybe because I'd been the one to give it to him.

I'd left Tray's photos alone, too.

6

I hid in the bathroom until one minute before workshop was due to start. I'd been so flustered after seeing my mother's photo in his office I'd taken the poems for class, instead of leaving them in Nathaniel's office as instructed. I confirmed I had them now, all properly collated, and took a deep breath, steadying my hand on the door handle before opening it.

I'd imagined, for some reason, class would start late, but Nathaniel was already talking. Eight students. Reg and Liliam, plus a handful of faces I recognized from the *Best of the New* event, including the reader of the never-ending poem. On the chalkboard, Nathaniel had written *Lizard Brain,* chalk strokes radiating off each letter. Every seat at the table was full. I scanned the room, panicking. There, tucked up by a podium housing a technical-looking box, was a folding chair vined in wires—that would do. The room smelled of body odor and wine. A few bottles were open on the table, paper cups in front of every student, Nathaniel too. Liliam looked at me, raising her little cup to her mouth. "Hi," she said, and sipped.

"I'm sorry," I answered.

"Ah," Nathaniel said, smiling with such genuine kindness I took another step into the room. "Wilhelmina is here with the poems." He clasped his hands and brought them to his chest, as if my arrival were something to savor. "Everyone, this is Wilhelmina Miles. My new assistant."

"Will, usually," I said. "Hi."

"Go ahead," Nathaniel said to me, in a more managerial tone of voice. "Hand around the packets. And close the door, please." His voice changed again as he addressed the class. "Personal and professional challenges this semester have made it necessary for me to secure additional help. Wilhelmina is here as recorder and notetaker—rest assured her transcripts will be for my eyes only." A few people nodded gravely. Did they know what he meant? He hadn't mentioned challenges during our discussion of my work; was that an excuse, or was he actually going through something? "As for her own work, I feel there's something in it that will round out the spectrum of voices here, a certain missing element. She's not yet in the *program*"—he said *program* with a twist of disdain, and they exchanged smiles, in on some joke—"but as poetry is the realm of exceptions and exceptional beings, this will be our first. And hopefully not our last." I was blushing, my heart pinging around. I wished he'd stop.

I dropped a packet onto Reg's open notebook. He'd written *Lizard Brain* as a header and underlined it twice. "Thanks," he whispered. Nobody else had looked away from Nathaniel. Most of their notebooks said *Lizard Brain,* too.

"My fear, my darlings, is that we can get terribly closed off, talking only to each other. So. Will. Let's welcome her, shall we? It should go without saying that her presence will not impact your workshop time in the least—but I'll say it anyway. Mostly for you, Leah." She made a face like, guilty!, and everyone laughed, a cozy elbow-nudging sound, Leah hardest of all. "And please, everyone, nothing of this to certain administrators. Wilhelmina is here to make my life *easier.*" More laughter. One of Nathaniel's superpowers—give him an hour and he could turn a room of strangers into his own personal army.

"Um," I said. "I am so glad to be here. Please let me know if I can help you with copies or anything." Nathaniel had not said anything about helping students, but I hoped the offer would ingratiate me with them.

"Hello, Will," mumbled a few from Nathaniel's spectrum of

voices. Nathaniel turned back to the chalkboard, where he wrote: *POETRY IS ATTENTION.*

I unfolded the chair and sat, the wires tapping my shoulders every time I adjusted the legal pad in my lap. Nathaniel had asked for nine packets—enough for everyone at the table, no extras. They leafed through the poems, leaned subtly toward each other, engaged in a collective conversation that progressed via glances and body language. After Nathaniel, Liliam and Reg, as a duo, were the power center. Leah radiated a stressful energy. She sat cross-legged on her chair, very erect, her curly brown hair in a high, tight ponytail. When the woman who'd read too long at *Best of the New* talked, the others tuned out. Liliam doodled on the corner of Reg's packet. Nathaniel didn't notice. Next to *Leah ask can revisions be workshopped* I added *L+R passing notes.* They were in, I was out. But he'd mentioned my work. I'd get my poems on the table if I played things right.

The way Nathaniel read! His voice was an instrument, as if the words were made for it, and not the other way around. When he recited "Dover Beach," I worried the others would see my eyes welling; it was as if I'd never read it before. After he finished a poem, he let a silence expand. At first, it seemed out of respect for the work. Then it very obviously became a test. The tension cranked higher and higher until someone offered an observation, usually about enjambment or another structural technicality (no one would dare say of work Nathaniel brought in something as anodyne as *I liked it*) and in the form of a mincing question. The universe flinched, waiting for Nathaniel's verdict. If the comment interested him, he'd stand up and attack the chalkboard, cracking the poem open to show us how the music was made. Exhilaration; epiphany. How had I never noticed the relationship between punctuation and the breath? Or the way the closing couplet of an Elizabethan sonnet rewrote what came before? My pen tip tore through the page. If Nathaniel thought an offering stupid, he'd blink, glaring at each student in turn, until someone lobbed a ball he could play with. Liliam, usually. At one point the silence went on for so long *I* almost spoke, just to put an end to it.

My hand cramped. I'd filled pages, most of them unreadable. I'd spent so much time reading poetry, but outside of a class in high school and a unit in the literature course I took at QCC, I'd muddled through it alone, following nothing but my own curiosity and the Nortons to each discovery. It was as if I'd been driving for miles in fog and rain, and Nathaniel leaned over and turned on the wipers.

By the time class ended, I was dizzy. From the poetry, I would have told you, but also, I was drunk. All class, Reg kept passing me tiny cups of wine—"Cheers, undergrad," he said, boldly turning around to hand me each one—and after two or three on my very empty stomach, the room had gone a little soft around the edges.

Later, at Net Café, I pored over my notes, trying to recapture the feeling I'd had in class—the flashes of clarity and insight, the urgent vibration that preceded the writing of a poem. Nothing. All that was left were the poems themselves, as opaque and mysterious as ever. In my inbox, a new email from my mother.

> *Hi Wilhelmina. I hope the weather is good there in the big city. I can't believe you've only been gone six weeks. Here it is already feeling like winter by nightfall. I put a suet patty out for the birds and in two days flat it was eaten whole.*

In her emails, my mother occasionally mentioned Tray, but never coming to visit.

> *Take care.*

That's always how she said goodbye, even when I did pick up the phone.

After every workshop, the MFAs went out drinking. Nathaniel never joined, though they always asked—according to legend, he'd gone with the students after every workshop until a handful of years before, and the recent groups felt slighted. Alehouse? they'd say, and there would be some discussion of drink specials and rounds owed as they trailed out of the room. No one invited me, though I caught Liliam looking my way after the third meeting, as if weighing the pros and cons of my presence. But I got to know them anyway. I heard them talking before class, in the halls. And I read their submissions. Their poems were more polished than the ones I'd found in the ancient copies of *The Rosendale Literary Review,* more contemporary, full of familiar detritus: beer and MetroCards, bad sex and longed-for sex (but rarely good sex, I noticed, as if that weren't a real, poetic possibility), Starbucks coffees and birds flattened on the sidewalks. But they were just as inadvertently revealing. After a few weeks I knew them better, I felt, than all those Greening kids I'd grown up with.

The seminar room outside of Nathaniel's office was their personal study hall, and I listened when he was out and they didn't know I was in there, putting his books in alphabetical order, dusting, or reading on the couch, because Nathaniel never gave me quite enough to do. In duos or trios, they talked mostly about each other. Larger groups talked about what they were reading, poets I'd never heard of, movies and TV more than I'd expected for a bunch of writers. But inevitably, the conversation would turn to him.

Is that true? Or is that what I listened to the hardest?

They had opinions about his moods based on what he was wearing, whether he drank a cup of coffee during workshop. Overtly political writing is propaganda, not art, they'd declaim, mocking him. Everything he said was so outdated, the best thing you could do for your work was exactly the opposite. Did you know he punched a man in the face at a poker game hosted by Philip Roth, who called in a favor to keep him out of jail? His apartment has a big-screen TV and no books at all, except his own. He loves jeans. Skirts, too, jackets, doesn't matter. A few years ago—before your time—a first-year tried to seduce him by wearing a pair of denim overalls with a jacket, Canadian Tuxedo-style; it worked, no, he called her out on it, no, it did work, but he told her after they fucked that onesies were for babies. He's obsessed with women's volleyball, and suggested to Randall Wilbur, whose thesis was about porn addiction, he try that instead. For almost a year, struggling with an undisclosed health condition, Nathaniel ate only adzuki beans. He had to eat them every three hours, I mean imagine how hungry *you'd* be. He'd sit there in class with a Styrofoam bowl and a plastic spoon. In the old days, before he stopped caring, his seminars lasted eight, ten hours, deep into the night. Students would piss themselves they were so nervous about interrupting him to go to the bathroom. Last year he asked Tim to read out loud from a Flannery O'Connor story, and he skipped over a slur, you know which one, and Nathaniel held forth for an hour about judging the time, not the work. He had a kid with some woman before Vilma; the guy grew up to be an accountant. There's a famous rock on the campus of the Tumbledown Mountain Writers' Retreat, where he used to receive blow jobs from his choice scholarship recipient. I've sat there—of course, I didn't *know.* I wouldn't *now.* That's why he doesn't get invited anymore. He was a draft dodger. No, a conscientious objector. No, he went to Vietnam but was sent home before even leaving the States, because someone in his troop shot him in the foot during basic training. It was an accident; no, he paid the guy. He always gives money to homeless people—take a walk with him, you'll see. He wrote his first novel blackout drunk. He wooed her over email after *Beauty and Mud* wrapped, we're talking novel-length letters, she scrolled through one for Leah at last year's MFA Christmas party. Yeah, I've met her. She's not as pretty in real life. More normal, like someone hot from high school. A lot of celebrities are like that, especially women—the camera does something to them. He's a millionaire. He can't pay his rent. Vilma cheated on him. He's obsessed with her still. They wrote each other's stories, just to fuck with people. Vilma's the only woman who's ever left him.

They loved him, they hated him, they wanted to kill him or eat him or put on his skin, all of it at once. Sometimes people pretended they didn't like his work, but he was the most famous teacher in the program, its biggest draw. Hired for poetry, he still primarily taught in that genre, but everyone wanted to take the memoir class he almost never taught. God, I loved his poems when I was kid. There's just something about them—so direct, like they're just for you. A gateway drug. He never forgets a student—just last year, he helped a grad from, like, the nineties sell his first book. Slipped it to an editor at Knopf, one of the old guys, at the end of a long dinner. Two weeks later, book deal.

They condemned his bad behavior, but almost affectionately—it was part of his lore, something to be accommodated, like a therapy dog. The price everyone paid for proximity to greatness. Or former greatness. Once I heard Leah talking about how many times Nathaniel had asked her where she was from. He means, like, my people, she said. He asked if I would describe my skin tone as swarthy. I could hear him asking this; he'd asked me a similar thing, after all.

In every case, the anecdotes revealed the author. Some were self-oriented, humblebrags in disguise; others, overtly literary, an attempt to prove they belonged. Some of the women loved the shocking and gross, as if to remind everyone they cared more about the art than the behavior, that it was all a big joke, except for what he wrote on their poems. Liliam never added, only prompted. Reg's stories were always amusing, and often about Nathaniel's eating habits. He was a monster, a pathetic old man, a luminary, the only legitimate writing teacher in the whole sorry business, a challenge to overcome, worth it in the end. Did Nathaniel know what they said about him?

I believed them—and I didn't. Hadn't rumors followed me all through Greening, started from nothing, a bra left under a pool table, one silly girl saying to another that I liked "it" in two holes at once? Whatever Ralphie had said. All it took was a detail; you could make any story you wanted. He'd had wives, a famous girlfriend, the same job for twenty years, apparently even an actual child. How bad could he be? I'd only been in New York for a couple of months, a blink, and more had happened to me than in my last three years in Greening combined—that was thanks to him. Everything else, from the pub to Net Café to my boring, anonymous classes at Barth, was just a placeholder.

Barth had a therapist but no medical center. One rainy fall day after anthropology, I made an appointment at the urgent care nearest campus. "Sometimes my heart beats fast," I told the receptionist when she asked me why I was there.

"Is it right now?"

"No. It's just, at random times."

Three hours later, I repeated the same thing to a doctor in a gray closet not much larger than my bedroom. "I don't do prescriptions for Xanax here," he said. "Try the doctors at your school. Or deep breathing. That sometimes works."

The visit was out of network, $159. I paid with cash.

7

"You're not spending enough of my money," Nathaniel said. Two months, and I'd charged around five hundred dollars total to the Visa—I had a special notebook, a tiny spiral one that flipped open from the top, where I kept track of my purchases. I made sure everything I bought would be considered practical, or writerly. His card was for used books, for coffee—my biggest splurge had been a handful of pens from a luxury stationery store near the subway stop at Lex and Eighty-sixth. "I didn't do the math," Nathaniel said, "but it's not what I owe you. Don't be shy. Buy yourself something nice. A dress or a haircut." He looked over at my corduroy parka, the warmest thing I owned, draped across the couch like a dead animal. "A coat." I was wearing a pair of black pants that would carry me through an extra shift I'd picked up at the bar. They smelled, when you pressed your nose right into the polyester, like onion rings. My socks did, too. My hair, the creases of my elbows. I showered after shifts but it was no use; I didn't have time to get ahead of my laundry, and I was always a little bit dirty.

We were in his office. Now that the whole city is covered with his fingerprints, it's funny to remember how in those early months we only met there. I want it to be evidence of the one thing that still—God, yes, *still*—matters: What happened between us was different. I was on the floor, filling out the squares of a giant monthly calendar he wanted me to hang on the wall. "Put Lili's research days on there,"

Nathaniel said. "Use some siren of a color. Radioactive green. When that woman shows up and I'm not expecting it, it gives me the terror." I loved when he talked about Lili like this; it made me feel trusted, approved, a feeling that dissipated as soon as I was in a room with the two of them. When Lili was present, Nathaniel didn't really pay attention to anyone else. He liked that she wasn't easy on him, and all three of us knew it. "Oh, and lunch with Maxwell. Next Thursday. Friday. No—yes, Friday. Two P.M. at Elaine's."

"Should I make the reservation?"

"He already did. I think. You can call and check."

Nathaniel often gave biographical summaries when he asked me to schedule meetings. At first, I'd thought this was so I could follow along, get to know the players in his world, but I came to see he took pleasure in luxuriating in his familiarity with high-status people. Yet another thing his students made fun of him for—while hoping to use it to their advantage—but it inspired in me a kind of sisterly tenderness. Rosendale or not, it was something, having come all the way from that creaky attic bedroom in Janet's house, grace every night over cold potatoes, to a life of Manhattans with film directors, late dinners near Lincoln Center after *La Bohème* with last year's winner of the Pulitzer for fiction. ("An uxorious lunkhead," Nathaniel said of the novelist, who'd written six famous books.)

Maxwell seemed to be in some other category. He'd come up before—once when I'd poked my head in his office to find Nathaniel on a call. "Not now," he'd hissed, "it's Maxwell." As if the name meant something to me. But when I came back a few minutes later, after hearing Nathaniel bark goodbye into the phone, he didn't tell me about Maxwell's books or awards, his acquisitions, or his clients. He just sent me away with another bag of laundry.

"Is Maxwell—I heard you have a son," I said, selecting a hot pink marker to color in Lili's alternating Wednesday shifts.

"Who told you that?"

"I guess I overheard some of the others talking about it."

The others. What a thrill, to use words like that with him, drawing verbal lines that sealed the two of us off. "Ah yes, my personal life. A favorite topic." He said it with total neutrality, as if the way they orbited him was no more irritating or worthy of comment than a late F train. "I do. He's in his thirties. Much older than you."

"I didn't know."

"Why would you?"

"I just, I've read—"

"He doesn't like me to talk about him in public. He's afraid of poetry, of the very concept of an inner life. And yet he thinks everything is about him! Imagine, walking around ashamed all the time of an old man's scribblings."

"What does he do?"

"He manages a grocery store in Islip, the kind of place that sells tinned mussels from the coast of Portugal and olives that taste like sex. You'd be surprised, how much a job like that pays." Olives that tasted like sex. I had never thought of sex as having a taste. "He's always very angry with me, even though I really had nothing to do with his upbringing. I sent checks, I did always do that. We have lunch once a year, if that. He has his mother's, sort of . . ." He made an angry face, showing off his radiant teeth. I laughed, but only to please him.

"The others said he was an accountant." I was not surprised a job at a fancy grocery store paid well; maybe there was one hiring somewhere around Barth.

"His work does involve accounting."

"It doesn't bother you, what they say?"

"Some of it is probably true." He looked at me. "Poor Greening girl. You can't bear it, the whispers. But don't let them get to you. When you're the subject, it means you're doing something interesting." The pride I felt when he said that! "Maxwell, sad fellow, has never been the subject. That's why he's always raging at me."

I finished the calendar, hanging it on the back of his door, and asked Nathaniel, as I always did, if he wanted to see my notes from class. Every week I typed them up at Net Café—I'd never gotten comfortable in Barth's computer lab—just in case he said yes.

"Not right now," he said, and then got up to take a closer look at the calendar. "I like the pink—I won't miss it. And yellow for yourself, interesting choice. I would have selected blue." Blue? Was that good? His body was warm; he smelled like the cleanest of the socks I'd sniffed my first day as his assistant. When we stood side-by-side, my slight advantage in height seemed garish; I tried to shrink. If I'd tilted my head a couple of inches in his direction, his eyebrow would have kissed my temple.

"Nathaniel? I don't know if you've thought about it anymore, but I have a poem that's ready to submit, if there's ever space for me to workshop."

"Of course you do," he said, still looking at the calendar. "But there's not. Go now. And for the love of God—spend some of my money before the Department of Labor shows up at my apartment."

I choose a steakhouse near Genesis. By the time I got there, the two-hour break before my bartending shift had shrunk to just over one. I requested a table in the back and ordered a Manhattan, Nathaniel's drink, which I'd made before but never tasted. Crab cakes to start. For the main, I choose the middle-priced steak, cooked medium rare, following the suggestion of the waiter, whose black pants were clean and pressed and made me rub at my own with a damp napkin. When the check came—it would be over a hundred dollars, with tip—I put down Nathaniel's card. My heart had started to rev and flutter about midway through the Manhattan, but I finished it anyway, swallowing hard. At a nearby table, a little boy—two, maybe younger—was sitting in a highchair between his parents, chewing a piece of steak in his fist. The boy pulled the meat from his mouth—chewed to gummy oblivion, it draped over his pudgy fingers—and offered it to his father. The man pretended to take a bite. "Bite," the boy shouted, upset now. The mother was laughing; the father relented, with a shudder of disgust.

Father. The word had returned to its original meaning, the one I'd given it in childhood: a blank, a question so thoroughly without leads there seemed no point in asking it at all.

8

I always showed up for class early, in case Nathaniel needed last-minute copies, and because I believed it kept the others from talking about me—as they entered the room, one by one or in pairs, I was already there, listening, waiting. I sat in the chair in the corner, next to what I'd learned was a projector Nathaniel had never once used, trying to look confident and unobtrusive at the same time. It was Halloween; everyone was annoyed Nathaniel hadn't canceled class.

There was a party after, some recent grad's annual thing. They'd been discussing it for weeks. The theme—for the writers, Halloween wasn't enough—was "train wrecks." Leah and the writer who'd read the never-ending poem at *Best of the New* were dressed as Britney Spears from different eras. Leah was the Spears of 2007, her hair tucked into a pinkish swim cap the color of her skin, wearing a sweat suit that was tight and velvety, not at all like the schlubby hoodie Britney had worn in those grainy photos. Never-Ending Poem wore the school uniform from the ". . . Baby One More Time" video. She had the Barbie-ish legs of a much hotter girl, too tan for the season and covered with goose pimples; Nathaniel also seemed struck by them. "Someone needs a blanket," he said, staring, when she walked in.

Liliam and Reg had, in their cool way, adhered to the theme with the smallest possible effort. Liliam, her hair long and loose and freshly reddened, was Lindsay Lohan. She'd smeared some crusty makeup under her chin and on the front of the wifebeater she wore with jeans, to look like dried vomit. Reg was Paris Hilton, though his costume required Liliam for context: all he'd done was put on a trucker hat. Next to Reg, a quiet blond guy whose poems had so much white space they were basically wordless, was draped in old sheets plastered with strips of orange construction paper. His head poked out of the top, bland and pleased.

"And you are?" Nathaniel asked.

"The Hindenburg," he said, snaking his arm out of the sheet to scratch his nose.

"I see. Let's start with yours, what's it called? Ah yes. 'Time Is a Knife Is a War.' Not . . . untrue. Please read."

The Hindenburg began. "Knife," he said, and then paused. "Of tree branch . . . of things you never told me . . . of the sound of the car door . . . not sharp until . . ." Nathaniel's button-down had gone lemony in each underarm. Every time he shifted, a flash of color. White vinegar might help—it had worked on my mother's work shirts, the ones she had to wear for fancy Rosendale events. The Hindenburg was repeating the word *into.* Lucky 999 paid no special attention to Nathaniel's clothes—but I could get the stains out in the bathtub at my apartment, maybe, if I let the shirt soak for a while. *"Oh how long . . ."* the Hindenburg said, looking up from his draft.

The room filled with silence. Finally, Leah said, "Okay, so, whoa. Very visceral, strong imagery. I'm interested in the violence in that repetition of *into.* But I guess my question is, who is *you,* here?"

That was enough. Everyone jumped in, voices overlapping, all of them trying to articulate something that would bring Nathaniel into the conversation. Except Liliam, who was bent over one of her own drafts, writing.

People who were up for workshop put their copies in a wooden tray on the radiator by Friday at noon for workshop the following week. The tray was referred to, with affectionate fear, as the Box. Sometimes I caught people riffling through it, as if to gauge, in advance, how their work stacked up against the others. Liliam was also up tonight—her third workshop, already. It sucked for the Hindenburg, having to workshop alongside Liliam. Every now and then, Nathaniel would ramble on about how workshop wasn't a competition, but the winners and losers were always clear. You won if Nathaniel liked your poem enough to talk about it—even better if he asked you a question. If he let the workshop ping comments around for fifteen, twenty minutes without interruption, the poem had failed to capture his attention: It, meaning you, had failed. If it was a very big disaster, he'd just let the time run out, offering almost no feedback at all. Let's move on, he'd say, and the writer would gather up their stack of slashed drafts. Usually, Nathaniel picked the worst poem to workshop first and saved the winner for last. He didn't seem bothered by everyone's awareness of this. Just the previous week, asked to start things off, Leah had read her draft visibly holding back tears.

"We're out of time," Nathaniel said. The Hindenburg drooped. A few of the paper flames were coming unstuck from his costume, and they fluttered to the floor as he collected marked-up copies of his piece from the people around him. I wasn't interested in his poem, but it did bother me, how often Nathaniel withheld the solution—surely there was some way to make the piece better? The blankness more productive? The metaphors less obvious?

Liliam, once again, was up last. "Sorry, guys," she said. "I made a few changes. I'll read the corrected version. Hopefully you can follow along."

Liliam's poems were odd and precise, usually one single sentence you sort of tumbled down, no line longer than five words, white space used not randomly, as the *Hindenburg* did, but as a breath, a turn. They made you work for the feeling, but once you got it, the poem knifed you in the gut. "Socks," Liliam said. I pictured Nathaniel's office drawer, full of socks; now that I was here, they were all neatly balled together. She'd only read the title, but already Nathaniel made that hum in the back of his throat, like a child sucking on a piece of candy. No one ever got that sound but her.

Nathaniel spoke first. "Smart, to get rid of the question mark after *rainstorm*. It torqued the sound too much—there's a menace there, now, in the flatness of the line, the way the sound doesn't float up as expected."

I didn't really know what he was talking about, and no one else seemed to either, but Liliam said, "Right? I'm glad you heard that." Her workshop turned into a conversation between the two of them, just as her last one had. In theory, the workshopper was supposed to remain silent during the discussion, but that rule didn't apply to Lili. The rest of us waited for it to be over. I had a compulsive vision of myself standing up, pulling Nathaniel's sock drawer off its tracks, and dumping it all over the seminar table. On the clock, the minute hand was three lines past nine P.M., then six, then eleven.

"Oh!" Nathaniel said, interrupting himself. Liliam put her pencil down. "But I'm keeping you from your night of debauchery, am I not? Someone, please, stop the old man next time." Laughter, and it sounded genuine, though, as usual, I couldn't quite tell what was funny. The *Hindenburg* was already so drunk he steadied himself on his chair as he stood. "Remind me, who is putting poems in the Box for next week? Reg, Stephanie, Tim?"

"Yeah, me, but I'm going to pass," Reg said. "Wilhelmina can have my spot."

"Reg, what! You can't," Liliam said. "You just finished that suite. You need the feedback."

"You can give me notes," he told her. And then, to Nathaniel: "She's here every week, making copies and everything. It just doesn't seem fair. I mean"—he turned to me—"you do write, don't you?" Now they were all staring. My first impulse was to say no. That's what Nathaniel wanted me to say, I could feel it. But what had he told them, that first meeting? *I feel her work has a certain missing element.* What was it? How else would I find out? I already knew he wasn't going to just tell me.

"Yes, I write. I would love to submit something."

Nathaniel shifted, flashing his yellow armpits. He was radiating the same spiky wavelength as the time I'd brought him a salad with balsamic instead of the mustard vinaigrette. "I can't give you an extra workshop, Reg," he said.

"It's cool," Reg said. He seemed oblivious to the chaos he'd inspired: Nathaniel's annoyance, the rest of the room's confusion, my exhilarated fear. But as he bent down to collect his backpack, he glanced at me, as if to confirm the rightness of what he'd done. I tried to send him a message back, but he looked away too soon.

"I would be happy to read her work," said Never-Ending Poem.

"Fine with me," said the *Hindenburg*.

"Yeah, as long as she's not, like, officially in the workshop, I guess it's okay," said Leah, separating her ponytail into two chunks and pulling it tighter against her head.

"Wilhelmina?" Nathaniel's voice was tight. He was looking at the clock, an object he'd never once paid any attention to.

"It would be a dream to hear what you all think," I said, already weighing which of my poems would be the most impressive offering.

"Fine," Nathaniel said. "Will, copies in the Box by Friday at noon, you know the drill."

As usual, Nathaniel vanished into his office the second class was over. I'd developed a habit of lingering until everyone was gone, gathering extra copies, the wine cups scattered across the table and even the bookshelves. While I neatened, I'd try to compose the perfect question: urgent and sharp, like ones the MFA students brought to his office hours. But all my questions, from the genuine (How do you know what to leave out of a poem?) to the most try-hard (Is the objective correlative the best way to impart meaning without abstraction?) seemed only to give away how little I knew, and I was afraid if I drew any attention to that fact, he'd banish me to laundry and copying duty forever after. "All good here?" I'd say. "Go home, Will," he'd say. After class, his face seemed to deflate, except for the skin around his eyes, which puffed up. Standing half in his office, the window dark behind him, a weak glow coming from his desk light, I was electrified by the fact of our aloneness together. The flirtatious energy I'd picked up at the reading, at our first meeting in his office—ever since I'd fixed the curtain rod, it was gone. It made me feel I'd done something ugly or wrong, and that only increased my eagerness to please, to get his attention.

Usually, he left his office door open, but that night, he shut it. Why was he so irritated? Hadn't me submitting been his suggestion in the first place? The students filtered into the hall, talking about the party, and I went through my usual lonely routine, skipping Nathaniel's goodbye after staring for a second at the severe face of his door.

The writers had gathered in front of the bathrooms. "It's gotta be a sex thing," said Leah. She was practically shouting; drunk, at least a little. I stepped back toward the rounded entry to the seminar room, not so much to listen as to wait them out. The writers were always performing for each other in the halls and forgetting other people existed.

"No way," said Liliam. Was she going to defend me? "She's too meek for that. She barely even talks. I bet they're related, or it's like a family favor. I heard them talking about Michigan once."

"Or she's his actual assistant," said Reg. "Remember how out of it he was last year?"

"Shh," said Leah. "He's going to leave any minute."

"Three times last semester he forgot my name," said the Hindenburg. "Once this one. I'm keeping track."

Never-Ending Poem emerged from the bathroom, wearing sweatpants. "What are you guys talking about?"

"Nathaniel's concubine," said Leah.

"Maybe she's, like, a really exceptional poet," said Liliam.

Everyone laughed, even Reg.

"I guess we'll find out," said Tim, who was so blandly affable I sometimes forgot he existed.

"Nice of you to sacrifice your workshop for the cause, Reg," said Leah.

"I just don't need that workshop static in my brain right now," Reg said. "It's messing me up."

Eventually, they made their way down the hall to the elevator bank. The doors slid open and swallowed them up and the building quieted, except for a faint ding as the group descended to a lower floor. The hallway lights went out. Still, I hovered near the seminar room, one ear cocked for Nathaniel, trying to figure out which of their stories about me was true.

9

Nothing I'd already written would work. I would have to write something new, and it had to be the best thing I'd ever done. It had to prove I belonged in the room, it had to frighten and awe the other students, make them regret every bitchy thing they'd said about me, and it had to make Nathaniel pay attention to me as a writer, not just a reliable person to dispatch with any task that came into his mind. I began writing it as I walked to the bus stop through the buzzing purple city, I wrote it as I clung to the strap on the crosstown bus back to the East Side, woke up writing it the following morning, even as I wiped someone's pubic hair off the apartment toilet, bought a bagel with a crumpled five a man had thrown at me the previous weekend, and then all through public speaking, cutting limes and lemons at the pub, on the margin of my notepad beside a drink order for a pushed-together table of twenty middle-school teachers, I began again and again and again, one word and then another, a few crossed out, a few more added. Sitting in Nathaniel's workshop had taught me how little I knew about poetry, but when I looked at draft after draft I could not call up a single lesson, only the image of Nathaniel at his desk, the sound of his voice as he told me to add, to the recommendation letter I was writing for a former student on his behalf, "Samson is a young writer of originality and verve." Verve! The poems I'd written before had arrived as a scent does, a thing you notice once it's already there. I'd picked them up and put them down on the page—the hard part wasn't sourcing the feeling; it was the act of translation. But something was wrong with my nose.

The day before the poem was due, I decided, in a panic, to write something formal-ish; a few weeks earlier, Nathaniel had railed about how young writers were indifferent to form, how you couldn't expect to write free verse if you couldn't write a sonnet. I picked quatrains, an ABAB rhyme scheme. The image that came to me was of the marina in Quincy, the fancy one on Lake Michigan. All those sailboats, with their bimmies and jibs and mainsails; I knew he liked them, because of that impenetrable novel. I'd never been on a sailboat, so I made the speaker a thief, stealing one. I called the poem "Apparent Wind." By the time I printed out copies for the Box, I expected to see actual calluses on my hands, that's how tightly I'd written myself holding the rope.

10

The night of my workshop, class started, as it always did, with craft. Nathaniel seemed in rare form, standing up to write on the whiteboard, laughing until he slapped the table at something Lili said, stopping the discussion for a second to find a specific Berryman poem in a book buried deep in his office. He called Never-Ending Poem up first, a workshop I was not really present for, because I was so happy I hadn't been tapped for the loser's slot. After the break, as we took our seats, Reg's hand skimmed my arm. "Good luck," he said. When Nathaniel didn't call my name again, I believed, for almost forty exhilarating minutes, that I'd won the workshop. Nathaniel had saved me for last!

To introduce each workshop, the workshopper read their poem. As soon as I said the first word, I knew I'd gotten it wrong. Before I even got to the last line, Leah was trying not to laugh. Liliam was writing all over my handout. Reg was biting his pointer fingernail. Tim was texting. The Hindenburg's eyes were closed, as if to concentrate, but his breathing was very rhythmic. Nathaniel's expression suggested I'd just asked everyone to do something very silly, like take off their shirts. "Well," he said.

"I'm kind of into the rhyme scheme," said Never-Ending Poem. Brave, considering how her workshop had gone. "You can tell the writer worked hard on that."

The Hindenburg opened his eyes, as if summoned. "Plath-y, but without the urgency," he said, feedback that particularly stung, because usually he didn't speak a word during critiques. It also confused me, because Plath mostly wrote in free verse. All class I'd ignored the wine but I reached for it then, balanced up on the podium where Reg had left it for me, an offering.

"I'm not getting Plath," said Liliam. Electric-blue slashes lengthened her eyes. Hair middle-parted, and in a patent leather minidress, she looked like she'd just returned from Woodstock on an alien planet. I was wearing jeans I'd had since ninth grade and one of Dev's most benign sweaters—a body-hiding outfit—as armor. "And there is urgency here, in the way the content strains against the rhyme scheme, the tidy quatrains, the almost-iambic pentameter, like it doesn't want to be controlled. For me, it feels like the influences are outdated, and not really processed yet—"

"Yeah! It feels like it was written in 1779," Leah said. "Like what is *that* doing?" She went on for a long time. A piece of gum was stuck to the underside of the seminar table, glistening like a tiny, evil brain.

"You know what I do like," Liliam said. I looked up; she was looking at me, too. "The title. Apparent wind. Doesn't that mean something, in sailing?"

"It does," Nathaniel said. "Not the actual wind, but the wind as felt by the sailor, a mixture of the actual wind, the *true* wind, and the boat in movement. It can result in miscalculation, even disaster, if a sailor doesn't know what he's doing."

"Okay so if that's what it's about," the Hindenburg said, on a roll, "just, explain this part to me." He read out loud a stanza that mostly described the texture of a life jacket. No one spoke. I couldn't have answered him either.

Reg stayed quiet, as if he'd done all he could. The rest continued to have their way with me, until a silence fell.

"A potentially good title in search of a better poem," Nathaniel said, eyes on the clock, which had not yet reached nine P.M. "Probably one for the can." He waved his hand to dismiss us. One for the can. He said this all the time, even about his own work. *Spent all morning working on one for the can.* Feeding the can was noble; it was the road that led up the mountain. All writers had to do it. But had Nathaniel ever closed someone's workshop with that line? Someone he'd called up for critique *last,* in the winner's slot?

They collected their things quietly, as if trying not to trigger an angry parent. Never-Ending Poem sent me a long, sad look of commiseration—her workshop had been a bloodbath, too. I averted my eyes. I didn't want to be anything like her, even if it would make me less alone. "You coming?" Reg asked as they moved in their weird eight-person body toward the door, a group of people linked forever by Nathaniel.

"I'll get your drink," offered the Hindenburg, not quite making eye contact.

"You need one," Leah said.

I was too miserable to register my first true invitation from the group. Instead, I stayed at the table, staring at the stack of drafts they'd handed back. Nathaniel's was on the top. It had very few markings at all—a long looped slash, a short question, a single check. He was already in his office, the door shut, waiting, presumably, for me to leave. A muffled hello: Now he was on the phone.

By the time he finished, it was just after ten. I was in the same seat, holding my packed backpack on my lap as if it were a child, or I was.

"Jesus," Nathaniel said. "You're still here." His eyes had that after-class look. He was probably noticing that mine were red, from trying and failing not to cry. "Walk with me," he said, switching off the seminar room lights, and so I stood. Was I going to get fired? The building had the air of a drained bathtub; echoey, cold. In the older parts, the lights stayed on all night, but the renovated hallways had motion-detecting sensors that flicked to life after we entered and reminded me of the practice rooms at Rosendale. In one of the dark seconds, just before we exited the building through a door I'd never seen before, I reached out to touch his coat.

I had to know. Why, if I was so bad, had he let me submit at all? Why had he made me think I was special? But before I could say anything out loud, he turned and held the door open for me. The streetlight above us blotted out his face. "Do you like scotch whiskey, Will? When I was a child, you could order it from the diner, with your pancakes, though I do believe that was against state law in those days. It's rather Greening's drink, isn't it?"

Rather. That was not a Greening word, though he was right about the whiskey. Nathaniel had just turned sixty-two. Oh, I knew what he meant by the question, just as he knew what I meant when I said: "I do. On the rocks." Men had been asking me some version of it since I was a girl. What I'm trying to say is I understood what I was allowing to happen. Hadn't I suspected it was coming since our first conversation in his office? I'd showed up anyway, asked him again and again to read my poems. Hadn't I already agreed? We traveled ten blocks south of the famous campus as he pointed out things he liked—the restaurant with the good branzino, Don's historic bar, the bookstore where he'd found a pocket watch in the stacks. "Good to know," I said, as if I often sought out excellent fish, or Tom. Finally, after turning onto a quiet side street, we reached an apartment building, generic except for a stone arch over the entry. "Here we are," he said. As the elevator dinged shut, I felt no excitement, but no dread either—instead, the kind of dull satisfaction of inevitability, the plane taking off right on time, everyone on board.

His apartment was on the eleventh floor. Neither of us spoke the whole way up. The lobby was nice, grand even—lots of old marbly tile, a doorman in a suit—but his apartment was a large bland square, sparsely furnished. When we got inside, he slipped off his shoes, so after a beat, I did, too, nudging mine against a pile of sneakers that all looked very much like the pair I'd retied. A couple of full bookshelves, more paperbacks stacked against the walls in narrow, wobbly towers. A kitchen in the corner, set off with an island. A hallway, to somewhere I couldn't see. Nathaniel left the overheads off and switched on a floor lamp standing alone near the living area.

I folded myself into the corner of his couch, right up against the armrest, and dropped my backpack onto the floor. So this was where the great writer lived. The windows offered an improbable slice of New Jersey skyline. My vision was staticky with nerves, but there was no denying we'd moved past some layer of formality, where I could now say some of the things I really thought. "Why were you so mad? When Reg gave me his spot." I poked my toes between couch cushions—there were holes in both my socks. I wished I'd worn a better outfit. But Nathaniel didn't sit. Instead, he headed for the corner, where a console table held a record player and a bunch of records, some already out of their sleeves.

"Wilhelmina," he said. "You're a terribly sensitive girl." Sensitive. My mother called me that, too, sometimes—though she'd never use the word *terribly.* As when she said it, I felt silly and small and eager to prove the exact opposite. "I wasn't mad. I was concerned." Nathaniel put on something jazzy, the needle skipping a few times before it settled. "This arrangement we have. It's not the kind of thing the program looks kindly on."

"Why does the program care who your assistant is?"

"They don't. They would care, however, that I let you come to class. It might be hard to believe, but it's very competitive. You can't just waltz in and workshop. I didn't want Tilda to know, and now she will. One of them will complain." He'd moved over to the kitchen island, where he poured me two inches of scotch. "But you made it hard to say no."

"Oh," I said. "I'm sorry." I was moved, that he'd been trying to protect me. And I understood the subtext: We had secrets.

"Your name suits you," he said, handing me the glass and sitting down on the couch square next to me, inches from my toes. The same old Greening taste, though this was the two-hundred-dollar version. "It is German in origin, I believe. Your name. Will helmet." He rapped gently on my forehead, as if knocking on a door. "Yes, very strong."

I smiled. "There," he said. "She's back."

I still hoped that at any minute we might talk about my poem.

He leaned forward and dipped a pointer finger into my glass, all the way up to his middle knuckle. "Hand?" I didn't know what he meant, and he laughed. He held out his as an example. A few droplets of scotch dripped onto my jeans. I put my drink on the side table and extended my hand. He pressed his wet finger into my palm. "Rub them together," he instructed. "Great. Now breathe in deep. Like this."

I smelled the rubbing alcohol my mother used to clean scrapes when I was a kid. "Mm," I said.

"Peat. Delicious." Nathaniel tilted a few degrees toward me on the couch. He gathered my hands into his, held them to his face. "Like something just dug up. The potato of drinks, and appropriate, somehow, for a helmet." My palms tingled as he talked into them. "It'll activate your taste buds."

He released me, and I picked up my drink. When I finished it, he brought the bottle of scotch over. "I'm good," I said. "As you know, I have to work tomorrow."

"Play hooky," he said. "I'm sure your boss will understand." He topped us both off, leaving the scotch uncapped.

"You sure?"

"Positively."

I was drunk—I'd had wine in class, nothing to eat for hours and hours—but I felt clearheaded as he talked and talked about Greening, about an ancient cat he'd snuck into the dorms at Rosendale, Biscuit, he'd named her, how she was buried under a boulder by the lake, how I must visit her next time I was home. When he wanted to be, Nathaniel was easy to talk to. As I told Nathaniel how the Rosendale faculty looked straight through my mother when she was at work, even when they were asking her for something, his legs moved inch by inch, until his toes were poking mine between the cushions. Every time I shifted to hide my socks, he'd shift, too. At some point I realized we were quite close together, sitting face-to-face as we talked. "I'm warm," he announced. "Don't you dare laugh if I take off my shirt."

He unbuttoned his denim shirt slowly, revealing a great deal of chest hair, and threw it over his shoulder with a flourish. "I could never laugh at chest hair like that," I said. "It's a very serious business." He looked absurd, sitting there without a shirt on; it had the unexpected effect of making me more comfortable, not less.

"Don't be distracted by my beauty, either," he said, pouring me a little more scotch.

We were laughing, I no longer remember about what, and I almost blurted out the whole story. Wasn't the funniest part of all this how for so long, years and years, I'd held on to the teeny, creeping hope that he might be my *father*? Plus—the thought lurched drunkenly through my mind—if I told him, it would stop what was about to happen, the events I'd set into motion. It would have to.

Wouldn't it? i

I said nothing, and, of course, the transition came. It was clumsy; I am larger than Nathaniel, and I worried I might hurt him, even though he was the one pulling me toward him, tightening his arms even when I tried to lean back, to slow things down, so I could get a handle on what was happening. I remember a kiss with teeth, everything the wrong angle. I couldn't get quite organized on his lap—his waist is narrow and my legs are long and I reared over him like a horse. Eventually, we wound up longways on the couch, Nathaniel whispering beautiful, beautiful Wilhelmina into my hair as he palmed my breasts under my sweatshirt, which I still hadn't taken off.

It wasn't sexy, but also, finally, here was romance, in its way. No motorboating titties, no cracked-open window or muddy shoes on the bed. I'd never, in all my life, gone on a real date—Nathaniel had put on a record, given me a compliment. Those gestures, small and canned as they were, changed my view of the scene, as if I were switching the lights on my mother's vanity mirror. From embarrassing to sordid to goofily sweet. No matter how many women he'd been with, I doubted he'd told anyone about that Rosendale cat. And what about the other women? The actress, Vilma? *Can't sleep, can't work, my heart is cold, my brain is cold.* It made feel me safer, those other women and their love.

Nathaniel buried his head in my shoulder, and there was another phantom scent from home, haunting me in New York—the sweet puff the Rosendale vacuums released when you emptied the bags. Where did I put my hands? On his shoulder blades? The small of his back? His erection was hardish but durable, almost too long-lasting. Had he taken a drug? If so, when? There was no discussion of contraception. My eyes had adjusted to the light; the ceiling was lovely, an alternating pattern of triangles and squares. It would remain my favorite thing about his apartment. I traveled up to their dust-spangled corners. From there, I watched the flexing of his ass, slow and consistent, very unlike the agitated humping of the window boys. Somehow, Nathaniel communicated a desire to switch positions, nudging me. I flipped onto my stomach and he reached his hand around, his full weight pressing me down from behind. My throat went numb. I'd been elsewhere, a cobweb in the grooves of the ceiling, and then, without warning, I was body, my face pressed into the couch; the orgasm was involuntary, almost painful, my first ever with another person.

After, he turned on the lights; I recognized this as an invitation to leave. "Nathaniel," I said, slipping on my corduroy coat. He was standing in the hallway to see me off, already brushing his teeth. "Why did you have me go last?"

"Tonight?" he said, toothpaste foaming around his lips. "They were all for the can. But yours was trying the most."

It was half past midnight. I wasn't sure where the subway station was by his place, and I didn't want to get lost in Central Park, so I walked back to the East Side via the Ninety-seventh Street Transverse, a route I knew well from the bus, sticking to the unlit sidewalk-like path. Few cars drove by. I felt small and large at once, the way I often did walking alone in New York; if I turned the right magic corner, opened the right door at the right time, I'd be welcomed into the secret city, the vast, glittering party I could sense, always, on my periphery. Perhaps now I'd be welcomed, either by Nathaniel or because of him at my side.

I took the stairs two at a time, and when I reached my apartment, my heart was pounding. How many calories were in those glasses of scotch? In the bathroom, I stepped into the shower, so dizzy I had to sit. I hugged my knees, staring into the pale valley formed by my belly, my thighs. My life in New York was about to accelerate. I had given Nathaniel something; now I would get something in return. Dev banged on the door—"My toothbrush, Will!"—and snapped me back into myself.

"Just come in," I yelled.

He smelled like liquor, cigarette smoke. "I'm so late," he said, with his toothbrush in his mouth. "Are you *sitting* in there? Disgusting. You will tell me everything tomorrow."

Standing in my towel at the kitchen sink, I washed Dev's dinner dishes, a couple of dirty jam jars, trying out versions of what I might tell him. By the time I was in my room, the bottoms of my feet were gray again and it was almost three in the morning. I brushed at the dirt with a cleanish sock and got under my covers, adjusted my pillow against the lumped backrest of the chair, pretending it was a headboard.

Three texts since I'd last checked my phone before workshop.

Mom: It has been two weeks since I have heard anything from you.

Liliam: Oof, you okay? That was a rough one. Here if you need a beer.

Mack: can you come in tmrw? We need to restock and Robby called out

I answered Mack—*ok*—and sent an email to my Barth professors, saying I was sick and I'd have to miss class. After thinking it over for a while, I responded to Liliam, who could only have gotten my number from Nathaniel. *i'm working tomorrow.* I thumbed in the address for Genesis. *you could come around 4, before we get busy?* I'd been in New York for over three months and still my only friend was Dev, sort of. When Liliam handed back her markup of my poem, every line was red. But she'd stood up for me in workshop, sort of—or at least she'd taken me seriously.

Before clicking off the light, I fished for my backpack—my room was so small I could reach it from bed—and pulled out my critiques. Reading them, I was back in the seminar room, chair half pulled up to the table so I'd had to balance my notebook on my knees. To read

I don't understand what does this mean I can't see this who is the speaker here and read *lol a bit much no can these line breaks be more deliberate this image is both melodramatic and a little dull* and read *derivative hmm the emotion is right on the surface I'm just not sure who this work is for* was like gulping hot oil, a sick melting in my bowels as it hit again, again, the understanding that I, the exception, had proven to be the rule. In class, I'd smiled big, nodded. When I gathered their letters, I said thank you. This has given me a lot to think about. No questions for the group.

Now I was seeing Nathaniel dipping his arm below the couch, lifting my ratty yellowed bra and holding it up in the lamplight. I knew critique was necessary. I knew the point of workshop. There was a raw spot on the inside of my thigh, skin abraded by one of the patches of fur on his legs. The poem, it's true—it wasn't very good. But I hadn't understood until their scrawled notes, their coffee spots and ink stains and endless question marks, that this wasn't just about my work—it was about me being in the room at all, and what they assumed it meant. A sex thing, as Leah had said, yes—but was that what they were angriest about? Or was it that my presence suggested there was a different set of rules for some people, depending on what they were willing to do? Maybe Reg had given me the workshop slot to test a theory. And now they were right. Nathaniel hadn't used a condom and when I swung my legs to the floor clots of semen glided unevenly toward my knees. *Start over,* Nathaniel had written at the top of my poem, drawing a faint pencil stroke down the middle. He'd circled one single line, near the end, an image of a mushroom sprouting between the pages of a book below deck. *Maybe keep this?* I wiped lamely at myself with a tissue from a box on the side table, before pulling my underwear back on.

But then, as sudden as my uncomfortable orgasm, the molten shame inside me cooled, turned diamond-sharp. They could say anything, do anything. But they couldn't stop me from trying the *most.*

11

Liliam showed up minutes after my shift started. I was alone behind the bar, checking my phone repeatedly for a sign of Nathaniel; Mack would be in the upstairs office until five, everyone else was in the back, eating shift meal. Liliam stood outside for a while, squinting at her phone, then up at the sign; I could see her through the front window, wearing a biker jacket and cigarette jeans and boots with spiked toes, a curved tusk for a heel. Her outfit looked like two months' rent. She shoved her phone into her back pocket and I swirled to face the liquor bottles, trying to look busy.

"Hey, bartender," she said, straddling Mr. Dougal's corner stool—he'd tip me zero for not saving his place—and draping her coat and bag on the seat beside her, instead of using the hooks. Well-dressed women often did this; I couldn't tell if it was because they were trying to keep people from sitting next to them, or if they just didn't care about making room for anyone else. In Greening, the unspoken rule most women followed was to take up as little space as possible. The bar was empty, but I didn't ask her to move, a choice that cost me fifteen dollars.

The two wings of black eyeliner, her photogenic face, transported me to the seminar room my mind seemed never to leave. She might as well have asked: "Are we on to the critique portion yet?" Liliam looked up at the chalkboard. "I'll have a Cosmo. The Friday night special."

I think she was trying to be nice, but it was an annoying order. No one except tourists ever went for the specials, and tourists didn't frequent Genesis, a bland Irish pub with a menu of utterly basic food and only Guinness, Smithwick's, and Harp on tap. It was a long room like a train car, with a handful of pocked leather booths split lengthwise by the bar. A few high-tops near the window. We mostly got by on regulars, beer and whiskey drinkers all, probably exactly why Mack had chosen Cosmos for our five-dollar drink. "Are you old enough to bartend?" she asked as I set a dusty martini glass before her. I filled a shaker with ice. Why had I invited her? I still couldn't handle more than four customers without backup, let alone on a Friday night, let alone on a Friday night while Liliam tried to engage me in a workshop inquisition.

"No one ever checked," I said, trying to smile. "But yes. Bartending age is eighteen here, like most everywhere." What came next? I picked up vodka from the well, dumped it in, added three seconds of cranberry. There was something else. Lime juice? Maybe at a nicer bar. Liliam watched my hand flit above the various bottles, as if trying to divine the right one through extrasensory perception. Triple sec! I tipped it in, counted to two again. I shook the metal canister and in my eagerness to get her to stop looking at me, forgot to strain the ice. I poured what I could into her glass, a heaping pink mound, and left the shaker beside her, praying she'd finish it before Mack came downstairs.

"Are you doing okay?" She took a sip, ice collapsing against her upper lip, and looked up at me over the rim, like, I love this perfectly normal drink. "That was a hard one. Wretched. Honestly, I hate when Nathaniel just doesn't say anything at all." Liliam had the accent of a rich person. Many of the writers had her placeless drawl—I'd heard it at Rosendale, too. Some special quality to the enunciation, as if every word were so delicious it must be chewed twice: once to release the meaning, the second time for subtext, flavor. *Wretch-ed. Hon-est-ly.* It evoked location less than it did milieu; cocktails on a wide lawn under a starry sky, horseback riding and wide-brimmed hats. "I texted him after to yell at him. Probably sulking. He doesn't like to get slapped on the wrist." *Sulk-ing.* Nathaniel had left his phone on the coffee table, face down beside the scotch, Liliam's chiding voice inside. Kirk, one of our regulars, pushed open the door, sat down as far as he possibly could from Liliam; from there he stared at her, his shoulders drawn to his ears. I slid him a Guinness. In class I hadn't noticed it, but there at the bar, pinned by Kirk's ravenous eyes, Liliam herself looked hardly old enough to drink.

"How old are you?"

"I thought you said no IDs," she said. "Twenty-four. Now you."

Fair enough. "Just turned twenty-three." For my birthday, Dev had brought me a chocolate cupcake with a lit toothpick as a candle. "Aren't you a little young for an MFA?"

"I'm here a year out from New Haven. Never bought into that whole get some life experience under your belt before grad school thing. I have plenty to say. I don't really need to flail around in some entry level publishing job to gather material. Waitressing or whatever." She stopped, flicked a look at me. Hurried to recover. "How do you know Nathaniel?"

"New Haven?" I asked as I checked for new arrivals, the level of Tom's drink. Liliam had drunk most of the liquid from her Cosmo, leaving behind a mound of pink rocks.

"Yeah. Yale."

"Oh," I said, confused about why she hadn't said Yale in the first place. I'd spent all day at Net Café and had barely eaten. My stomach shrieked, a sound midway between an infant's wail and a fart; I tried to cover it up by plunging the silver shovel deep into the ice, but in the process, I knocked a wineglass—the one I'd been drinking seltzer from—directly into the ice basin, where it shattered. "Shit," I said, but Liliam didn't seem to have noticed. Why had I been drinking from a wineglass?

"I thought he might be a family member of yours or something. We've all been speculating. But it's so his, like, anti-institutional *thing,* to just let in some random assistant from outside the whole MFA circle jerk."

"You seem to know him pretty well." I would have to water the ice—and then I would have to find Mack, get him to cover the bar while I ran downstairs for another bag. Robby, who was everywhere when Mack was also behind the bar, was nowhere to be seen.

"I got the research fellowship at the end of last year. It's fine, it's a part of my funding. I get a monthly stipend to assist him with, basically nothing. I thought he might give me something good to work on, but no dice."

"Weren't you excited? I mean, it's Nathaniel Fellow." I was trying to fish out the pieces of glass without stalling the conversation.

"Sort of? I like the old stuff. Sometimes he talks to me about what he's reading, just offhandedly, and it hits me—this is Nathaniel Fellow. But it wears off. You realize there's a real person behind the writing, and the real person isn't as good as what's on the page. Or what *was* on the page." She slurped some of the pink runoff from her martini glass. "Or, I don't mean isn't as good, I just mean, it's different. There's, like, this gap."

A gap. I thought of the spaces between all the Nathaniels I'd already known and imagined: the poet, the famous writer, the runaway father, the Greening boy, the boss, the teacher, and now whatever we were becoming. A crescent of glass slipped through my fingers, and then there was blood on the ice, blood unfurling from a little mouth on the side of my index finger, pretty, pulsing in time with the pounding behind my eyes.

"Are you okay? Will, you're bleeding."

"I'm fine," I said, turning on the hot water like I should have in the first place. At the far end of the bar, closest to the door, a middle-aged couple sent me hello-idiot-we've-been-waiting energy, shifting on their stools. The ice was melting slowly.

"You sure?" Liliam asked, before launching into a deeper analysis of the difference between Nathaniel the writer and Nathaniel the man. I stuck my finger under the burning water, knowing Mack was coming, feeling it in the air around me. Time in a restaurant is measured by little shifts in atmospheric pressure, the way light falls against the window, the sound of street traffic, the texture of the clangs in the kitchen, the happy gasp of the door as the after-work drunks start to push their way in. And by the manager, who was now behind me, watching as my blood swirled into the thawing sea of ice.

"You need new ice," Mack said.

"I know, I just—there was no one to cover the bar."

"I said you need new ice. Can you hear?"

"No—" I started, but he'd already seen it: Liliam's tragic Cosmo, the shaker with most of her drink standing tall beside the thumbed glass.

"Excuse me," said the male half of the couple down the bar. "Can we get a drink here?"

"One second, sir," I said. A group of three swung noisily in through the front door, took the high-top near the window.

"What is that?" Mack wasn't even looking at Liliam's drink—he was looking at me, but his awareness was so focused on the martini glass it was as if he'd picked it up and was wielding it directly in front of my face.

"You mean my Cosmo?" Liliam said, leaning over the bar and looking up through her eyelashes. Mack's awareness trembled, turned. "I know it's so gross. But that's how I like them! Will was so sweet to indulge me."

"You like your Cosmo on the rocks?"

"I can't help it. Holdover from one too many teenage parties. The ice slows me down." Liliam deployed a huge, toothy smile, and Mack took a disoriented step back before leaning closer in.

"Right after I help out those folks down there, I'm going to make you a proper drink," he said. And then, four degrees louder: "Will. Ice. Now."

When I came back upstairs, my finger wrapped in a Band-Aid, Mack and Liliam were chatting away as she sipped at a squat amber drink. She winked at me, a glassy sheen over her eyes. She was either a lightweight or she'd had something before she showed up. Reg appeared around an hour later, in the middle of the rush. He swooped onto the stool next to her, still empty thanks to her bag (Mr. Dougal was four seats down and giving me the silent treatment), and ordered a Jameson.

"What happened to you wasn't fair," Reg said. For a second, I thought he was referring to what happened *after* workshop. "I liked your poem. Nobody tries to rhyme anymore, not because it can't be good, because it's too hard."

"Thank you," I said. Did he mean it? He was wearing a beanie, his hair smooshed flat on his forehead.

"Get rid of that hat," Lili said, pulling it off.

"So what have you guys been doing without me?" Reg took his hat back and folded it neatly on the bar beside his Jameson.

"Talking?" I said, sweat trickling from my temples. I hurried to fill an order—two Guinnesses, one Smithwick's, three Harps—for one of the high-tops.

"Miserably failing the Bechdel test," Liliam said. I didn't know what the Bechdel test was but understood I should not admit that. They turned their attention to each other while I ran back and forth behind the bar. Whenever my peripheral vision snagged on them, they were laughing. Nathaniel still hadn't texted. Finally, they asked for the check. I only comped one of their drinks, so terrified was I of Mack, and when I slid the leather folder to Liliam she pulled out the receipt, then held it up with some confusion before handing it back with her card.

"Should I?" Reg said, gesturing toward his wallet.

"No, no," Liliam said. She signed with a flourish, left it carelessly on the bar, took her copy, crumpled it, and dropped it into her purse. "Thanks, Will," she said. On the right side, her eyeliner was smudged into a dense black bruise. "Some advice?" The slur in her voice was subtle, but it was there. "Don't flirt with Nathaniel. If he gets the wrong idea, he'll never leave you alone. And you're not reading the right poets. I'm going to give you some books."

It rattled me, her warning, coming on the heels of my night with Nathaniel, as if she'd somehow sensed what had happened. I cared more about her finding out than what she was implying. I didn't want him to leave me alone. And hadn't I seen her flirting, or something like it? I didn't consider she might be, in her Lili way, trying to look out for me. She'd left me 20 percent, not a cent more, not a cent less. Maybe she wanted all his attention for herself.

No word from Nathaniel. I picked up brunch on Saturday as a distraction. Genesis was not a destination even on weekend nights. Brunch was a dead zone, a desperate attempt for customers who never came. Hours could creep by with no more than a couple of tables, everyone ordering the western omelet or the almond French toast, made with flavored syrup and stale soda bread from the previous week. I'd make thirty bucks if I was lucky. Outside, people in some other narrative passed by—the old women with beautiful hairdos and toddling dogs, the babies in their strollers who appeared to tug their tired mothers behind them, the group of teenage boys I could hear through the glass, not Nathaniel, not Nathaniel, not Nathaniel. I looked at my phone. What if I texted him something simple? Like *hi,* or *I had fun*? Or a joke, like *hope your shirt's okay!* I seemed to be having a delayed chemical reaction to the orgasm. When it happened on Nathaniel's couch, I'd been startled, almost scared. But remembering it turned me on, the first true feeling of arousal attached to the experience, confusedly present and two days late.

Dev was home when I got back from my shift. I laid it all out for him. He was almost thirty, the only person I'd ever met who was attracted to both men and women. ("Now, Will," he'd said when I told him that. "I know you're not an idiot.") I believed he knew everything on earth about sex. I ordered us Thai food, a blatant attempt to get him to sit with me longer; it cost most of my morning's tips.

"Mmm the daddy thing is weird," Dev said. "I knew you were a freak when I met you. You were too polite to be normal." Now Dev was the only person in the city who knew the whole truth about how and why I'd come, and we'd never once hung out outside that cursed apartment.

"You're making me feel worse."

"No but really, I was in a situation just like this when I moved here." The staccato of an emptying shotgun filled the air every couple of minutes; Cody, our other roommate, was playing video games in his room.

"Yeah?"

"I got a job working for this Russian lady I met on Craigslist. She had a shopping addiction. I took pictures of clothes she bought and then wrote captions—Proenza Schouler dress, never worn, original tags, shit like that—and she sold them on eBay and bought new stuff with the money. Rinse and repeat. She lived in one of those Gramercy apartments on that park with the key. I have never in my life to this day seen such a thing—the whole apartment, kitchen, bathrooms, had carpet. In New York! My eyes will never forget."

"How is this the same?"

"One day she opened this nice bottle of red and we were trying on stuff, trying to decide what to post next, and, you know. We fucked. She was old hot, huge biceps, a little off her head." Dev took a long drag of his Thai iced tea. "I worked for her for like another year. It was a great job. So easy."

"Did you have sex with her that whole time?"

"You know, I can't really remember," he said. "At least once or twice more. But not like, every day." He reached over and forked some of my pad thai. "In a situation like this, it's important to know what you want."

"What do I want?" I couldn't articulate any of it to myself. It was too big, too raw and tender. All the usual things a lost and drifting young woman might want from a successful older man—attention, approval, to be chosen, yes, for him to recognize something special in me, call it talent, call it whatever would rescue me from my mother's fate, Rosendale's walk-in freezer clicking shut. And underneath that, something wilder, too bold to admit. I wanted to learn how to speak, and how to make people listen when I did. I wanted to become someone who mattered. Someone like him.

"I can tell you what you don't want. You don't want to lose that gorgeous credit card. Play that right and you won't be working at a craphole bar very long."

"You think he's going to fire me *now*?" I hadn't even thought of that.

"I think you're a liability if you start to get all girly on him. Just be chill. Act like nothing happened."

"How the hell am I supposed to do that?"

"Step away from the phone. Don't fall in love or get sex-high. He's done this a million times, and most of them the girl got crazy, I can promise you. You need to be different."

A million times. I knew Dev was probably right; it hurt anyway. My total count, when it came to sex at least, was four, including Nathaniel. He'd lost patience with me before—when I complimented him at the reading, and in his office when I did the same thing. He liked flattery as much as any writer; that couldn't be the sin. What, then? On workshop nights he'd sometimes fade, his gaze going inward, until someone asked an unexpected question—then he'd pick up his pen, point it at them, even stand. Boredom. Was it that simple? I'd bored him. I would try very hard never to do that again. My life in New York, my life as a writer—I wasn't going to let it end before it started.

Cody exited his room, wearing a pink bathrobe and flip-flops. "Thai food, yum," he said. "I would have ordered." He stood above us. The diamond stud in his left earlobe glittered when he leaned over to pull a spring roll from an open takeout container. "Talking about your writer?" He was always trying to get me to put stuff for the apartment on Nathaniel's Visa. On my mother's advice—she was worried I'd blow it all or get robbed or evicted—I'd prepaid six months' worth of rent when I got my financial aid refund, covering me from November through April. Cody thought I was rich. "I googled him. Did you know he dated that actress from *Beauty and Mud*? Think you could get me her email?"

"My God, Will," said Dev. "That practically makes you famous."

The next day, Nathaniel texted me. *W, you big wonderful helmet head. Because I know you're wondering: I let you in because you're really very good. I'll behave tomorrow if you will.*

Really very good! I assumed he meant my poem. Four hours later, I texted back: *Thank you.* Capital *T,* period. I was grateful he'd acknowledged what happened before my next morning with him.

And I do appreciate your helpful personality, he sent, about a second after my message went through.

But when I showed up at his office on Monday, he wasn't there. The faint smell of him in the air, the sight of the nameplate on his office—I was overcome, lit like a match. I burned, a heady combination of longing and fear, shame and infatuation, or maybe just the force of my own determination to make our new circumstances a step on an upward path. I texted Nathaniel a single question mark. Right away he wrote back: *Sorry something came up last min. Will pay for both today and Fri. Spend as if full days!!*

I went to Gristedes. Pineapple, dark chocolate, deli turkey from the counter, whole milk, frozen shrimp, a loaf of fresh rye, avocados, cashews, a twenty-two-dollar hunk of cheese I couldn't pronounce, because the sample tasted like the smell of Rosendale Lake when the algae blooms washed up on shore. In New York, you could get any fruit or vegetable you wanted no matter the season, all of it bright and misted every few seconds with fresh water. Once you get used to certain pleasures, it's hard to go backward. The total came to $274; around $150 more than he owed me. I handed over Nathaniel's card, feeling like someone.

Thursday evening, a week since I'd left his apartment. I chose my usual chair in the corner.

"No," Reg said. "You can't sit there. You've workshopped. You're one of us now, whether you like it or not."

No one else said anything. I moved my chair up to the table anyway—maybe it would be good for Nathaniel, who was almost ten minutes late, to see me there. Liliam wasn't there either.

"You ever think about how, if you take the standard tuition, each minute we're in here is worth like a hundred dollars," the Hindenburg asked the room.

"Did you get an email," Leah said. "I didn't get an email."

"Per person, I'm saying," said the Hindenburg.

"You should write a poem about it," said Reg, but not meanly—like he really thought so. It wasn't a bad idea—not the Hindenburg's petty construction, which also gave away that he'd received no funding—but I could sort of see how you might write it, an actual, precise valuation of each minute and its cost. If you switched every student around the seminar table out for a pile of singles representing how much they'd spent to be in Nathaniel's presence for three hours, even accounting for fellowships, all their tuition awards, most of the chairs would disappear under piles of cash. Except mine: I would simply disappear, leaving nothing behind except Nathaniel's Visa.

Liliam entered first and held the door for him. Nathaniel was grinning, his chin tucked into his chest. It was so obvious, how he flirted with her. It made him seem like her grandfather, her pediatrician. "My apologies, writers," Nathaniel said. "I was detained." He took his seat, a normal man, and a confused pulse started between my legs, some tepid mixture of agitation and horniness and social anxiety. He wore a long-sleeved green T-shirt; devastatingly uncool. "Okay, everyone. It's that time again. I'm soliciting for *Best of the New.* Send me your best poems by December eighteenth. No more than three; no, linked poems do not count as a single poem."

"Is there going to be a fiction section this year?" Leah asked.

"No, there is not."

The bad poets, who all identified as fiction writers, groaned.

Liliam blew around the room, her arm flashing between us, distributing stapled packets of poems and a schoolmarmish floral odor.

Why hadn't he asked me to make the copies? She dropped herself into the chair next to mine and unwound her long scarf, intensifying the scent. She slid one of the last packets onto my lap, and with it—"Your makeup looks pretty," she whispered—an understanding clicked into place. He flirted with her like that because there was nothing to hide. She thought she was his favorite, and maybe that was true, but she wasn't his secret.

"Sorry," Liliam said, leaning forward until her chin hovered over Never-Ending Poem's shoulder.

"Yes?"

"It's just, Will and I are kind of squeezed out of the circle." It was true. Our chairs were wedged too close together, at an awkward distance from the table. Nathaniel met my eyes for a second, and I read the amused spasm of his eyebrow as a reaction to my lipstick, a color I'd chosen, in part, for its ability to be seen from far away.

Over the course of an unnecessarily long and noisy minute, chairs wiggled closer together, slowly encroaching the giant parentheses of empty space around Nathaniel. I did not envy the Hindenburg, who was now elbow-bumping distance from him. For the rest of the term, whenever the Hindenburg lifted his hand to speak, Nathaniel wouldn't notice; you're in my blind spot, he'd say, when really, he was punishing him for being too close.

"That's better," Liliam said to herself or to me once we'd squeezed ourselves in until our chairs connected at the bottom, a bench for us two. "Now we're at the table."

The next morning, I showed up at Nathaniel's office for my Friday shift. A few minutes before ten and he was there, his door ajar. We hadn't yet been alone since I'd left his apartment; after class the previous night, he'd exited with the others. "Hi," I said, trying to sound cool, as if it were any other day.

"Wilhelmet." The collar of his pink button-down was half up. "Good morning and come in. You look like springtime, very nice on such a cold day. I regret to inform you that I need to send you to the post office." He gestured to a several separate piles of books on the couch, each with a Post-it on top. It was the most organized task he'd ever given me—so he was nervous, too. "It will be at least a few trips."

I filled a tote bag with the first two stacks and heaved it onto my shoulder. I was already halfway out the door when he stopped me with my name.

"We got a bit carried away the other night, didn't we?"

"We did," I said, but did not turn around.

"You're all right?"

I looked back at him then. He was giving me the face you might present a child who has fallen and hurt their knee—gentle, concerned. An acknowledgment of the sting, but carefully calibrated not to make the crying worse.

"Nathaniel," I said, with my sunniest smile. "I am just fine."

I really believed it.

12

Liliam blew into Genesis, unraveling her scarf, asking me what I was reading, and didn't I think those chutes funneling steam out of the center of the city, right up through the middle of the street, looked like whale blowholes? Or maybe cartoon buttholes, just blasting one. It was a Sunday afternoon, the doldrummy stretch between brunch and happy hour.

She'd started coming to Genesis now and then, texting me twenty minutes before she showed to confirm I wasn't too busy to talk. I think Liliam liked that I wasn't one of them. How little I knew about the scene, or her portion of it, how fascinated I was by their ambition, their oddities of personality: Leah smoked cloves while she wrote, and sometimes wore a Chaplinesque bowler hat for good luck; Never-Ending Poem was the granddaughter of the person who invented a foam tile that was ubiquitous in suburban Midwestern basements, and Nathaniel had let her in to court a big donation, or so Lili said; Reg wrote one poem longhand every morning, first thing when he woke up, and then ripped it into pieces he threw into a wicker basket (named, of course, the Can). This was an exercise, he said, in writing as a practice, in removing the ego, in getting to the invisible sacred core we all—and I do think this is what we were after, in those early days, before any of us had published a word outside of *Best of the New*—believed poetry could touch, if we worked hard enough, wrote honestly enough, took in Nathaniel's feedback and revised our poems into the sharp, brilliantine creatures he promised they could be. Poet, Liliam taught me, was as much an identity, a choice about what kind of person you were in the world, as it was a commitment to the art and act itself. Public weeping, fantastic clothes, ludicrous non sequiturs, alcoholism—calling oneself a poet made such quirks not just excusable but exalted, the symptoms of the extraordinary, covetable disease of talent.

I soon realized Liliam was also short on real friends. She had Reg, but he was half in love with her, and she was irritated by his dreaminess, his lack of drive. (Reg was famous for having never submitted a poem for publication—Nathaniel had forced him to hand over a workshop piece for the previous edition of *Best of the New.*) You couldn't ask Liliam to do anything, come to anything—you had to extend your fist, wait until she approached and sniffed. Show eagerness and you were dead. Even her position as the workshop's center was uneasy. Leah, especially, would sometimes grow sullen around Lili; during Lili's workshops, a hateful, reverent energy often crept into the room in the seconds after she read. But I couldn't hate Lili. It was wonderful to stand behind the bar quartering limes as she talked, leaping from one thing that interested her to another. That was also the impulse she followed in her poems; my strategy so far had been to try to mimic what I'd read in the Nortons.

That day, Genesis was empty except for us and a guy who'd been staring at *The New York Times* at a four-top since we'd opened at noon. I'd checked on him four times. Men always made me nervous when they didn't leave or drink. I felt like they were waiting for something, and like they wanted me to feel that way.

Liliam was talking about her hometown in Massachusetts, where a nineteen-year-old girl she knew distantly—cousin of a friend's stepbrother—had just been convicted for setting fire to fourteen different barns within a fifty-mile radius. For a long time, the fires had been a mystery, but then someone saw her—a girl with a can of gasoline and a match, leaning toward a bale of hay. Skinny, with a crab apple face, Lili said, and big, dry pores that made her look older than she was. Kind of a crappy family, missing dad, brother in jail. Lili had met her once. When the police asked the girl why she did it, she told them she was lonely, and bored, and she wanted something to happen. The fires look pretty at night, she said.

"I'm going to write fourteen poems, one for each barn," Lili told me. "I just need to get the voice right. I wanted something to happen! God, I relate to that so much. That response, all by itself—that's basically my ars poetica. When I was a teenager, I made a noose out of a clothesline and put it around my neck, just to see what it felt like. That's the kind of hungry for experience I was, a real devotee of Sexton, Plath, Rich, all the sad lady poets. I wish I'd set fire to a barn. Fourteen! My version is just pathetic."

I could tell Lili about Rosendale, about how long I'd carried around the dream that Nathaniel was my father. Or about the night I called Brian B. back on my mother's landline, curious about hooking up, sure, but also so tired of the story happening to me, instead of me happening to it. I'd shared it all with Dev, and easily, once I got started; but no matter how many secrets Lili disclosed of her own, I kept my worst to myself. There was something about me she admired, though I couldn't tell what it was—what if the truth ruined everything? "Me too," I said. "I relate to it, I mean."

"Gonna go work," Lili said when people started showing up and taking my attention. She meant write. She left her scarf on the floor, a puddle of gauzy cotton, embroidered diamonds buried in the folds. I tucked it into my purse.

Did I leave my scarf

Didn't see it, sorry—ill look tomorrow

At home, after my shift, I pressed Lili's scarf to my face. It carried some of her spark, along with her smell. I wore it to Net Café the next morning. "Oh!" Ditya said. "I love that scarf." In my months of bumping into Ditya at her dad's café she'd never looked at my clothes with anything but puzzled sadness. I opened a new document. Ditya disappeared behind the counter and into the back room. Within minutes, she and her dad were yelling at each other—her voice a screech, his low and controlled. I tried not to listen. "I hate you," Ditya was saying, and then a door slammed.

Big, dry pores. The observation played on a loop, probably because my pores were also big and dry, different in some intangible way from Lili's. Good skin took money, the consistent application of money over a long period of time. Loneliness, boredom. My whole life, until New York. The girl didn't need to try on a noose to know what one felt like. That's why she started the fire.

There was no one to tell, so I started typing.

I hate you, Ditya was shouting. I hate you I hate you I hate you.

Hello Wilhelmina, I thought email might be a better way of reaching you, as you have not answered my last several phone calls. The snow came on Halloween and keeps on coming. On Wednesday we got six inches overnight and Tray hurt his ankle so I was out there for a while shoveling. It's not so bad, the cold smell reminds me that the holidays will be here soon. I guess you are not coming for Turkey Day. Are you coming home for Christmas or not? It would be good to know for our plans. Take care. Mom

The week of Thanksgiving break, work for Nathaniel canceled while he was upstate, Lili gone, I took his credit card to a nail salon. As I got my nails done, a man stood right up against the glass, masturbating underneath his sweatpants, while the aesthetician draped my toes in pink and we laughed at him. After, I wondered if our laughter had egged him on. I began seeing dicks everywhere I went. Cody and his girlfriend had a fight, and he seemed to always be at home, walking around the apartment in boxers, sitting right next to me on the couch, knocking on my door at all hours and asking if I wanted to watch a movie. Like a sillier, younger version of Tray. His dick—Dev and I had discussed it at length—was vast and pendulous, straining against his flannel shorts, an ever-present outline, Cody's familiar. Dev himself asked me to look at a peculiar spot on his shaft, concerned it might be herpes. (It was a pimple.) On a crowded 1 train, a bearded man wearing khakis and a thick gold wedding ring pressed his dick right up against my lower back, rocking into me as it hardened. And then there was New York City itself, dick after dick after dick, all the tall buildings thrusting toward the sky, every person pushing to make the train, to cross the street, to nab a taxi or cut off the line or get the best table, the whole throbbing fucking island. I wanted to go home—no, not home, not where Tray was, though my mother asked me every couple of days about my Christmas plans, but at the very least, somewhere else. Instead, summoned by a text—*Will, back early from Hudson. What if you did your Monday today, at my apartment*—I went to Nathaniel's for the first time since he'd dunked his finger in my scotch three weeks before.

This is what grown-ups do, I thought when I saw his text.

Read to me, he said, after a few minutes of small talk, handing me James Salter's *A Sport and a Pastime,* page folded to the scene just before Dean and Anne-Marie have sex for the first time. You're such a cliché, I said, like a girl who would be cool with absolutely anything. That's the idea, he answered. It was a Saturday afternoon, around one P.M., his apartment bright and sunny, dust everywhere, a piece of old toast sitting plateless on the counter. Me on one end of the couch, him on the other, his feet resting on an ottoman and crossed primly at the ankles. A few minutes in, he unzipped his pants, shooting me one coy glance—*okay?* I nodded. It wasn't what I expected, specifically, but I'd recognized what he meant by inviting me to his apartment. *Game,* wasn't that the word people used? Here was another side of him; accepting it would bring us closer. Nathaniel trained his eyes on some spot in the middle distance where, perhaps, the scene from the novel was unfolding. His dick was a jaunty, hairless creature playing peekaboo with his hand. I entered a kind of alternate headspace, pretending, as I read aloud, that we were somewhere normal, like the park, and his hand wasn't moving at all. After a curiously long amount of time, maybe ten pages, Nathaniel came, reaching, just before it happened, for an embroidered dishcloth draped over the armrest on his side. It seemed less an escalation of the night we slept together than a movement through some shadowy side door, a new duty in my ever-evolving job description. You read well, he said, crawling over and kissing me on my forehead if I'd just correctly recited my ABCs. He tried to touch me, but I pushed him away. I had to leave for the pub, and I intuited (perhaps because of the Salter, or Dev's advice) that leaning backward would better keep his interest.

The bar was busy. I didn't cash out until a little after one A.M.; fragments from earlier—the plateless toast, the awareness of Nathaniel's moving hand—jarred out of focus every time someone asked for a refill, an order of buffalo wings. I was alone on the floor, just Mack left upstairs, probably asleep on the dusty twin mattress wedged between his desk and the safe. The kitchen staff was long gone—food stopped at eleven—and I'd told Juan and Robby to leave, said I'd spray down the mats, carve the stuck wax out of the candleholders, finish closing up. I had just licked closed the little yellow envelopes that held Juan's and Robby's cuts when I checked my phone. There—his name. The full thing, *Nathaniel Fellow,* that's how I had his contact saved, as if I wanted someone else to see it. Or maybe it was just for me, just for the moment when I ticked through my contacts list and saw him there within instant reach. One missed call.

His missed call had been there for *hours,* and I felt something inside of me unfurl, billow fat with wind, set sail into the chop. He never called me. To prolong the feeling, I didn't play the voicemail until after I was well into my early morning walk home, rats leaping out of my way as I skirted the plastic trash bags waiting for the truck along Third Avenue, nearly a hundred singles rubber-banded together in the inside pocket of my coat. It had been a good night. *But, Will,* he said, as if we were already in the middle of a conversation, *have you read the whole thing? You should have told me. I'll bring it to class for you.* I played it only once; it was oddly mortifying to hear his voice, and the only reason I didn't delete it was that I wanted proof. That would come to mean something very different to me later, but that night, I relished this evidence our secret meant something to him, too, that he thought about it when we weren't together.

In class the following week, he slid the book across the table.

"Catch, Will," he said, and I flushed, because the declaration accompanied by the book—the very same one I'd held just days before, a talisman from the looking glass world of his apartment—well, it was as if he'd drawn a diagram on the chalkboard outlining our last encounter: where I'd sat, how he'd looked away from me, the buttery smell in the air that flared when he released into his hand.

I waited for the others to leap upon me, snarling.

"God, I love that novel," Liliam said with a little smiling sigh, no barbs as far as I could tell. Nobody else seemed to notice.

But the thing is, I *had* read it. I'd read it my first year at QCC, checked out at random from the Greening library. The novel had made a precise impression on me; I carried its story around like a memory, vivid still, but faded at the edges from touching. I hadn't had a chance to correct him. I suppose I could have called him back, though his voicemail didn't invite that, really. And anyway, I wanted his personal copy, which now held within it not just Salter's story of sexual awakening, overlaid with questions and phrases in Nathaniel's spidery cursive, but also the crystallized memory of Nathaniel and me that afternoon, a memory my own narrative impulses hadn't yet been able to solve. I was looking for a way to make it okay, or to make myself okay with it.

Though I'll admit I was hurt that he hadn't been able to discern my familiarity with the text from my joke about his choice being cliché, or the sensitive way I'd read it aloud. I was still so new. I hadn't learned yet that many men, famous men, men Nathaniel's age, men who have been at the head of the table for a long, long time—well. Men like Nathaniel don't really believe a young woman has read a book unless he gives it to her himself.

13

They were sitting on the steps of the Angelika. It was early December, sunny and so cold my ears ached in the wind. Leah saw me first, all the way across Houston. She looked twice, confusion twisting her smile, and I knew Lili had not told them she'd invited me on art date, a tradition I'd heard about during one of her afternoons at Genesis. Most Mondays, Leah, Lili, Reg, the Hindenburg, sometimes Tim or Never-Ending Poem, went out into the city looking for inspiration—art dates could not involve literature, and always ended at a bar. I'd come straight from Nathaniel's office to meet them for the afternoon showing of *Black Swan,* skipping my baroque art class, the last meeting before finals review. I didn't bother emailing the professor, who didn't know my name.

Lili leaped from the bottom step, waving, and walked to meet me as I crossed the street.

"You didn't tell them I was coming?"

"I told Reg," she said, linking our arms. She was wearing an enormous fake fur, the reddish orange of a fox pelt, if the fox were from a kids' movie. "I thought it would be funny to watch Leah shit her pants."

"Funny for you, maybe." My entire side warmed against her fur. "Is Reg coming?" He wasn't on the steps—maybe telling him I'd be there had scared him away.

"Sup," the Hindenburg said when we joined him and Leah. Under his winter coat, he wore pair of mesh basketball shorts.

"How crazy," said Leah. "The city can be so small sometimes!" She dug her hands into the pocket of her peacoat, a deep green color with a rounded collar. If it weren't for the cigarettes she started packing against her palm, she would have looked like an American Girl doll.

"I invited her," Lili said.

"Oh," said Leah. "How cool that you were free."

"I just came from Nathaniel's," I said. "He had so much for me today, I almost couldn't make it." That wasn't true—all he'd asked me to do was continue alphabetizing the books in the seminar room. We still hadn't addressed what happened the Saturday I'd read to him at his apartment; our interactions since then had been benign and slightly formal—*how was the rest of your weekend fine mine was nice too looks like rain can you print this again in a larger font*—except for the way my body registered his every movement. It was not so different from those Mondays at Greening High, Brian B. or one of the other window boys nodding when they passed me in the cafeteria or on the way to the gym, as if I didn't still have a wad of their chewed gum stuck to a bookmark on my bedside table. That day, Nathaniel had left a few minutes before I did. When he came out of his office, he watched as I sorted books into piles. You're doing a good job, he'd said. You work fast. He put his hand on the small of my back as he talked and I thrilled a bit to his touch. My old brain, he said, stutters on tasks like this. You're not old, I said, meaning it—I didn't think of him that way, not really. He was someone who'd lived, who already knew what I wanted so badly to find out.

"So much, huh," said Leah, exhaling a ring of smoke. "I want to know what you do for him. It must be so boring."

"Well," I said. Lili's arm was still linked through mine—it made me brave. "It really depends on what you're *into.*"

Lili laughed. Jokes like that were part of why she believed my relationship with Nathaniel was professional, or at least as professional as he could be. The same principle as hiding something in plain sight.

Despite the rumors, being Nathaniel's assistant gave me clout—I'm sure it's why they let me hang around at all. "Let's go inside," she said. "My tits are freezing off and knowing Reg he'll get here halfway through previews."

Prime work hours on a Monday but the theater was so full we had to take a row near the front. Leah filed in first, then the Hindenburg, Lili, and me, at the end, beside an empty aisle seat for Reg. As the lights went down, the ground rumbled, sending vibrations up my legs. "What is that?" I whispered to Lili.

"Subway," she said, stuffing a Twizzler into her mouth. "Keep your feet up—last time I was here a mouse ran over my shoes."

The logo trailer filled the screen. Behind us, a couple was arguing about Aronofsky's filmography. Shh, someone hissed, loud enough that they were hushed back. If you wanted to go to the movies in Greening, you had to drive thirty minutes to the multiplex outside of Quincy, where you could pick from recent franchises only.

"Hey," Reg said, sliding into the empty seat. Natalie Portman was in a cone of bleached light on a dark stage, her arms outstretched, winglike, as the camera panned to her feet. "What did I miss?"

"Shut up," Lili said, leaning over me to hand him a Twizzler. He stuck one end in his mouth and ate it without using his fingers.

"Good so far?" he asked.

"Intense," I whispered back.

"Shut up," Lili said.

"I like intense movies," Reg said, putting his arm on the armrest we shared.

"Seriously," Lili said.

Whenever something surprising happened, Reg took a deep, shocked breath; when Nina and Lily kissed, he yelped out loud. I couldn't imagine it, being so unaware of or unconcerned about bothering others, and so open with my own unfiltered reactions to a piece of art. I was embarrassed on his behalf; I also envied him. "Whoa," he said when the movie was over, putting his hand on my leg and shaking it gently.

At the bar, after, they argued about the movie. Reg loved it, Lili thought it was too on the nose, the Hindenburg thought Mila Kunis was hotter than Natalie Portman most but not all the time, and Leah thought it was hard to focus on the story because of the aggro lighting and that Natalie Portman was one million times hotter, one of the hottest people ever. As for me, I thought of the small miracle of that very moment: sitting at a table with a group of friends, talking intensely about a film. I felt affection even for Leah, who had accumulated a pile of fry ends on a napkin beside her beer, because she only liked the middles. "And what about Will?" Reg asked, dunking a fry into a ramekin of ketchup.

"I'm not sure," I said. "I think I agree with Lili." That wasn't wholly true—the imagery did seem on the nose, but the depiction of obsession gone wrong had unsettled me the way good art did; I knew I'd keep thinking about it. But I couldn't figure out how to say that in their incisive, quick-witted, reference-heavy way, and so I didn't.

The five of us stayed at that table for hours, comforting the Hindenburg as he moped into his beer about how he only ever got form rejections when he submitted to the slush pile, as Leah talked about her on-again, off-again boyfriend's psychotic mother, as Reg laid out all the evidence of paranormal activity in his apartment, as Lili humblebragged about her internship options for the spring semester, two offers from prominent literary magazines. At one point, misty with beer, the others in a different conversation, Leah pointed a fry middle at me. "Will," she said. "You're, like, one of us, and I don't even know where you're from, what you're studying. You're a woman of mystery! What do your parents even do?"

I knew those things about Leah, I realized, just from being vaguely around them—she was from the tech part of California, went to USC for undergrad, and her father was a Stanford professor, something biomedical, whatever that meant. I ignored the first part of her question. I didn't want to remind them they were hanging out with an undergraduate. "My mom works in a private school cafeteria," I said. "And I grew up in Michigan. Same town as Nathaniel, actually."

"Oh my God," Leah said, squeezing my hand. "Your mom is a lunch lady? No wonder you have so many jobs."

Art date cost me, all told, almost seventy dollars—a little more than what I made in a shift at Nathaniel's, about the same as a Sunday night at the pub.

Hi! Will! Remember me? Your old friend, Tilda, from your first days in the big city. A little birdie told me you're working with Nathaniel Fellow. How is that going? I was friendly with Gerry, his former assistant, and I know he can be . . . a lot. Would love to take you for coffee sometime to chat. Hang in there! xT

I got the email the morning after art date, my hangover so bad I spent all ninety minutes of my Tuesday morning yoga class at Barth in child's pose, my forehead pressed into the loaner mat. I told myself I'd write her back, but a day went by, and another, and I never did.

At the end of the last workshop of the semester, Nathaniel gave a speech. He congratulated all of us—I pretended he was addressing me, too—on doing the work. We'd set off on a difficult, twisting road, one that led only upward, with no clear end point, and we'd all reached places in that journey we couldn't have anticipated on day one. The writers looked at each other, pleased and shy. But he wasn't done. It was important, Nathaniel continued, to remember this: No one should try to be a writer unless they would die without doing it. He said *die* with grim emphasis. But there was good news! Our focus and commitment to each other, to the page, signaled to him that we were all serious writers or could be, and therefore destined to bear forever the heavy responsibility of keeping ourselves alive by writing. It was a burden, but we had all been called to it. And was there any more important work? Several people in the room were nodding. When he finished talking—"I will always be in your corner," he said, "for the rest of my days"—everyone clapped. It was inspiring in a scary way. He sounded very moved; I believe he was.

I planned to meet the rest of the class after, at the bar—Lili had nagged me to go, and when Reg said, during the break, it wouldn't be the same without me, I was convinced. But I lingered until they were all gone, my usual routine, wiping up the crumbs scattered across the table from the muffins Never-Ending Poem had baked for the final class.

"You sure you don't want to come," I called, so Nathaniel could hear me in his office. "It would make everyone very happy."

"Not tonight." He shuffled out a few minutes later, wearing his winter coat, gray wool and blankety, not very warm-looking. "You don't need to do that, you know," he said. "There's a janitor."

"You could have told me that before." A feeling passed between us, quietly, the way light changes the saturation of a room. Not sex, exactly, but closeness. When he spoke, I expected him to invite me back to his apartment.

"I'm sorry, Will, but I can't have you in class again. I'd love to keep you on, and it's nothing you've done, but someone did complain." Leah. Who else? "We may have to reevaluate how things work next term. I've got a full dance card over the holidays, a lot of travel. Take tomorrow off and we'll work it out on Monday."

It was, I assumed, the beginning of the end. I swallowed a noise of despair, a sound I'd never been driven to make before and haven't since. The paper plate in my hand shuddered and a piece of muffin fell to the ground. "Should I give you your card back?"

"I am still in your debt," he said. "We'll figure it out next week."

I could run into his arms, beg him not to fire me, do something brazenly seductive like unbutton my shirt. Would any of it work? He was already heading toward the passageway that led to the rest of the building. "Nathaniel," I said, coming up with a better idea. "Can I ask you a question?"

He turned to me, patiently, just as I'd seen him do for Lili, for Reg, even the Hindenburg. Nathaniel was a good teacher; plenty of questions bored him, but I'd never seen him ignore one. The right side of his face looked slightly lower than the other—not in a medical way, but as if his body were getting tired in separate pieces. "I am about to register for my second-semester classes. At Barth. There's a poetry course, it's an introduction. Should I take it, do you think?"

"If you will allow me to be honest?" He'd forgotten his scarf. I knew it was draped over the back of his office chair. "I don't think you should bother. The wrong class, the wrong teacher—it can predispose you to a certain way of thinking," he said. "And in the end, most of what we learn about writing, we learn from life," he added, even though it was the subject he taught.

I thanked him, and pretended I needed to look for a book, because I couldn't bear walking out together.

The last night of workshop, for me, forever. Nathaniel's poetry class was the only one I ever took.

14

A complaint had traveled from a student to the graduate program director, and Nathaniel had been called in for a meeting, where he was told my participation in class made people uncomfortable. He sensed Tilda's fingerprints on the whole thing and was getting whiffs of Gerry, a situation that had ended messily, one he was not eager to repeat. That should have been the end of our story, or close to it.

I would have shown up on Monday, the university quiet, classes over, grading already underway. He'd be at his desk with his thermos; he'd pour me a cup of milky coffee, just as he had my first official day, ask me to help him clean out his office mini fridge in preparation for the break, run one more bag of laundry to Lucky 999, and pick up his dry cleaning on the way. I'd hand him back his card; he'd give me a check for five hundred dollars, more than he owed me but not enough to make me feel like he felt guilty. I would try not to cry, and I would succeed, at least until I left his office.

And then the rest of my life would start—my life without him, my life as a student, a terrible waitress, a woman with two, maybe three real friends, a note from a stranger named Vilma tacked to her bedroom wall, where eventually it would mean less and less and less. What would she have had to say? What would she have written?

Because in the true story, that conversation with Nathaniel on the last day of workshop wasn't the beginning of the end. It was the swerve.

Almost four in the morning—I'd just finished a wild Saturday at the pub, my feet so swollen my arches had nearly disappeared. In my backpack, $123 in cash. On the climb to my apartment, my pulse accelerated until I could feel it in my throat.

I didn't turn on the lights when I unlocked the apartment door lest Cody emerge from his room and try to talk or, worse, force me to sit at the foot of his unmade double bed and watch him annihilate Big Daddies in *BioShock.* Just for a minute, he always said, come on, asking so many times I just gave in—I'd learned that if I didn't, the next time he asked he'd say, you owe me, as if it were known to all the universe that my rightful place was watching him play video games, and any hours spent elsewhere were to be made up for later. He always seemed to be awake, the dim laugh track of a sitcom emanating from underneath his door. I dropped my backpack in my room and went straight to the bathroom, shutting the door but leaving the lights off.

My period had started during my shift meal. I hadn't bothered with Plan B after sleeping with Nathaniel—it was expensive, and wasn't he too old?—but I was glad to see the stain in my underwear. The shower eased my cramps, the first relief since the distraction of the Saturday night frenzy for Jägerbombs. I picked up a bottle, squirting out a melon-scented dollop so minuscule Dev wouldn't, I hoped, notice I was using his shampoo, and in the darkness misjudged the distance to the shower caddy. The bottle clattered into the collection of containers that ringed the tub. I bent over to pick them up, and as I stood, something happened to my heartbeat.

"I heard a crash," Cody whispered. The door opened a crack. We didn't have a real shower curtain, just a see-through plastic liner. His form was a different texture than the shadowy hallway behind him. "You okay?"

I tried to steady myself but my palm slipped against the shower tile. I was on my back, a clanging in my skull that almost distracted me from my heart. It was beating so hard I could see my breasts vibrating when I looked down. What, exactly, was a heart attack? And was it possible for someone my age to have one? Cody slid open the shower curtain. I didn't know if it creeped me out more or less that he hadn't turned on the light.

"You fell," he said. "One too many?"

Would I be able to talk?

"Ha," I said, and gracelessly, as Cody watched, tried to pull myself into a sitting position while bottles rolled around under my ass and water streamed into my eyes. I felt like I was eating my own heart, like it was trying to exit my body, I could hear my heartbeat, feel it in my eyes and fingertips, I was certain, without fear or panic, that I was dying. I leaned forward and turned the shower handle until the water stopped. "Towel," I said, and one slumped into my lap—his, I could smell it, syrup and mold. I wrapped it around myself, feeling stronger as I did so, strong enough to stand. Probably, I would bleed on it. "Leave," I said. "Now."

"Jeez," he said, backing up. "You ever heard the expression, don't bite the hand?"

I walked an icy mile down the hallway to my room, Cody's towel keeping my heart inside my chest. I inserted a tampon and pulled on a pair of sweatpants, my vision not blurred but buzzing, almost hyper-clear. I had the feeling, leaving the building, that Cody had entered my room. He would say his towel was the reason he was sifting through the clothes on my floor. Mount Sinai was nearby, north and west and right by the park, but how many blocks? The city was empty. Even the trash was cleared away, the streets swept, cars drowsing along the curb. When the body has an emergency, everything becomes very simple. I turned onto Madison Avenue. In the valley between buildings, the darkness was fading to the deep blue of very early morning. How many hours until my next shift? Five? Six?

The double doors seemed official and right, Mount Sinai stamped above them in a reassuring font: This was a place people went for help. Behind a glass partition, a nurse stared into a computer. She didn't look up when I approached, and for a blink I wondered if I was already dead.

"I think I need help," I told her. "I'm having some kind of heart problem."

"Do you have a history of panic attacks?" the nurse said, clicking her mouse.

"Maybe?"

"Have you taken any drugs tonight? Been under extra stress lately?"

"I don't know. Yes—kind of? The stress part, not the drugs. I'm sorry—I can't—I'm having trouble concentrating." Now that I was still, I could feel I wasn't breathing right—I was letting out too much air, or not taking enough in. Neon spots were arranging themselves in lovely lapidary patterns in my peripheral vision. Who would tell my mother?

The nurse reached through a window in the glass wall between us for my wrist. Her thumb roamed around my tendons, feeling for a pulse. "Oh," she said, and then things moved very fast.

Stickers, first, on my chest, forearms, ankles. Followed by wires. When I was all plugged in, the EKG—though I didn't yet know to call it that—bleated, a long, high alarm, the screen full of spikes. My heart rate was 280 bpm. "I'm sorry, patients say this makes them feel very bad," a nurse said as the first injection of adenosine went into my arm and her face melted, dripping with me into the molten core of the earth. A little death: All electrical signals halted for an instant that could have been any length of time at all, the heart gone into blackout mode. It didn't work. The doctor—the only man in the curtained-off area where I was dying, or whatever this was—seemed startled.

"Again," he said. "Twelve milligrams this time."

"Sorry," the nurse whispered, plunging the needle. A hand, ghostly, touched my shoulder in the dark. It shook me once. Silence, for a second, as the fingers scuttled away. The EKG beeped on: 277, 254, 268, 284.

"Huh," the doctor said, and conferred with some of the many people ringing my bed. Eventually, they got out the cardioversion machine. In middle school, Theresa had once dared me to long-jump the distance of three wide cafeteria tiles—I landed flat on my back, gasping without sound, while a group of preteens looked down at me. The shock felt something like that. The numbers on the EKG fluttered around and then descended to 102. "There we go," the doctor said, as if he'd reached into my chest himself. My bones hurt. For a week, I'd have two squarish burn marks on opposite sides of my chest, outlined in brighter red, as if someone had tried to carve windows into my skin.

They asked me again about drugs and took more of my blood. "No, I can't be pregnant, I'm on my period," I told someone new, the hundredth time I'd said that sentence. "May I please go to the bathroom?" I asked a nurse adjusting my IV. The doctor had left some time ago; I had no idea what I was waiting for, or what had happened. The nurse looked at me with kindness. "We can't have you walking around right now." She slid a bedpan under my ass, which I could barely lift; her disinterested hand dabbed between my legs.

"Excuse me," I told the nurse, the next time she whisked into the room. "How much longer will I be here? I have to go to work."

"Honey, we're checking you in. We need to run some tests."

I texted Mack. It was barely seven in the morning, but he responded right away.

this is unacceptable
how am I supposed to find cover in four hours

I'm really sorry. I'm in the hospital

oh
Hope you okay let me know if you will be out more days

I called Lili. No answer. She was almost definitely asleep. On non-class days, she liked to write until early in the morning and sleep past noon. Next, I tried Dev, who also didn't pick up.

I flicked to my mother's last missed call, and then to our texts. Our exchanges were mostly updates from her, announcements of how long it had been since we talked. The last three:

Hello
three weeks and counting are you alive
Wilhelmina, I don't know what to say

There was no one else.

Nathaniel, I tapped into my phone. *I think I need help.*

A few minutes later, it rang.

Nathaniel appeared around eleven, an hour before my shift at Genesis would start without me. In one hand, he carried a brown paper bag—inside were two poppy-seed bagels, untoasted, with scallion cream cheese (his order)—in the other, a cardboard drink caddy with two steaming cups of coffee.

"Can you have this?"

"I don't care," I said, taking the coffee. When I sat up, the monitor around my neck pulled on the wires attached to my body. I adjusted them, reached for the bagel. I was in my own room. I'd presented no insurance—I was still covered by my mother's (I'd marked that on my Barth application, at least, because insurance was required for registration), but I had no card—and no ID, as I'd brought nothing to the hospital but the clothes I was wearing, and my keys. All I'd been told was that I'd had an attack of supraventricular tachycardia, a relatively common and usually benign episode of a high heart rate that can typically be corrected by bearing down or blowing into a tiny straw. I remembered, when the doctor said that, how the triage nurse had handed me a straw and a balloon, told me to blow—it had been so utterly strange I'd dismissed it the moment it happened. They were checking for structural abnormalities in my heart.

I reported all of this to Nathaniel.

"This has never happened to you?"

At my first steak house dinner. On the bus to New York; I'd had my period then, too. In class, when Nathaniel turned around to write *Listen with your eyes* on the rolling whiteboard, angry with every writer in the room for their muddy imagery. In bed with one of the window boys, I'd woken with a start, my chest vibrating. Just before I hit the Genesis tile. For a half a minute, two, four, every few days, and then two weeks of nothing, before it woke me up again, that same dream of racing my mother down a hill, wondering which one of us was going to trip first.

"I went to urgent care a while back. They said it was anxiety or something."

"Doctors cannot listen. It should be a job not so different from a writer's—reading signs, making connections—but their personalities make it impossible." Nathaniel shook his head, took a big bite of his bagel. He had a twist of toilet paper stuck to his cheek with a speck of blood—had he shaved, before coming to me? "You're a young girl, why would they listen to you?" He asked this with outrage, as if he'd spent his life taking young women seriously. A laugh bubbled up, but I swallowed it. He was here, after all, wearing the same dingy blazer he wore so often to the office, where he did things like sit behind a desk, listening with full attention as Liliam described the tiniest edit to a single line of a poem. He did take girls seriously. Just not me, not in the way I wanted him to. Not yet.

"Hi, Dad," said the doctor, and I almost laughed again at the strangeness of it all. With his beard shaved, Nathaniel's skin looked floury, as if touching it would leave a mark. This was a new doctor—young, with a cheerful voice, wearing lilac scrubs under his white coat. "We were worried about this one for a minute." They talked about me as if I weren't there. Listening, I learned I had something called Wolff-Parkinson-White syndrome—essentially, an extra electrical pathway in my heart, which conducted the superfast beat. The prolonged episode of tachycardia had left me with elevated troponin, the same protein that spikes after a heart attack. I would feel tired, maybe for as long as a week. I could take a beta blocker every day, though the doctor didn't think it necessary for a person so young—he suggested a wait-and-see approach, regular visits to a cardiologist, and, if the episodes started to interfere with my "daily life," a procedure called a cardiac ablation, which would burn off the extra pathway causing all this funny business. "We can get them done in a couple hours," he said, still looking at Nathaniel. "How's your ticker? Sometimes this stuff runs in families."

"Mine's like a metronome," Nathaniel said. "It must be the fault of her mother's people."

"Luck of the draw," the doctor said. He looked at me. "You'll be fine. Try the vagal maneuvers next time, and if you can't make it stop, come back here, okay?"

We were alone in the hospital room, waiting for the discharge papers to come. Nathaniel dragged his chair toward my bed until he was close enough to rest his head on my lap. I wasn't sure what to do with my hands. Carefully, I put one on his shoulder, and the other in his hair, that thinning red-gray tangle of curls. His scalp felt hot and alive, like the belly of a dog; I scratched it with my nails, and he burrowed a little into my legs.

"I was worried. I didn't expect that," he said. "To feel so worried."

"I'm okay. But I'm glad you were worried." I'd meant to say it casually, flirtatiously, even, but my voice almost broke.

"Yes," he said. "Will. I have an idea about you."

He sat back up, fussily adjusting my blanket until it was smooth, and then tucking it around and slightly underneath each of my legs. "I hope you won't mind me saying. What if instead of all those morose, derivative poems, you try writing a story?"

It took hours for them to bring the papers—Nathaniel stayed the whole time, stepping into the hall to cancel a few appointments. I filled out my name, my address, my phone number. No one asked me for any money. In the insurance section I wrote Blue Cross—those words were all I could remember about my mother's plan—my Social Security number, and, in the field for Member ID, N/A. Outside of Mount Sinai, Nathaniel hailed a cab. "To yours," he said, and waited for me to give the driver the address. I hadn't been in a cab since my very first day in the city.

He insisted on walking me to my front door, up all four flights of stairs.

"Thank you," I said, standing on the landing, where there was barely space for the two of us. The overhead bulb flickered, as if we were on a sinking ship, and the light coming through the stairwell window was dim and sour, the glass thickly coated with pigeon shit. The deranged carnival music of *BioShock* emanated from behind the door, along with the apartment's olfactory essence—thrift store dust, unwashed bodies, pasta plates crusting in the sink.

"When I was your age, it was much easier to be poor," Nathaniel said, looking around. "You're not going to show me your room?"

I assumed I knew what he wanted. I was so tired I was having trouble forming words, and could smell my own armpits, but it seemed a fair trade for how much time he'd given to me, for making him worry. My underwear was stuffed with a gigantic pad, the kind for postpartum mothers, all the nurse could find. I would shower first; I'd fold my bed up into the chair it was meant to be, and he could sit there and wait.

"Okay," I said. "But you have to hang here for a minute. My room is a mess and I don't want you to see it like that."

"You think I haven't seen a messy room before?"

"Please," I said. "It's not professional." That made us both laugh.

I slid into the apartment, leaving the door cracked. In my room, I unstuck Vilma's letter from where I'd taped it on the wall and tucked it, folded, into a narrow blue vase I'd found on the street. I piled all my clothes into the corner, stacked my books, and folded up my bed. I flipped my pillow over to hide Goofy's face. The poems I'd tacked all over the walls looked childish—*morose, derivative*—but what could I do? The *BioShock* music stopped.

"Okay," I called, hoping Cody would hear Nathaniel's voice and decide to stay away.

Opening the front door blocked the entrance to my room, so it took a bit of shuffling before Nathaniel was standing in the doorway.

He'd become Nathaniel to me, the way New York had, without fanfare, become the difficult place where I lived instead of the city of my longed-for escape. And yet, just as New York could still crack me open with wonder in the most banal of moments—as when an express train whooshed by in a blur of people, people, people, the miracle of all of us, with our singular destinations and dreams—so could Nathaniel. *Now,* even, standing there in worn jeans I'd seen him slide to his ankles, he was both himself, concretely, and also a million other things at once: his teenage poems, those words I'd loved and followed all the way here; the name on the spine of the serious, decorative books on my mother's shelf; those mornings in Rosendale, summer sunlight and the opening up, as I read, of some vast possibility. You could love someone for that alone. For holding both who you once were, and who you wanted to become. I could. I went to him, and he wrapped his arms around me, transmitting nothing but comfort—a first for me, that kind of hug, from a grown man. I saw Cody over Nathaniel's shoulder and closed my eyes. When I opened them, Cody was gone.

"I don't understand," said Nathaniel after I pulled away. "Where is your bed?"

"Here," I said. I demonstrated how it unfolded into three sections and fit exactly between two walls.

"This room is appalling," he said after a couple of itchy seconds. "I suppose I didn't really think of it, but if I had—well, it's worse than my imagination could muster, by miles. I've lived in some loathsome places, but all of them had windows that opened. And who is that *person,* skulking around?" In in the kitchen, Cody was noisily washing the dishes.

"My roommate. I have two."

"Why won't he show himself?"

"He's probably scared of you," I said, knowing Cody was listening.

"You can't stay here."

"Where am I supposed to go? It's hard to get on a lease when you're mostly paid by credit card." I'd meant it lightly, in the same spirit as "It's not professional," but he frowned. This more direct reference to our relationship made him feel implicated—for Nathaniel, that was a very quick on-ramp to annoyance.

"Bring some things," he said. There was an edge to his voice that made me not want to push. "For now, you'll stay with me."

"I couldn't," I said. What I meant was, I don't want to. In that instant, all I wanted—and I wanted it so badly—was to be alone. But he was already picking up my backpack. I stuffed some clothes, the blue vase, and a few books into my laundry bag, and then we were headed back down the stairs, me following him. I expected to return within a few days, but I never saw that video game chair again, or the Goofy pillowcase, a fixture of my bed since my fifth birthday, so faded from washing the colors looked bleached.

The cab smelled vibrantly of raw onion, waking me up. Nathaniel had an extra room, plus he was leaving in a couple of weeks to spend the holidays in Santa Monica. He wouldn't be back until late January, a few days before the new semester. I was to make myself at home, we'd figure it all out when he got back. Passing through the park, from east side to west, signaled, as it always did, the transition between my world and his. I'd traveled the narrow, intermittent sidewalk of the Ninety-seventh Street Transverse on foot, the night I left his place—through the cab window I spotted not a single pedestrian, just that fence of worn stone, holding the park away from the road.

That day, I must have been wrong even about what I wanted: Look how quickly I step into the cab when Nathaniel holds open the door. He nudges the backpack between us to the floor, slides over and takes my hand. A dozen feelings clamor for my attention, but the only one I let in is relief. To make it real, to scare the darker ones away, I say it out loud.

"Thank you," I tell him. "Thank you, thank you."

15

In the entryway of Nathaniel's apartment, the floor was so gritty I could feel it through my socks. Papers covered the kitchen table; pencils drifted around on the floor. A bouquet of screamingly fresh lilies dripped pollen all over the record player, masking a different smell.

It was afternoon, his apartment full of light. "How should we do this?" he asked, still holding my backpack. "You look dead on your feet. There's the extra room." I followed him to it, my laundry bag skimming the floor. The spare room contained a bare twin mattress and a dozen manuscript boxes. "There's also mine—the bed's nicer in there. Of course it's up to you."

His room was neater than the rest of the apartment, empty except for the king-sized bed and large photorealistic painting of a horse, so textured I could see every hair of its mane. His sheets smelled like apples. He tucked the blankets around me, drew the shades, turned off the light. When I woke, it was dark. Leaving his room to enter the rest of the apartment, I felt I should knock. Nathaniel was working at the table—his desk, I learned.

"There's Chinese on the counter," he said. I microwaved some noodles, hoping the beep wouldn't disturb him, and sat down at the end of the table least covered in paper. "Would you like to hear?"

He read from one of the legal pads for a long time. It was a story, as far as I could tell, about a man who kept talking about needing to see another man, a breeder, about a dog. The dog was special and rare, a replacement for one the narrator had loved very much; it was unclear if the man truly wanted to find the dog, or just wanted to search.

"Is it new?" Were we working? I tried to think of something more insightful to say. Was the dog a metaphor?

"Yes," he said. "Maybe nothing."

"I don't think so!"

"What interests you about it?"

I had to think about this. "I am curious to know whether he'll get what he wants."

Nathaniel laughed. "I don't write very much anymore," he said.

"Lili told me that. Why not?"

"Do you feel uncomfortable?"

I was sitting on the edge of the chair. Most of my plate was untouched—I hadn't wanted him to see me eat. I saw him noticing that.

"I used to have a very hard time being a guest," Nathaniel said. "Especially in situations that were . . . unequal. When I got here from Greening, when I started publishing, traveling. I can't think of a single time, in all my life, my mother invited someone over to break bread. I didn't know the etiquette of it. For a long time, at another person's table, I felt I was stealing."

When he said things like that, I felt he understood me better than anyone. "Do you still?"

"Now I have a lot of practice," he said. "I can get comfortable anywhere. And it got much easier once I realized something. People like to give. I want to help you. I have the space. I find you easy to be around. Maybe you remind me of home."

"Thank you," I said. I felt inordinately pleased by the compliment, and didn't, at the time, understand what he really meant: that I never asked for anything he didn't already want to give. At twenty-three, I had no clue.

"You are a beguiling person," Nathaniel said. "I have no idea what's going on in your head. But I want to be clear, right away, so that this can work. I have my own life, my own entanglements, as I imagine you do, too." There was a worm-shaped stain on the breast of his gray T-shirt—sauce, probably, from the noodles. Some people dirty the clothes; some people wash them. I thought it in my mother's voice. "We can be respectful of each other's freedoms, I hope."

"I respect all freedoms," I said, trying for lightness. He wasn't in love with me—oh, I knew that. I'd had a lifetime of training myself to have no expectations when it came to men. Still, I refused to let it go, the smallest balloon in the bunch, even as I told myself it didn't matter: I wanted something else from him.

Later, he stood in the doorway, watching me brush my teeth in the bathroom connected to his bedroom. "It goes without saying, I am sure. But obviously, don't speak of this to Lili. This isn't the kind of situation she'd understand. Lili's never really needed help." I assumed he meant financial, and nodded, spitting out my toothpaste as prettily as I could.

Not a love story. Instead, an arrangement.

I slept in his bed that night, but when he kissed my shoulder, I stopped him. "I'm so tired," I whispered, and showed him my back. He was confused—I could hear it in his breathing. Then he put an arm around me and fell asleep, his breath warm on my neck, his chest hair prickling my shoulder blades.

We were still working out the terms.

IV

HERE'S MY HEAD . . . I LIED IT OFF

1

That first morning, both of us half asleep, he reached for me again, and my body responded before I had time to think, time to consider what I looked like, what he did, what any of this meant, where we even were—his bedroom, where I'd later scrape an inch of dust off the horse painting's frame, my little room in Greening, Gerry's note still waiting on my desk, the library alcove in Rosendale, or some other plane altogether, created by me, by all that time I'd spent reading and thinking about him, the same unlikely dream place I made, sometimes, when I wrote. "I don't like to kiss in the morning," he said when I tried to fit our mouths together, a flash of boldness I regretted, and then he was doing something with his hand, angling the crotch of my underwear aside with his wrist, a confidence and insistence to it, yes, even in its disregard for me, that made me cry out.

After, I held my breath as I traced my fingers along his arm, connecting sunspots to freckles to white patches, to the divot where, I'd learn, he'd had a basal cell carcinoma removed. His arm. It seemed the most intelligent, interesting thing I'd ever touched.

Sex high; Dev had warned me. I wonder how much it had to do with the brute fact of the orgasms, a new discovery, that my body could respond like that to someone else. I hadn't even aspired to one, with the window boys—what we'd done together was so outside the realm of that kind of pleasure it would have been like trying to take a boat to the moon.

Pleasure, yes. I must add that to this story, to the knot I can't untangle about us.

Nathaniel got up, naked, and pulled a pair of shorts from an overturned laundry bag from Lucky 999; he hadn't bothered to put anything away. His arms and legs were lean and compact, as if he were a runner, though he wasn't and had never been. He kept two ten-pound dumbbells on his radiator and liked to do his stretches, but his belly was soft and rounded and friendly. Sometimes when we sat on the couch, reading our separate books, I'd lay my head on it and listen to it gurgle, imagining his blood traveling from his feet to his brain and back again, keeping the machine alive.

He was awake, so I had to be, too. Wasn't he also still my job? As I dumped the rest of the clean laundry onto his bed, listening to him sing Tom Waits in the kitchen while he scrambled eggs, I felt almost afraid of my own power. I was naïve, but not so naïve that I hadn't already heard this story, both of us fitting neatly into our roles. Except he didn't know how hard I'd worked to get here. And in that way, I almost felt I was taking advantage of him, some balance between us restored.

There was a pair of leggings mixed in with his laundry, obviously women's, size small. I made the bed and left them at the foot, folded. I joined him for breakfast, and when I came back in later, to use his shower, they were gone.

I called my mother. It was confusing to know where to start, so I began with the diagnosis and worked backward.

"I had that funny fast beat before," she said. "A lot when I was younger. I'd bend over to get a can from a low shelf, and blam. It's no big deal. Ignore it and it goes away."

"But it wouldn't go away. I couldn't make it stop. They couldn't make it stop, they had to get paddles. They said they never have to do that."

"You probably let yourself get all worked up. Don't tell me those doctors scammed you into a million tests you don't need."

"Of course not," I said, remembering how they'd buckled the straps connecting me to the table, swiveled me around like I was on a carnival ride. "But it's something I'm supposed to monitor."

"You've always been very healthy," she told me. "There is nothing wrong with you. Doctors are always trying to make money. Have you made your Christmas plans yet?"

"I don't know, Mom. Plane tickets are expensive. I don't have time to take the bus because of work. The doctor said it can evolve. Usually, people need the extra pathway burned off."

"I certainly wouldn't let someone fiddle with my heart like that. Cause more problems."

In the kitchen, Nathaniel's toast was burning.

A few days after the hospital, I was sitting at Nathaniel's kitchen table, peeling an orange and reading the submissions that had trickled in for *Best of the New*—everyone from workshop, except Reg and Lili—when Vilma opened the door. She didn't knock or ring the bell, and there was no buzz from the doorman—she came right in. It was noon. I'd just finished cleaning the apartment from top to bottom. Nathaniel always left his doors unlocked; she'd either counted on that, or she had her own set of keys. "Oh," she said. "Is Nathaniel here? I tried to call, but no dice. I need to speak with him—it's important, though not urgent. I was in the neighborhood."

"You must be Vilma," I said, because it seemed like something a grown-up would say to another grown-up, and implied it was normal for both of us to be in Nathaniel's apartment without him.

"It is remarkably clean in here." Vilma walked fully in, dropped her purse on the table next to me. She was wearing long, elegant gloves, a silky black material, the kind a woman tugs off one finger at a time before sitting down to share her case with the private investigator. Her body was sturdy and strong, her face lined deeply around the eyes. "Usually, the first thing I do when I get here is open the windows." She wandered past the table and into the living room, as if gauging the quality of my cleaning work. I wanted to look and look and look at her. She seemed so complete, so decided about herself, from the black trench that fluttered around her legs to the white sneakers she wore sockless, despite the cold, to her utter lack of interest in me. I couldn't imagine her smiling unnecessarily, or apologizing for opening her mouth, or following anyone around.

"I don't think he'll be back for a while," I said. "Can I make you some tea or something?"

"No. I'll be on my way."

"Should I tell him you stopped by?"

"If you want to," she said, already moving toward the door.

I waited for her to ask me my name, but she did not.

When I turned up for my next shift at the pub, Robby was power-washing the sidewalk. I stepped over the blue river of soap, and he grabbed the door for me. The apologetic look on his face tipped me off before Mack said a word. But still, I pretended I didn't know what was coming, even after Mack asked me to take a seat. Instead of sliding behind the bar to polish bottles or refill napkins—Mack never had a conversation at the bar without doing several tasks at once—he took the stool next to me.

"I wanted to give you a chance, but this isn't working out," he said.

"Mack—no. Please don't."

"You'll get another job. Try hostessing, somewhere downtown."

"I don't want to be a hostess." I didn't really know what a hostess did, but I knew it was a demotion.

"This is my business," Mack said. "What you want doesn't matter. I can't have people sitting for five minutes waiting for a beer. Chattering with your friends, falling down, disappearing for days. I don't have work for you here anymore."

"The regulars will miss me."

"Not for your service."

Mack handed me a couple of twenties—my shift pay from the previous week. I stuffed the clothes from my locker into a Duane Reade bag and carried it into the kitchen to say goodbye to everyone. "Qué lástima," the cook said, with an unmistakable note of relief.

"Maybe it's a blessing," Nathaniel said. "That job seemed dismal." It was lunchtime—we were eating BLTs I'd made. I'd just turned in the last of my fall semester papers, except for a two-page reflection for yoga about releasing trauma in pigeon pose. "What was that man's name? Your superior? Rack?"

"I was terrible at it."

"I worked at a bar once," he said. "I drank a great deal and have almost no memory of that time."

"You were probably great."

"I probably was! Too bad it's all lost in my big beautiful head."

With the twenties from Mack, I had roughly four hundred dollars in cash. In my bank account, another forty-two, all that was left of my financial aid refund after prepaying rent and buying books. Plus Nathaniel's Visa, the one he'd given me, and knowledge of where he kept one with a different account number: in a kitchen drawer that otherwise held buttons and matchbooks and an inexplicable knitted baby sock. Knowing rent was taken care of for a while, I'd been careless with my money from the pub. Now that I was fired, this seemed unbelievably stupid. How would I ever save up enough for a security deposit and first month's rent for a normal room? Even with the next semester's financial aid refund, I wouldn't have enough.

"Maybe I could get some other kind of job. Like in an office or something. Do you know of anything?" I was just thinking out loud, but when I heard the question in the air, I remembered he'd helped Lili with her literary magazine internship—a letter of recommendation and a personal email—and that position paid twelve dollars an hour. "Maybe something with books?"

"I will think on it. But in the meantime, you can take on more for me. If that appeals. There's always something."

I trusted he really would think on it. Clean, I liked his place—the decorative ceiling in the living area gave it character, and the leather sectional was worn in a comfortable way. In a closet off the hallway leading to the bedrooms, the smallest washer and dryer I'd ever seen were stacked on top of each other. Why do you pay for the laundromat, I asked him when I saw it. Who has time to fold, he answered. I washed every sheet and blanket and towel he owned and arranged my blue vase on the windowsill in his spare room, Vilma's letter still inside, and hung my mother's best dress in the tiny closet. I made the bed in there, too, bought a new pillow, though I'd slept with him every night that week except for one, when I came back after he was asleep. That night I'd woken in the twin bed with my heart speeding; I tried every vagal maneuver, knowing Nathaniel was just behind the wall. They didn't work, but after thirty minutes, my heart returned to normal on its own. Even with my uncertainty about what Nathaniel wanted, or might ask for, or how long any of this would last, I felt safer than I had in years, maybe since before Tray had moved in with my mother.

"I'm good with that," I said. "Until I find something else."

We settled on twenty hours a week, my allowance on the Visa raised to $750 a month; about as much as I'd made at the pub. Half of my hours would fall under the umbrella of "housework"—he liked the apartment better clean, too. He wrote the terms of our professional arrangement down on a blank page of the legal pad, and seeing it listed in his handwriting, with no mention of how we slept together, answered a question I hadn't known how to ask. My job was one thing, our relationship was another. Given the circumstances, there'd be some blurring, but that was a side effect. Or was the job a side effect? I couldn't quite make it out, but I was comforted by the numbers, the details, his professional nonchalance as he logged me into his university email.

The password was BiscuitFellow1234, after his Rosendale cat. I'd kept a calendar for him at his office based on what he wrote down, but now he wanted me to check his email, input important appointments into his online calendar, *and* record them on a physical one I bought that day and hung on the fridge. I was to take over all fan mail. "What little there is," he said.

"Do you want to see it?" I asked.

"No," he said. "It gums up the works."

Anything from a student, especially one I knew, I was supposed to leave alone. Ditto for university business, though eventually he'd dictate his responses to me from the couch. But he got a lot of emails from strangers about his work, forwarded from his agent. People wrote about his memoir almost exclusively, sometimes sharing personal stories I never knew how to respond to. Sometimes people wrote him for advice about their own writing. Samson, who I was always revising rec letters for, wrote to him at least once a week. Almost no one wrote about his poems. I was still under the impression that even outside of Greening, in Nathaniel's universe of readers and writers, poems were of the highest value. As soon as I was alone with his inbox, I snooped. It was surprisingly boring; a soup of logistical details about readings and meetings and speaking engagements. Another education, those emails, in the life of a professionalized writer.

Nathaniel was a careful deleter. I found only a couple of emails from Gerry, including what seemed to be her resignation note, dated—could that be right?—the day I left Greening.

> *Nathaniel, I'm done talking. I'll make sure the books are dropped off at the event and that's it. I expect a letter of recommendation.*

He didn't respond. I checked his drafts. Nothing. Had they slept together, too? I felt more curious than afraid. She was gone; I was here. Part of me thanked her for leaving. The other part didn't want to look.

One more informal element of payment: If I finished a story, I could leave it for him on the table, by his legal pads. He'd be happy, he said, to tell me what he thought.

I didn't like Nathaniel watching me write. "Working?" he'd ask every time he saw me sitting on the couch with the legal pad he'd told me I could use. Working, not writing, like Lili. I felt painfully aware of how fast my pen was moving. Net Café was open twenty-four hours, and some nights I'd head there after dinner and stay until one or two in the morning, returning when I knew Nathaniel would be asleep. One night, deep into a story about a woman who starts misplacing her clothes, item by item, until her closet is empty, only to find them out in the world, on the bodies of strangers—no saving this one, Nathaniel would say, just try again—Ditya pushed through the glass door, the little bell tinkling. She slipped off her heels. Arjun was asleep. When I'd arrived, he'd popped out briefly to say hello, and had given me a parfait on the house, a cup of hot tea. He looked relaxed; Ditya was spending the night at a friend's, and he was going to watch *Seinfeld* as loud as he wanted. "Only if it doesn't disturb you," Arjun said.

I couldn't hear the show, but within a few minutes he began to snore, a calming sound, very regular, like waves crashing along the shore. Behind the checkout counter hung a shower curtain printed with sunflowers—behind that was a small rest area, a landing, really, where Arjun kept a couch, a TV set, and a mini fridge. A set of stairs, I now knew, led to the basement apartment he shared with Ditya. When the bell tinkled, his snoring hitched for a moment but then resumed its regular cadence.

"God, why are you here?" Ditya said. "Are you, like, homeless?"

"I'm working."

"Don't you have your own computer?" Her eye makeup was smudged.

"No."

"Wow. Even I have a laptop." She sat at the computer next me and shrugged off her coat, swiveling back and forth in the chair. She was wearing one of those halter dresses from American Apparel, tight and green, with no bra or tights, even though it was freezing outside. The knot behind her neck had loosened, and one of her breasts was dangerously close to spilling out. I smelled alcohol.

"Are you okay?"

"I just got dumped," she said. "So no, I am not okay."

"Your dad said you were at a friend's."

"My dad." She said *my dad* with such disdain I felt almost afraid of her. "My dad doesn't know anything."

"He just worries about you. It's nice. Trust me, you miss that when you don't have it."

"He wants to control me. There's a difference."

She got up and tottered to the bathroom, shutting the door behind her quietly. I didn't hear a flush. When she reappeared, she slipped behind the counter, bending down to check for something on the shelves. She stood, a few bills rolled in her palm.

"Why are you staring at me?"

"Sorry," I said. "Are you leaving?"

"I can't stay here. He thinks I'm at Monica's. And he would shit a brick if he saw me in this dress. I'll just walk around until morning, when one of my friends wakes up."

"Ditya, that's idiotic. You're drunk. Just wake him up—he'll be mad at first, but he'll understand. He wouldn't want you out in the city in the middle of the night."

"I've done it before. And I am *not* drunk."

All my financial aid money going to waste, the room paid for, no one there at all. It filled me with light when I thought of Ditya putting the space to use; maybe Nathaniel had felt something similar, hailing a cab to the hospital. For once, I could be a help, instead of begging for scraps from people with more than me. "You can stay at my place." Ditya looked at me skeptically. "My old place. I don't—it's complicated, but I am not staying there right now. There's a bed, even some clothes. You can use anything you want."

"Where is it?"

"Just a few blocks from here, over on First, right before that playground. I'll walk you. Give me a second." I texted Dev and told him I was helping a friend, to keep an eye out for her.

Not home baby but whatever, it's your room

It was after midnight, a Tuesday, and the streets were quiet except outside of the bars, where men stood in clusters, smoking. They watched us go by. A few whistled at Ditya, but she didn't seem to notice. I blushed as I always did, hunching into myself. Outside of the apartment, I checked the vestibule to make sure no one was sleeping in there and handed her my key ring. The apartment's windows were lit. Cody, playing *BioShock* as usual. "My roommate Dev is great, and he knows you're coming. Cody can be unpleasant but just ignore him and he'll go away."

Ditya was swaying a bit. She looked tired, and sad, and, in the glare from the vestibule's overhead, extremely young. How old was she? Sixteen? Seventeen, tops? I considered dragging her back to Arjun. But then she threw her arms around me. "Thank you," she said. "I really didn't want to sleep in a diner tonight."

"It's the room on the left, right when you walk in. You have to shut the door to see it." I punched my number into her phone. "Listen, I should warn you. It's not very nice. The whole place—it's a shithole."

"Will, I share a one-bedroom apartment with my dad in the basement of a decrepit internet café used only by illegal immigrants and weirdos like you. I'm sure it's fine. Also—hello? I've met you. I didn't come here thinking you lived in a palace."

"In the morning you go straight back to your dad."

"Duh," Ditya said. "I'm not, like, running away."

She pushed through the inner door, and then clattered up the first flight of stairs, disappearing into the building. I waited a second longer. There was a subtle variation in the quality of the brightness radiating from Cody's window. Maybe Cody had paused the game—he'd go to the kitchen first, pretend he needed a snack, and find some reason to travel down the hall. I felt a flicker of unease. But Ditya had marched through the wave of catcalls without even a flinch. She could handle herself.

2

"We probably shouldn't go together," Nathaniel said. It was the night before he was leaving for his month in Los Angeles, and we were on our way to Lili's for her holiday party. We'd just gotten out of the shower. This seemed to me a wildly sophisticated thing to do—shower with my older lover, the small tenderness of exchanging places under the showerhead. Lover. Was that a fair thing to call him? Even the undefined nature of our relationship seemed sophisticated—we were adults, playing an adult game. An arrangement; an affair. He looked handsome, tugging his belt through the loops of his jeans, his face pink from the hot water. The loose flag of skin under his chin, the way his eyelids drooped—these were, to me, enhancements, more evidence of my writerly adventure, really, my dedication.

"Does it really matter? They know I work for you."

"It's eight at night, Will. It will look a certain way."

"Who cares? You've gone out to dinner with Lili and Reg. I'll just say we were eating."

He'd asked me to wash his hair, and it was drying fluffily around his ears. Those first days at his place, I'd been afraid he might have a fetish, that he'd have me reading to him at all hours while he jerked off or worse. But so far, his sexual imagination proved straightforward: missionary, lots of soap, a hand on my ass when he passed by in the kitchen.

"No, it's best if you wait," he said. "The complainer will be in attendance, I am sure, ready to launch the next missile. By next semester no one will care, but I'm not eager for more meetings."

I waited exactly thirty minutes, most of it spent trying to wing my eyeliner like Lili's, and then I left. By the time I showed up, the party was already sloppy.

I was nervous, walking through the door. I promised I wouldn't look for him, but Nathaniel was the first person I saw, sitting on the floor with his back against Lili's couch. Leah shouted my name. She hugged me, splashing eggnog on the back of my dress. "I am so glad you're here." I didn't take it personally, that she'd complained to Tilda—Leah believed in rules. Nathaniel held a glass of bourbon the Hindenburg was actively filling with more booze.

Lili rushed over to hug me, too. "You're late, you're late," she said. "Now we're only waiting on Reg."

Nathaniel didn't look up; I felt the effort it took him, and it pleased me.

Lili's apartment was off Fifteenth Street, a one-bedroom with a galley kitchen and big windows and a walk-in closet. It would have been charmless except for the fairy lights she'd strung around the ceiling, the walls of books, the rug with its neon pattern of palm leaves. The dining room table was covered with beer and wine brought, presumably, as offerings (I'd come empty-handed, like a fool), and a giant bowl of punch. "That will absolutely annihilate you," the Hindenburg noted sadly, as he watched me ladle some into a Solo cup. The party included everyone from workshop, plus some writers from the cohort above and below Lili's, people I'd seen around but hardly knew. There were also two other faculty members from the MFA program: a regal poet whose gray hair cascaded halfway down her back and a farmhand-looking man of about thirty, a former student of Nathaniel's, there to teach the next semester's fiction workshop. Neither acknowledged me.

I took my drink and went to stand by Leah, who was deep in a conversation with a bunch of writers I'd never met—men mostly, with dark hair and glasses and four-day beards. They were talking animatedly about a book it was clear Leah had not read, though now and then she threw a question into the fray, with real interest. "Is it his first novel?"

"Yes," said one of them, before turning back to one whose shirt was blue. "It's so depraved. Imagine *The Human Centipede,* but as a book. I love that shit. I just need a novel to do something new, you know."

"Totally," Leah said. What was new about depravity, I wanted to ask. But the one in green flannel was already talking. That's how it often went in class, too—the men seemed to compete only with each other, while the women competed with everyone. Lili was an exception, but not entirely; the men grudgingly conceded to her position as the best, but it seemed easier for them, that she was not the best *and* male. Reg, too, was an outlier, for being wholly uninterested in writing as attached to any goal.

Nathaniel heaved himself up off the floor. He passed our group, clapping one of the guys on the shoulder, before the Hindenburg appeared to refill his drink. Standing there, just a few feet away from him, my body urgently awake like it always was in his presence, a teenage girl from one of Nathaniel's stories marched through my mind. She shows up at the forty-two-year-old widower's door with her knapsack full of dollar candy bars, her business just a pretense for what she's really after: someone—anyone! him?—to take her virginity. A whole story, just about that. But Nathaniel was a Genius, with a capital *G,* certified by the people who made those choices; and hadn't I also laughed at that story, rooted for the sad, lonely dad? Nathaniel's blind spots were courage, honesty, art. Unlike, say, Leah's—or, I assumed, mine, though I knew my problem as a writer, as a person, was that I could not yet grasp my limitations fully. What if my blind spot was him? The question floated up, and I smacked it away.

"Finally," Liliam said when Reg appeared at the door. "Reginald has graced us with his company. Now I can do the toast." She drummed on the small section of the tabletop that wasn't covered with alcohol containers and someone turned down the music. "Thank you all for being here. Cheers to everyone in my cohort for another marvelous, challenging, unforgettable workshop—and especially to Nathaniel, our fearless leader, for showing us the way. I can't believe how lucky I am to get to be read by all of you." Lili's eyes were wet. Usually, she held herself at a remove from all of it, but I saw now how that distance was pretense; she needed them as much as they needed her, a star to orient themselves around. Nathaniel looked damp-eyed, too, standing there with his real glass, the only one in a sea of Solo cups. "Cheers," everyone shouted, and then Lili turned up the music again.

Reg was standing alone by Lili's bookshelf. He pulled a pack of cigarettes from his pocket and moved to the window, already open, where there was a fire escape.

"Can I have one?" I asked as he was threading himself outside.

"Sure," he said, looking over his shoulder with some surprise.

The Hindenburg's punch must have gotten to me, because instead of standing in the opposite corner, I wedged myself against the brick, right next to Reg. It was also a strategy to get Nathaniel to notice me; eventually, I was sure, he'd realize I was gone. I wanted him to have to look.

"I'm so sorry you smoke," he said. "It's very disgusting."

"I don't, really. I just couldn't be in there anymore."

"You get used to it."

"If you hate all this stuff, why are you even getting an MFA? Like, what's the point. If you don't want this."

Reg exhaled, his breath mixing with the smoke.

"There are a lot of ways to answer that. I couldn't get a job after college. The economy sucks. My dad is the saddest person on earth. This is the only program that gave me money."

"Why do I feel like none of those are the true answer?"

"Are you sure you want to hear it? It's corny."

"Yes, I do."

"I just want to learn how to do it, you know? To write one really really good poem. If I can do that, that's it—I don't care if I grow up to be a plumber. All of this will be worth it. I don't think anything in the world matters more."

There was an intensity in his voice that reminded me of how I'd talked about poetry to my mother, growing up—it felt private, like something you shouldn't hear. "But you write beautiful poems all the time," I said. "I've read every single one of your workshop pieces. I can't believe your work has changed that much in what, a year and a half?" And Reg would never grow up to be a plumber. His parents were doctors—his mother, a pediatrician; his father, a general surgeon. They appeared in his poems, the mother who could make any baby laugh, the father in the operating theater, elevated and estranged from his only son. Reg's stipend was twelve thousand dollars, plus four grand for each class he taught. He lived in a studio apartment, alone, held no other job.

"You didn't see the crap I was writing before."

Our cigarettes were gone, but neither of us made any move to go. Reg's hand was dangling near my own, and his fingers tapped mine once, twice, before he hooked his index finger around mine, and then our hands were knotted together, his thumb traveling the outer length of mine, from base to nail. He smelled resoundingly of whiskey. I wasn't sure how to interact with an overture like this, landing like a bird in my periphery, waiting for some crumb. I was so distracted by questions of interpretation I didn't have room to explore what I felt about the frisson of our fingers colliding, a physical conversation in a different key than the one I'd been playing in for days with Nathaniel. Nathaniel, who believed in freedoms and entanglements. Nathaniel, who was so easily bored. Did I want him to catch us?

"Excuse me," Nathaniel said, from inside the apartment. Reg dropped my hand. "Sorry to interrupt but, Reg—I want 'Seastorm' for *Best of the New.* I need you to sign permissions."

"Can I say no?" Reg said, crouching down until they were face-to-face. What did they see when they looked at each other?

"You can," Nathaniel said. "But you won't. Good night, you two. Stay out of trouble."

He meant the last part for me. His flight took off at nine-thirty A.M. I'd booked him a car to LaGuardia with a seven A.M. pickup time. If I didn't leave soon, I might not see him at all before he left—would that bother him? It bothered me, but caring in that way did not seem part of our terms. I slipped out an hour or so later, when a woman whose name I didn't know started reading everyone's tarot. Back at Nathaniel's apartment, the lights were all off, and his door was shut. I got the message and slept in the twin bed.

Freedoms were okay, as long as he decided what they were.

He texted me the next day. *Landed safely. Thank you for the car. Will miss Will. Makes me happy to think of you tooting around in the apartment while I'm caramelizing in LA.*

I was forgiven, though I wasn't sure for what. Flirting with Reg? Staying out late? Pushing back when he said we should go separately to Lili's party?

Or maybe not. A few hours after the text, an email:

> *Will, I am sorry I cannot take "Leash" or "Notes on Not Giving Up" for Best of the New. Good changes. But I think you know why. Meanwhile, I do look forward—with great eagerness—to reading a story, should you write one. With regret, and supreme confidence in your wisdom and understanding, N.*

But I think you know why. Because the poems were bad? Or because it would link the two of us in a public way? I tried to tell myself it didn't matter, but I couldn't shake the question.

"God, he was wasted," Lili said when I told her Reg had tried to hold my hand. "That was a seriously sloppy night." We were in the Midtown Apple Store, two days before Christmas. They were having a holiday sale—I'd seen the signs in the window. I wanted a MacBook, a white one like Lili's. The store's gleaming spaceship interior and technology I didn't know how to use intimidated me—I'd brought Lili to help me blend in.

"I still can't believe you don't have a computer," she said.

The store was crowded, everyone buying last-minute gifts. We joined the massive line. What if Lili saw Nathaniel's name on the credit card when I brought it out to pay? Did anyone look at someone else's card that closely? And if she did, how would I explain? I hadn't told Nathaniel I was buying a computer, and I'd maxed out my allowance for the month already—the day before, in fact, when I'd sent a few gifts from Amazon to my mother. But I also wanted to see if he'd notice, and if he did, what he'd do. I told myself it had nothing to do with his rejection of my poems. He hadn't reached out since that email; maybe I just wanted to get his attention.

"Lili, you don't have to wait here with me," I said as we crept closer to the counter, wishing I'd thought about the card issue before inviting her. "It's going to be forever."

"I'm fine." She was staring at her phone.

"I forgot; I've got to call my mom."

"Right now?"

"Yeah, I'm sorry. It's sort of private. Can you give me a minute?"

Lili ducked out of the line and headed over to the window, where she sat on the broad ledge and curled herself up against the glass. I called my mother for real. It seemed easier than faking a conversation.

She picked up right away. "Wilhelmina," she said. "Is everything okay?"

"I'm good, I just wanted to call you and say hi and Merry Christmas and everything."

"Oh. Hi. What's that noise? It sounds like you're in a bus station." Hope in her voice.

"No—it's the Apple Store. It's slammed. Holiday shopping, I guess."

"Like the laptop computers?"

"Yeah, I'm getting one. For school."

There was a pause, one of our special ones, brimming with a conversation neither of us knew how to start. "How much are those?"

The line ticked closer to the front—I was only a couple of people away. "Probably more than a plane ticket, but what do I know."

"Mom—"

"It's okay," she said. "If everything's fine, I have to go. Tray and I are about to head to Meijer before the whole town shuts down."

I listened for a few seconds to the silence on the other end.

When I handed the cashier Nathaniel's Visa, I held my breath. If he asked me who Nathaniel was, I would say my dad—I'd see Leah do it, at Alehouse, when she put the whole cohort's drinks on her parents' tab. I blinked, ready to say the line. The receipt was already printing.

The cashier slid me a pen, and I made an unreadable scribble—not Nathaniel's name, and not mine either.

3

The three of us were standing at the foot of the Rockefeller Center Christmas tree, staring up at its universe of lights. When Lili heard I'd be in the city for the holidays, too, she told me the tree was required reading. Christmas Day, late afternoon, the wind already picking up—it would start snowing after midnight and keep going for twenty-four hours, filling subway stations and stranding cars, painting the whole city in deep drifts of snow, as if Greening had decided to travel to New York so I'd stop missing, in a quiet aching way I was trying to ignore, my mother.

"Corniest thing in the world," Lili said, "but this tree really gets me. If I had a more joyful essence, I'd start caroling."

"O little town of Bethlehem," sang Reg. He was Jewish, but had skipped his family's annual pilgrimage to the movie theater just for this. His teeth were purplish, from the red wine in his flask. "Will, you grew up in a churchy place. What's the rest?"

"How still we see thee lie," I said, wishing I had gloves. A soft, powdery snow was beginning to swirl, the kind that never seemed to land, only float. Stores were closing early, not just because of the holiday, but because of an advisory warning people not to travel after six. The sky was a depthless gray.

We walked to the Russian Tea Room—Reg's idea—and slid into a booth, Lili and me on one side, Reg facing us. Underneath the table, he extended his legs between mine and the wall. Our calves touched.

A waiter came by, and Reg ordered three "filthy" gin martinis, extra olives, and the caviar tasting, as I anxiously calculated the bill. "How do I eat this?" I asked when the food arrived, the caviar in its special tin, the garnishes in their separate bowls, the tiny, unappetizing pancakes. Reg and Lili laughed. For them the whole day was kitsch, a joke I wasn't quite in on.

"I love taking you places," Lili said, making me a blin. "You're like our very own Nell. It reminds me how much I like the world, seeing it through your virgin eyes."

I smiled, without understanding the reference. I wasn't just reading the wrong poets, I was always out of step with their pop culture touchstones, too, as if I hadn't just grown up in an out-of-the-way place, but another era. I ate my caviar like a good student. If I wanted to like it someday, I had to practice. As Reg drank more of his martini, the pressure of his leg against mine increased.

When we left—he'd paid, thank god—snow was falling in clumps. "Do you think I'll ever get a cab," Lili said. She was meeting up with someone from Yale and being cagey about it. I got the sense it was a person Reg didn't like. "Reg, do you want to ride downtown together?"

"What are you doing?" he asked me. His hair was full of snow, just like the window boys, but there was nothing secret about what he was asking.

"I think I'll walk."

"You are so crazy," Lili said as a cab drifted over to the curb, ignoring several other people with their arms out. "Even when it's not a major weather event, that's one thousand miles."

"I'll join you for a bit," Reg said. "I don't want you to get eaten by the blizzard."

"Merry Christmas, freaks," Lili said from the cab's open window.

Reg and I headed back uptown, toward the park. Reg didn't know where I was supposed to live—I'd veer off at some subway station well before Nathaniel's. We were talking about our mothers, which turned into talking about being only children, and then about poetry. He was still drinking from his flask of wine. I slipped in slush and he threaded his arm through mine.

"Will," he said. "Wait. Don't you live on the East Side?" When we hit the park, I'd turned west, toward Columbus Circle. "I swear Lili told me that."

"Oh, I do," I said. "I must have gotten turned around." I looked around with slight exaggeration, as if I had no idea where we were.

"You'll get the hang of it," he said. "I got lost so much when I first moved here."

Up ahead, the entrance to the A train. When I talked to Lili about poetry, she treated me a bit like a student; and Nathaniel was Nathaniel. Only with Reg did I feel like we were two people interested in the same thing, in the same way, on a similar level. I wished the night didn't have to end, but I couldn't muster the energy required to lie my way through it. "I'm sorry," I said. "I am freezing. And my socks are soaked through." That last part was true, though I hadn't noticed it until we stopped. "I think I'll take the subway back."

"You want me to ride with you? It's getting kind of late."

"Reg, it's seven P.M.," I said.

"I meant late . . . for Christmas. And the storm."

I laughed. "You know I take the subway alone every day, right?"

"All the more reason for someone to come with you?"

And then, so there could be no further conversation: "I'm pretty tired."

"Okay," he said.

After we swiped our MetroCards I saw him on the other side of the platform, waiting for the A going the opposite direction. He lifted his hand, but before I could wave back, his train barreled in. I rode uptown seething at myself for the lie about being lost, and for always acting dumber than I was, and for feeling—wasn't this the stupidest part—resentful of everyone for assuming I really was the person I pretended to be.

At Nathaniel's, the doorman—a kind middle-aged man named Jamal, who never once made me feel unwelcome—stopped me in the lobby. "This came for you, miss," he said. It was a large bouquet, a little gaudy, lots of blue cone-shaped flowers that looked slightly artificial. They must be from Nathaniel; Dev was the only person who knew my secret, and he was too broke to send me flowers. The tiny envelope taped to the vase undid my bad mood. Maybe Nathaniel had written me something, a line or two. Up in his apartment, snow obscuring the usual view of the skyline, I slid it open.

HO-HO-HO, it read. MERRY CHRISTMAS, WILHELMET.

4

I didn't get a bill from Mount Sinai until Dev brought it over one gray Sunday afternoon in late January, a couple of days before Nathaniel came home. I'd had my Barth information routed to Nathaniel's apartment, though I left my address as is everywhere else, uncorrected even with my mother.

"I don't hate it," Dev said, shedding his coat on the back of a chair. "It's very grumpy old man needs a woman's touch. Great view, cool art." I'd hung a painting I'd found in the closet of the spare room on the wall over the kitchen table—a large canvas dyed indigo, with arguing mauve and yellow slashes. "Maybe you can convince him to hire a decorator. I'll make a fake business card. I'd be good, you know I would."

I made us a pot of Nathaniel's imported English breakfast, and we sat on his couch.

"So what are you going to do when Daddy gets back," Dev said, blowing into his mug.

"It seriously upsets me when you call him that."

"I'm just teasing. Do you miss him?"

"It's nice to be alone," I said. "But yeah, I do." Did I? "I just wish I knew what happens now. What if he wants me to leave?"

"If you want to come back to the apartment you need to hurry up. Cody sends eighty emails a day trying to fill your room.He thinks he's a genius for trying to get double rent."

We moved on to Dev's dating life, a tangled network of men and women who all seemed to be in love with him—the problem was, he could never decide which one he liked the best. "I wish I could date them all forever," he said.

"I get that," I answered, thinking of Reg standing on the other side of the subway platform, his cheeks still red, thinking of Nathaniel lifting his jacket off the plastic hook stuck to his hallway wall, the slope of his back as he turned toward the door.

Dev stayed until the sun started to set. "Hey," he said as he hugged me goodbye. "Are you really okay with this? You don't have to be."

His concern threw me—if anything, I thought he'd envied my situation. And compared to Dev's stories about sneaking out of a married woman's apartment window via the fire escape, avoiding entire blocks of the city so as not to run into lovers current or former, I'd felt almost boring. What was I missing, for him to ask me that? "Of course I'm okay with it," I said, aiming for a version of his bravado. "I've been in New York less than six months and I live in a doorman building with a famous writer. My *favorite* writer. Imagine where I'll be in a few years?"

"The girl has a point," Dev said, and I was reassured.

After he left, I opened the bill. The original balance had been $42,000, but insurance had brought it down to $36,000—my mother's insurance was some Michigan-oriented plan, where you had to see local doctors to be in network. They'd given me a pregnancy test, despite my period. It had cost $343 dollars, none of them covered. There was a $7,200 charge for something called "critical care." I looked it up. *Provided to a patient experiencing imminent or life-threatening deterioration.* Critical care was not associated with any service or treatment, but instead for the category of urgency they'd assigned to me—I felt a kind of retroactive fear at the words "life-threatening deterioration." I'd had a handful of episodes since, all of them impervious to vagal maneuvers, the straws and clenching, but they'd at least resolved on their own. The rest of the charges were for the tests and the hospital stay, including the tray of Jell-O and reconstituted eggs they'd brought to my room a few minutes before we left. I half expected to see a line item for the menstrual pads. It was an unfathomable amount of money; I would simply never, ever be able to pay it.

The only other mail was a card from my mother. A stock image of a decorated tree, *Hope This Christmas You Get Everything You Want* printed above it in gold cursive. On the inside, my mother added: *Miss you! Love, Mom.* And then, in another pen color, but still in her handwriting, Tray's name. She'd included two twenty-dollar bills.

Will, happy new year! Following up on my note from a while ago. How you doing? All okay? Here if you want to talk or take a walk or anything. -Tilda

I didn't just ignore Tilda's email, which came the morning Nathaniel was due back. I deleted it, hearing Dev's voice as I did: Are you really okay with this?

I refreshed my inbox. There. Tilda's name was gone, and with it, the specter of Gerry and whatever had happened to her.

5

The elevator dinged down the hall and I arranged myself at the island with my performative glass of wine. I'd put on a Duke Ellington record, gotten fresh flowers, made spaghetti with tomato sauce and lots of chopped basil, all of it paid for from my allowance, not with Nathaniel's apartment card. I was wearing jeans and a black T-shirt; my hair damp from the shower. I wanted to look fresh, and like I hadn't tried that hard, but the preparation had taken most of the day. I'd printed out my first short story at Net Café and left it beside a stack of Nathaniel's legal pads. It was twenty-four pages and called "Flash Forward"; how had I ever thought that was a good title? Nathaniel entered, dragging his suitcase, wearing a leather jacket, his jeans loose around his hips, as if he'd lost a few pounds. "Smells good," he said a bit tiredly. "It looks good in here, too. Hi, Wilhelmet."

"I bet you're exhausted," I said. It was almost midnight. The stubble on his cheeks, the faint suntan, the freckles on his forearms when he slipped off his coat and hung it on the handle of his carry-on—his physical reality was so concrete I closed my eyes and blinked them once, trying to get the image to render. "I made some food. I'm sure you want to rest. I can give you some space."

"You're still here," he said, and then he was behind the island, pulling me against him. I hunched my shoulders and bowed my neck so my head would fit, in the feminine way, between his chin and shoulder. "I thought you were a dream."

This was possibly the most romantic thing anyone had ever said to me. As he ate the pasta, he talked about what he'd been reading on the plane: a new book by an old friend, subconsciously conformist and mediocre, people doing things people always did, the literary equivalent of stroking a baby's head. I listened, rapt, to exactly the lessons I'd come there for. "This is good, Wilhelmet, but next time less garlic," he said, lifting a spool of noodles with his fork.

I had trouble falling asleep—I'd grown used to his big bed, alone, and Nathaniel was snoring, a sweet, whiskery sound, like a drowsing rabbit. There I was, twenty-three, in his dim, comfortable room, almost nine years from the summer I'd found his poems at Rosendale. I hadn't expected love, but his affection was clear. Whether it was for my youth, my body, my potential, sex, plain and simple, in the end, if I got what I came for, what did it matter? I already knew the first thing I'd change in my story, after the title. But what did he mean, when he complained of his friend, writing about people doing things they always did? What else was there to write about? His sleeping form revealed no answers; he was on his back, covers pulled up to his collarbone, mouth hanging open.

The next day, over coffee, as he flipped through one of his legal pads, before even saying good morning: "I hate writing on a laptop." Talking less to me than at large. My story was exactly where I'd left it, unacknowledged. "I've always found it better for the cadence of a poem, to write the first draft by hand. Sometimes I think that's the problem with student work. No feel for the texture of words, the verbal surface, and the typeface makes everything look better than it is."

That was all he ever said to me about the new computer.

Most of the time, I kept it hidden in the bottom drawer of the dresser in the spare room, as if it were stolen goods.

As for the story: It was for the can.

The weeks before Christmas had been so novel and charged, so stuffed with final papers and holiday events that kept Nathaniel out of the apartment, I hadn't had time to register how it really felt to live there, with him. After he got back from LA, I slunk around like a trespasser, eating toast over the sink, washing my plate as soon as I finished, waiting to shit until he'd left for the day. If he was working, or cranky, I left, or hid in the spare room. Always, I tried to be useful, to look busy, to leave everything more pleasant than I found it. At night I slept in his bed unless I got back late from somewhere, or he did—but I waited to be invited, a specific look on his face, or more often, a question: I am tired, Will. Aren't you?

Back from the university early, he once opened the door to me eating a Subway sandwich a few inches away from his legal pads. I was in pajamas; it was almost two P.M. "I'm sorry," I said, brushing lettuce off what was probably something brilliant. I felt the usual embarrassment about my purchase—I'd never seen Nathaniel eat food from a chain restaurant.

"For God's sake. Stop acting like a bank robber every time I talk to you. It's all right. Sit. Eat. Your sandwich dribblings aren't going to make those four sentences any worse."

It's amazing, what a person can adjust to. Depending on how you read it, my life with Nathaniel was either the most unexpected situation I could find myself in, or proof of the existence of fate. Except for the occasional moment of disorientation so profound I feel it still—as when, one evening, happy about the four new poems he'd written that week ("your good influence," he said into my neck), he waltzed me around his apartment, showing me first how to follow, and then how to lead—by February it was almost routine.

Ours went something like this.

Every night I washed the coffee maker and set it to brew for seven-fifteen A.M., a few minutes before he got up. When I first moved in, I'd felt very strange, peeking through half-closed eyes as he stepped from bed, listening to his piss hit the toilet, as he shuffled around for clothes, unsure if it was correct for me to be resting when he was not. But Nathaniel didn't like to talk in the morning. He took his supplements and ate something small, an apple, a piece of buttered toast. In the early winter, he read admissions for the MFA program, a massive sandwich of binder-clipped files he kept in a special backpack. It took him two weeks to winnow them to thirty. I carried the throwaways to the trash chute, flipping through the transcripts and letters of rec, wondering where I would have come out in the stack.

On Mondays, a day neither of us had class, he'd go to the park for long walks with former students, friends, Vilma. I often went to the grocery store; before long, I didn't need a list. "Wilhelmet," he'd say, pointing at me with a cucumber, "look at this bounty!" Midweek, we went to our respective campuses and didn't see much of each other—Nathaniel never entertained, but several nights of the week he had dinner plans, theater tickets, somebody's reading, party after party after party. "Can I come?" I would ask him, sitting up against the pillows while he tried to decide between two equally bad sport coats.

"Just another obligation," he'd say. "A bunch of geezers. I'm saving you for something good."

He was right about how much there was to do: calling the super about the broken flusher in the half bath; scheduling and rescheduling physical therapy for his knees, a weekly appointment he could never manage to make at its original time; keeping track of events, and whether he was attending as guest, reader, interviewer, introducer, emcee, or something else; reminding him about the overdue foreword for the small publisher reissuing a book of poems by an obscure Australian writer he admired, then reading the book and drafting it for him, an assignment so consuming I skipped class for a week, capped off with an afternoon correcting typos in his rewritten version before sending it on his behalf; putting his office hours appointments on the physical calendar in the kitchen, and, increasingly, adding a line about what the student mentioned wanting to discuss; plus the various items from his personal email that he reported to me, like that dinner at Jim's on Wednesday, or the weekend in Vermont with the Myersons, for which he would need train tickets and a pair of better hiking boots.

I kept his baseboards dustless.

Even with these tasks, I had more time to concentrate on class than I did working at the pub, but Barth felt somehow less real. *Thin,* wrote one of my professors after the final paragraph of a paper on Maslow's hierarchy of needs, for a class called Theories of Personality. I got a C. I was taking four courses that semester, mostly trying to get math and science out of the way. Geology, college algebra. When classmates asked where I lived, I described my old apartment. I didn't make a single friend; probably, I was protecting myself, and him. I showed up and when class was over, I left.

As for my allowance—"your stipend," Nathaniel was always correcting me—for a month or so, it was hard to spend it, and then too easy. I put my cellphone on autopay. My monthly MetroCard was my next biggest expense. The rest went toward food, or coffee, or books, or nights out with Reg and Lili and the rest of the poets. There was no record of unspent money carried over except for the one I kept myself, in a notepad of my own, that Nathaniel never asked to see—but there was also no tabulation of my hours, only a schedule I loosely set, unless Nathaniel had a specific request. In early February I got another refund from my financial aid. For a very long time, that eleven hundred dollars was my primary source of cash.

One day, late again for Theories of Personality, I left my dirty egg plate in the sink, along with the pan and his dishes from that morning. When I got home later, he was standing at the sink, washing them noisily. When I said hi, he didn't say anything back.

I was always trying to catch him writing. I thought maybe seeing him do it would teach me something. But the few times I did, he just looked like a man, lost in his head.

Lili and I got in a habit of writing together on Saturdays. "What'd you do this week?" she'd ask, staring at her laptop, a Nerds Rope hanging from her mouth, if we hadn't seen each other since the previous session.

"Class," I'd say, or I'd describe some task Nathaniel had set me to, emphasizing its bookishness, because I knew she thought it weird I worked out of his apartment, which I'd let slip accidentally. That spring he had me coordinating the production details for *Best of the New,* which would bore Lili, but I was also helping him track his reading for the Selden Awards, which would not.

"Oh shit," Lili said. "Who's in the pile?" The annual contest was for emerging writers at the "frontier of literature." Winners were "nominated" by judges, but nominees first had to make it into a pool of finalists, whose selection was very secretive. Nathaniel communicated with the administrator via his university email; if he talked to the judges, it was through his personal account, and I never saw it. Each winner received thirty thousand dollars. Ten thousand less than my mother's annual salary. Enough to wipe out more than half my medical debt. In the ballpark of a single year's tuition at Rosendale. He'd received a big box full of books and a few bound manuscripts. One of my jobs was to sift through it and mark which ones were by former MFAs. "Isn't that . . . obvious?" I asked. "What?" he said. "I like to give money to people I know have done the work."

"Totally unethical," Lili said, switching to Swedish Fish. "But selfishly, I can't say I hate it. Read this for me?" She emailed me what she was working on. I sent her a poem of my own; with Lili, I always wrote poetry. We kept going until it was late, stuffing ourselves on candy and then ordering a pizza. I silenced my phone four times after making sure it wasn't Nathaniel; debt collectors, calling about Mount Sinai.

"Thanks for coming to my place again," she said. "Next week we'll do yours."

"Oh no," I said. Cody would bother us, and where would we sit? It was too far, a long walk from the subway. Her place was so much better. Eventually, Lili stopped asking. She knew I didn't have a lot of money. Probably she didn't want to embarrass me; but wasn't it easier for her, too, how our friendship was conducted on her terms, when and where she wanted me?

Nathaniel's apartment was quiet and dark when I got back. He was in Vermont, breaking in the hiking boots I'd spent hours selecting. On the kitchen island, a stack of torn pages from his legal pad, next to a loose piece with a message for me: *Type this up, notes welcome. Short one for* New Yorker *special issue—curious what you think. Back late Sun.*

I spent the whole night deep in his story, trying out suggestions, typing it once, twice, and then again, just to feel what it would be like to write like he did. It was three pages typed, almost a prose poem, the story he'd read me about the man looking for the dog distilled to its funny, tender essence.

"Thanks," he said on Monday morning, looking at the printout with my precise comments penciled in the margins. No other mention of my notes, whether they'd been useful or completely idiotic. But when the issue came out a few months later, he left it on the table, open to the story. I read it, breathless. He'd taken my suggestion to switch the order of the images. His draft had ended with the imagined dog; in the final piece, the real one.

That might have been the first time I felt like a writer.

6

For a while, every story I wrote was for the can. He didn't even mark them up. Start again, he'd tell me. You'll learn more from that, he said, than trying to resuscitate something that was never alive to begin with. And so, I did. Over and over. Until one afternoon, late March, when he dropped a draft into my lap while I was reading on the couch, covered in notes. "I have a dinner," he said. "We'll find a time to talk about it this weekend, if you like."

The story was about a thirteen-year-old girl whose mother has a new boyfriend—a dentist, younger than her mother, with some of Tray's mannerisms. Nathaniel had written *good* beside the opening image: an old-fashioned vanity, the kind with its own stool, a drawer with an ivory handle, no rotating spotlights. Unlike my mother, the fictional parent was meticulous about her makeup. Foundation within thirty minutes of waking, brow pencil and lip liner and blush the color of persimmons. *Makes no sense coming from narrator,* Nathaniel had noted. *She's a thirteen-year-old girl in northern Michigan: What does she know about persimmons?*

The dentist meets the protagonist's mother at work—she's in his chair, squinting under the bright light, while he probes a soft spot in her back right molar with his pick. An omniscient POV, to telegraph seriousness. As I'd thought he would, Nathaniel loved the teeth, the intimacy of rubber against tongue, the mother trapped in the chair, but more needed to happen, and the structure was too symmetrical—it began with the daughter watching the mother apply her makeup, staring into the vanity mirror, and ended with the daughter, alone, staring at her own face. *No real transformation,* he wrote. *But there's a sensibility. In the next draft, put the dentist in a scene with the girl.*

Back at my laptop, I deleted *persimmons* and let blush be blush.

I don't know how long it would have taken Nathaniel to tell me about Sarah if I hadn't come home early one Thursday night. He'd asked, in the morning, if I had plans, and I told him about dinner with Reg and Lili, about the reading after, a young poet whose work he liked. "So not back until late, then," he said.

"Yeah." He didn't usually ask me what I was doing unless he wanted to go to a movie, take me for dinner, but I didn't like to be too available. "The reading is downtown, so I might stay at Lili's."

"Have fun," he said.

It was one of the scene-y readings, not at a university or in an auditorium but a bar with its windows open to the street. May and it was already hot, Reg's arm slick against mine. We were in some kind of flirting limbo I didn't understand. The poet sat on a stool under a spotlight, no stage, and did things to language that defied logic and created something new, right on the thrilling edge of sense. When I told people at those readings what I did for work, some gushed, and most asked me what he was like. A few said, "Who?" But for others, Nathaniel was something between a punch line and the joke itself. It didn't bother me. Even the people who dismissed him, who said he hadn't written a good book in years: Didn't they all, ultimately, want what he had? The job and the awards, the apartment paid for with Hollywood money from the memoir adaptation, the friends with houses up and down each coast, editors eager to publish every story, every poem?

Halfway through the second poet's reading, my heart did its flip and race, and I pushed through the crowd out to the sidewalk, where I sat down against the brick and put my head between my knees.

"You okay?" Reg said. I hadn't noticed him following me. The curls around his ears dripped sweat onto his T-shirt.

"I'm okay," I said. "I just feel weird." It seemed like too much to explain. I'd tell him if the bad rhythm didn't stop.

He joined me. "I get panic attacks, too," he said. "Just take a deep breath."

I did, to humor him. He tapped my knee with his, trying to get me to look his way. I was very uncomfortable, my pulse so fast my body rocked; could he not see it? He launched into anecdote about the Hindenburg, trying to make me laugh. "Reg, stop," I said. It came out meaner than I meant it to. "I'm fine."

"Okay," he said, standing. "If you need help, I'm just inside."

As I hovered at the top of the subway stairs, trying to decide whether to spend my allowance on a cab, my heart snapped its fingers and returned to normal. Just before nine P.M. when I opened the door of Nathaniel's apartment—not early, but not late either.

He and Sarah were on the couch, in a position I remembered from my very first night at his apartment: facing each other, her back against the armrest, his body in the middle and cocked in her direction. "Hi?" I said. Even after all his talk about freedom and entanglements, it took me a minute to understand.

"Will," Nathaniel said, with faux surprise that should have been a clue. "This is the lovely Sarah. I believe you two corresponded about my author shoot?"

Sarah. The photographer. I'd handled the scheduling, made sure his outfits—one formal, one casual—were clean and ready to go, verified the time of his haircut, and gotten him out the door. She was much shorter than me, plump in a huggable way, somewhere in her forties.

"How nice to meet you in person," Sarah said. "Thanks for your help . . . before. Are you just dropping by?"

"No," Nathaniel said before I could answer.

"No," I echoed. "I . . . I forgot to bring Nathaniel his book. I was going to leave it with the doorman but he sent me up. I know you need it for tomorrow."

"At this hour! True dedication. I need an assistant like you." There was a note in Sarah's voice: amusement, maybe pity. Did she think I had a silly crush? The idea made me angry. There were two books in my bag: *A Mask for Janus* by W. S. Merwin and the Swedish thriller so ubiquitous that year you could buy it at Duane Reade. I'd been hiding it from Nathaniel all week. I pulled out the thriller.

"You needed that first thing?" Sarah said to Nathaniel, wondering now, very obviously, what was going on.

"Thank you, Will," Nathaniel said. "I'll check in Monday."

I placed the book on his worktable. It was the only thing in the scene that was obviously mine; how strange, to live somewhere and leave so few traces of yourself. I sank with the elevator to the lobby. Jamal, the doorman, pretended not to see me, an act of kindness.

Outside, I walked. I couldn't go to Lili—she'd want to know what happened. Or Dev, who'd tell me to pull it together. And Reg? What did he even *want*? My phone rang twice; unknown numbers. The collection agencies liked to try me at night, which seemed illegal. I turned onto Broadway and followed it downtown. I stopped at a crosswalk, undone by a couple at a sidewalk table across the street, the tender way he offered a bite from his fork. Around eleven P.M., Nathaniel texted. *My apologies, Wilhelmet, for that bit of awkwardness. Sarah is gone now, please return.*

I kept walking. *Please?* Near midnight, as I ate a falafel sitting on the fountain at Lincoln Center: *Will. You're not hurt are you darling? It's a different sort of thing.*

The streets quieted when I reached the shopping corridor below the park, turning interstellar at Times Square and then lonely again near the famous Macy's, all the lunch places shuttered and dark. As the city changed, so did the storm inside me, as if we were in conversation. Dodging skateboarders in Union Square, I went, all at once, from feeling sorry for myself—so clearly being replaced by this more interesting, experienced woman, possibly on the verge of losing a place to live, my *job*—to sorry for Sarah. Hadn't I gone into our arrangement with my eyes open? She was the one being lied to. Nathaniel and I *were* different. Like everything special and rare, we couldn't quite be described. Getting the good parts of him meant getting the bad, too. Like his students, whispering about his behavior, like the administrators at the famous university, like who knows how many other people, I would accept the conditions of his brilliance.

Still, I didn't return until after one A.M., hoping I'd made him worry. Before I let myself in, I could hear him snoring from the hall. All the lights were on, as if he'd been waiting up. On the kitchen island, two dirty wineglasses. I washed them both.

People were wrong about New York—it wasn't lonely. It was just the easiest place to lie.

"That was very bad of me," Nathaniel said the next morning, pouring me a coffee from the pot he'd made for both of us. "And I'm sorry it hurt you." He added exactly as much milk as I liked; I didn't know he knew. "Let's take the day. Do something fun."

After I canceled his physical therapy, we rode the subway to the East Village and spent the morning on a tour of his past. At one point, I laughed so hard tea dribbled from my nose; at another, he took my hand, in plain view of everyone on the street. We sat on a bench in Tompkins Square Park and he pointed at the top floor of a redbrick building. "The flat of Lucerne. Don't look too closely in case she's still there and senses us, the witch. I lived with her for fourteen ludicrous months. She was narcoleptic, a condition even more inconvenient than you can imagine. Once, she tried to make me box her, right over there." He gestured to a dog park full of people my age. "Told me the only way we'd be equal was if I hit her, like a man."

"Did you do it?"

"What do you think? Later she threw all my notebooks right out that window. Now she's just a story I tell, like I'll be for you someday."

"How would you like me to tell it?"

"He was unspeakably handsome," Nathaniel said. "There, a free first sentence." When we passed a young man nodding out, Nathaniel pulled two twenties from his wallet and tucked them into the man's sleeve.

I followed Nathaniel into the basement of a restaurant that, he said, made the best hummus in town. We took turns dipping pita into the bowl in the middle of the table, whole chickpeas nesting on top, still warm, as he told me his theory of relationships. The reason people were often so unhappy in love was because they believed that channels of romantic connection were tainted by one's feelings for others. That's a belief that makes for good fiction, he said, but not for good living. Here was the secret to happiness: remembering that relationships don't take from each other. That's why Sarah had nothing to do with ours. I would get it in thirty years, he promised, signing the check. In the meantime, we needed to sort a few things out.

On nights he brought Sarah back to the apartment, I had to find another place to be. Usually, I stayed with Lili. Cody has a new girlfriend, I told her, and she's so annoying. Nathaniel never asked where I went.

At the time, I took this as a sign of respect.

A few weeks after the Sarah encounter, I was at a coffee shop near Nathaniel's place with my laptop; they were at the apartment, but not until late, never late, as she only had a babysitter for her six-year-old until ten-thirty P.M. I had a few hours to go. In Nathaniel's inbox, there was a beautiful letter from a former student. She'd been thinking of him as she drove through Utah on her way back from a residency, where she'd finished the attached poems. What did he think? I wasn't supposed to read notes from former students, but how did he expect me to recognize them based on names and subject lines? I read the poems again. Then I hit delete. His students bothered me more than Sarah. They got the best parts of him, his most serious attention, without having to also wash his bedsheets.

In my inbox, there was an email from my mother. *Hi Wilhelmina, in just a couple months it will be one year! Everything in your room is just how you left it.* She couldn't mean the trash bags over the windows, too. *Hope the semester went well.* I'd just squeaked the grade point average required to keep my Barth scholarship. *Do you think you could come home before your senior year?* I could. Nathaniel would be gone a lot of the summer. But every part of me rebelled against the idea of returning to Greening, of seeing Tray, even if it meant seeing my mother, too. *I never imagined going this long without a visit. Take care, Mom.*

Why didn't she ever say *love?*

Hi Mom, I wrote back. *I miss you, too. I'll try but I'm not sure. -Will.*

My heart tripped, and then it was off. I fished around in my backpack—no wallet. I could picture it on the windowsill in the spare room, Nathaniel's card tucked inside. I had seven dollars in cash. Not enough for a cab to the hospital. The beginning of June. Reg and Lili were with their families, not back for weeks, and even Dev was on vacation, an all-inclusive cruise to the Bahamas. I gulped, trying to keep my heart from coming out of my mouth. The nearest ER was Mount Sinai, across the park, over a mile away. At every don't walk sign, I plugged my nose and bore down, hoping the episode would resolve by the time I got there. It didn't.

I stood outside the ER's entrance, willing my heart to slow, afraid of the bill. By the time they hooked me to the monitors—280, 284, 279—it had been over two hours. This time, the adenosine worked. I plummeted into a well and the lid slid closed. When it opened again, my heart was normal. I texted Nathaniel from the hospital bed. Thirty minutes later, he was there. It wasn't even ten—I never asked what he told Sarah.

I added the bill to my running total: $65,000, give or take a few hundred.

7

In my next draft for Nathaniel, I put the dentist in a scene with the girl. She goes to the vanity in her mother's room. She can see the dentist in bed behind her, watching TV while she plucks her eyebrows. His hand moves under the comforter. Her mother is downstairs washing the dishes. The girl is wearing the pajama set her mother bought her after they moved in with the dentist, her whole body hidden in fabric. The daughter sees movement, but does she really? Maybe he's just scratching his belly, adjusting the fold of the blanket. There's no sound. It's not what she thinks, and she doesn't want him to know what she thinks—maybe *she* doesn't even want to know what she thinks. So she goes back again and again, sitting on the little stool in the dim room, closing the tweezer's edges around hair after hair.

"Atmospheric," Nathaniel said, "but nobody is doing anything." He'd taken me to the ballet, and I'd spent the entire show in rapture. Now we were eating pork dumplings dipped in chili oil so spicy my eyes and nose streamed water. A normal Wednesday night: The girl who'd discovered his poems at Rosendale wouldn't have been able to imagine it. "He's watching, she's watching, so what? Tell me what you're really trying to say."

I put down the chopsticks he'd taught me how to use and told him about Tray. About the sound outside my window, about how I still didn't know what my mother knew, about the photos, how, after I found them, I could feel them vibrating inside the glove compartment of Tray's car, almost giving off a sound. The garbage bags, my already-dying feeling, how I had to run. Why I couldn't bear to go back, not even for a few days, just to see my mother, who was the only person in the world I really had. He'd told me to start with what I couldn't stop thinking about, and that's what boomeranged back. Neither of us connected the image of the dentist's moving hand to Nathaniel.

"Oh, Wilhelmet," he said, taking my hand. "That was a bad house. What he did to you, the real crime, is taking up all this space in your brain." He went on in this semi-comforting way. "But this," he said, tapping the manuscript, which I'd carried around all night, even to the ballet, hoping we'd talk about it like this, "isn't a story. It's a feeling. Maybe there's a story in what you were really afraid of. That he would rape you, right?"

The word frightened me coming out of his mouth. "I mean, yes. Something."

A scene came as he talked. The girl, standing in the dentist's garage. She opens an unplugged fridge; inside, guns, just like the ones Tray kept in ours. She pulls the smallest from the vegetable crisper. She knows it's empty, and she knows that in an ice tray in the freezer, there are bullets that fit it perfectly. A bad house. Was it, my home?

"Photos," he said as he was signing the check. "I wouldn't mind seeing those."

I laughed; wasn't it a joke?

Later, hair rippling around my face from the box fan whirring at top speed, because Nathaniel's bedroom AC was on the fritz, he cupped my cheek. "I wish I had a magic wand to make you three inches shorter," he said. "Then you'd be the perfect fit."

He got up and went to the bathroom, leaving the door open. "Can you ask Tilda for anything but August for *Best of New*? That's the real cruelest month. The city's a dead zone. Gerry could never talk her into it, but she didn't have your persistence."

"Who's Gerry?" I said as neutrally as I could.

"The old you," he said. And then, hearing himself, he appeared in the bathroom doorway. "No, that's not right. She was the blueprint, you're the mold breaker."

The line had the quality of something he'd said before to someone else. There were days when every second with him felt like work.

When I asked Tilda if she might consider September for *Best of the New*'s launch, adding a breezy line apologizing for missing her previous notes, she responded: *No. The school year is booked for actual program events.*

For me, it was a happy night, even though the crowd seemed smaller than the year before. I wore one of Lili's dresses, a black tube-shaped piece of fabric that cost four hundred dollars off the rack. It'd still had tags. I didn't look like myself, my hair in loose curls (also Lili's doing), wearing lipstick the shade of my nipples, a tip from the girl at the Sephora. In the corner of the room, the chair cart, exactly where it had been one year before. One year. I could almost see our outlines, me with my six chairs, Nathaniel's cheesy attempt to help. I wished I could whisper a message to that girl. Your real life is about to start, I'd say.

"You look good," Tilda said as I arranged books on the sales table. Nathaniel was already by the stage, talking to a group of contributors.

"Thanks for helping us with this," I said. "And sorry again I didn't answer your emails."

"Life is busy, I get it. How's it all going?"

"With Nathaniel?"

Tilda put the cashbox down next to the tallest stack of books. How old was she? Thirty-five? Pretty and cool, in her gray jeans, with her tape roll bracelet and visible tattoos. "Will, I know him." She said *know* in a way I didn't like. I put a book on a bookstand, apple core out. What did any of this have to do with her? Why did people think I was some doe-eyed baby, instead of a woman who'd made a choice?

"Me too," I said. "It's the best job I've ever had."

When Nathaniel took the stage to give the introductions, he thanked me, using my whole name, for my "tireless attention." The room filled with claps and whoops—not just Lili and Reg, though they cheered loudest—but the contributors, too. I turned a red I hoped no one could see in the dark, and stayed very still, trying to hold on to the feeling. The reading started. Voices, applause, stage lights bouncing off someone's black plastic glasses. Goosebumps, and then a period of stupefying boredom that felt almost transcendent, a kind of micro death, absolute stasis. When it ended, my spine tingled. Applause, applause, applause.

I'd invited Dev, but he was late, and I didn't see him until it was all over, standing by the wine table with a plate full of grapes.

"What did you think?" I said.

"Cool scene," he answered. He was still wearing the black button-down from his shift at an Italian restaurant in Midtown. "Capital-*P* pretentious, though, don't you think?"

Maybe it was Sarah. More likely, it was the vampiric rhythm of Nathaniel's sexual interest, which required new bodies. Or it was our life together, with its very domestic patterns. I can always tell your toothbrush, he'd say, because it's been chewed by a beaver. Do people with veneers even need toothbrushes, I'd say back. The night after he returned from Labor Day weekend in the Hamptons, he held me, but didn't seem interested in anything else. I realized it had been a long time since he'd followed me into the bedroom with that dopey look on his face, saying, "Will, I have an idea." I hadn't missed the sex. I liked our new dynamic better, watching a film on his laptop with my head on a pillow in his lap. We'd reached some deeper underlayer; if I imagined the future, I imagined I was there to stay.

8

My second Thanksgiving in New York was a week away. Nathaniel wanted me to pick up a present for Sarah's daughter, who was about to turn seven. I was dragging Lili through the Union Square Barnes and Noble—we'd just finished a writing morning.

"This is cute," Lili suggested, holding up a board book about triangular people chasing a bird. Sarah seemed to have relaxed Lili when it came to my job with Nathaniel. She'd stopped asking if it was awkward to work with him at his apartment; she'd even eased up on asking me if I'd started looking for fall internships.

"She's seven, not one," I said.

"I don't know anything about kids. This is why I don't want to be a mom."

We settled on a stuffed bunny ballerina and an illustrated hardcover of *Charlotte's Web.* I paid with Nathaniel's card, not bothering to hide it. I was on official business for my official job. My instinct that day in the Apple Store had been correct: Lili, who noticed everything, immediately spotted Nathaniel's name. "You ever get an impulse to take that thing and just go wild?" she said. Most of the MFAs were struggling to get hired at all, let alone in books, but Lili had landed an editorial assistantship at *Belvedere,* the literary magazine where everyone wanted to publish.

"Yes," I said. I wanted to show off, prove to her my job was important, too, that Nathaniel would accept misbehavior because I was essential to him, to his process.

And so we did.

I came back with the presents for Sarah's daughter already wrapped, wearing an expensive cashmere sweater from a boutique Lili had steered me to. We'd gotten blowouts, my first one, and my hair was rippling down my back, overstyled. "Jesus," Lili said, looking at us both in the mirror. "You could look like a completely different person if you wanted to."

"Your hair looks obscene," Nathaniel said as I packed the presents into a tote bag so he could carry them easily to dinner. They had a reservation at Aquavit. I'd had to call multiple times.

As he puttered around, getting ready, I put on a pot of tea, settled myself on his couch.

"You know, Wilhelmet." Nathaniel was speaking from the hallway bathroom now. "I've been asking around about apartments."

"Yeah?" I stopped breathing. Was it Sarah? Did he somehow know how much I'd charged that day on his card, over five hundred dollars between the sweater and the two blowouts? Or maybe it was the latest draft of my story, about which he'd remarked, only the day before: The point of a revision is to *improve.* "Any leads?"

"A few," he said. And then, jokingly: "But don't worry. I won't abandon you. I need your help too much."

I had started to cry, without knowing it.

"Oh," Nathaniel said, coming over. "Oh, Wilhelmet." He sat down and I leaned against his chest, curling my neck the way I always did so I could fit more neatly against him. He stroked my hair until his shirt got so wet he had to change. "It might not make sense to you now, but I'm doing this for you."

It took him a little while, but right before Christmas, Nathaniel found a studio in Hell's Kitchen, the New York landing spot of a Rome-based sculptor who never came to town, maybe because his apartment was so bad. In exchange for free rent, I had to clean it and get out of there whenever—if ever—the sculptor came back. "I haven't seen him in this country since the nineties," Nathaniel said. "You might be able to retire there."

I coordinated the details with the sculptor. *There is a tub in what I will generously call a "kitchenette" but the only toilet is in the hall. The bathroom will not bother you. Most of the other apartments have their own. You will find sometimes drunk people will take advantage of its convenience, but other than that it is all yours except for one old woman who may not be alive anymore.* The sculptor loved Nathaniel, or owed him a favor, or both—he called him Natey, and confirmed, when I double-checked, thanking him exuberantly: *no rent, just electric.* Nathaniel told me to put it in his name, not to worry, I could just add some hours to my weekly schedule.

He didn't help me move in. "This is best for both of us," Nathaniel said, "but it does rattle my old heart. I would prefer to facilitate from afar." I'd lived in his apartment for almost a year. I was in the shower when the keys arrived from Rome, and he left the envelope on my bed. He placed a torn-out sheet from his legal pad on top that read, in his distinctive half cursive: *A new adventure for Wilhelmet. I will force myself to look on the bright side—I still have you twenty-five hours a week. Yours always, N.* My hair dripped, bleeding the ink.

He was gone—he had a physical and then lunch and the movies with Sarah and her daughter, and then a meeting with his agent, which would turn into drinks and dinner. I packed one of his old backpacks with my clothes, and the rest of my necessary items in a couple of totes. I took the subway. The building, just five squat stories, was between a lumber warehouse and an abandoned pile of bricks topped with a crumbling AUTO SERVICE sign. It was not a residential area, and the apartments, as I ascended the stairs, were silent. But the bathroom on the fifth floor (I never saw the old woman) was clean, or clean enough. Cleaner than Nathaniel's, the first night I'd stayed there.

By any rubric, the sculptor's studio was worse than my old room—not only because of the apartment itself, but because it was a fifteen-minute walk to Penn Station, the nearest subway. The narrow room's low ceilings were made even lower by shelves that extended the length of the space. It would have been possible to crawl from the lofted bed, along one of the shelves, all the way to the front door, if they weren't so crammed with stuff: leatherbound legal texts; dozens of curvaceous renderings of women from waist to knees, cast in something white and porous; a massive ship in a bottle; a box of dilapidated toiletries, including a bottle of Listerine with a label so retro I wondered if it might be worth money. The bathtub was opposite what passed as the kitchen—a sink, a refrigerator, and two cabinets—which you walked through to get to the underbed area where I'd eventually put a child's school desk, just before the only window.

And it was filthy.

I used the Visa to buy cleaning supplies. I found two mummified mice underneath the twin mattress in the loft, another behind a dresser. By the time it was clean enough to sleep, it was nearly midnight. People in the nearest building were going about their lives: pulling a sheet pan from the oven, flicking on the TV, standing in the center of a room, practicing lines. New York wasn't an island of skyscrapers, tethered by bridges, its heart the gentle hills of Central Park—it was a million tiny rooms and the people inside, their desire mixing with the wishes of everyone who had once passed through. I could have stood there with my head outside the window forever, just watching. The actor, noticing me, closed the curtains.

I ordered a mushroom pizza and sat in the bathtub, eating it. The only other person on earth with the keys was an entire ocean away. I texted Nathaniel:

Mouse coffin was the best you could do?

There's always a catch.

It's okay I fixed it.

Of course you did.
All writers should live alone at least once.
And you know I love helping you, poor little fiddlestick

you already miss me huh

Hush, Sarah's over.

But overnight, it rained, and by the next morning, it hadn't stopped. I thought removing the mouse bodies would solve the bad smell. But the humidity did something to the wood floors, and the apartment filled with ammonia—in the daylight, I stepped on a litter-box-shaped stain, right beside the ladder to the bed. The odor was so strong, I asked Nathaniel if I could come back for a night or two, just until the rain was gone. When he reached for me that night, a T-shirt of Sarah's watching from the corner of his room, there was a sweetness to it, as if we'd restarted a book neither of us had wanted to end. I fell asleep curled around his back.

I left in the morning, but a few of my shirts were tucked into the dresser in his spare room, holding my place.

In January, a couple of weeks after I'd started staying at the sculptor's apartment most of the time, an editor from a journal run by a low-residency MFA program in Vermont wrote to say they were accepting my poem "Leash." *What at first seems like a speaker struggling for independence reveals itself to be an unexpected meditation on the stickiness of home,* they said. *We would be honored to publish it.* I would receive a fifty-dollar honorarium. My heart revved, and I got the spins. It took a minute to identify this as joy, not tachycardia.

I met Reg and Lili at Alehouse to celebrate. Reg was sitting at the window alone when I got there, drinking a dark brown beer—he slid it my way when I sat, and I took a sip. I had no idea what it was; I had been an atrocious bartender. "Congratulations, author," Reg said, and quickly, as if Lili could already see us, he kissed me on the mouth, pulling away almost as soon as our lips touched. We'd had a hundred tiny encounters, his leg pressing mine under the table at the diner, his hand on my hip as he passed me another drink, all so brief I couldn't gauge the current that passed between us. And now, this. He smelled like dryer sheets, like a boy whose mom still washed his clothes.

"What?" I said dumbly. The kiss was almost unrecognizable as a kiss, a different species of contact. Feeling came rushing in, now that I knew for sure what his signals had meant. All light and froth, like the bubbles on top of his beer; maybe that's why, even as I enjoyed the simplicity of an appropriate, reciprocal crush, I couldn't take him seriously. What I had with Nathaniel was knotty and uncertain and destabilizing—it was dangerous, and it could hurt me. Those were the qualities, freshly twenty-four, I associated with love.

"I think I like you," he said. Think. Such a Reg qualifier. He was dear, and mostly kind, but he was also a flake. This was the only time, since I'd met him, he'd arrived somewhere before me and Lili. "This is my third beer," he said, as if in explanation. "And you look so pretty, all flushed from the cold and proud of yourself."

"Come on," I said. "I know this doesn't impress you, Mr. I Write to Serve the Muses."

"No, I don't need you to get published to think your poems are good. But I know it matters to you."

"Thanks," I said. He put a hand on my leg, looked at me like, is this okay? I turned my knees toward him. It didn't feel like a betrayal of Nathaniel; if anything, it was a way of diluting my feelings across subjects, so neither could destroy me. Reg always touched me like that—a question, with a long pause after, that I was expected to fill. Maybe that's why the kiss had taken so long.

"Tomorrow morning. Meet me in Washington Square? I'll buy your breakfast. Maybe lunch, too, if you play your cards right."

I smiled. Classes were over for the holidays. I didn't have anything but Nathaniel; on Fridays, I usually cleaned the apartment. I was also waiting for notes on another draft. And Nathaniel wanted to go to the movies, which meant sleep over—he'd mentioned it yesterday. I could try to meet Reg before, but Nathaniel would want to know what I was doing; he also knew I didn't have class. "I would love to. But I can't. Sunday?" So much easier, lying to Reg than Nathaniel.

"I'll be in Philly."

"Then when you're back."

Reg made a big deal out of shaking on it. Lili knocked on the window. She was standing on the sidewalk, her pink peacoat glowing in the streetlight. She held up her phone in one hand and raised a finger.

"She'll be twenty minutes," Reg said. "You can tell—she's talking to her mother. Watch how she paces." She *was* pacing back and forth, turning when she met the stairs to Alehouse's entrance and beginning the cycle again at the entrance to the hair salon next door. It was delicious to tease Lili, a way of proving we were closer to her than anyone. Then, just beyond Lili's stomping pink blur, I saw Ditya.

She was walking down the street with a man—older than her, with a scraggly goatee. His arm was clamped around her shoulder, and they hobbled, four-legged, one of those couples who won't stop touching. "Oh no," I said. "No way."

"What?"

I was out the door, into the cold. "Ditya," I called, and she turned, unhooking herself from Cody.

"Oh, it's you! Hi, Will. My dad asks about you all the time. Too good for us now, I guess."

"I've been meaning to come by—I finally got a computer." But that wasn't why. I'd just gotten more comfortable at Nathaniel's. Now that I'd stopped them, I had no idea what to say. Cody was, I knew, closer to thirty than twenty-five. Even with eyeliner on, her hair in the same messy bun all the college girls wore, Ditya looked like the high school student she was. Her eyes were bloodshot, as if she'd been smoking weed, or crying.

"Is everything okay?"

"It's fine," Cody said.

"I didn't ask you," I said. "Ditya?"

"What?" She snuck an arm through Cody's and leaned into his side.

"Is everything okay?" I felt like an idiot, standing there in my T-shirt, repeating the same question. I wished I had Arjun's number. But what would I tell him when he picked up?

Ditya rolled her eyes. "He's my boyfriend, Will. Get over yourself. Running out here like you're going to save me? You think just because you have two conversations with someone you know anything about him?"

"You're right. I don't know very much about him. But you can do so much better." The movie line was pathetic; I knew I'd lost her.

"You were always a bitch," Cody said.

"He's dating you because he can't get anyone his own age. You're smart enough to understand that."

Ditya cocked her head. Had I gotten to her? But then she grinned. "Wow. Really interesting hearing this from—what do they call your line of work? Sugar baby? Or do you prefer—well. I'm not going to say it." The word rang in the air between us anyway. I hadn't yet let it enter my story, at least as I was telling it to myself. But there it was, as if it had been there all along. Ditya looked a little sorry. Dev must have told them. He was the only person, besides me and Nathaniel, who knew.

They turned away and I stood there, watching them go. Lili appeared next to me—how long had she been listening?—and I followed her inside.

"God," she said, taking the seat next to Reg so she was in the middle. "There's nothing more depressing than a woman with zero self-respect."

"I agree," said Reg. "Who are we talking about?" As soon as Lili sat down, it was like the kiss hadn't happened. It stung.

"A girl I know from Barth," I said. The lie about knowing Ditya from Barth was unnecessary, but simpler than explaining how we were really connected. When your entire life hinges on a great big lie, small ones happen without thinking.

"So weird she was just walking by. Why does that happen all the time in New York?" Reg said.

"The guy is a certified underground creature," said Lili. "Sometimes I wish I could scoop up every teenage girl and put them in a cozy padded box until they prove they won't date the first guy who shows interest in them."

I watched Lili all night. If she'd clocked what Ditya said, she didn't show it. But for a long time after, years, as my lies piled up, I'd picture her in that pink peacoat, standing a step behind me with her phone in her hand, and wonder: How much did she hear? How much did she know?

I filled out my financial aid paperwork, registered that winter for spring classes, but I had a job, a place to live, friends, forty-two pages Nathaniel said had "something." What did I need Barth for? I withdrew in late January, after a week of classes, nine credits shy of a bachelor's degree, with the vague intention of finishing later. I was learning so much more from books. Hadn't Nathaniel himself taken years to finish school, bouncing around the city from odd job to odd job, gaining the experience that made his stories and poems so alive?

I already had a teacher.

V

WE WERE VERY TIRED, WE WERE VERY MERRY

At the Selden Awards, you're Nathaniel's guest, with your own seat at the best table. Two years and change, you say to the woman who asks how long you've been in New York. People are starting to know you now, at least by sight: Nathaniel's assistant, his special girl. He is giving a speech about what it feels like to be emerging, and how it never really stops. Wilhelmina Miles. Your name sounds like a stranger's when Nathaniel thanks you onstage. Someone interesting, important. That very morning, you caught Nathaniel reading your new pages before you even asked.

After the event, you walk through the frigid December night to one of the writer bars. You admit to Samson, who has already found four reasons to mention how surprised he was that Nathaniel nominated him, that you're writing a book. Good for you, he says. I liked yours, you offer, and this relaxes him. You did look at it for a long time, imagining what it would feel like to have Nathaniel say, in print, *magnificent,* about you. About you, or about your *work*? It will be years before these memories make you cringe—though, in the very back of your mind, that trapdoor behind which people like your mother live, isn't it there already? Your awareness that this isn't exactly right, your place here, and how you've gotten it? That you've made a bargain, without knowing how you're paying?

There's Nathaniel, by the door, talking to a guy you vaguely recognize; Lili, sitting on a barstool with that impenetrable ring of space around her, even as three separate people try to get her attention; Reg, listening to the Hindenburg with his eyes on you, then Lili, then you again. Samson tells you it's impossible to write a book. That he couldn't give you a piece of good advice if he tried. It needs to burn itself out of your guts, he says, tongue darting toward a speck of foam on his lip, and then you must be strong enough to wrestle it into shape. The way he says *must* and *wrestle* and *guts,* looking at your waist, then your hair, then your breasts, you know he doesn't think you're writing anything at all, that if you have managed a sentence, two, they're slush, about dolls or blood or other girls, about your silly little self. You're Nathaniel's assistant, Samson tells you. Good man. I should see if he needs a drink, you say, thinking, go ahead, dismiss me. Burn itself out of your guts. Your brain gives his words Nathaniel's red slash.

A couple of months later, another reading, another bar just a few blocks away from the last one. In line for the bathroom, Reg kisses you, tasting of gin, and then you're in a cab going over the Manhattan Bridge, your hand on his zipper. Nathaniel, Reg, Nathaniel, Reg. Then it's summer, and you're crashing at Nathaniel's place—the sculptor, surprise!, is back in town for three weeks. At a book party Nathaniel ducks out early—my head, he says, and whispers in your ear: See you tomorrow. He's no longer dating Sarah, but there's someone—his shower drain was clogged with long brown hair. It doesn't matter. Really, it doesn't. What's between you is secret and lawless and yours. His key in your purse, credit card in your wallet, the spearmint taste of his Italian toothpaste in the back of your throat. You sleep together, nights you're at his apartment—Thursdays, always, because you clean on Fridays, and any time you stay for dinner, and whenever you're uptown—but you can't remember the last time you had sex. Is this weird? You like his hand around your waist, his clean sheets you washed, he likes your eggs in the morning, to give you his thoughts over coffee, how you fold the towels, one of your Rosendale tricks. Sex, he says, does it ever make you weary? All that wet and slap. Your legs are in his lap. He puts one finger at a time between your toes. Sometimes I think my panting years are over. You try to remember what it felt like to want him like that. The memory slithers away. But you still make sure you smell clean and sweet, vanilla sugar scrub, something that tastes good to bite. You would let him. You both know that. But more and more you talk like this, about sex, about his women. Once, he even takes you out to lunch with Vilma. When he's in the bathroom you ask her if she was ever afraid they weren't important, literary enough, her stories about women and all the things they think and feel. Jesus, she says. I thought your generation would be braver. Actually, you're worse.

You even talk about Reg, who kisses you and then disappears, who's in Vienna, sending you letters, or France, sending you silence, or in Brooklyn, texting you to come over, please, I can't stop thinking about that space where your collarbone divots, if it still tastes like snow. Nathaniel says, well, little Wilhelmet, you're not exactly available either, are you? That's probably why he keeps coming back.

Nathaniel says, he's a poet, what do you expect?

Your mother finally comes to New York, a three-day visit, after she gets a Xanax prescription for the plane. The days before she arrives you yearn for her, a desperation returned from childhood, those afternoons you couldn't wait for her to come home and begin chopping onions for dinner. You put her up with Nathaniel's card in a Holiday Inn in the Garment District, an anonymous location walking distance to many chain restaurants with food you know she'll eat. You don't show her Barth, or the sculptor's studio, or any of the bookstores or bars where you spend your non-Nathaniel hours reading, reading, reading, sometimes putting the book down for coffee or wine with Lili or Dev. Your mother walks with her arm looped tightly through yours, an intimacy she only allows herself because her fear of the city is greater than all the unspoken bitterness between you. On the subway, she clutches her things. She doesn't ask you anything, and because that hurts your feelings, you ask her nothing in return, as punishment. After her first twenty-four hours you count the minutes until you can leave her at LaGuardia, and then, even as your heart aches, you're waving goodbye as she rises on the escalator beside her hulking suitcase, bought for the sole purpose of visiting you.

Every emergency room in the city is the same, and the adenosine is the same, too: doom, then exhausted relief, the bruise in the crook of your arm where the drip went in, the flutter of your heart before it pumps once, starts again. The bills vary, even though they're always for the same thing. You've long stopped keeping track of how much you owe. At Maimonides they give you Xanax when you arrive, Xanax when you leave, as if this faulty mechanism is something your mind should be able to control. Is it? At Mount Sinai, they test every time for drugs. Vilma publishes a strange, slim novel about marriage, darker than her other books—you read it in a hospital bed, waiting for discharge papers, Nathaniel barraging you with texts. In the book, the wife eats her husband. She doesn't cook him; she eats him raw, but with a fork and knife sharpened using a special device she built herself. It's described graphically and for many pages, but before the cannibalism, the book read like a domestic drama. You can't put it down, and when it's over you don't know how to feel. The book, you realize, doesn't care. Vilma wins a prize in the UK that Nathaniel has never even been nominated for. He repeats that fact over and over. He takes Vilma to dinner to celebrate, and for weeks afterward he's gloomy and cold.

Don't you ever want to do something else with your time, he snaps, coming home to find you pruning expired food from his pantry. Buzz buzz buzz, you're just *here*. Your chest empties, fills with ice. As quiet as you can, you close the pantry door, pick up the trash bag, and leave. You stop using his card, eat peanut butter toast and cheese cubes from party trays for a scarily long amount of time, weeks, so long you think maybe the whole thing is over, start wondering if he's going to cancel the electric for the sculptor's studio, applying for executive assistant jobs that never reach out for an interview. You have no degree, no work experience except for whatever you're doing with Nathaniel. One night you google cleaning services, the phrase "maid for hire," consider applying for a position that clearly involves sex work. When Nathaniel asks you to come back, you cry with relief. When's the last time you truly cried? Still, you make him ask three times before you agree to meet to talk.

That night, after two bottles of wine at dinner, after Nathaniel's apology, after he tells you he needs you, after kissing sloppily in the elevator, you have sex. It's been a long time, so many nights with Reg in between, a couple of strangers, too, but you feel tenderness for Nathaniel when he bends to retrieve his T-shirt from where it's fallen off the couch, the freckled curve of his shoulder, his baby powdery smell, the way it takes his penis three tries to get hard and stay that way. You expect something when he leaves to catch a flight—a kiss on the mouth, some return to how it was in the beginning between you, but having sex only rewinds you part of the way, back to where you'd been before your break, companions, sexless husband and wife. He ruffles your hair, tells you to order a takeout, stay at his while he's gone, reminds you to type up his old notebooks so they're easier for him to read. It almost makes you sad. Nathaniel's lukewarm desire seems to have less to do with you—my God, Wilhelmet, he'd said, when he unzipped your dress, you're in full bloom—than with the way he has begun to drop his sentences right in the middle, repeat the same story twice.

Your phone rings. You don't answer. Some days the calls come every few minutes. On the other end of the line, there's a person whose job it is to call only you—that's how much money you owe. Do they strategize the pacing, four calls in a row with an hour break, or what area to code to use, the most sensitive time of day to deploy the one from where you grew up? Will they get a reward if you finally pay? You wonder how much they make, what their health insurance is like. Would they garnish your wages if you had a W-2? That happened to Tray once; you remember your mother telling you. You learn to keep your phone on silent. Popular, Reg says, watching it light up on the bar. And then months with no calls at all, so long you start to believe maybe the hospitals just gave up. But they always, always start again.

It happens overnight. Oh, everyone says, with the exact same note of awestruck heartbreak, how is it *fall* already? You meet Lili at a speakeasy near *Belvedere*'s offices in Dumbo to toast to her promotion. She dresses all in black now, most days, or big oversized button-down shirts over skin-tight jeans, her vintage dresses and hats pushed way back in her closet. To the associate editor, you say, watching the olives jounce as your martinis collide. Nathaniel buys you a new scarf, cashmere, the color of the frost on the Great Lawn of Central Park.

Your book is sixty pages, then zero, then eighty-two, one hundred, a single radiant chapter, halfway done, almost finished, roughly twelve pages, eighty thousand words. No, you don't have an agent, you say, when people ask you at readings, at parties, but you do have Nathaniel, Nathaniel who reads every version, Nathaniel who tells you, when you really think you're truly done, to set it aside, to write it again, like a real writer. You've completed the practice rounds, he says. But, Will, this is real work! I am so proud of you. You bury your head in his chest when he says this, so he can't see your face, how happy it makes you. When you start again, you write slowly, you aim for poetry in every line. Purple, Nathaniel writes in the margins. Breathe. You're in a rush, but you're also not. You're only twenty-what, five or six, still Nathaniel's assistant, his very best girl.

Your job has swelled and swelled. Do you ever feel, you ask Lili, like something odd is happening with time? Now you manage Nathaniel's life, you make it bigger, busier. You're working with his agent on a new selected—prose this time. And he's got so many meetings, Hollywood things you schedule that never seem to pan out, he likes for you to send gifts after, cocktail shakers, personal notes. You write recommendation letters for his former students, blurbs, spend a week researching mattresses for lower back pain and coordinate the replacing of his bed, the installation of blackout shades, the doctor's appointments, the insurance claims, the copies for his classes, groceries, dinner, shoes to the cobbler, the first draft of the book review, the speech, the questions for the interview at the 92nd Street Y. Sometimes you pick out his clothes. He likes to keep baby wipes on the toilet tank, just in case. He wants you to record him talking about screenwriting, for a craft book. He wasn't trained, you know, he learned it all himself. Why is he always out of bananas? He doesn't trust transcription services, wants you to do it by hand. He never asks you about health insurance, even when he collects you from the hospital, even though he knows about your heart, the urgent care visits you sometimes pay for with his card. You'll be done with the book when Nathaniel tells you you are.

Best of the New, same as every year, Nathaniel's students switched out. You sit in the front row. Tilda nods hello, but at some point, it's like you never knew her at all. When you pick up your plastic cup of wine, she doesn't even nod, doesn't try to meet your eyes.

In the winter, the best part of the bar after the reading is the second bar after the reading, the group whittled to an unlikely handful shuffling through the snow, you and Reg coming up behind, slipping away to smoke and make out in the cartoonish whirl of flakes—wait. Pause here. This time was different, wasn't it.

Reg stops. You look at each other, eye to eye. He kisses you again, both of your eyelashes full of snow, the kiss you dreamed of as a girl, or would have, if you hadn't been thinking so much about poetry. It's been six months, more, since you last touched. Reg, who'd started doing things like taking reporting trips, had been on one of those, or Nathaniel was being extra needy, or Reg had a girlfriend, or you were dating Nathaniel's agent's forgettable assistant, oh, who knows. "Come with me," Reg says, and he hails a cab crawling slowly through the sheets of snow, the only car in sight. When it stops, you're not at his place in Greenpoint, you're at Prospect Park, the grand entrance near the library. You stumble through the snow—it's coming down too hard and fast for the plows to keep up, and anyway, why would they bother, when you and Reg are the only two people in the whole city. Snow is in your boots, melting down your back, it's in your bra, your ears, in the crevices where your fingers and Reg's fingers meet. Everything glows. In the circles of light cast by streetlamps, the flakes are sparks, so bright they hurt your eyes.

"Where are we going?" you ask, and he tells you he doesn't know, that he wanted to be somewhere outside of the city with you, and this was the best he could think of.

"I thought you were made of snow, Michigan girl," he says when you stop to brush a thick layer off your hair. And you're annoyed, just a flicker, because he's wearing one of those expensive puffer coats with cuffs that extend to the knuckles, a wool hat pulled below his eyebrows, waterproof Chelsea boots. You're in one of Lili's old coats, wine red and fuzzy, with torn silk lining and plastic buttons shaped like daisies. Tights, faux leather cowboy boots a quarter of an inch taller than the snow you're walking through. He pulls you with him toward a break in the trees, and Long Meadow opens out before you. No one. Just a plain of empty, alien white, as if you've traveled somewhere impossible, like Greening, or the surface of the moon. You don't even see the tracks of a squirrel, or a rat.

"There," Reg said. "We made it." See how he looks at you. "Remember your first Christmas here, when I tried to walk you home?" Feel the wobble in his hands as he turns yours over, unfurls your fingers from your palm. He kisses your forehead, then puts his hat on your head until it covers the place his mouth touched. Neither of you are drunk anymore. In the story you've told yourself, Reg was the one with the crush, who, as soon as you showed interest, couldn't commit. Reg was the one deciding where and when and how, but here he is, looking at you like he's been waiting outside your door for years. "Will," he says, "I really like you. I like you so much. I've been an idiot. I wasn't ready. But I think I could be now. I got stuck on you a long time ago and it just doesn't go away."

You try to think of one thing you've ever asked of him, and you come up with nothing. Wasn't that Nathaniel's advice? Let him come to you? It occurs to you only there, snow in your mouth, that's exactly what you didn't do with Nathaniel. It's taking you too long to respond. You both feel it. "Took you long enough" is what you finally say. What you mean is, why didn't you tell me before it was too late? (Later, when it really is, you'll see that, of course, it wasn't too late at all.) And then, because you want it to be true, because you've slipped out of time together, onto this blank page with no record of your mistakes, you say: "I could be ready, too."

In Reg's bathroom mirror, you look older than you do in Nathaniel's. At Nathaniel's, you're always a girl of twenty-two, begging the great writer to take you seriously, because that's what he needs you to be. Here, you're someone else. Who? Back in Reg's bed, he tells you, haltingly, as he fiddles with a hank of your hair, that your job with Nathaniel makes him uncomfortable. That he knows what Nathaniel is like, and even though—"Even though what?" you say. Reg stops, tries again.

"You've been his assistant forever, as long as I've known you. Don't you want to do something else?"

What Nathaniel is like. The worst part of that line, and you've heard it so much, is what it assumes about you: that you're either delusional, a sweet little girl who tripped and fell sideways into a trap, or something even more pathetic, a woman who takes any crumb she can get. "I want to write. That's it. Who else will give me my mornings free? All those days off every month when he travels?" It's too hard to explain. It's not something Reg would ever understand. Maybe you had other ways of getting here, but would they have worked? You also don't say the next thing you think: that Reg only knows you because of Nathaniel.

"I know," he says. "And I'm not one of those crazy jealous people. I just don't like how much he—it's like you're his pet or something, or he sees you like that, like he can just . . ."

It's almost possible. You could tell Reg about the Visa, your debt, how you're nine credits shy of a bachelor's degree. You could tell Reg about your mother, about Tray, about your dreams of Rosendale, how they come to you still, as if part of you is already banished there, hands dishwater raw, bleach in your hair. As if part of you never left. How Tray never touched you, but how he *made* you think about what he imagined, how you still feel him outside every window. How in your book, Nathaniel says you need to write it plain, but you still haven't figured out what that means. How he feels—even with Reg right there beside you—like the most solid thing you have.

In the morning, Reg kisses you before either of you has brushed your teeth, like Nathaniel never would. It feels different, this time, like Reg is trying to tell you something he doesn't know how to say. Sweat pools in his lower back, the curve of his neck, and when it's over, both of you are damp, breathing hard. He has to go to the office to file a piece. He says he'll see you after work. He whispers something into your hair, that word again, and you reach for him, confirming. But when he calls, you're at Nathaniel's, putting the salmon in the broiler.

You text back, *sorry Reg, I can't now. Talk later?*

Samson is, somehow, always there, at the reading, at the bar after the reading, at the second bar, the diner after the nightcap at the editorial assistant's shockingly well-appointed apartment, the used bookshop on Twelfth Street in the middle of the afternoon, when everyone else is at their normal job. One night you kiss him back half-heartedly after Reg shows up at the Housing Works holiday party with a date, a bony butterfly of a girl who works in marketing for *Time Out.* Samson hasn't written another book—no, that's not right, he's still writing it, he had that story, Nathaniel took him out for a beer, it's been a struggle. He gets some help from his parents, but just a little—really, he hardly gets by. Most of the time he says nothing to you, either that or you wind up gossiping furiously in some dark corner after you've both had too much to drink. At some point you realize you're not so far apart in age, you and Samson, him perpetually at work on book number two, you promoted to typing up Nathaniel's archives, the stacks of impenetrable legal pads from the past he thinks might hold a kernel that can become a new novel. Sometimes, when it's late, his handwriting very messy, you let yourself write, a little, in his voice. When you show him the pages, you wait for him to notice where you took over, but he never does.

Are you different? You're twenty-seven. There was something you were supposed to do by now—what was it? You measure your face in Nathaniel's mirror. Nathaniel says hair is youth; you let your eyebrows creep toward each other. You cut your hair, let it grow back out. Your mother gets sick, but she doesn't tell you until after she's better, stage 2 breast cancer, nothing chemo couldn't fix. For a while, you call more frequently, but the long silences, how neither of you can ever seem to find a way to ask a question of the other that elicits more than a single-word response—it's too much for you to bear, and you're both comforted, you tell yourself, when you slide back into the rhythm of talking once a month, less, on holidays only.

Nathaniel's taking his new Lili out for dinner. She's Chinese—he tells you this over and over—and writes like her head is on fire. What would he say about how you write? A year later it's a different girl, a blonde with crooked teeth and a Southern accent. He reads you one of her poems out loud. For two months, he's out almost every night with a brassy girl from Queens, tiny with humongous breasts; the next semester, you hear through the grapevine, she drops out of the program. Sometimes the Lilis make you jealous, but there's never another Will. You read every single draft. You let yourself into his apartment on a Saturday morning, so you can be there to show the super the noise the toilet makes when you flush it, and find a young woman, no more than twenty if you had to guess, eating a bowl of Kix at the kitchen island. Just his assistant, you say, and scoop up his laundry, throw in a load of wash while you're waiting. The girl is gone before the super arrives, and you never see her again. It takes you a few days to realize—you never asked her name. Whenever you find women's clothes mixed in with his, you fold them carefully, leave them on the foot of his bed. Once, you steal a pink cashmere sweater, hip length and so soft; when the radiator breaks at the sculptor's studio, you sleep in it.

Reg and Lili, even Nathaniel, they transform, transform again. But you, it's as if the monumental effort of finding your way to him, of turning yourself into the person Nathaniel needed you to be, blasted your power source, got you stuck in this endless loop forever, pairing his clean socks, fucking him a couple of times a year, as if performing routine maintenance on an antique car. Writing and rewriting the same book, publishing your secret poems here and there, for usually zero, sometimes fifty dollars apiece, hitting ignore when your phone rings. But you have an apartment, a job, Nathaniel's notes in the margins. This is the story you tell yourself: There is no life in the city without him, not for you. Isn't that why you dodged Reg for months after that night in the snow, let your relationship slide back into an uneasy friendship, why you never let him talk like that again?

Reg writes a piece about ghosting that goes viral, starts getting bigger and bigger assignments. He goes to Flint to report on lead in the water, texts you a selfie from the Detroit airport. In your home state, he writes, and you don't bother trying to explain that Detroit is as much of a different universe from where you grew up as New York, that you've never even been there. Lili becomes the managing editor at *Belvedere,* starts dating with great seriousness one of the hedge fund guys from the board. It seems like you only hang out with him three or four times before she's engaged, before you're at her wedding, telling people over and over, no, you don't know Lili from college, you met through poetry. Her husband, Jake, is forty-one, a tasteful age gap, with a dimpled chin and earnest political opinions, eager for children. He's never once made you laugh. He seems double Lili's height. Sometimes he picks her up and cradles her in his arms like a baby. Maybe that's his appeal. Lili, who stopped writing after her second promotion, wins the Selden the year of her wedding, for a chapbook she published two years prior. You know Nathaniel nominated her. You want to ask her what she's doing with the money, where thirty thousand dollars goes when your husband is a hedge fund manager. You're supposed to attend the ceremony as Nathaniel's plus one but you tell him you have the stomach flu, and then you lie to Lili, too, pretend you were so sad to miss it when she shows you a photo later. But you're also happy for her, truly—you hope it will make her write again. You miss her poems; you never feel closer to her than you do when you are reading them. The exact opposite of how you feel about Nathaniel's work, which you still value unthinkingly, even when it bores you, makes you squirm.

After the election, everyone is shocked. You are, too. But when you press against the feeling, are you, really? You know, without ever asking, that your mother and Tray probably didn't vote at all, but if they did, it was for the man. On the subway the next morning, the atmosphere is funereal; an elderly lady sitting across from you openly sobs. You go to the Women's March with Reg and feel inspired, yes, but mutely so. What has to happen in a life to make a person believe that if they say no loud enough, the bad thing will stop? That rescue will come. Was it something someone was supposed to teach you? Where was that teacher? Was it protest, what you did, leaving Greening and refusing even to visit? Taping the bag over your window?

Then, a miracle. Nathaniel tells you the book is done. You're in Paris, just the two of you. He's there for a festival and he brought you along. I can't believe this is my life, you think, as you follow him around the city. You watched him read your latest draft on the plane. It's the shortest version, barely one hundred and fifty pages. No fat, all scene, a numb third person, lots of white space. You had a feeling he liked it because of how he was breathing, his irritation when the flight attendant interrupted to ask what he wanted to drink. When he tells you, you're at a café in the 11th arrondissement, hallucinatory with jetlag, sharing a plate of cheese so pungent that forever after, whenever you see your book's title, you smell mold. Even after Nathaniel passes the book to his friend, the publisher of a prestigious small press you've read for years, after he calls to offer you three thousand dollars and a contract, tells you during your first meeting how the book reminds him of *The Sun Also Rises* but with a distinctly female point of view, you smell mold, mold, mold, as if the cheese were still melting on your tongue.

You and Nathaniel eat it all. On bread, it is delicious, veined with blue, crumbling at the edges. You press it against the sponge of yeast until your fingers stink. The two of you stop at a tabac for a Kir Royale, and then another, for another. You attempt sex in the creaky bed near the window, which looks like a doorway, opening outward. It doesn't work. You tell Nathaniel you're tired, you want to stop. "I'm sorry," he says, and you almost laugh. Is it possible he thinks this was ever what you really wanted from him? The next morning, standing by the steps to the pop-up stage, you help him adjust his clip-on mic. He stops your hands before you switch it on, puts his palms on your cheeks, says,

"You are very dear to me, Wilhelmet."

"I know," you tell him back. And you do.

How will you account for all these years? You're nobody's poor little fiddlestick anymore. When your book comes in the mail—in a cardboard box, like it could be toilet paper, a sheath of lightbulbs, a replacement filter for Nathaniel's air cleaner—the first thing you can't believe is your name, in silver foil, slick against the matte cover. Wilhelmina Miles, almost as large as the title, as if the publisher wants you to be the thing the reader remembers. You pick it up—there's that taste again, fecund and earthy—and flip to the first chapter, the fourth, the very last page. You swallow, trying to clear the taste from your mouth. The endpapers look expensive, too, especially for a small press, and when you crack the binding for a flash of a second, you're in Nathaniel's office again, begging him to let you in, you're widening the hole in the neckline of Reg's black T-shirt, you're listening to the shrieking EKG, you're at Rosendale, trying to outrun Tray. Turn back to the first page. There you are, just behind the text. Alone in the sculptor's studio, writing down a word that becomes a sentence that becomes a story.

For so long, you've been watching yourself try to figure out how to live. Is it writing that does that, skips a person a little off the track of their own existence, or something broken in you? You pick up another copy. Wilhelmina Miles. You wouldn't take any of it back, even if you knew what came next. Look, you say out loud, though there's nobody in the sculptor's apartment to hear.

Look how far I've come. Look at what I did.

VI

BAD? HOW COME?

1

We were in the waiting room at Nathaniel's primary care doctor. He'd had some new shortness of breath, only on the longest of his long walks. This was a follow-up to talk about how the inhaler was going. I'd always helped with scheduling, but lately he liked me to go with him to his appointments—he complained of a funny weakness in his left hand and believed it the sign of another impending stroke, though his blood pressure was under control. I checked my phone. In my inbox, an interview request. It was August, six months since my book came out, and those, along with event invites, had mostly trickled out. My publicist, who'd moved on to other projects, said there'd be more action around the paperback.

"Must you always be on your phone," Nathaniel said.

"I need to answer this."

I'd love to talk, I wrote. *Whenever you're free.* The interviewer responded right away. *Great! Is today too soon? Like 5pm? And quick question—you still work for Nathaniel Fellow right? Is he off-limits?*

Five is great! I said. *Ask away!* Her question about Nathaniel didn't strike me as odd. Nathaniel was the first person I thanked in the acknowledgments. His blurb was on the front cover ("sublime, strange, and beautiful as an ice storm"), so his name, in smaller print, was right beside my own. Interviewers often wanted to know what it was like to work with him.

"Who are you flittering with on that thing?"

"Nathaniel, I said it was an email."

"All right," he said, and then a nurse with a clipboard opened the door and called Nathaniel's name. He got up, raising himself in his new way, sort of pushing off from his knees. He reached her in seconds, not very old from behind, not in that leather jacket, burnished to a shine at the elbows. Observations like that comforted me. Nathaniel had always seemed younger than his age, but lately he seemed much older than sixty-eight. I heard the nurse laughing at one of his jokes as the door closed. He'd let me pick up his Lipitor refills or his acid reflux meds, even call a doctor for him now and then, but he didn't like me in the rooms, to hear whatever it was they told each other about his brain, which according to him was just old, softening a bit at the edges, not terribly out of the ordinary for a man nearing seventy, not necessarily a sign of anything. My cognitive is on the decline, he teased. *Mild* was the word he said they used. It did run in his family, on the paternal side: In his memoir he wrote movingly about how his father died, wandering out into the Greening cold on an October night, sundowning and confused. Poor Janet had found the body. Doesn't it worry you, I asked him. He pointed at his books. The words will shore it up, he said, and patted his head.

Nathaniel needed sleep, protein, to keep up with his morning crossword. To drink less, to watch his diet. Teaching was actually good, the healthy kind of stress.

He was quiet after the appointment, didn't want lunch. Back at his apartment he went straight to his room. I emptied his dishwasher, cut up an apple and sliced some cheese, putting the plate in the fridge. "I'm heading out," I called, but waited a minute in the entryway, listening for his response. I could feel the expectation in his silence. He wanted me to come check, slide under the covers with him, rub his head, but I needed to get back to the sculptor's apartment before my interview.

I stopped at a grocery store on the way home. Two weeks until the end of the month and I was roughly fifty dollars from maxing out my allowance. I bought a loaf of bread, a bag of discounted oranges, whole milk, and peanut butter. A little under twenty; thirty left. I did other gigs for cash—regular dog walking for two old women in Nathaniel's building, occasional babysitting for people Lili knew, and sometimes I sold pictures of myself in my underwear holding a burning cigarette, face outside the frame, for a guy who paid me fifty bucks a pop and didn't seem to mind that they all looked the same except for the color of my bra. Dev had sent me his way. But it probably wouldn't be enough to get me to the first of the month without going over on Nathaniel's card.

I'd worked for Nathaniel for a long time. Too long, Lili said. Weirdly long. I'd been promoted to literary manager, a title Lili loved to tell me was made up, which of course it was, by me, after three years of assistantship, with the vague idea that it would look better for the résumé I didn't have if I got a promotion. My allowance was fifteen hundred dollars a month; around the time of my "promotion" Nathaniel made me an authorized user on his credit card, so I'd be able to build some credit of my own, and because I was sick of paying for things with something that didn't say my name. Once, when I was younger, a bartender had chased me down, shouting, don't forget Daddy's card! Lately, they thought it was my husband's.

We'd never changed my hours from the twenty-five a week we'd set when I moved into the sculptor's apartment five years before; some weeks I put in more, some weeks, especially when he was away, I answered a few emails on his behalf, dusted the apartment, and that was it. A few years before, he'd started giving me a check at Christmastime for one thousand dollars. Nineteen thousand dollars a year under the table; without rent or utilities, with the extra I picked up here and there and Nathaniel's silence when I exceeded my allowance, I was comfortable enough. Sometimes I felt lucky. The credit card meant I couldn't really save or prepare for the future—but I'd never expected, with all my debt, to have any real money. It was a sacrifice that had led me to my book, had given me continued access to his world.

But now the book was out. Soon, I would be thirty. I couldn't lie on my taxes forever. I'd started a retirement account in a fit of anxiety two years before: It had six hundred-ish dollars in it. Samson was the only person I knew who wrote full-time; even Leah had gotten a job in marketing. Everyone had started splitting checks down the middle, no matter what people ordered. Dev worked at an event planning start-up and was saving for a down payment; Lili, after acting allergic to them as long as I'd known her, had gone and had a *baby,* Reg, any day, would tell us he was engaged. When I'd looked toward the future, I hadn't looked further than now. Nathaniel seemed to think I'd work for him forever. I knew we both had the same worry. If I ever did leave, who would take care of him?

The interviewer worked for a literary magazine that threw sloppy issue launches in their offices. In the winter, the pile of coats by the door grew so deep you had to wade through them to get to the beer table. It was always hot, and the fire escape groaned under the weight of people shoving up against each other to smoke. The editor in chief's office looked like a bedroom. According to lore exchanged at every single party, even though everyone had heard it before, there really was a Murphy bed in the wall parallel to his desk. I'd been to many issue launches over the years, mostly with Lili—the publication was a friendly competitor of *Belvedere*'s, and as managing editor she had to mingle. I didn't remember meeting the interviewer, but she spoke as if we were at least acquaintances.

She'd read some of the poems I'd published—this was unusual—and quoted my sentences back to me, wanted to know why, given the novel's exploration of trauma and sexual assault, I'd chosen a cool third person, very rarely giving the reader access to the protagonist's mind. I almost told her Nathaniel's joke—nobody likes it when a woman talks about herself for too long, no matter the genre—but I caught myself, told her I wanted a little space between the protagonist and the narration, so the reader could see around her better. The

POV, I said, if it's working right, should position the reader as a watchful outsider, mirroring the dynamic between the dentist and the girl. Sometimes when I said stuff like that, I sounded just like him.

I'd taken all his suggestions, writing in crisp fragments, the longest passage only a few pages. The rapes happen off the page, but they hover in the white space between sections, pressing on every sentence. He helped me dial up the details, figure out how to say something without saying it. The book is quiet—reviewers called it lyrical, restrained—so the shooting comes as a surprise, even after the daughter's attraction to the gun, even knowing, of course, that it's in the book to kill the dentist. Nathaniel suggested readers would like the Old Testament pitch of redemptive violence, especially in contrast to all the early domestic scenes, and he was right—they did. I gave the mother my mom's long, sooty hair, set it in Greening. Stolen details, to give the feel of the truth. The daughter shoots the dentist in his office. Blood on the tray of cleaned instruments, the X-ray machine, the pedal that adjusts the level of the chair. It's a ridiculous scene; I knew while I was writing it.

I heard the interviewer typing. Then, a pause. "Just one more," she said. I expected her to ask what they always did, though usually closer to the beginning, some version of: How much of what you wrote is true? Even knowing it was coming, I didn't like that one. I gave a different answer every time. The more I was asked, the more disoriented I became. Once I said, laughing awkwardly, obviously I've never shot a man. Another time, I blurted, to a room full of college students, the entire story of waking up in the morning in Jerry's party barn. My boobs were freezing, I said, sensing I had gotten too dark. A boy raised his hand. But there's no party barn in this book?

"Okay, so," the interviewer said. "In this difficult political moment, a lot of women, myself included, are reevaluating their relationships with certain men. I keep thinking about my high school basketball coach, how when he'd wrap my knee after a game—was that even his job?—he'd feel the whole way up my thigh. I always thought it was just medical protocol or something, but why were we alone in his office, you know? And Nathaniel Fellow, your mentor and, I think, your boss?—maybe you can confirm that—is someone who has a reputation for complicated behavior with women."

I didn't hear a question, but I rushed in to answer anyway. Lili was always yelling at me after events, telling me to take a beat. "Oh, yeah, totally. So yes. I'm—I've worked for him, helping manage the nuts and bolts of his writing life, for a long time," I said.

Complicated behavior with women. I thought I knew what she meant—the students he panted after, the relationships that blurred together, the clip from the talk at the Strand where he found five opportunities to mention the interviewer's exquisite skin. Gerry, whose whole story was a still a mystery. Nathaniel was a cad. I'd started to pity him for it; there was a growing mismatch between his sense of himself and the way women saw him, and yet he still talked to every twenty-year-old waitress like he might have chance, even with me sitting right there. But how can I explain? In a relationship, there's what you know, what you don't know, and what you don't want to know.

"Nathaniel's given me everything. I really can't speak to his relationships with other women, other students, but I would never have written this book without him. Or published it. He's the reason we're talking—that you want to talk to me. From my personal experience, I think some of that stuff is overblown. Nathaniel really invests in his students. He asks a lot, and that expectation pushes people to do good work."

Nathaniel never read my interviews. And even if he did, he'd never come across something that existed only online. But just in case, I wanted him to know, as if it were ever in doubt, that I was—as he would say—partisan.

"All right," she said. Her voice was clipped, as if another person had gotten on the line. "I think I have everything I need."

2

The sculptor, vacationing in the Pontine Islands, drank an entire pitcher of frizzy table wine with his supper of linguine vongole and decided, stumbling along the waterfront, to rent a fishing boat. It was already dark when he took it out into the chop, and he was old, with no boating experience to speak of—the fisherman should never have rented it to him. The sculptor's glasses had been left at the restaurant, folded on top of the signed check, their beaded string dangling over the lip of the table. A pontoon of tourists found him the next morning, his body bobbling in an eddy of water between outcroppings of rock. A few days later, the boat drifted, unharmed, into the bay. An estranged son, the sculptor's only living relation, had inherited all his assets, including the Hell's Kitchen studio, which I learned when a realtor and a locksmith opened the door one Wednesday afternoon in September to find me in the bathtub rereading Vilma's second novel, *The Exhale of Stars,* my mouth gluey with M&Ms.

I'd done a lot with the place, over the years: packed the detritus into carefully labeled file boxes, saving everything, even the ancient Listerine; repainted the walls and cabinets a soothing butter yellow; cleaned between the floorboards with a toothbrush, installed bookshelves, patched holes in the drywall, hung prints and broadsides and a giant black-and-white photo of Lili, Reg, Leah, and a random none of us ever spoke to anymore standing near the carousel in Brooklyn Bridge Park. I'd replaced the twin mattress in the loft, fixed the closet hinges, carved my name into the underside of the child's desk by the window, where I'd written much of the final draft of my book. I had an excellent hotplate and an electric teakettle Nathaniel had ordered from Copenhagen. The room only stank when it rained, and I'd long been on a nodding basis with the actor whose apartment I could see from the window.

The sculptor had come back a handful of times since I'd lived there. Grazie, signorina, he would say, when I met him to hand off the keys. His head came up to my chin, his skin soft and tan and as wrinkled as a palm. I couldn't have guessed his age for a million dollars. You have made this place so charming, I almost like it now. When he left, there was always a gift for me on my desk—a tiny birdlike form made of sandstone, a torso in scratched onyx that I used as a paperweight, a hunk of bluish stone pocked with irregular divots, each object ineffably alive. His initials scratched into the bottom.

The sculptor's son wanted back rent for the years I'd lived there. He was requesting a sum of $125,000, which, he claimed, was far below what market value would have dictated for the place. This seemed more or less true. People had been asking me for money I didn't have for so many years that the letter, written tersely by a lawyer, inspired in me almost no reaction. Now I would be sued. It didn't seem, really, to matter—I had no money either way. I showed Nathaniel the letter, and his lawyer responded so forcefully we did not hear from the son again, except to confirm the dates of my immediate departure so renovations on the apartment could begin. Nathaniel's lawyer told me I had grounds, having lived there so long and with the sculptor's blessing, to refuse to leave. In New York, he said, it is very hard to remove someone who has established residency in an apartment from the premises, if they object. Did I? If so, he could send another letter.

I told Nathaniel's lawyer that wouldn't be necessary.

W, the sculptor wrote, after I sent him an early copy of my book. *It pleased me beyond words to receive your novel, and to imagine that dreadful hole we have in common transformed into a place for an artist to do their work. I myself could never do anything there but despair—I admire your tolerance for suffering, which bodes well for your future artistic endeavors, and eagerly await your next book. Bravo.*

Except when he came to town, or we had to hammer out some detail, or when the light in the apartment turned the torso into a tiny, temporary mirror, I thought of the sculptor rarely, though he'd been, in his own quiet way, as much a part of the atmosphere of my last five years as Nathaniel himself. I packed the teakettle, wrapped each of the sculptures in brown paper, shouted farewell to the actor across the air shaft. All these years, I'd considered the apartment something Nathaniel had given me, was giving me, when really, it had been the sculptor's offering all along.

Before I closed the door for the last time, I stood for a while in the threshold. Now I would join the apartment's ghosts; I'd met it a girl fresh from Greening and was leaving a writer, with a real book. Funny how the thing I thought would change everything—writing a book—had required so much of my life to remain frozen.

With such short notice, there was nowhere to stay but Nathaniel's. Lili would welcome me, but she was busy with her one-year-old son, Ansel, and often went days without answering her texts. Reg lived with his girlfriend, a short redhead (she reminded me a bit of Lili in her MFA days) who worked for some podcast—I saw him maybe once a month, sometimes less. It was no comfort that it seemed difficult for him, too, whenever we were alone. I had other friends—Dev, Leah, Samson, who sent me a meme almost every day—but no one in the category where I could ask for housing. As I stacked my books on the table in his spare room, I told myself—and Nathaniel—it would only be temporary.

"Of course," Nathaniel said, sitting on the twin bed. His knees were bothering him. Twice, since I arrived, he'd told me there were treats in the "closet," by which he meant ice cream, in the freezer. "Stay a day, stay forever. Stay as long as you like."

3

A few days after I moved back in with Nathaniel, my mother called to tell me Janet Fellow had died, at ninety-four, in her sleep. Nathaniel hadn't yet heard. Janet had always gone to our church, but my mother had gotten to know her well over the years—after I left, she'd joined the volunteer team that helped single older people with various daily tasks. There would be a service for Janet at St. Joe's in less than one week's time. I hadn't seen my own mother in almost three years.

"You tell him," my mother said. "You tell him, no matter what she acted like, she would have wanted him there. I know Janet was hard, but not a day passed she didn't think of Nathaniel."

"If that's true, why did she never call him? Email him?"

"Janet didn't know how to use a computer."

"Okay, send him a letter, then. I process his mail. I've never even seen a birthday card."

"The things he wrote about her—"

"In his *fiction.* About mother *characters.* In his poems. He has a persona, Mom."

"Not the one he wrote they made into a movie. Based on a true story, right up there with the credits." In the background, Rosendale's dishwasher turned on. "It's despicable, a despicable thing, to drag the private life of a person out there for anyone to see. And I know most of that was an outright fabrication. Janet loved that boy."

We weren't talking about Nathaniel anymore. I hadn't told my mother my novel was being published until I got the advance copies a few months before the release date. I wanted to surprise her. Here it finally was, bound and printed proof that my leaving was worth it. I mailed her a copy with a few positive prepub reviews printed out and tucked inside. The day the package showed as delivered, I waited for my mother to reach out. I didn't hear from her for three weeks—every day I checked—but I refused to ask if she'd seen the book. Finally, she called. I don't understand, she said. Why did you give the dentist Tray's tattoos? Why would you write something so vile about the people who love you best on this earth? About your *home*? She was referring to the layout of the dentist's house, identical to ours. There was a picture above his dining table of a beach at sunset, sky blending into water—we'd had one of those, too. And the setting, which was Greening. And the mother, who was her twin. What was I supposed to say? Because Nathaniel told me to? It's art, Mom, I'd said.

"I'll tell him, okay? I'll tell him."

"It's time for him to show some respect, take some responsibility. He's what? Seventy years old? You tell him."

"I will!"

"It's over now. She's at rest. It's the least he can do."

I waited an entire day. Who else would reach out to let him know? At the end of her life, my mother said, Janet had few visitors, except for a full-time nurse paid for with Medicare. She didn't speak to Maxwell either—her only grandson!—for reasons I didn't know. Sometimes Nathaniel would ask me, vaguely, for the "report from Greening." What he was really asking, I knew, was if his mother was still alive.

Nathaniel and I were coming home from IFC. The film was Romanian, about a father who tries to fix his daughter's exams, guaranteeing her entrance to Cambridge. It was full of scenes of the two of them in the car. Nathaniel, who used to sit at the theater leaning forward, with his chin propped in his hands, tracking every detail on screen, had fallen asleep. He'd been doing that lately. I woke him on purpose on my way to the bathroom, about twenty minutes from the end. "Lovely," he said when I asked him if he liked it. "Just lovely." We stopped to watch the basketball game on the corner of West Fourth. The players, a group of teenage boys, shone with sweat. Every now and then the ball slammed against the chain-link fence, parallel with our faces, and we both flinched. October, and the sun was going down, though it was still hot as a summer afternoon. The West Village was starting to buzz.

"Nathaniel," I said. "I got a new report from Greening."

"When?"

"Yesterday. I was trying to think of the best way to tell you."

"Oh my," Nathaniel said, tracking the ball as it bounced it off the rim. "Can you believe. I felt it. I did."

All through dinner, he was quiet. His hair—how had I never noticed this?—had turned entirely gray. I told him about the funeral arrangements. I said I'd already looked into flights, I had the best one saved on my laptop, ready to purchase as soon as he gave the all clear. He could stay at his mother's—I'd make sure it was unlocked for him—or there was a new hotel in Quincy that seemed nice, with lots of four-star reviews. It would probably make sense for him to say something. I would type it up for him if he liked, enlarge the font. She wanted a Catholic service, but if he had an opinion about the music, readings, I could figure out whom he should talk to. Janet had paid for it all in advance, for the plot and her casket, too, even a few flower arrangements. She would be buried—this was her wish—beside Nathaniel's father in Greening Cemetery. Nathaniel laughed when I said that. He ate a few bites of chicken parmesan, left his wine untouched.

We rode up the elevator to his apartment in silence. He went in first, a few steps, and then stood there in the dark, as if he'd forgotten something. I switched on the light, helped him shrug off his denim jacket. His arms were floppy. There were a few flecks of red sauce on his T-shirt, near the collarbone. I made a pot of mint tea. Eventually, Nathaniel sat down on the couch. "Sleep in my bed tonight," he said when I gathered his empty cup. I didn't take it to mean he wanted sex.

But I hadn't been sleeping in his room since moving back in. It had seemed like a boundary I should hold, a way of underscoring what I'd promised to both of us: temporary.

"Yeah, okay," I said. "Tonight."

He turned to me, and I steeled myself, even as I let him work my tank top over my head. I was grateful, as ever, to have a place to stay. It wouldn't take long. After our first time, rarely, during sex, did I think of Nathaniel as old. When he forgot things, or fell asleep at the wrong time, or flinched when rising to stand, then I thought it. But his body was just Nathaniel to me. I noticed it in relation to itself, fluctuations in his weight, for example, or his smell. Or when I slept with someone else and was shocked by the comparison—not young versus old, but new versus Nathaniel. He was the baseline; others were the variation. But I thought it that night: Nathaniel was getting old.

Nathaniel was also urgent. I was taken by surprise. I'd read something about this, seen it in a movie—how grief can make people desperate for sex, desperate to stake their claim in the world of the living. When it was over, he asked me if I came. I said yes, like I always did, even though I had not. He fell right asleep. I went to the kitchen for a glass of water. Nathaniel still had the same couch from the first night I went to his apartment. The leather looked identical, maybe a little more cracked in the corners. I tried to remember. What, exactly, had happened, after his breath on my palm, before I was on his lap. To be on his lap—a position, is it not, of control? I'd said something. What was it. No? I rubbed my shoulder. Let's slow down? He'd bitten me there just minutes earlier, and the mark throbbed. I willed it to stop, and it did for a second. But then it started throbbing again.

In the end, Nathaniel refused to go, and I went in his place. I told him if he wasn't going to attend his own mother's funeral, the least he could do was write something for her. Everyone in town would be expecting it. "Fine," he said. He wrote something on the back of an envelope, slid it to me. "My mother," it read, "scared me every day of my life. She seemed from my earliest memory to already be dead, and extremely angry with everyone around her for it. Perhaps it will be a comfort to those of you who considered yourselves her friends that she, like all very nasty thoughts, will most likely prove unkillable. I know I, for one, will never go a day without thinking of her."

"Nathaniel," I said. "No. How would you feel if Maxwell said something like that about you at your funeral?"

"Maxwell will say kind things about me, if only to elicit sympathy. He'll probably pretend we were close. My father, the writer, blah blah blah, the time we went to the zoo. And besides. Indifference is worse than cruelty, especially when you've taken pains to disguise it."

"Are you sure it's not the other way around?"

"So you write something, then. Say it's by me. Say I'm too addled with grief to show my face." And then he flew to LA for six days, even though there was nothing on his schedule but a single meeting with a washed-up producer Nathaniel called, in our private conversations, the flimflam man.

I booked myself the four-star hotel in Quincy for three nights. Seven years since I'd been home. Whenever my personal feelings toward Nathaniel got unruly, I forced them into place by reminding myself that he was my *job:* I took pride in my ability to do that, a hard-earned professional skill. At the airport bar, I ordered a twenty-six-dollar glass of prosecco, opening a tab with his card. This was the only way I knew to lash out—spending too much—and I even did that timidly, staying in the lines unless his behavior had been egregious. It wasn't that he'd asked me to go to Greening for him. It was that he hadn't, not once, acknowledged what it would mean to me: seeing my mother, the hurt creature between us fat and slobbering after years of being fed on silence and my refusal, even after she got sick, to visit. Tray, whom I couldn't imagine reading a novel, but who must have heard, even just from my mother's face, about the dentist's tattoos. Driving past Greening High, recipient of the unofficial superlative biggest slut, to get to the stuffy church of my childhood, where I'd have to climb the stage and read as Nathaniel, the dream come true all wrong. As the plane climbed into the sky, there went my heart. It was a short connecting flight from Detroit; but at least planes had defibrillators, unlike the subway, as far as I knew. I attempted the vagal maneuvers and then stood, trying to get it to stop, annoying my seatmate. Sorry, I mumbled, sitting back down. Perhaps my compulsion to apologize to men would someday be my actual cause of death. I angled my body toward the porthole. Its edges were frilled with ice. My heart didn't normalize until I was in the line for the rental car.

I'd written a whole book set in northern Michigan and never mentioned the air. I marveled at it, driving to the hotel, the windows down. Sweet and clear, ample with light. All the trees along the road, blazing with autumn, looked like they might glow in the dark. It was a beautiful place, and unlike the city, where the pleasure came from discovering, every second, a world that had nothing to do with you, here every leaf felt like mine. I'd gotten it all wrong. I'd written a landscape of ice, dormant and bitter even in summer. But this was an alive place, as intricate and intelligent as New York. I felt a bit ashamed.

Nathaniel would have liked the hotel. It had cork floors and a deep bathtub, a view of the lake. Instagram had reached Quincy, too. I wondered if it would be that way in Greening. At the hotel you could get avocado toast and shrimp on squares of crispy rice. I ordered both and pulled up Facebook. Four in the afternoon. It felt like something big should be happening; I'd finally returned. But really, I had nothing to do until the following day, when I was supposed to help my mother and her volunteer group clean out Janet's house. I was meeting her there at ten A.M. A work shift. My mother had offered to pick me up, invited me to dinner at the house. The image of sitting at our old table, passing the pasta to Tray, made my stomach lurch. "I can't," I'd told her. "I have some things to deal with for Nathaniel." When she pushed back, I told her it was a "work trip." *Work*—that religious word that excused everything in the city and meant nothing to my mother.

I scrolled through the faces of kids from Greening High, boys who'd climbed through my window, mean girls, Theresa. She wasn't very active. Her last post had been years before, after she got her nursing degree. I sent her a message anyway. Almost instantly, she answered.

Oh my God, she wrote. *You're here?*

She met me at the hotel bar after putting her kids to bed. She had three: ten-month-old twins and a six-year-old. When she walked into the lobby, she looked exactly as she always had. "Wow," she said, laughing. "Seeing you makes me feel like I'm thirteen. That"—she pointed at my wine—"should not be allowed." She told me about her kids, her husband, her job; I told her about my book, about Nathaniel, about the city, leaving out a great deal. "Your life is so glamorous," she said. "You did everything you wanted to do." I didn't correct her. It was nice to experience my story through her eyes—I could pretend it all still felt like a choice.

We talked until close to midnight, exchanging memories of things I'd forgotten, like how the boys didn't just unclip bras—they used to steal them from the locker room so girls would have to go without after gym. "When I think of my kids," Theresa said, "I'm just so glad the world has evolved since we were teenagers. It feels like, finally, things are going to be different. Remember how it was a sin to be a prude, but also if you went too far you were a slut. But also everyone was like, girl power, except the main important thing was to be hot. And that rumor about you and the party barn! So insane. Ralphie bragging about sleeping with you when he was so drunk he could barely talk." She looked radiant, wearing no makeup at all. Her husband was a roofer named Jeff; a good guy, she said. The best. "You got the worst of it. But look at you now!" She was smiling and shaking her head, like this was stupid stuff we'd put behind us.

Was it possible that all this time, I was the only one who really believed the things they'd said?

"Utterly shameful," my mother said, for the sixteenth time since I'd arrived. She was pulling white plates from Janet's kitchen cabinet and stacking them into a laundry basket lined with a bleach-splattered towel. All of Janet's things, including her house, were being donated to St. Joe's. Upstairs, three church ladies I vaguely recognized were taking inventory of the furniture and linens. "The writer," they clucked when they saw me, and I looked around, for a split second, for Nathaniel. I was supposed to be cleaning the fridge, but it was almost spotless except for a few algaeic flecks of lettuce plastered to the bottom of the produce drawer. Janet had dishes for six, but there was no excess anywhere else I looked. A single dish towel piously folded over the rack, one black plastic comb behind the bathroom mirror, one rag rug on the living room floor, which she'd stepped on to leave her insurance-issued hospital bed.

"He was just too sad to come," I said, trading the sponge, which was no match for the petrified lettuce, for my thumbnail. "I've really never seen him like that."

"My ass," my mother said. She never talked like that on the phone with me, in her terse emails, on her tense trip to New York. Only in Greening. Maybe that was why she hated to leave; it was the only place where she could use her real voice. She looked good, my mother. She'd just turned fifty-three; I'd missed her birthday. Her biceps were defined, and her hair was still long and glossy, skunk-streaked in a few places with white. She had put on a few pounds since her breast cancer diagnosis and had obviously spent a lot of the summer at the lake. I'd braced myself for how much older she'd look, the signs of her inevitable decline. Instead, she seemed stronger. When I pulled up to Janet's house she'd been hauling a trash bag out the front door. You made it, she'd said, without putting down the bag.

"I don't know what to tell you, Mom. You can't make people grieve the way you want them to." The last bit of lettuce worked its way under my nail and I closed the drawer, and then the fridge.

"I don't care what you've accomplished in your life," she said, wrapping water glasses in newspaper. "If you miss your own mother's funeral for any reason other than your own death—especially after putting her through hell and high water—you leave this world a failure."

She was moving on to me now, her favorite indirect subject, so I grabbed an empty box and took it to the bureau in the living room, a hulking, dustless piece of wood with a dozen drawers and tiny compartments. My phone buzzed. The interview was up. I scrolled through quickly—I hated reading my own voice. The interview closed where our conversation did, except hadn't she cut the last bit of my comment? Online, my answer ended with: I just think some of that stuff is overblown. But I knew I'd said something about his high expectations, because I'd added it for Nathaniel—on the off chance he ever saw the interview, he would have liked me saying that, and it was true of him, as a teacher. But otherwise, the article was fine. I posted it on the Instagram and Twitter accounts my publisher had urged me to make, where I had very few followers and only shared things about my book, and then began trying to separate a massive knot of rosary beads into their distinct strands.

When I finished, there were fourteen different rosaries. Most were the crappy plastic ones they handed out after confession to the kids, but a few were special. One had heavy metal beads; another was strung with large pebbles of blown glass. How had they gotten so tangled up? Janet in her rocking chair, pulling from the drawer of beads, saying so many prayers the strands started winding together. Asking for penance, or something else. Something small, and simple, like for her son to come home and forgive her.

In the bottom drawer, there was a scrapbook, the film lifting in places so the clippings shifted when I flipped each page. Nathaniel, a baby in a frilly christening dress. Nathaniel, twelve or so, holding a baseball up to the sun. Nathaniel and Janet, standing next to each other in front of the ROSENDALE sign, arms not touching. All in black-and-white. Reviews from his first few books—it seemed like she'd tracked down every outlet, from a tiny alt-weekly in Denver to *The New York Times.* A postcard from Nathaniel, sent from Belgium. *Dear Mama,* it said, *how loud the church bells ring here! Love, Nathaniel.* The date was worn away, but his handwriting looked unsure, like a teen's. A few more loose photos, including a picture of Nathaniel and Vilma kissing outside of city hall. Vilma wore a fur coat.

Nothing about the memoir, or the movie, or any of the novels, and few pictures of Nathaniel as a man older than his mid-twenties, except there it was: the entirety of the *Vanity Fair* feature, Nathaniel in his navy suit. She'd had it laminated. I hadn't seen the photo since I was a girl, looking at an old man. But now, he seemed so young, barely older than me. He was uncomfortable, his smile strained, something robotic in the position of his head. It must have been the outfit—it was not something he would have picked. Who had been his assistant then? I packed everything into the box, alongside the rosaries. I'd ship it back to New York, and if he refused it, I'd stack it with the rest of his documents in his office.

I wound each rosary and tucked them between different pages of the scrapbook, hoping to keep them from tangling again. Maybe Janet had been praying for the grace to forgive him.

The night before the service, I tried to write something for Janet, but even though I'd written as him a million times, I couldn't ape his voice, not about her. Sometimes it felt good to hear him onstage, asking an author of a book I'd loved questions I'd written, to see his writing in print, cleaned up by me. I was still learning so much. But this—it was too much. Wrong. The only thing I could think of was a story he'd told me a couple times, how one night, when he was a small boy, five or so, he'd opened his eyes in his cold bedroom, moonlight an aching shimmer all around him. There was Janet, sitting beside his bed, holding a pillow to her chest. Tiny hairs glinted on her chin. I'm praying, she'd told him, but he said he knew, with full conviction, she had been thinking about putting the pillow over his head. The story had all of Nathaniel's major themes. After seeing that drawer, I was sure it had never been true.

The next day, I climbed the steps to the altar, where the microphone was set up beside a cardboard photo of an unsmiling Janet, a single, cheeky curl poking out from underneath her black cap. Not a huge crowd, but a respectable showing. Everyone looked familiar. I hadn't thought of them for years, but there they were, the Karstus and the Hausers and the Boyers, Maud Bitterson from the hair salon, Jim no-one-knew-his-last-name from the bar and the bench outside the grocery store. The boy who'd struggled so to find my clitoris, now a man with a neck beard, wearing a flannel shirt and holding the hand of a pious-looking woman whose stolid physique I knew Nathaniel would call podgy. A few of my elementary school teachers, in somber cardigans. The church ladies, two whole pews of them. Theresa and her husband each wore a baby in a carrier. Her six-year-old sat between them, playing on a tablet. In New York, time had always skipped forward, never quite happening; but here, I could see the measure of the years. My mother, in the first row, a chief mourner—I'd been surprised, following her into the church for the service, when she strode all the way up to the front. Tray was beside her, refusing to look at me. Staring down at him, at his hand on my mother's knee, I understood how people could be capable of murder. That part of my novel, at least, I'd gotten right.

I pulled a piece of paper from my back pocket.

"Hello, everyone." My voice flickered. "It's nice to see you all again, after so long." Theresa smiled, fluttered her fingers over her baby's head. "I'm here to read some words on behalf of Nathaniel Fellow, Janet's son, who could not be here today and sends his regrets." My mother scoffed, loud enough for the whole church to hear. "My mother could be a difficult woman"—a few people laughed—"and I think we didn't understand each other very well. I am sorry about that, especially now. It seems like something I should have tried harder at. When I was a little boy, sometimes in the winter the moon would shine so bright into my bedroom window it woke me up—you know that winter moon we get here, when it's really cold, all rung around with light from ice in the air?" A few people nodded. I didn't sound like Nathaniel at all, but I kept talking. "One night it was like a spotlight on me. When I opened my eyes I could see my breath coming out of my nose. I didn't think I had toes anymore—I couldn't feel them. My mother was already there. She'd warmed up a pillow by the fire, and tucked it under my blanket, right over my chest, so it would keep me warm. When I woke again she was still watching to make sure I didn't freeze in my sleep. My mother tried to do what was right, to take proper care of everybody around her, as anybody who ever trick-or-treated at her house and came away with a celery stick or a piece of carrot surely knows." Loud laughter, from Theresa. "That's more than a lot of people can say. I will miss her, and I hope she rests in peace."

Bored applause. My mother was looking at me strangely; the Halloween detail had probably been the giveaway. Jim no-one-knew-his-name was already out of his seat, and when his coat brushed mine as we traded places, I smelled whiskey. "Janie never passed me without giving a buck," he said. "Thank you, Janet Miskner! Maybe you all didn't know I known her since she was a little girl with a braid down to here." He made a slashing motion with his hand at about his belly button. "Never thought of her as difficult. I believe she is already in heaven, laughing at that picture of herself they put out for this thing. Don't look like her one bit. If she picked it, you better believe it was to screw with us." And then he creaked down the steps again.

My mother was a coffin bearer, so I found myself standing beside Tray, looking at the room they'd dug for Janet in the dirt. Nathaniel's father's worn tombstone had partially fallen over, or been kicked. It was early October, a brisk, sunny morning, the trees red and gold. As people started to wend their way back to their cars, Tray put his hand on my arm. I thought he was just trying to steady himself, but then he squeezed.

"I didn't do anything to you," Tray said. My book had made him say it. Or maybe the way I'd looked at him.

I didn't exactly disagree. My mother was hugging one of the church ladies. The sun was in my eyes. After my mother got me those new blinds all those years ago, she'd made a big deal of telling me to keep them closed, to turn them up, not down, because that made it harder for people to see in. She stood in my room, twisting the plastic wand one way, and then the other. *See? See how the gap closes?*

"Is that right," I said, my memory shifting to Nathaniel's joke about the photos.

Tray had nothing to say to that, and I walked away, again.

The Quincy airport had one gate. It cost almost a thousand dollars more to fly there instead of the bigger airport ninety minutes away, but that was Nathaniel's problem.

I was sitting in a bank of chairs, scrolling through Twitter, waiting for my flight back to New York to board. A lot of people were tweeting about the media mogul who'd been accused, by dozens of actresses, of sexual assault. I retweeted a few comments about how disgusting it all was.

Then I saw that my tweet about the interview had four likes, one reply, from just a few minutes earlier.

@willmil overblown, huh

I refreshed my feed. One person liked the reply. A few minutes later, so did someone else. I clicked on the tweet, and then the profile of the poster. Her avatar was a square piece of pizza, and her handle was @fuxboi. She had a few thousand followers, and many interactions with the writer who'd interviewed me. Should I answer?

I typed out a response, repeating the bit from the interview about my experiences just being my experiences, but when I read it to myself it sounded defensive. I couldn't take back overblown. I deleted the message and hearted her tweet instead—this seemed a good idea, because I was new to Twitter, and terrible at it. The whole thing was awkward, but really, I was glad @fuxboi was calling me out for saying something ham-fisted. No matter what it sounded like, weren't we pretty much on the same side? So much context was missing. I hadn't meant it like *that.*

4

A couple of weeks later, at Lili's, Ansel was trying to walk. He got himself into a standing position and bounced on his feet, like a shy guy on the sidelines at a club, his arms dangling. He lifted one foot and then tumbled backward onto his play mat. He gave Lili and me a look of profound betrayal and then crawled over to his plastic cellphone and began ramming the buttons with his webby fist.

"All right, buddy," said Lili. "Next time!" And then, to me:

"So do you think he'll do it?"

"Nathaniel? He'll be thrilled. He never gets asked stuff like this anymore."

This newest Lili, Lili the mom, had brown hair with reddish low-lights, cut into a cute, wispy bob that kept sliding over her ears. She no longer seemed to travel more than a ten-block radius from her brown-stone near Prospect Park. A few weeks before, I'd pointed that out to her, trying to convince her to come with me to a reading at the 92nd Street Y. Ansel was adorable and funny, but I missed my friend, alone, without her kid. "So weird," she'd said. "I guess you're right. But no, I'm not doing that. I actually think that sounds like hell."

Sometimes, when I came over or caught up with her at the park, she looked sort of accidentally chic, the way Brooklyn moms often did. I found her once curled up under a tree with Ansel in her lap, dressed in a shapeless linen A-line, zero makeup, like a rich nun-in-training. But sometimes she looked messy and careless, the way I could when I'd been writing a lot, and that worried me—the stained or even smelly T-shirts, the pilling leggings, the time she opened the door in her bra, dried breast milk scaling her belly. Behind her, deep in the house, Ansel was yowling. Lili, who'd always cared about her presentation, suddenly did not. And on top of that, Lili, who'd first been obsessed with poetry, and then obsessed with her job, now did not write or work at all. *Belvedere* had no maternity leave policy. They'd given her twelve weeks unpaid. "I'm going to be losing my goddamn mind," she'd told me over dinner, hours before her contractions started. Lili getting pregnant had seemed almost like performance art—thirty was a regular age to have a baby anywhere but New York, where it was transgressively young. "Twelve weeks staring at a wrinkly, leaking football who can't even talk," she'd said, looking frightened. But four days before her time was up, she called her boss, Andrei, and told him she wasn't coming back. "Of course you won't get it," she'd said to me, nursing Ansel. One of his fists, the size and shape of a walnut, rested on top of her breast. He opened and closed it, his fingers mashing into her flesh. "But the idea of paying someone more than my salary to hold Ansel while I sit in Andrei's office and try to explain to him why he needs to use the intern's correct pronouns—I just can't do it. Some things are so much more important they aren't even on the same planet."

After that conversation, I emailed Jake an article about postpartum depression. One of the symptoms, the writer said, was loss of interest in activities the mother once enjoyed. Lili texted me later that day.

cool move
going to my husband like it's nineteen fifty
I swear to god will you are so weird about men it gives me the creeps sometimes
I AM FINE okay
save your concern for someone else
it's called having a THREE month old BABY

Lili was famously mean when she was angry. Once, in a crowded restaurant, she'd shouted at Reg that he was "the pussiest-ass piece of milquetoast" she'd ever seen; none of us could remember what set her off, but we still said it to each other now and then, the kind of inside joke that becomes more necessary when the stretches of time between hangouts start to grow. Pussiest-ass, Reg would hiss in the stilted silence after a movie, and we'd laugh until tears welled from our eyes. Or I'd say it to Lili, when she was being grumpy: You're being very pussiest-ass right now. I apologized for sending Jake the article one more time and waited. A few days later she sent me a picture of a yellow smear on the wall—evidence of Ansel's projectile poop—and I knew I was forgiven. But there was something new between us, a prickly burr of resentment. With my mother, it was anger, with Lili it was whatever this was, with Reg it was sadness, and regret, and longing. Only with Nathaniel, perhaps because we'd always been so uneven, did I feel truly comfortable. And more and more, with my less intimate friends, the people who were always at the readings and book parties, like Samson, who was forever down for a last-minute drink or to go to that thing at Housing Works. I tried not to let it bother me that he'd never once acknowledged my book. Once, at a reading, a bookseller asked me, right in front Samson, if I could sign some stock. Samson moved down the aisle and didn't reappear until I was done.

Good*bye,* howled Ansel's phone. He threw it at Lili, and she slid it back to him. He picked it up and began to murmur quietly into its face.

"Hello? Mr. President," I said. "Is that you?"

"I'd like a large pepperoni pizza," Lili said, imitating the actual president. "The most beautiful one you've got. A pizza the likes of which—"

"No more, God."

"Ga," Ansel said, copying me, and we laughed.

"I just need an angle on the Nathaniel piece." Lili had taken on a freelance assignment from *Belvedere,* her first since quitting; I hadn't seen her so fired up in a while. "New poetry collection after a quarter of a century is not the hook Andrei thinks it is. And Nathaniel's already had the full-blown *Belvedere* Great Talks treatment. I don't want to do a repeat of the whole, like, boppity-bop, talk to me about your journey through the genres, from poet to novelist to reluctant memoirist to screenwriter and back again—we know, we've heard it, he's done it."

"I mean he would love to talk about that. And when was the last one? Fifteen years ago? Definitely before *Beauty and Mud*."

"Nathaniel Fellow, exactly how much of your writing and correspondence is actually generated by your extremely talented assistant, Wilhelmina Miles?"

Nathaniel's forthcoming collection was a fifty-page volume of poems I'd salvaged from his dozens of notebooks.

"Stop. And for the record, it's literary *manager*."

"Right."

Ansel raised both of his hands, clenching and unclenching his fingers, like he was tugging on an invisible udder. Lili scooped him up and arranged him on her lap, pulling her breast through the collar of her shirt as if she were taking a utensil from the drawer. Ansel watched me while he drank, his eyes big and wet and blue, his lashes obscenely long. It was the same vaguely threatening stare he often sent my way. It meant stop talking to my mama. I smiled at him, trying not to look at Lili's gigantic breast.

"What about mentorship," I said. "How many of Nathaniel's former students have had books out in the last few years alone?"

"Nathaniel as teacher. Huh." Ansel reached up to bat at Lili's chin. "Gentle with our bodies," she said, and then she kissed his hand with a loud smacking noise. "Yeah, that's a good idea. Moves the focus off him. Would be cool to mess with the Great Talk format a little bit."

Belvedere Great Talks were deep dives—long-form interviews with distinguished writers, usually following a major prize or near the end of an illustrious career. Very few writers were asked to do one. It was rarer still to be asked a second time. They required massive preparation; *Belvedere* asked the interviewer to read the subject's entire oeuvre, conduct and transcribe the conversation, and write an introduction for an honorarium of five hundred dollars. Back when Lili was at Belvedere, it was her least favorite thing to coordinate—interviewers were always dropping out. I'd wanted her to ask me, to somehow intuit my eagerness from the way I talked to her about possible subjects, but she never did.

"Nathaniel is such a weird choice for this," I said.

"Tell me about it." Ansel detached himself and climbed out of his mother's lap, headed again for the phone. "But Andrei loves this kind of provocateur move. That's what *Belvedere* was built on. Old white men, desperate to prove they still matter. Actually kind of hilarious that he thinks Nathaniel Fellow is some kind of fuck-you to the literary establishment. Like, dude, this is not the flex you think it is."

"Well, they did ask a woman interviewer."

"Ha," she said. "It's pretty offensive, honestly. How he's using me to make the whole thing palatable. To get the interns and the rest of the staff on board. He probably told them I'm the one who wants to do it."

"You could've said no."

"Yeah. I could have." She watched Ansel. "Don't eat that, baby. Not yummy." Ansel dropped the TV remote, shiny with saliva, and Lili leaned off the couch to swoop it up. "I don't want to go back. I really don't. I just, it's the first thing Andrei's offered me. Five years, pretty much running that entire magazine, and he just let me walk away. I couldn't even look at the issue they published after I left. And can you believe, I answered a phone call from him about trim sizes from the fucking hospital, like four hours after Ansel was born?" I'd heard the story of the phone call a thousand times, but I made the sound of outrage she wanted and deserved. "I kept expecting him to reach out, fight or something, invite me to write a piece. I don't know what I'm saying. I could say no. I probably should have. I just want to keep the door open." Ansel was standing again. "Oh shit," Lili said. "He's going to do it."

He was standing in the same way—a partial squat, dangling arms, bobbling from foot to foot—but he had a look on his face, almost angry, his mouth screwed into a little knot. The same expression Lili used to make during our Saturday writing sessions, when I'd glance at her across the table, having it out in her mind with a poem. I felt I could see Ansel's future, how much he would make possible through will alone. That was something he'd learned from her. Maybe it was something we all learned from our mothers. Lili slid off the couch and crouched to his height with her arms out, so he only had to take a couple of steps before she'd catch him.

"Come on, bub," she said. "It's okay if you fall. Just try."

Ansel squatted almost to the floor and then bounced up. "Lo?" he said. He lifted one foot, put it down, lifted it again.

"He really is," I said. "He's going to do it."

And just like that, he took a few wobbly steps. Right before he fell, she caught him.

Lili sent an email to the MFA listserv. *Did you get it,* she texted. Forgetting, like she often did, that I wasn't an alum.

no!! send or screenshot

Hi MFA-ers, I hope this finds you well in writing and in life. I'm interviewing Nathaniel—yes, our Nathaniel—for Belvedere's Great Talk series. Would love to talk to some former students about his influence. Looking especially for people who worked with him in the early days of the program, or who've published in multiple genres. Got a story to tell about some wild thing he did in workshop? Let me buy you a drink, or a coffee. Phone is cool, too. Cheers, Lili (poetry, '11). P.S. Oh—on or off the record, up to you.

looks good
on or off the record a nice touch
bet you'll get some weird ones

that's the plan
really want someone to verify pissing their pants in workshop
remember that story

The next day, there was a big piece in *The New York Times* about the mogul and the actresses. Come up to my room, he'd say, so we can talk about your career. Sit down. Anywhere. What can I get you to eat? Are you cold? Would you be more comfortable without your sweater? He asked them to watch him shower. Soap frothing in his chest hair, the functional way he moved his hand between his legs. I clicked the piece, closed it, read half, closed it again. Every time I opened the news. The woman trucker whose codriver laid on top of her while she was taking a nap, the news anchor who'd sent pictures of his penis ten twelve fourteen times a day to the girl at the front desk, the photographer who'd touch women wherever he wanted as he got them into position—the stories made my brain swim, they made me turn off my phone, sit staring at the blank white walls in Nathaniel's spare room, where I'd never, after all those years, hung a single picture.

Sit down?

Okay.

What can I get you to eat?

I'm good with anything. Whatever you're having.

Would you be more comfortable without your sweater?

I guess I would. I'll hang it up.

Will you watch me shower?

Some of the women in the stories had said no. No, they'd said, no, no, no. Sometimes it didn't matter, and whatever they'd said no to happened anyway. Sometimes they got to leave the room, but it cost them jobs, money, friends. An entire career: a life, wrenched off one track and onto another. Some of the women said yes, but most of their stories were between the lines.

Once I'd invited a senior boy—popular, smart, with shoulder-length brown hair—to climb through my window, after he made me laugh a couple of times on AOL. When he got there, he asked if I liked to be hurt. I don't know, I said. Can I try, he asked. I bit my lip so hard blood filled my mouth, but I didn't ask him to stop.

I wondered about the women who weren't in the stories. If any of them thought, here is what is being offered to me. If any of them thought, I'll take what I can get. What they were thinking now.

The senior left before my alarm rang that morning. A few hours later, in class, I rolled up my sleeve to look at the bruise. I pressed it. Look, the feeling said. Someone was there. Someone wanted you.

remember how N used to have me come to his office for those, like, two-hour tutorials where we'd talk and talk about one fourteen-line poem? We'd talk about it so long I'd feel crazy, like I had no idea what we were saying anymore, and I'd want it to end but I didn't know how to get out of there without hurting his feelings, or maybe it just seemed like it was his call to end it, like I had no say in the matter whatsoever, and sometimes he'd be like should we continue this over dinner and I'd say yeah for sure, even though all I wanted to do was go home

and then I'd sit there with him while he drank and drank at Crow's or that Italian place with the plastic buttercups and the more he drank the longer he'd leave his leg against mine and then when we were standing to go he'd come around to my side of the table quick before I could get my purse coat

and put his hands on my waist just for a few seconds and once I was wearing a dress with cutouts on the side and he put his fingers sort of up the sides against my skin and I just froze

I kept thinking about how he'd picked up the fried mushrooms

one hundred percent clear what he was trying but part of me is thinking no, don't make such a big deal out of it

but THEN some reflex kicked in and kind of loud I told him stop being a perv!!! he pulled his hands away but with this cranky bitchy look

real fucking mad at me

there's like an epic twitchy second with true violence in it between us

BUT THEN HE STARTS LAUGHING

like uh-oh, got me, like it had all been some kind of joke

but what if I hadn't said anything you know?
???

I'd received Lili's texts at two A.M. And then another round at four, as if she hadn't been able to sleep:

and after that we just went right back to normal
I am pretty sure we had dinner again after the cutouts just us two like a week later
I am trying to remember but I think this happened first semester my first year???
before I was even his fellow
I think for all this time I really just thought it was a funny
and I was flattered too
remember how back then it was cool, to be the one your teacher wanted like that
especially him

I read them at eight. I'd just put the coffee on at Nathaniel's. I could hear him peeing, a trickle that started, stopped, started again. I took out the half-and-half and poured an inch of it into his mug. The carton was almost empty, and I wrote *half-and-half* on the grocery list I kept taped to the fridge. Now I knew, for sure—he *had* tried Lili first. The coffee was done. I took a sip. It came back up my throat, a little. I swallowed. Why did the coffee taste so bad. I tried to push the voice out of my head, mine, it was my voice, that wanted to write back to her, to say: That's it? That's all he did to you?

And with it, another question: What did I think he'd done to me?

My publicist kept sending me links. Almost overnight, or so it seemed, my book was all over the internet, appearing on reading lists from *Cosmo* to *The Atlantic* to NPR. "Books to Help You Make Sense of the Current Moment." "A Reading List for the Conversation All Women

Are Having with Their Friends." My publisher wrote to tell me they were going to do another reprint. I retweeted every list. On the top of my profile page, I'd pinned only the hashtag everyone was using. There were dozens of comments, over a hundred likes. Lots of hearts, breaking and in solidarity. Many people seemed to assume that what happened in my book was my story.

you are so brave @willmil thank you

I can't imagine what it took to write this [prayer hands emoji]

Then, @fuxboi responded.

so survivor2survivor is it overblown to be pissed about NF behind me at KGB with his hard dick rammed into my ass or

I thought of the plateless toast on his kitchen island the afternoon I'd read him Salter, the ten minutes he'd spent touching himself, how I swung from horror to hilarity to a tickling sense of power to horror again. I tweeted back, feeling it in my gut: *I'm so sorry that happened to you.* And yet, that cold voice again, almost Vilma-like, but undeniably mine: That's it? Have you ever ridden the subway? I wished the voice would get out. I couldn't figure out how I felt about any of it with her in there. A bunch of people chimed in—some were mad @fuxboi for jumping on me (@divena: *THIS is exactly why men have been getting away w this shit so long, stop fighting about the wrong thing*), and some were outraged about my comment in the interview. I stopped interacting. Within a couple of days, the thread went quiet.

"It was a callous thing to say," Lili said. "But I don't know why @ fuxboi is breathing down your neck about it. Isn't half the point of this whole thing that all of us thought exactly that for so long? You just said it at a supremely boneheaded time." She'd come from a coffee with one of Nathaniel's students and was dressed like she used to in the pre-Ansel days: pleated pants with a little brown belt, a tucked-in white t-shirt, gigantic earrings in the shape of the Eiffel tower. Her boots, which she balanced on the bottom rung of my barstool, were hot pink suede. Even better, she'd met me in Manhattan.

"I'm so happy to be having dinner with you," I said.

"Me too," said Lili, picking up a shrimp.

I felt, in a big gooey rush, like I might cry. Nathaniel was on sabbatical. His new poetry collection was a few months from release, too early for much publicity. He hadn't sold a screenplay in forever. He had spent most of the day on the couch, making vague and maddening demands. First, he wanted me to read him the day's headlines but not the articles (that man is a monster, he said of the mogul), then he needed a specific book from his office that turned out not to be there. For lunch, he wanted a BLT, but when I picked it up from the bodega, he said the bacon was too wet, and he wanted me not just to ask them to make it again, but to take the bacon back and show the guy how it was stretchy and pale in the middle, how it had no snap. When I came back from tossing the sandwich in an outside trash can because he didn't like the smell, he was asleep on the couch. One of his feet was bare; on the other, his sock had rolled nearly off his foot. I hated seeing the treacherous map of purple spider veins between his heel and ankle. In the open notebook on the coffee table, he'd written, in Sharpie: FISH BOAT WITH SPRING LOAD.

When I covered him with a throw, a scent wafted up like salted meat, bologna when you peel back the plastic film. I answered a few emails as him—yes to an event invite, yes to the same former student who needed their letter of recommendation updated and sent around again every couple of months, no to a request to blurb a new novel by a magnificent new voice. I'd opened a PDF of the novel—within minutes, I was bored. I browsed apartments on StreetEasy; to live alone, you needed to make forty times the monthly rent, and you needed to be able to prove it, with pay stubs. Next, I checked Craigslist. Everyone looking for roommates was twenty-five. They all sounded bit like Cody. I wrote to one that sounded promising—forty-something woman seeking quiet, nonsmoking single woman to take the smaller room in a two-bed in Harlem for nine hundred dollars a month—but I got a response within minutes, asking for credit card information for the security deposit. When I left around four, Nathaniel still hadn't woken up.

Lili finished her wine, ordered another. We talked aimlessly for a while, about Ansel, who, now that he could walk, refused to even look at his stroller, about Lili's mom, who commented on Lili's weight every single time she saw her.

"I have to find a new apartment," I said. Lili would have ideas—she loved a project.

"Why?"

"Something came up with the sculptor's son." Technically, everything I said was true.

"Wow. End of an era. Want me to post on the MFA listserv? Sometimes people have sublets."

"That'd be great."

"Maybe it's a good thing? That place is putrid."

"Yeah, maybe." Lili had asked me for years why I didn't move into an apartment with an actual bathroom. I can't afford it, I'd remind her. Oh yeah, she'd say, like it was new information every time.

Why aren't you seeing anyone, she wanted to know. I'm trying to start writing something new, I said. Everyone on Tinder is an animal. Next, she wanted to know why—Lili loved this topic, especially since quitting her own job—I was still an assistant. Still *Nathaniel's* assistant. It seemed she'd come to dinner to needle me: Something was bothering her.

"Literary manager."

"Okay but, Will—that's not a career. People have literary agents. They don't have literary managers. It is literally made up. Like, how is this going to translate—how are you going to get another job, if Nathaniel . . ."

"What?" I said. "If he what."

Lili swiveled around on her stool until she faced me, our knees bumping together. "There's no easy way to talk to you about this," she said. "I know how close you two are."

After her first email, requesting stories about Nathaniel, a few women had responded angrily. So Lili wrote a different one. She built the list of recipients with one of his former students, and the contacts spanned decades. Why hadn't she sent it to me? There it was, a worm of pain, starting in my gut, inspired by the wrong thing. Lili asked people to keep the email private, but to forward it to other women who might have something to say. Anyone who wanted could contact her directly. She was talking in a soft, slow voice I'd only heard her use with Ansel, as if I, too, were her sweet little baby, hearing something I'd find hard to believe. Her eyes were damp.

Many of them had been his favorites. It started with phone calls, long emails, the exchange of personal stories or the deployment of an inside joke. It started with listening, a hand on a shoulder as he walked around during class, mid-lecture, the way he might correct your shirt collar, observe a change to your hair or, more compellingly, your poems. The dinner invitation no one else got. The extra workshop letter. The request, coming near midnight, for your feedback on a story of *his*. The way he thanked you for your notes. Nathaniel has a basic misunderstanding of his own power, a woman had written, describing how he'd eviscerated one of her workshop pieces after she rejected an invitation to his apartment. It's so easy to see what you want, he'd told another woman, coming around his desk, bending down to kiss her while she was pinned in a chair. A publicist, the one for the memoir, twenty-six, accompanying him on tour. Up to his room for a wind-down scotch—*scotch,* I could taste it when Lili said the word—he'd argued her into taking off her shoes, sitting on the opposite bed, just lying down, nothing has to happen, a conversation that went on so long and twisted in so many directions she honestly couldn't tell you if she consented—she might have, just to get him to stop. Lili paused, took a deep, wavery breath. I waited to feel sad or disappointed or scared or hurt. Anything. I waited to feel angry. I knew this was when I should; here it was, permission. Instead, I had a funny, creeping feeling Nathaniel was listening, somehow, his ear pressed up against a seam in the space-time continuum—that he was listening, and shaking his head, the way he did when people at a party who had to be indulged said something about art that he considered banal, or untrue.

Lili was gathering their stories, but for now, it was all off the record. She wanted to make a space where we could sit together with this. She'd gotten over twenty responses. This, she said, could be her take on a Great Talk. *This* was Nathaniel's legacy—what these women had to say, not what he'd written.

"When you first showed up in class," she said, "and this was back when I lived for his approval, sending him revisions at all hours, earnestly reading everything he recommended—I remember thinking, hmm, this is not right. The rumors were part of his mystique, and we all kind of rolled our eyes, but there you were, this girl going in and out of his office, sitting silent in class. It was weird." She'd never told me any of this, at least not in this way. All along, all these years, there'd been a story snaking through her mind about me, so different from ours together, or the one I thought she believed. "At first I thought you must be his long-lost niece or something, I contorted myself trying rationalize it, because he was Nathaniel, and surely he wouldn't be so obvious, and also you were so cool, so serious and focused about writing—the more I got to know you the more I just felt like, well, she knows what she's doing. And maybe I was even jealous, which is a gross thing to admit, about the special relationship you two had. I went to talk to Tilda about it, just to see what she knew about your situation—"

"You talked to Tilda?" It wasn't Leah who'd complained. It was Lili.

"I figured, if there *was* something weird, she'd suss it out and the school would intervene. And when nothing came of it, I was so relieved. And you kept working for him, and that made me trust him, that you did, if that makes sense."

Maybe, if I'd been a student in the program, her plan would have worked. I wasn't angry with Lili; I would have been, years ago, for how it kept me from his classroom. But I wasn't anymore. People trying to help. I knew the impulse, and I knew the ways it could all go wrong. Wasn't that the thing about my life? I'd either been rescued or trapped.

"But, Will," Lili said. The restaurant was full and noisy but I would have heard even if she'd whispered. That was something the city taught you, how to be alone with someone anywhere. Several women had told Lili to contact one of Nathaniel's former assistants. Geraldine Keene. Lili had emailed her several times without getting an answer, and the way Gerry kept coming up, it made her think about *me*. What my job really was. "God," she said. "I'm sorry I haven't brought this up more." More. Because she had. And every time she did, I deflected with a story or a joke, changed the subject, moved the topic to her work, to what we were writing or trying to, to what we were going to eat or how we were going to get there, to our mothers, to our bodies, to all the things women talk about when they don't talk about men. "I just keep thinking—that shit he pulled with me, what must he have done with you?"

"He's Nathaniel, Lil," I said. My phone was vibrating in my bag—it was probably him. Perhaps I should pick up, let him answer Lili for me. What would he say? Wilhelmet? There's nothing I haven't done for her. "I don't have to tell you the things he says. There's been plenty of that. It's not awesome but I'm used to it."

"He didn't ever?"

I waited for her to say it outright, but she wouldn't.

"No," I finally said. It was easy to lie. I'd been doing it for so long. Just a few months before, Nathaniel wanted me to go with him to the Grolier Club, where they had a special exhibit of Yeats facsimiles. I'd been wearing a tank top. I was leaning forward, with my elbows on my knees. The train lurched and I sat back against my seat. One of those old cars with the orange and yellow seats that make an L shape, each of us sitting on our own bench. Nathaniel reached out and grabbed my right breast. Honk honk, he said, squeezing it a little. Across from me, a teenage girl watched, headphones muffing her ears. Don't, I told him. He tried the other one. Honk? I pretended to laugh. He took his hands away and rooted around in his pocket for his phone, sent someone a text.

"Maybe because I was always there," I said. "I don't know. He just kept that side out of things with me."

When Lili's face relaxed, my stomach turned over. The question had been eating her. "I knew you'd tell me if there was something," she said while I studied the bar top. "But I was really in a spiral." The bartender disappeared the shrimp plate, overpoured Lili a new glass of wine. "The stuff I've heard, Will. We've got to do something."

She talked for a long time. What if I'd just told her, right from the beginning, the truth? Now it was too messy to explain, a network of lies going back so far that confessing them would undo every good memory of our friendship.

When we said goodbye, I promised I would help. For penance. And because Lili was right.

It started raining while I was on the subway, headed back to Nathaniel's apartment, and when I opened his door even my socks were wet. "I knew you'd forgotten an umbrella. I was sitting here, thinking, Wilhelmet has gone out without her umbrella, just as she always does, and will come home wet and cold. And I was correct." Water was in one of my ears. I slipped off my wet shoes, my socks, and my feet made tracks into the kitchen. On the top shelf of the fridge, right beside the Greek yogurt, was Nathaniel's cellphone. I brought it to him, along with a beer for myself, and sat beside him on the couch. "Stop looking at me like I spit in your soup," he said. He tapped my legs until I lifted them off the floor and deposited my wet feet in his lap, feeling like a traitor, and, at the same time, like I was home. "Tell me what you wrote today," he said. He was in a good mood, clear and himself. Despite everything, I liked to see him like that.

"Nothing. I was very busy with somebody's BLT."

"The longer you wait to start, the more impossible it will feel." My big toe cracked. A new unknown number appeared on my phone. It had a New York area code. My voice messages were full; I kept them that way, so debt collectors couldn't get through. I wanted them to think maybe I'd died, or the number wasn't in use. I denied the call.

"What did you write today?"

He pointed at the notebook, and we both laughed at FISH BOAT WITH SPRING LOAD. Back in his apartment, I'd reentered the timeline from before Lili, the closed-loop world of Nathaniel and me, with its own set of rules. And yet, a memory came to me, unbidden—of a time, the year I'd lived with him, that I came back from Net Café just after midnight. As I crossed onto his block, I saw him outside the Duane Reade in a strained conversation with a woman, not Sarah, both of their voices raised. She was drunk, swaying on her feet. Student, I'd thought, though I wasn't sure why; I couldn't see her face. For his sake, and mine, I stopped in the middle of the street, turned the other way.

"I will tell you," he said, "about a time I was very stuck. I was in Rome. Vilma was having an affair. She has still never admitted it, but she was, with a young Rasputin named Hadid. The boy had ears like saucers and she claimed he was around all the time to fix her bad energies. This was one source of my despair, but it was the surface one, the agitation on top of the water that hides the deeper disturbance underneath. That's why I left her in New York—I had to see what was under there. *Autumn Legend* had been a bestseller, *The New Yorker* took that mean little story about the couple mincing around the kitchen at night, and of course I'd had the poems, but I was on the upswing, as I saw it, and there was this tremendous pressure to write something that would pin me to my place in the firmament. I knew no one, spoke no Italian, walked around all day looking very idle indeed, while inside me the furious machinery of my soul was in mutiny against itself! It was the hardest work I've ever done, that month of not writing. I walked and walked, up and down the banks of the Tiber, from dawn until it seemed an acceptable time to start drinking, which in Rome was noon. Then I walked with a bottle of white wine, because it helped me think. One day, a boy passed me, riding his bike harum-scarum down the rooty path. He kept lifting his hands from the bars. I was sure he'd end up in the river, riding as he was, no hands one moment, then jerking his handlebars into the sky so his front tire skittered off the stones. I believe he was trying to get—what do they call it?—air. Then the little fellow fell. Flew, really. Flew over his handlebars, several feet, straight into the crumbling wall marking off the steps to the road above. I could hear howling before he even hit the ground. I was the only one around. By the time I reached him, he'd disentangled himself from his bike, palms clapped over his knees. I could see from the blood underneath them how he'd hit—palms first, and then his knees had caught up with his body and made impact, sliding down the wall with him. The child was staring up at the sky, rigid with terror. You see, he was afraid to look. I knelt and helped him slowly remove each of his hands. His knees were awful. Worse, actually, than I thought they'd be. But once he saw the wreckage, he bounded up, righted his bike, and started riding again." My other big toe cracked.

It occurred to me, with an adenosine-like rush of doom, that it had been a long time since I'd had my period.

"Of course, the thing under the water was fear. Not fear that I couldn't do it, but fear that I could. Fear, perhaps, of what it would take. That's what it always is."

"No," I said. "I'm not afraid of any of that." Why were Nathaniel's stories always so easy?

"What, then?"

"I'm afraid of you."

Nathaniel smiled, gave my foot a squeeze. I swung them back down to the floor. Was I one week late, or two? "Wilhelmet, I'm old. I know a lot less than I think I do. You can decide to, just—" And then he waved a hand in the air, like he was batting away a fly.

A few days later, Reg hosted a dinner party. "He's going to tell us he's engaged," Lili said as we rang the buzzer at his garden apartment off the Smith F stop. Reg's girlfriend, Alice, opened the door. I saw the ring right away; of course I was looking. A trio of glittering gray stones. Reg appeared over her shoulder, and then we were inside, everyone smiling and laughing, happy, happy, happy, such beautiful news. He hugged Lili first, then me.

"I heard you're helping with the Nathaniel piece," he said into my hair. "I'm so proud."

Reg, I wanted to say, wait. But of course, by then, it really was too late.

5

We really didn't know how many would say yes. Lili had been meeting with them, buying them lunch and coffee and dinner, traveling all over the city to their apartments, wherever they felt safest talking. A couple of them, already, had told her they'd go on the record. Most still weren't sure. She wanted to do it as a group interview, maybe with answers from Nathaniel wound in. She wanted it to be read. It wasn't just about information; she wanted to make everyone *feel* what he had done. Andrei would object, but she'd find a way. The interview usually went up online before it was in the print issue—maybe she'd do the whole thing straight, and then add the women's stories as a comment, get Reg to send it to some of the magazines he wrote for. Maybe she'd go around Andrei, straight to the board. Tell them *Belvedere* could have the piece, or someone else, but it was going to be out there either way. She'd contacted a journalist at the *Times,* but they kept blowing her off—Nathaniel, who'd always loomed so large to us, was not famous enough to make them jump. If she had to, she'd publish it herself, one hundred and forty characters at a time, on Twitter. She was so angry. Where had that anger been, all those years in the MFA and after? Waiting there, trapped behind some fence, and now the boards were being torn down. It separated us, Lili's anger; it almost scared me. She was taking the next forceful step toward something she'd always believed: There were things, from men, no woman should have to accept. I was still on the other side, peeking through a knothole. My life in New York had always been infused with secrets, because of him. But now it had split. On one track, with Lili, I was weeks away from exposing Nathaniel, from quitting my job and freeing myself, from helping to make sure he could never do any of this again. On the other track, with Nathaniel, things went on precisely as they always had.

When she told me their stories, I could tap into something raging and powerful, but as soon as I was alone, the surge was replaced with an exhaustion so complete I'd go to sleep minutes after eating dinner, while Nathaniel was getting settled in front of his laptop, where he'd taken to watching prestige TV. Lili met with two or three women a day. She met with one several days in a row. They talked about Nathaniel, but at some point, with almost everyone, they talked about everything—childhood, the dreams that still came to them, their bodies, their children, their work. Lili hired a nanny to watch Ansel, or she took him with her, let him nap in the stroller while she talked, while she listened. She was going to have all the women over, the local ones anyway, just to connect, but also to make sure they were okay with the piece itself, to gauge how many of them might add a name. Who might help, in a more public way, to turn the shame around so that he was the one who carried it, not all of them.

We had fifteen RSVPs for what we were calling the gathering. Lili was checking every single one to confirm they still planned to attend. I was in her kitchen, stuffing dates with almond butter. The smell was making my mouth sweat. My stomach was weird again. I was pretending I didn't know what that meant. I'd told Nathaniel I was finally starting to write; I needed a day to get some momentum. Wonderful news, he said. He was sitting at the dining table, no book, pencil but no paper, no phone. When I left, he was standing in front of the open refrigerator.

I lined the dates up in a circular pattern on a tray. Ansel was clipped to the kitchen island in the floating high chair, his legs dangling freely. "You," Ansel said, offering me a puck of orange Play-Doh.

"Why thank you, kind sir," I told him, and took a fake bite. The Play-Doh's kindergarten smell was worse than the almond butter, or they were bad together. Lili, in the living room, was telling someone she understood. Yes, she did. This was difficult. This was impossible. Please don't be sorry. The last thing on earth she wanted was for her gathering to be a source of any additional pain or stress. No one should come unless they thought it might help. I strained to hear. Something about how hard she found it, trying to process what had happened between her and Nathaniel alone—it was only listening to others, the sheer volume of stories, that she fully understood. That was the idea behind tomorrow. From there, she hoped, it would be possible to achieve justice, whatever that might look like, and to move on. Yes, of course—next time. Anytime, she was here to talk. To listen.

Lili blew back into the kitchen. She stood behind Ansel's chair, running her fingers through his blond fuzz like she was going to pull it into a nonexistent ponytail. I could see just what she'd been like at *Belvedere,* those late nights closing an issue. How she'd charged through the office, carrying proofs. How if something broke, it would be such a comfort to go to Lili to fix it. She wouldn't be afraid—or if she was, she wouldn't show it. She'd just get out her pen, start making the necessary corrections. "We lost one," she said. "But that's okay. Everyone else is coming." Her skin was flushed, as if she'd been jogging. "I need to ask you something."

"Okay," I said.

"I need your name." I hadn't sat for an official interview—she'd never asked me, maybe because we talked about him so much. "A lot of people will want to be anonymous. But it's going to have a bigger impact with names. And yours—people know you and him. It'll send a message."

"You don't think that's unethical, or something? If I don't have a quote?"

"I want you to add something. You can write it, if it's easier. Take your time. I realize you need to give your notice first. There's no rush. But things he said count, too." She pulled a bit of Play-Doh from Ansel's mouth and he started to cry. "I think I'm also worried if I don't get your name you'll never leave him."

I already missed her. Which probably means I knew what I was going to do.

6

The F had stalled for forty minutes just before York Street, and by the time I got to Lili's, I wasn't just too late to help her with the chairs, the ice, the tray of sliced cucumbers, the sensitive work of welcoming women at the door; I was officially late for the start time. At her brownstone, the cobalt door was propped open with an accusing brick. I could see women moving in the big bay window—they'd come, then, most of them. I stopped just inside the gate, looking up. I'd counted, with Lili, every single RSVP, but I'd never really believed in this moment, the women together like this, all their stories of Nathaniel intersecting at once. I was afraid. Both of that collective story, and what character I was in it.

I stilled the part of myself that wanted to run. I did it for Lili, not for me. I slipped inside, leaving my bag underneath the console, where a fresh bouquet of flowers I couldn't name, each one the size of my head, dripped white petals onto the marble. The day before she'd had sunflowers delivered; they must be in the trash. It was the kind of thing that would have kept her up all night, the fear she had the wrong flowers for this, and I knew she'd called her florist that morning, probably before Ansel was even awake, to ask if they could make something less cheerful, a little more austere. No problem about the fee for a rush order, delivery before noon. I brushed some of the petals onto the floor. Inside, it was loud as a bar, women talking over each other. A somewhat shocking amount of laughter. My phone vibrated in my back pocket. Lili was already coming toward me. "It's good, Will," Lili said as she hugged me, hard. "I really think it's good. I can't believe so many of them came. The courage is astounding."

"It truly is," I said, or something like that, and followed her all the way in.

I knew them, even the ones I met for the first time as I followed Lili around the room. They were tall and short, mostly white, the youngest twenty-five, the oldest in her late forties. They were tired. Several were already tipsy—Lili had placed open bottles of something yellow and French in ice buckets all around the room. One was talking about how she had to leave soon, for pickup. Two others said they had nannies who did that for them. From the neck of one's T-shirt climbed a lushly drawn tattoo of a vine. One carried a cane. Another had a scar curving from forehead to dimple, twisting through her left eyelid so that it barely opened. Two were of moderate renown; one was, in certain cultish literary circles, probably more famous than Nathaniel.

They sat side by side on the deep sofas that faced off in the long and narrow room, or hovered, standing, near the passage to the foyer, or perched on the edge of the chairs Lili had dragged from the dining room and arranged in a half circle near the window. An ageless woman with long hair the color of ginger ale described returning to the apartment she and Nathaniel had shared after a girls' weekend and opening the trash can to discover, resting among the eggshells and coffee grounds, a tied-off condom filled with semen. She was from before my time, a poet I'd only heard about, the one Nathaniel called "the crazy javelina." He'd lived so much life before me—for him, I was barely a chapter—and yet he made up so much of mine.

I even knew some of their backstories, or could guess, or overheard them talking about it in that very room, how they were born rich or poor, to CPAs and pediatricians and the guy who mowed the grass at the community college, to parents who stayed and parents who disappeared, they'd had inspired fathers and absent ones and the movie regular kind, who stood at the door on prom night and warned the young man in his rented tux to drive safe, which really meant, don't even think about touching my girl. Nathaniel loved girls from the sticks, girls with something to prove. The mother who had to leave for pickup called someone; the woman next to her cheered when she said she could stay, grabbed the nearest bottle of wine, and refilled both their glasses.

By the dining room table, a handful of women, led by Lili, were talking about sex. How many of them experienced pain during intercourse with men, one during deep penetration, one at the moment of entry, a searing stab that made her tense her whole body but went away as fast as it came, and the rest as electric bursts or steady, thudding aches or howling, mind-seizing torture in certain positions or at specific times of the month or when they were feeling low or just sort of always except now and then, doctor-stumping pain that one treated unsuccessfully with antidepressants and another, to more success, with benzodiazepines and Yellow Tail Shiraz. A weird coincidence, that so many of them had lost their mothers, two within the year, each without ever telling her what happened in his office in the back of the cab in the hallway at night so fast she wasn't quite sure after the party in the corner at the bar when her boyfriend was right there after two years of dating one night when she was sleeping. "Ha," said one of the ones who'd told her living mother. "I was advised to forget it. She said, are you sure? Did you perhaps have too much to drink?"

Somehow, Lili wrangled the whole group into a kind of circle, all fourteen of them. I positioned myself at its outer edge, halfway in the threshold to the kitchen. She thanked everyone again. I knew she meant every word, but it was theatrical, and it made me think of Nathaniel, all the ways he'd rubbed off on her. She was grateful they'd come, shared their stories—she knew how hard it was, how scary, and she hoped this could be the start of something big and real, that would keep what had happened to them from happening again, to other women. I thought of the bruises on Nathaniel's legs, from bumps he couldn't remember. How his erections faded after a few minutes, without medication, and sometimes with it, too. In that room, these thoughts were compulsive and awful, like imagining hurling yourself down the subway stairs. They kept coming. My phone buzzed once, then again. "Can I just," Lili said, and then she asked how many of us had been on his payroll.

Four hands went up. I didn't raise mine. I had the strangest sensation that I wasn't really there.

More than half had considered themselves in a relationship.

Most had never told a soul and never planned to until they got the email, forwarded by someone who'd been in their workshop, on the program staff, at the conference, Lili herself.

"Former students?"

All but two raised their hands, including the woman who was almost his age—perhaps she'd taken one of his classes at the Y? I kept mine down. Lili looked right at me, and so I raised it. Was *former* the right word?

"You don't have to answer this next one," Lili said, "I'm just trying to see something."

Eight. Eight had been assaulted before, if that was the word, in college high school on the playground with their brother's friends at a sleepover we called him uncle or Mr. F or the name escapes me now, he was my teacher best friend ex-boyfriend cabdriver boss, can you believe he was the guy who drove the ice cream truck like in an awful movie on one of those channels you only watch in the middle of the night.

The woman with the vine tattoo, who hadn't raised her hand once, abruptly announced that she was fine, she could orgasm in seconds, she could *think* herself to climax, she was so sick of this narrative, sex and trauma, women as victim, he had no power over her anymore, she'd come here just to say that. "To be honest," she said, "and don't take this the wrong way, but I just wanted some like-minded company. I'm not really interested in whatever *this* is." When she stopped speaking another woman clapped. Lili kept her face neutral, but I knew she thought it a vile position, a betrayal.

The youngest woman wanted to know: "I'm not sure I'm really supposed to be here? Does it count if it was just something he said?

Because maybe it doesn't, but why do I dream about him so much?" She sounded like she might cry, and one of the moderately well-known poets hugged her.

"Honestly," said a woman with an uneven gray bob. "Screw this. What he did wasn't okay, but I was no lost lamb either." When she rose from the couch, only the lower half of her face moved, while her eyes stayed wide-open and perfectly still. "Ladies," she said, "don't kid yourselves." About what? That all of us were victims? Or that anything would ever change?

"Thank you for coming," Lili said genuinely as that woman split off from the group, the one with the vine tattoo following. And then Lili pivoted to talking about her piece. After outlining next steps, the timing for another meeting, Lili thanked everyone one more time. A wave of applause. Lili was clapping too. The circle disintegrated slowly as a few women got up to refill their glasses, and others gathered their things to leave. I heard one woman telling another she'd mostly come to network. Not including the famous writer, three had published books, several poems and stories here and there, but few of them wrote anymore.

My phone buzzed again. I fished it from my pocket, and it clattered to the floor. When I bent over, my heart stopped. The usual surge of panicked vertigo. Bad timing. But was it more dangerous if I was pregnant? Nobody noticed my shirt fluttering over my chest. I swallowed hard. *I need you to come home,* read a text from Nathaniel, just before the notifications for his missed calls.

I met Lili's eyes and tipped my head toward the kitchen, where there was a half bath, done floor to ceiling in cerulean tiles she'd hand-selected on a trip to Athens, freshly stocked with Kleenex and makeup-removing wipes. Instead of using the bathroom I let myself out through the slider into her backyard, past Ansel's sandbox, through the gate where her housekeeper had dragged the bins—one sunflower peeking from the compost lid—and into the chilly November evening, joining the trickle of Brooklynites winding toward Prospect Park. My phone was still buzzing.

"Nathaniel," I said, picking it up, my breath shallow. "Stop. I'll be there soon." On his end of the call, a funny clunk, as if he'd dropped the phone. The last time he called me over and over, he'd gotten lost near Battery Park. My heart was still in its bad rhythm.

He'd been twenty, a few years from his first book, twenty-five, a bright young thing fresh off his first big prize nomination, thirty and more handsome than ever, thirty-eight and on set with the famous director, catastrophically hungover as he explained what he'd meant on page seventy-four. He'd been forty-two in Rome on the fellowship everyone wanted, fifty-seven and visiting campus for the semester, sixty-five at the head of the seminar table, with his expensive sweaters and his mothy office and his calcified habits, the bistro on the corner, the bodega where they called him boss, the aisle seat he liked at Film Forum and his way of making everyone, even the most nondescript, talentless girls, feel seen. I couldn't bear for it to have been random—any girl, anytime, anywhere as long as no one was looking. As I closed the door of the cab, it hit me. Not random, of course not. I couldn't understand, and then all at once, how stupidly obvious. The office assistant, the cooking show host, the surly teenager who manned the counter at his bagel place, me—every one of us had loved his work.

The drive from Lili's place in Park Slope to Nathaniel's apartment on the Upper West Side would take at least an hour. Much longer than the subway, which meant more time for Nathaniel's crisis to escalate, more mess for me to clean up. And fifty dollars, minimum. Almost half the price of a monthly MetroCard, a handful of used books or about as many boxes of tampons, roughly a quarter of an uninsured dental cleaning, and on and on. The habitual math was almost soothing, fifty dollars a good-sized bucket, big enough for wants and needs. But I didn't like to go underground during an episode, in case a train got stuck.

where you what the hell

sorry Lil it was just a lot. call you later

are we really going to do this piece

I looked at her messages, thumb hovering over my phone, and then dropped it back into my tote. I bore down with my nose plugged. In response my heart rate accelerated. In the rearview, the cabdriver regarded me without curiosity. "When people throw up in my cab," he said, "I really don't like it." Perhaps I'd groaned. Two hundred bpm, I guessed, or close. The car stopped again and again. The meter ticked up. Already at $27.42, almost an overdraft fee. I didn't feel faint—instead, I was gripped by the adrenalized clarity that often overcame me during an episode. First, I'd sort out Nathaniel, who was probably, as my cab detached itself from cars in front and behind to drive illegally up the shoulder, pulling every book off his shelf, looking for something only I knew how to find. Then I'd call Lili. I'd say, Lil, I have something to tell you. By then my heart would be back to normal. "Okay," she'd say. "I'm ready to hear it."

When the cab eased over to the curb outside of Nathaniel's building, my heart took a sickeningly long hiatus from functioning and then resumed a normal sinus rhythm. Relief washed over me: I'd made it through with no ambulance, no thousand-dollar injection of adenosine, no mandatory pregnancy test that accompanied every ER visit, with its potentially life-exploding information.

The world around me wobbled, then righted itself. I nodded at Jamal and rose in the clanking elevator. No smells in the hallway of smoke or cooking—good. Lately, the journey down its benign, carpeted length to Nathaniel's door made me feel like I was neither alive nor dead, a physical space akin, psychically, to the front matter of a book. When was I going to turn around, go back, start something else? "It's you," Nathaniel said when I opened the door, beaming at me from his leather sofa. Dust sparkled in the sunlight falling through the windows behind him. He'd pulled out most of his suits, shirts and jackets and pants draped over the radiator and the kitchen island and the coffee table. His floor lamp was wearing a pin-striped vest I hated. "Black tie, I know, but tell me, what's been out of rotation?" When he looked at me that way, as if I alone knew all the secrets of the world—

wasn't that the way I used to look at him?—he reminded me of Ansel, holding out a leaf for Lili to inspect and approve.

"Last time," I told him, gathering suit pieces into my arms, Armani and Brooks Brothers and Ralph Lauren, some gifts from publishers or producers in the old days when they gave gifts like that, some bought with another version of the same card I had in my wallet, "you wore the beigey one. It was just a few weeks ago. The *Spectacle* party."

"I was handsome." He'd looked rumpled, actually, but charming in his Nathaniel way, brown tie loosely knotted, a restless, joking look on his face whenever he caught my eye. I was immune to it by then, but others weren't, and they circled him, laughing, young and old and in between. Loyal fans, his very favorite people. He still had some. So sharp that night, quoting Wallace Stevens from memory, whispering, during the toasts, about the publisher's divorce, about the time he'd gone to an MMA fight with the magazine's newly former—and disgraced—editor in chief.

"You were okay."

"Okay?!" he said. "My speech is in the compartment. I have to thank the library, can you add that in somewhere? No. Not compartment. Pocket. The inside pocket."

I piled up the clothes on the dining room table and began running a few pieces at a time back to his closet, where I slid them onto hangers, the suits following each other down the rack. No speech in any of the pockets—just twists of Kleenex, a plastic bottle cap, twelve wadded-up singles.

"It is tonight?" Nathaniel slumped against the armrest, the feathery plume on his crown in disarray, a gluey cast to his eyes.

"You know?" I sat next to him and took his hand. "I think it's next month." A fat green vein traveled up his forearm and curled around the base of his middle finger; I dammed it with my thumb. On one side, it swelled with blood. On the other, the vein disappeared.

"Yes, yes," he snapped. "Wednesday."

It *was* on a Wednesday—this year's Selden Awards. "Hands of a bowler," Nathaniel said, glancing at mine curled over his, trying to paint over the confusion he'd felt just minutes before. "Broad, but squat. Very unfeminine. And you have such a nice face." Would the blood keep pooling there, stretching the flimsy walls of his vein until something snapped? Or would it travel backward, eventually, toward the source? And did the Selden check come in installments, or did they dole it out all at once? Every year I wondered. I pressed harder, but gently, and then released the pressure, watched Nathaniel's vein rise again where it met his knuckles, the sparse hairs I'd once kissed. There it was. The fatigue didn't hit or wash over or bludgeon me, it didn't knock me down or out. It oozed, spreading from my core outward, until even the strands of my hair felt heavy. For a moment I almost couldn't see.

"Are you very tired, dear?" Nathaniel turned his hand around so our palms touched and squeezed mine.

"I had an episode. Almost two hours. Stopped on its own."

"That is, what? Three in almost as many days?" I moved my head, yes-like. It confused and touched me, that he'd kept track, the things that stayed in order in his mind. "You'll go to sleep early. We'll order a takeout. Tomorrow I'll talk to my heart guy, see what he says about all these new ones you're having."

And so I didn't call Lili, or answer the text messages from her that flashed one after another on my phone's lock screen, punctuated, around eight-thirty P.M.—Ansel must have fought bedtime, I thought—with four calls in a row. My best friend. That's what we said—at Lili's wedding, in the acknowledgments of my book, when we introduced each other to strangers—but there was so much Lili didn't know about me. My debt, for one. Or how I'd discovered Nathaniel's work, the mystery of my father and my foolish childhood fantasy. In Nathaniel's spare room, the pillows already stained with my drool, the nightstand buried under books he wanted me to read, clothes in the dresser squeezed between the foot of the bed and the wall. Tomorrow. I'd call. No—I'd do it in person. A bottle of wine—maybe not wine—and tacos on her stoop, like a thousand nights before, like the night we'd talked about reaching out to the other women. I'd tell Lili everything.

I understand, she'd say. I forgive you. Family is complicated. Then I'd tell her the rest.

Nearly four A.M., but in the twenty-four-hour Duane Reade it was always the same fluorescent hour. Behind the checkout, the indifferent cashier tipped another sour straw down his throat, opening and closing the cash door with his free hand. A woman in business clothes cradled liters of Pedialyte in her arms. I cut through the makeup aisle, where an old man stood near the mascara, rattling his dented walker. I smiled at him. "Don't even think about it," he told me in return. In Greening no such place existed; if a predawn crisis befell you there, you dealt with it alone.

Time was falling down around me. All those women, and their stories. Nathaniel snoring on the other side of the wall. I felt a kind of gathering up, as when the air tenses, slightly, before the stick hits the drum. A change in the quality of the silence. It drove me out of bed.

I needed to get the proof part over with.

I chose the most expensive test on the shelf, using my debit card so Nathaniel wouldn't see the charge, even though it's not like the pharmacy bill would be itemized.

Piss on my hand, some on the floor, my foot—the test was high-tech enough to display the word, so why couldn't they design it better, a funnel or something, a wipe that changed color? I pulled up my pants. Pregnant.

The stick hit the drum. The song was already playing.

VII

OFFICE HOURS

If you want to know what a poem is, Nathaniel said, go down to Fulton Fish Market at dawn and watch the fishermen spreading their hauls across the ice. Think about casting the line before sunrise, the hook through the cheek. Packing the coolers, driving in from some raggedy town on the coast, back home at dusk with a roll of tens and scales under your fingernails. But you're still thinking about the hook in the cheek—I can tell from that look on your face. When what you need to do is consider, deeply, the real work of the catch.

Nathaniel said Liliam was a natural writer, but she was spoiled, and like all spoiled things would curdle eventually. By thirty, he said, you won't recognize her. You are not spoiled, Nathaniel said, but you might as well be if you don't stop mincing around and learn how to take what you want. The result—failure, disappointment; the crime of bad art—will be the same. Go to the river with stones in your pocket before adding to the noise, though with all the hackneyed manuscripts I've helped bring into the world, only to drown out the good stuff—but that, Nathaniel said, is something I must live with.

On a park bench, iced coffee sweating in his hand. Women dress like that because they want to be looked at by men like me. You're not allowed to say it, but if it isn't true, why else? Well? When you put on a pair of high heels?

To start, Nathaniel said, walk ten miles a day, like Hart Crane, up and down the length of the city. Following the rivers. Then you'll know what a poem is.

Always, Nathaniel said, I seek the feature. The physical detail that expresses, via the exquisite particularity of its construction, the personality in essence. Interestingly, never a breast. Though once, a nipple, just the left, oblong and the pale brown of early wheat. A single sprig of coarse black hair, very lively against the tongue.

C-O-M-E, Nathaniel said, not C-U-M, a red pen in his hand, trying not to laugh. What genre do you think this is?

A novel should start with flight, a pebble launched from a sling. The thing it hits—and the chaos that follows—that's the story. A poem, Nathaniel said, can start one of two ways: meter or image. The second way is what all of you want to do. But that's foolish. The first way is how poets make something that lasts.

He said, think about it hard and then release it from your mind, a dove from a cage. That's how to write an ending; you must trust the bird to come back.

Never, ever, Nathaniel said, order french fries for delivery.

In the shower, over the sound of running water, operatically: Help, I need somebody, help, not just anybody.

My father? After I wrote about him, I never thought of him again.

Hubris, Nathaniel said, that's what it is, thinking you have something to say. So you start with the masters. *But when the blast of war blows in our ears, / Then imitate the action of the tiger; / Stiffen the sinews, summon up the blood* . . . Who could hear that and not thrill to it? *Dishonour not your mothers; now attest / That those whom you call'd fathers did beget you. / Be copy now to men of grosser blood, / And teach them how to war,* Nathaniel recited, out of breath. I don't know why I even bother.

The story with Vilma is she wanted to eat me. How could I stay married to someone who wanted to cut me up into tiny pieces and swallow every single one until I came out her other end?

You're so beautiful. So beautiful and young.

Looking not at my eyes, but my fingers, before he bit them.

His preferred instrument, Nathaniel said, was a wooden spoon. The long one, burned here and there where my mother let it sit on the pot rim too long. Among other things, it was a useful early lesson in how sound makes you feel.

At the opera, just before the lights went down, clapping his hands like a child: They say there will be a real live horse!

Nathaniel said where in the fuck are my keys have you seen my did I answer the can you help me, Will, can you help me for just a minute, I keep forgetting—

Yellow is not your color. But, Will, Nathaniel said. I fucking love you in pants.

See, Nathaniel said, how he breaks the line after *attest*?

When I was a child, I had to work, Nathaniel said. The old farmer paid me five cents for every cow pie I found, and on a good day he handed me a single seamed and grimy bill, which he fished from the pocket of his Wranglers. The spade I used for this purpose was kept on a dedicated shelf in the barn. It had a nicked wooden handle precisely the length of my palm. What I did was stand in one spot, a swell in the pasture, and look for disruptions in the tall grass. It only took finding one to get a start on it. The pies tended to cluster together, and once you found a family of them—it'd be one, then one two three four five all toppled together, then one, one two, a few feet before the squirmy-shaped one—you could clear the whole field on scent and detail alone, just reading the land, the tension in a cow's belly that said something was coming soon. I walked slowly, looking, and crouched to scoop them into a plastic feed bucket to be used later to fertilize the zucchini and cabbages. Sometimes they'd be stuck to the grass and I'd have to get down on my knees and dig them out. Those didn't smell like anything at all. The farm didn't do much. There were the cows, and a few dozen fish-belly cabbages, and some balding chickens the foxes were always after. That was my first job. When I got home my mother looked at the bowl on the table and waited until I put the coins there. She asked the farmer later how much he'd paid, so it's not like I could skim any. All the cow pies had the same stuff in them, hay and the dense, seedy particles that all living and once living things are made of. I'd squeezed a dry one before, felt it turn to powder in my hand. The farmer's name was Roland Karstu. He was born old and died old but when I worked in his field, he was twenty years younger than I am now. He's been dead awhile, since before the last time I was in Greening. I'll tell you the problem with my students. They haven't touched shit. Have you? Have you ever knelt in the dirt, drowning in your own sweat, and then, unthinking, mashed your fingers, the shit you'd just picked up, right into your own eyes? You have to be low, the lowest thing on earth, to write the truth—that's how you see it. By looking up, at everything. You have to be so low you can't miss a single fleck of shit.

Your lips are your best feature, Nathaniel said, handing over the floss. Weakness and strength, full, but just the slightest bit dry and bitten. Your teeth, though. They tell me where you're from.

Of course you're not smart enough. Nathaniel said, don't worry about that. It's not a matter of thinking, though one can always be a better thinker. It's a matter of listening—of letting the words vibrate in the space between mind and ear until, just like that, they bloom.

Wilhelmet, Nathaniel said, or Nuunuu, when he was tired. Coconut, in the morning, my pajamas still on, hair unbrushed. Little Peach, Darling Girl, Sour Patch McGleason. Wilma the Magnificent when I said something smart; Chuckwagon when I was mean.

Nathaniel said Reg couldn't kill a bear if you drugged it first, loaded the gun for him, and then pulled the trigger. I'm not sure about you. Somehow you seem like you couldn't, but I wouldn't put it past you. How, for example, did you come to live in my house?

Mothers, Nathaniel said, disgust everyone, even themselves. Someday I'll tell you the story of how mine tried to kill me.

Lipstick, Nathaniel said, pulling a twist of napkin from his jeans pocket, makes you look like a clown. Then he leaned forward and brushed the paper flecks away with his thumb.

Of another famous poet, standing at the podium in a long flannel coat, Nathaniel said: Poor man. He used to know how to write, but then he drank too much. Now you can poke a finger right through his poems, like a piece of bad fruit.

Will, what are you doing with this first person? Let me give you some advice: No one wants to listen to a young woman declaiming things about herself for pages and pages. One grows suspicious.

Second person? Absolutely never. A jazz hands move, for charlatans.

Your kindness honors me, Nathaniel said to the woman at the front of the line. Thank you. Thank you. Thank you. And how do you spell your name?

I've been married twice, Nathaniel said, pulling from the grocery bag the seedless grapes, the imported box of English breakfast, the chocolate-dipped almonds, the strip loin bleeding through its butcher paper. But for the first time, it's like I have a darling little wife.

When you get older, Nathaniel said, you'll learn that relationships are never as simple as the words we use to describe them: Friend, lover, mother, father, teacher, pet. Sometimes it's better not to try to name them. To just let them be what they are.

Of New York, Nathaniel believed what E. B. White did and said it all the time, as if he'd written it himself: No one should come to New York to live unless he is willing to be lucky.

Oh, I don't know, said Nathaniel, maybe it's different for girls.

Foil lettering. I didn't know they could afford it. They must think it's good, Nathaniel said. And look. He opened to the back cover and put his finger on my face. There you are. Sign it for me.

You want to find out who someone is? Give them everything they want and then watch what happens next.

Nathaniel said don't make it so easy.

Nathaniel said don't make it so hard.

Nathaniel said write every day.

Nathaniel said don't force it.

Nathaniel said do you know what a poem is yet?

All right, Nathaniel said. Get a clean page.

Go on, Will. Try again.

VIII

THE ART OF LOSING

1

The ultrasound machine reminded me of a robot from an eighties movie—beige and child-sized, with a blockish head containing an image, in black-and-white, of outer space. Lili had already called four times that morning. On my way out the door, Nathaniel had gestured to my phone. "Someone's trying to get you," he told me.

"There," said the only OB I'd found on Zocdoc with a same-day appointment, "is the sac." He moved the wand. "That's a nice picture, for this early. You see it? The little head." I saw a smear, rounder on one side than the other, of pixelated gray. "Sometimes it's hard," he continued, "Oh! Nope. There it is. Hear it?" In the background, the whoosh-whoosh-woosh of a microscopic bit of electricity. It seemed very improbable it was coming from anything other than the machine. "The little-bitty heartbeat!"

I took the roll of ultrasound pictures on my way out the door. A smear, with a fast, flickering heartbeat. Four images. They all looked exactly the same. On the topmost one, in tiny block print: 7 WEEKS 1 DAY. The night after I'd told Nathaniel his mother died. The OB's office was out of network for my tier of Obamacare. The visit plus ultrasound cost $271. I put it on Nathaniel's card; I had no choice. There wasn't enough in my checking account. He probably wouldn't even notice.

Just finished a draft, Lili texted me that night. I was sitting on Nathaniel's couch; he was at dinner and would be back any minute.

> *I don't know where you disappeared to, but can you read*
> *most people are okay with me sharing some of their stories but only four on the record*
> *with you I have five, that's solid I'll list out everyone else who contributed using X or something*
> *unless you have ideas for a better way?*
> *but I do need your story / name*
> *you can just add it right into this doc wherever you think it fits*
> *ughhh call me too much to text*

There was Lili's piece, sitting in my inbox, right above an email from Jennifer Kestrel, subject line, *Congratulations.* I clicked that first.

> *We have been trying to contact you for many days to share the good news: You are one of this year's three winners of the Selden Award for prose. Usually, we like to congratulate our honorees over the phone, but you are a hard person to pin down. Please call me back at your earliest convenience so we can go over some details regarding the ceremony and the distribution of your award.*

The number in her email signature was the same one I'd been silencing for weeks.

After all those years I'd dropped hints, after nominating Samson, Lili, a handful of other students, never me, Nathaniel had done it: put me up for the Selden.

For one soaring moment, winning felt as good as I'd always imagined it would.

Still on the crest of the wave, I opened Lili's doc. She'd written it like an interview. Instead of an introduction to Nathaniel's work, she'd described her methodology—how many women had participated, how she'd assigned them each a number, how she was not attributing stories to specific names, to illuminate the ubiquity of the behavior. Of the harm. Women who were comfortable sharing their identities were listed at the bottom, as signatories. Then Lili gave a bit of biographical information: where and when Nathaniel was born, the number of books he'd published, screenplays he'd written, awards he'd won. She shared details like his university salary, which I couldn't figure out how she'd gotten and was higher than I thought, and how many students, roughly, he had taught in his nearly four-decade-long teaching career. How many of those students had gone on to publish, and how many of those who did identified as female, nonbinary, or male. Interspersed between their answers were questions she'd asked of Nathaniel, with his replies. I'd forgotten about their meeting, that she'd interviewed him, too, over a long breakfast at Cafe Cluny during breaks in her conversations with the women. He hadn't arranged it with me—he and Lili had always had their own direct line.

She asked each of the women the same question first: Where did you and Nathaniel meet?

1: In the classroom, on the first day.

2: When he called me, to tell me I'd gotten into the MFA program.

11: At a party at my mother's house—she was a painter, and I was seventeen.

7: He emailed me, to tell me he liked my work.

Lili: You've talked before about how you knew you wanted to be a writer from a very young age. When did it crystallize for you, and how?

Nathaniel: I was fourteen when I started writing. My parents didn't read or write or even talk but my uncle, my mother's brother, was a man of some success, on the board of a new day school that opened near the small town in Michigan where I was born, a place devoted to the arts, and he secured my admission. Hippie stuff, back then, hardly even a school, but they had books. Fourteen, fifteen. Harrowing years, all Sturm und Drang, a time when, I have always believed, the soul is very open to its assignment. It was Yeats, Yeats in the sunlight, on the shores of the brackish lake, one toe in the water, nibbled by fish. I thought, perhaps I'll give it a try.

Lili: You've won many significant awards. Can you talk about what a prize does for a writer, and how that recognition changed—or didn't—the way you work, how you move through the world as a writer?

Nathaniel: The thing to remember about an award is that it doesn't have anything to do with you, and you should not allow it for one instant to disrupt your inner machinery. Prizes have allowed me to keep some better foods in my refrigerator and have funded useful assistance of various kinds. Tremendous gifts. Otherwise, I try not to think about them at all, especially when I am winning.

Lili: Have you ever won an award for your creative work?

5: No.

2: I have won one award. When I was an MFA student. I don't think the program gives it anymore. After the ceremony, Nathaniel took me out for dinner. Under the table—we had both had a lot to drink, and I was flirting with him. I was. I was so flattered he wanted to be there, when he could be anywhere, with me. He told me he was the one who decided the winner. Under the table—first it was just our legs, and then he put a hand, and then he took it away. In between the entrées and dessert, he inserted two fingers between my legs. Into my vagina. No contest, he kept telling me. It had been no contest. Under the table—he had to reach, sort of under the table to do it, with his arm, and I was afraid people sitting near us would understand what he was doing. I was very aware of that. He kept his nails long for a man. It was something I'd noticed in class. He'd get chalk—he always used blue. I gasped. The sound, I tried to swallow it, and it came out wrong. I think he thought—

1: No.

4: No.

Lili: How would you describe Nathaniel's influence on your writing, and on your life?

There was more to read, but I couldn't. I slammed the computer shut. Before I locked myself in the twin bedroom, I dry-heaved into the toilet in the half bath, nothing coming up but bile.

Everything I wanted. I guess I'd finally earned it.

Will

are you okay?

I didn't get up the next morning until I heard Nathaniel leave. There was a note from him on the counter: *The coffee thingy is broken!* When I went to make a pot, I saw that it was simply not plugged in.

That afternoon, I took the F train to Lili's. It was dusk when I emerged from the subway, and feathery snowflakes had started to fall. I stopped at Taco King and ordered six carne asada tacos, extra salsa on the side, with chips and guac. Lili's order. Right before her block, I ducked into the organic wine store and bought a bottle of pinot noir. A nicer one than usual, as if to commemorate the thing that was about to happen. I paid with Nathaniel's card.

I rang the bell and then let myself in; she'd left the door unlocked for me. The house smelled like butter and cheese. Ansel, butt naked, was trying to climb up the side of the sectional in the front room while Jake laughed.

Lili was on her laptop at the island in the kitchen. I unpacked the tacos, opened the wine, poured a glass and set it right next to her typing hands.

"I'm sorry, one sec," she said. More typing. "Okay, sorry, hi." She shut the laptop. "You read it."

"I read it."

"You're not drinking," she asked, looking at my water.

"Not tonight."

"You're not pregnant, are you?" she said, and then laughed at her own joke. "So, what do you think."

"I think it's powerful, and you're amazing. I can't believe how quickly you got it together. It's"—my voice broke, even though I tried to stop it—"overwhelming to see all their stories in one place, right up against his voice."

"I'm only waiting on a few people to sign off. Do you think I should send it to everyone who came to the group thing, just as a courtesy? Oh, and I added your name to the signatories but I still need your contribution. Andrei won't do it, of course. But it's fine. *The Spectacle* is going to run it online, as a feature. They have a bigger following anyway, at least of internet people."

"You need to take my name off. I'm sorry."

"Not quite as satisfying as getting Nathaniel in his own backyard, but—" Lili looked at me. "You're scared about your job. But I promise, I will help. I've already sent like fifteen emails. Adam—remember him?—he needs an assistant, his current one is a grade-A idiot. He's very interested. And that's a real job, at an actual agency." I knew the kind of job she was talking about. It paid thirty thousand a year, on the books. There would be a background check. A documented place where the debt collectors could find me. Everyone in the office would have a BA or an MFA from schools up and down the East Coast. They'd want to know what it was like working for the great writer. After Lili's piece, they'd want to know exactly what he did to me—they'd ask, or they wouldn't. Either way, they'd think they knew. "I know you're losing your place—you can stay here, as long as you need. I can float you some money. It's fine. I'm happy to help. But you've got to get out of this situation. It's time, Will. It's way past time."

"I already lost my place."

"God, I'm hungry," Lili said, reaching for a taco. She took a huge bite, and some meat dropped out of the end back onto her plate. "Wait, what? So where are you staying?"

"With Nathaniel."

"For how long?" she asked warily.

"Since July. And on and off other times before that, over the years. For almost a year, when I first got to New York."

"A year? Hang on." She was speaking slowly, figuring it out. "So you lied about needing a place? And the whole time I've been talking to the women? You were just going back to his *apartment*?"

"I lied about a lot of things." It was a relief to admit it, even though Lili was looking at me like she'd never seen me before. "I do need a place. I don't *want* to stay there—"

"Did you tell him about the piece?"

"Of course not, Lil, Jesus." Did she really think I would? A vicious, wounded feeling streaked through me. I'd tamped it down before—when she underestimated my work, at all those restaurants when she ordered the fucking hamachi crudo and then told the waiter to split the check down the middle—but now I couldn't control it. I probably should have left then and there. Instead, I opened my mouth. "Honestly, though. I think you're being irresponsible."

"Oh, I can't wait to hear this." She leaned back, crossing her arms.

"It's horrifying, reading their stories. It makes me sick. But situations like these—they have nuance. There's another side."

"Whose side, Will? Yours or his?"

"I think you're trying to make something very complicated black-and-white." I didn't know I thought that, but saying it, I felt both cold and certain, and as radioactively ashamed as I had the morning I'd woken up in the party barn.

"What's complicated about this?" she said. "Spell it out for me."

In the other room, Ansel started howling. "Can you guys keep it down," Jake shouted as Ansel's wails migrated up the stairs.

"Maybe you'd know if you paid any attention," I said, because I couldn't answer her actual question without my life falling apart. "How many times, in the last five years, have I been to your place?"

"What are you talking about?"

"Like, hundreds? Would you say? And how many times have you come to mine?"

"That shithole you don't even live in anymore?"

"Three."

"You never invited me."

"Not true," I said, though of course it was.

"I have a *baby*. I can't just zip over to Manhattan."

"He's one! What's your excuse for the other years?"

"Wow. Now that I know you're a liar, so many things about you finally make sense. Let me tell you something. Your life only sucks because of your stupid choices. It's truly disturbing, how much you hate yourself."

"At least I'm not just some sad mom trying to use other women's trauma to make myself feel important. How long has it been since you wrote anything? Not including this."

"Just a mom," Lili said. Her voice had been deadly calm, but now there was a crack in it. I was the one who'd scared the baby. "Just a mom, huh."

"He touched your waist. Boo-hoo."

"Get out," she told me.

There was a flower arrangement on the console by the front door. Eucalyptus and lush white lilies and little crimson twisty things. Every week, she had flowers delivered. I saw the invoice once, taped to the brown paper wrapping, before she threw it away. $149. A small thing, but it brings me cheer, she'd said, switching the water. I did the math automatically: six hundred dollars a month, give or take a few bucks, $7,200 a year. Poor little Will, Lili had hissed, as I stood up to leave. She had a shred of cilantro on her gumline. Came to New York without a buck and tried to fuck her way to the top. I guess you'll have to find something else you're good at.

I picked up the flowers, vase and all, and took them with me into the snow.

When I got back to the apartment, Nathaniel was out, as I knew he would be—he had theater tickets. I put the flowers on the dining table, where his coffee mug still sat, a few inches of murk at the bottom. I picked it up, to load it into the dishwasher, and then I set it back down. In the spare room—my room—the bed was made.

In the end, I packed one of his rolling suitcases with almost nothing: clothes, a few books from his living room shelf (*The House of Mirth, The Complete Poems of Elizabeth Bishop, Giovanni's Room*), toiletries and my tennis shoes, some granola bars from the pantry. It seemed like there should have been more. I looked for a long time at the box of author copies of my book. I had five hardcovers left. I put them all on Nathaniel's shelf, and then I picked up the coffee mug, washed it in the sink, and placed it upside down on a clean washcloth to dry.

After that, I left.

At the Garment District Holiday Inn, I paid for a fourteen-day stay up front with Nathaniel's card. In case he tried to cancel it, whenever he realized I was really gone. The Selden check came in installments. Two. The first one, for fifteen thousand dollars, was distributed at the ceremony, along with a certificate commemorating the honor. I would stay at the Holiday Inn until the event. I could collect my check and find somewhere else to go. The second check would be mailed to me in January. Better for tax purposes, the administrator said.

When they asked me to confirm my mailing address, I gave them my mother's.

2

Lili's Great Talk went up the first week of December. The cover image was a group shot from the gathering we'd hosted, taken from the stairwell—Jake must have held the camera, at some point after I left, but I felt, looking at it, almost as if I'd taken the photo, so perfectly did it capture how I'd experienced them in the minutes before I walked away, glancing backward at the group before disappearing down the hall. They were unidentifiable, faces blurred, but you could get a sense of individuality from clothes and skin color, from the different ways they held their bodies. I wondered if their children would know them, their partners. Nathaniel.

For a period that felt very long while it was happening, Lili's article seemed to be the only story on the internet. At first the response was enthusiastic. Lili was brave; she was a hero. But within days, even people who'd celebrated the story expressed doubts. Why was it written this way? If these accounts are true, why did so many women leave off their names? Someone made a GIF of the last line of my old interview—*I just think some of that stuff is overblown*—over picture of a blond girl standing in a field while a fire roared behind her, and people on both sides started tweeting it. I made my account private. I stopped logging in. Some days, I didn't leave the Holiday Inn at all. The only person I saw was Dev. "You are going to be okay," he said, after taking one look at my face. I'd met him in Madison Square for the twenty minutes he could steal from work. "But can I just say? Lili is a badass."

When I got back to my room, I logged into Nathaniel's email. He still hadn't changed his password. Every day I checked.

The famous university asked that Nathaniel not come back for the spring semester until they conducted a review of the allegations from former students, referring specifically to the account of the prizewinner using only the vaguest language: table, accusation, touching. Once that was over, the dean assured him, he would be cleared to teach again. In the meantime, he'd be paid as usual. Nathaniel's lawyer said not to worry. This was all too common lately, and Lili's piece was nothing. From a legal standpoint, it was as relevant as—he used this example—somebody claiming they'd gotten a bruise from a bad dream. His lawyer told him not to talk about it, just to be on the safe side, with anyone. I read the emails, and if Nathaniel hadn't read them yet, I marked them as new. He got other emails, too. From women, a few men. He didn't respond very often. To one woman, who wrote only, all in lower case with no punctuation, *im glad this is finally happening to you,* Nathaniel responded: *I am sorry you feel that way. It seems we may have experienced our relationship differently.* To Vilma, who wrote, *you should sue,* he replied: *I left the bathroom window open with the door shut overnight, and in the morning the tiny cactus Will put on the tank was covered in frost!* He'd attached a blurry photo—he knew how to do that? The cactus in its pink pot looked as it always did. There was my shampoo, lined up on the rim of the tub.

I didn't want to, but I couldn't help it. I was worried about Lili, and I was worried about Nathaniel, too.

Nathaniel, who'd been on the not-so-secret panel of judges for the Selden Awards pretty much since he'd won one himself forty years before, had been removed from the ceremony, though not disinvited. Another thing I knew because of his emails. Jennifer Kestrel wrote him a cautious, apologetic message, explaining that recent feedback from community members had made the board reconsider their decision to have Nathaniel represent the foundation as keynote speaker.

They were sorry about the short notice, and they wanted Nathaniel to know they valued his many years of service. He would still receive his honorarium and was welcome to attend the event; however, everyone would very much understand if he chose not to, and could he please let them know soon what his plans were?

I could see her, Jennifer Kestrel, tucked away at a desk in some office on a middle floor in the lower reaches of Manhattan. How long had it taken her to write the email, to pitch each sentence just right—clear and to the point, but with curved edges, so as not to anger Nathaniel or the three men who were on cc. No one could say—regardless of how she felt, writing his name, entering in all four email addresses—that she hadn't done her job.

Will. Nathaniel texted. *Wilhelmet, I have wanted to be respectful of what is clearly a demand for space, but there are matters we need to discuss. Please, dear one. A walk. That's all I ask.*

Don't tell me you believe all this rubbish

And then, a little later. *Perhaps you think I don't know how to do things like check my credit card statements. I have never been helpless, Will. That was just a game I played for you. I know you are sleeping in that cheerless department store hotel near the flower shops. I know about the noodles you're ordering, the outfit you bought just yesterday, for the Selden event I presume, and without so much as thanks to me for either the item or the occasion at which you will wear it. Notice how I do not cancel the card? Notice how I let you pretend you are the director of what is happening now?*

Later, still. *You will be receiving a call. If you want your way out, I suggest you answer.*

In the middle of the night.

I do miss you oh yes I do miss you, your little smells and padding feet setting things right on all the shelves
perhaps
if you forsake me

I will have to move
change my whole life

3

There was the Morgan Library, spotlights roaming its stone face. I entered through the modern façade on Madison Avenue, following the noise of the party into the first-floor library room, with its walls of books reaching up to the ceiling. The ceremony would be in the lobby, which had been transformed into a dining room, round tables clustered around a raised stage. They brought the fake olive trees in special, too. At the end of the night, people like I used to be, before I was a winner—assistants, interns, the library's security staff—could take the flower arrangements home. The ones left behind went straight into the trash. But first, hors d'oeuvres and champagne amongst the books, and under the banner announcing the night's honorees.

My face was between the two other winners for prose, the size of a recycling bin. Reg had taken the headshots for my publisher, one sunny afternoon as we walked along the Hudson River. I looked a little astonished, but pretty, which was how I felt that day, how I often felt when I saw my book in a shop window or on a table at an event where I was to read. As if I'd just found something wonderful on the ground, dropped by someone else. My face was partly in profile, and it looked like I wasn't wearing makeup, though I was—expensive mascara, nipple-colored lipstick, something called a skin tint, layered glossily over my actual face. The dress I'd worn was red and covered with tiny white flowers, the fabric so thin it seemed cheap, but wasn't. When the sun started to sink over the river, Reg had been very worried I would be cold. I'm fine, I'd said, and he pointed at my arms, covered from wrist to bicep with goosebumps. Tonight, I wore black because I didn't want to be looked at. I had bought it new—Nathaniel was right. It cost $289 and was two long triangles of silk connected at the neck. Except for my shoulder blades, which were naked and pale, no part of my body could be deciphered beneath the fabric.

The other winners stood around a tall table, each holding a flute of champagne. Some of the guests looked their way with awe and envy. I remembered opening Bryan Millets's novel and putting it on the new release shelf in Nathaniel's office at some point in the late summer. Bryan was blushing, even though no one appeared to be saying anything to him at all. I hadn't read any of the others—I'd always taken Nathaniel's advice to heart, that to become a true original, one must be an apprentice not to one's contemporaries, but to the artists of the past—and as I joined them, this made me first embarrassed, and then sad, since they all seemed familiar with each other, friendly even.

"I really liked your book," said one of the poets.

"Thank you," I said. She blinked up at me, Lili-sized with buzzed hair and a nose ring, waiting.

I knew what I was supposed to say. "Your poems are so good."

"Champagne?" asked Bryan, his face turning a darker shade of red as he nodded toward the waiter at my shoulder.

"I'm okay."

"Do you guys know who nominated you?" asked the other prose writer, who was wearing, amazingly, jeans and a white T-shirt. On her feet, a pair of black high heels. She was pretty in exactly the way Nathaniel liked, and there it was, the usual boring pang—was she good, too?

"Not me," said Bryan. "Though I think it was maybe my MFA mentor?" When our names were called, a slide featuring our headshot and a quote from our book would appear on the giant projector behind the collapsible stage, and with it, in large letters at the top, the name of the writer who had put us up for the prize. When the emcee revealed the nominator, sometimes it got a bigger "ah" than the quote. Before the ceremony started, you could try to guess who'd nominated who based on the writers in attendance, a game Lili and I had liked to play in the years before Nathaniel nominated her, when she attended as a representative for *Belvedere* and I came to make sure Nathaniel didn't drink too much or, if he was speaking, lose track of his notes.

Across the room, floating between various tables, were several of Nathaniel's people, though I did not see him. Over by a lit-up case holding very rare and expensive books was Samson, talking to a group of flannelly MFA guys who were, for the night, wearing suits while they drank their whiskeys from the open bar. Andrei, Lili's former boss, appeared to be threatening a couple of older women with a small quiche. The poets were saying something about money. Bryan was talking about prepub reviews, and how his four stars had made all the difference. Vilma was sailing between tables in a purple jumpsuit that looked like a cross between pajamas and cruise-wear, with violets—I just knew they were real—twined into her braided hair. And then, Lili, late; she was grabbing a glass of champagne from a waiter when we saw each other. She didn't look angry, but she didn't wave or smile. Her dress was awkward, a shirt-y thing, floor length, tied higher than her natural waist. She looked worn out, her red lipstick bleeding slightly past the boundaries of her mouth. I raised my hand, but she turned away, grabbing the arm of someone else she knew.

Jennifer Kestrel ushered us, with much effort, toward the dining room, where we would be seated for the ceremony—the welcome and intro during the salad, the keynote and readings during dinner, dessert served afterward, buffet-style, while dance music turned the lobby into a nerdy club. A few donors sat in a place of honor at every single table, thronged by famous writers who'd gotten comp tickets, or former winners who could speak movingly about how much the money and recognition had changed their lives, or publishing industry people with their decadent, illicit gossip and funny asides. It was the publishing people, not the writers, who were the most fun to sit with—another of Nathaniel's opinions that I'd found mostly true. The winners' table was docile and anxious. A very old man and his beautiful forty-something wife, probably billionaires, smiled benevolently at each of us as we sat down.

"Too many teeth," yelled the wife, across the table at me. My novel was called *Hyperdontia;* I was surprised she'd read it. Her hair was as black as mine and stabbed into a sloppy pile on top of her head with a handful of ivory tusks. Were those actual jewels, glittering on her eyelids?

"That's me," I said. The writer in the T-shirt laughed. "Thanks for reading," I told her. I stuffed bread into my mouth before the swell of nausea could rise.

A waiter appeared, a divot of concentration on her forehead, and silently distributed the salads, fluffs of wet lettuce interrupted here and there by a whisker of carrot. I lifted my fork. Across from me, lettuce disappeared, one shred at a time, into a vast dark space between the old man's lips. I had the sensation, unique to pregnancy, of my tongue multiplying, and I put my fork down. Onstage, Jennifer Kestrel was giving the program welcome, and then she was introducing the director, and then the director was welcoming the keynote speaker, who was not Nathaniel—of course not, I knew that already, so why did I look up, pulse racing in a hideous, eager way—but instead, *Samson,* who, I'd forgotten, had published his second book after all, to excellent reviews and many longlists. The poet with the buzz cut gripped my arm, thrilled. Her fingernails were perfect ovals, painted brown.

Samson was overjoyed to be here. Samson was thankful to the Selden Foundation for giving him his start, his real start. Samson wanted to recognize the work of the foundation in championing underrepresented and diverse voices, like those of tonight's winners—he gestured to the banner, where some of the faces belonged to women, some were Black or brown—and then he thanked, in a genuine way that made me ashamed of my bitterness, the people who had paid for it all. This has been a year of necessary and long overdue reckoning, he said, especially within our own community, and the room got a little itchy, murmurs bubbling up and meeting surprise or silence, as people either nodded or pretended not to understand what Samson was talking about. These books, these writers, Samson went on, tackle with verve and courage the oppressive forces that limit our literature. The prose writer in the T-shirt leaned over to Bryan, asked him, without bothering to whisper, if he thought Samson meant she won because her book was sort of about rape. Bryan's face deepened to a new color. "Oh no," he said. "I don't think so! I think it's just, like, political work."

Samson said more about how winning the Selden had funded—along with his parents, he did not add—the writing of his second book, which was the reason he was standing before us all on this beautiful night. What one had to do was follow the secret voice within, even when nobody else could hear it. This was the truth only each of us special winners could hear—until we wrote it, that is, and gave it as a gift to readers everywhere. Following private truths was what all of us at the winners' table had done, and why we were here tonight, about to receive large checks that would be immensely relieving in the instant before they vanished, especially for some of us. Next to me, the poet's eyes glimmered. The bejeweled woman and her husband were almost done with the steak. The prose writer in the T-shirt was texting. Bryan looked like he'd seen God himself. On instinct, I cast around for Lili. She was listening attentively, her arm propped on the table, chin in her hand. Right. They were friends. We all were.

Samson concluded. Applause. On his way back to his table, he squeezed my shoulder, bent down to whisper: "Congrats." So, he had read it? If I could bear to stay one minute past dessert I vowed, once and for all, to ask him to his face. I tracked Samson back to his table, and there, in the purply dark, was an old man, with an empty chair to his left and a donor—you could tell by the clothes and hair—to his right. The man was looking at his plate. He was leaning across the table to say something to Samson, who ignored him. He was wearing a bad suit for the occasion—even in the dim light, I could see it was pin-striped, that he'd forgotten a tie, and I feared for his socks, which were almost certainly athletic, and visible beneath his pant hems. He did not seem to be looking for me, but when, after the three poets finished their readings, Jennifer Kestrel called my name, I could feel his eyes as I moved toward the screen, which still bore the name and face of the previous winner. I arranged myself before the microphone, glad the spotlight made it impossible to discern a single face. All the other winners had thanked rafts of people before they read. Gratitude, yes. Oh, I knew the feeling. I remembered how it shuddered through me every time I unlocked the sculptor's studio door. How it tasted, in the mornings after my first night at Nathaniel's for what both of us knew would be a longer stay. When he handed me a stack of pages, striped with red. When my phone vibrated, Reg or Lili texting me back. When I emerged from the subway, into the very city where I lived, as recently as that very day, the city I was about to lose. Gratitude, that's what I'd called it, pulling back the shower curtain, telling Nathaniel okay, you can come in.

The audience didn't like that I was up there without saying anything. I could feel what they wanted, even without seeing their faces; maybe that was my truest talent, shaping myself into whatever people wanted me to be. I thanked the foundation, and I began to read.

It had been hard, to select a passage of no more than three minutes that did not feel, in the end, like it had been written by Nathaniel, or for him, or for people who liked books like his. Because I hadn't taken any copies with me when I left for the Holiday Inn, I had scanned through my book—mold, mold, mold—in the Union Square Barnes and Noble. In the end, I settled on a description of Greening in July. From the first chapter, right before the protagonist's mother meets the dentist. Good—fine—a bit boring, Nathaniel had gone after it in the margins draft after draft after draft, but on his final read, he seemed to have forgotten or given up, and he'd left the passage alone. It pleased me, this little thing, all mine, I had shepherded all the way here, to a room of listeners I'd dreamed of since my days creeping around Rosendale. At the hotel, I'd re-created the passage from memory, and that re-creation was what I read—no more than six sentences, a shorter reading, even, than some of the poets.

"The blackberries had come early," I concluded. "Thank you." Uncertain applause. Somewhere out there, Nathaniel was, what? Clapping along? Shaking his head?

I was at the lip of the stage, on the bottom step, back in the darkness, where I could see that Nathaniel wasn't looking at me at all. He was leaning over, as if to tell a joke to his neighbor. Lili still had her hands pressed together before her chest, and was trying, it seemed, to meet my eyes. Behind me, Jennifer Kestrel was saying thank you for that. Saying, "Wilhelmina Miles, winner in prose." Oh, it thrilled me, hearing my name alongside *winner.* For one more second, even after everything, it did. And then: "Nominated by Vilma Wise."

I stopped, looked back. There was her name, at the top of the slide.

Applause again, louder and more sure-footed, and then Lili's unmistakable reading whoop, an abrasive sound that always embarrassed me but never failed to send a shock of good feeling through an audience. Angry as she was, Lili knew how much the Selden meant—when I heard her, I knew, even if we never spoke again, that she still loved me. Vilma was sitting a few tables away, perched on the edge of her chair as if it did not have a back. She lifted her glass to me but did not smile. Bryan's turn. There he went, up the stairs to the stage. Jennifer Kestrel clicked something over at the podium, and as Bryan fiddled with the microphone height, the slide changed, replacing my large face with his. At the top, right above the quote from Bryan's book, in glowing white type:

NOMINATOR—NATHANIEL FELLOW.

IX

HOME IS SO SAD.
IT STAYS AS IT WAS LEFT—

1

The boy didn't knock. I'd only just arrived and had left the office door—my office door—open. He came right in, saying hello as he crossed the threshold, and then, when I spun around from the bookshelves: "You are Wilhelmina Miles, right? The visiting writer?" He sat in the armchair across from the desk, forcing me to take the teacher's seat. The desk hadn't been cleared off before my arrival, and it felt intrusive to rest my forearms on the piles of student poetry from semesters past, watched by a family photo under the lamp. Two grinning teenage boys standing slightly ahead of their father, the man I was subbing in for, a hairy fellow of about forty-five with seventies sideburns, wearing a denim shirt Nathaniel would have liked. An unwrapped protein bar balanced, bridge-like, across an old mug full of coffee-ish murk, giving off a fungal smell. The tutor—that's what they called teachers, here at Rosendale—had recently been diagnosed with cancer, and was taking one semester, possibly two, of medical leave. I didn't know what cancer. But the state of the office. If I had to guess, it was a bad kind. I tried to sweep the thought away, what the bad cancer might mean for me, if I did a good enough job. I didn't even want to be here.

The office was ablaze with icy January sun, the eastern wall all window. So bright the boy was nearly invisible, a pair of colorless eyes blinking above the twin points of his Rosendale collar. Classes didn't begin for another two days. Why was he wearing his uniform? A cloud passed and he took shape—sixteen or thereabouts, milky wrists speckled with hearts drawn in pen, a copy of my novel in his lap, stuffed with wings of torn paper.

"Can I help you with something?"

"I loved your book," he said. "Usually the teachers here are, like, older. I had this feeling, when I was reading it, that it was talking right to my life." He leaned forward so that his tie, the skinny mauve one even the girls wear here, draped across the open mouth on the cover. I had an urge to laugh. Not at him, not really, but it was so strange to imagine this boy, with his tidy uniform and eager face, underlining sentences in my book about a girl who kills her mother's boyfriend after he rapes her. "When I saw your name on the course list, I couldn't believe it was you—that the author of *Hyperdontia* was going to teach here."

He was bullshitting, trying to plaster over his desire to win my favor with something he thought I'd like better, but I warmed to him anyway. It was impossible not to. Nathaniel, shaking his head after a student meeting: I don't know what they want from me. I'd read it as irritation, felt implicated by it—why wouldn't everybody just leave the great man alone, so he could write, or think, or just be!—but there'd been a note of something else in his voice, a little upward, marveling gust of wind. Hadn't he welcomed them, one after another, told them, go ahead, shut the door? "Ha," I said. "Well, it's beautiful country." Quoting Nathaniel, every time he visited a nowhere city.

I'd gotten in the previous evening, after waiting out the days until faculty moved in on the couch at Dev's new studio. At the Quincy airport I was picked up by a minivan shuttle, the driver an unofficial ambassador of Rosendale, giving me the full tour as he pulled into campus. "Really," I'd said, when he told me about the dance majors, their annual production of *The Nutcracker*. And then, when he pointed out Warren, "Good to know," as if my mother weren't somewhere inside, working on the welcome week menu. The minivan bumped down the unpaved road where my residence was tucked in a semicircle of pines. They were all the same, those depressing shoeboxes for the visiting artists, but when I dragged my suitcase up the steps and into the narrow room, I felt like I had my first day in New York. A twin-sized bed with mothy sheets, a wood-burning fireplace, a kitchenette, stocked with milk and bread and butter and eggs. Mine alone. A solid desk, underneath a sturdy window; a door that locked in two places. And free—or free-ish—a supplement to my stipend for the term, which was about 10 percent of a single student's annual tuition. I also had health insurance. The faculty plan; much better than my mother's. The co-pay for ER visits was one hundred dollars. For childbirth, at least in the state of Michigan, it was thirty-five dollars. I was telling myself it didn't mean I was leaning any way, how I'd checked that benefit first.

"There's the part," he continued, looking not at me, but at the Hopper print on the wall above my head, "where the girl, she wonders if what she feels is real—before anything happens. When he's only the dentist, sort of watching her a lot. That felt really true to me." Nathaniel heard things like this about his work from student after student. There's always another meaning directly behind what someone says, Nathaniel had told me once. I try to talk to that, in my work and in my life. The sky had gone overcast, and the room felt smaller, bookshelves towering against the walls. I could ask the boy. The question was in the air, an eager little creature with its own heartbeat, begging for attention. Did something bad happen to you? An older friend, maybe, a beloved uncle, a coach nobody expected. I could ask. He wanted me to; I could sense it.

"Thank you," I said. "Thank you very much for reading it."

The boy reddened violently—I wasn't sure what to make of that—and then raised his copy, pushed it across the desk toward me.

"Will you? I have a pen," he said, handing me one.

"Oh. Sure. To?"

"Benji," he said. "I'm a second-year junior. I'm in your poetry class."

"I'll see you in a couple of days, then." I handed back the book.

"Or maybe sooner. I come here all the time to write."

"Okay, then."

We looked at each other. "Okay!" I said, again.

He stood up slowly, as if waiting for me to say something else, and then trudged to my door, his salt-stained backpack hooked over one shoulder. I could feel I'd disappointed him.

On the other side of the window, the pine trees glittered with ice, a cluster of nuthatches rising in a swirl from the uppermost branches as Benji walked by swinging a knobbly branch. A girl in a red coat was a few paces down the road and Benji jogged to reach her, lifting the back of her coat with the stick so she swirled around, laughing, to face him. They veered off the road and into a path in the woods. I knew that path, those trees. The tacky lemon taste of my fingertips after I traced the initials carved into their bark, pledges from people I'd never met. The same taste as the cleaning fluid Mom used on the cafeteria tables, a flavor that started in the back of the nose. Hadn't I told Lili, the two of us tilted into each other on an A train in the middle of the night, on our way to or from some ridiculous party during those glowing years when we first became friends, that if I ever went back home it would be because I was dead, or because I'd failed so completely, I had no other choice? She'd put a hand right on top of my head, like she was giving me a blessing, her voice melty from a hundred plastic cups of white wine, and said, "You, Wilhelmina Miles, are destined for better things." There were so many times I could have told her the truth about Nathaniel. So many ways for this to have played out, instead of the story I was living.

On my desk, a paper strip had slipped out of Benji's copy. In fading pencil, he'd written: *Meaning of title? Too many teeth? Whose teeth?*

Hers, Benji. She's the one with too many teeth. She's not supposed to use them. She's supposed to keep her mouth closed, to sit with what happened for years and years, letting it change the shape of her bones while he gets up in the morning, goes to work, sticks his fingers in someone else's mouth. Instead, she shoots him.

One reviewer had asked: Isn't what she does worse?

The gigantic black phone on the desk bleated once, twice, and I raised it to my ear. It had a cord—an object, like this whole place, from the deep past. "Oh good, you're there," said the program director. She seemed out of breath, just as she had in the voicemail she'd left right after the Selden ceremony, following up on a reference from Nathaniel, about Rosendale's urgent need for a visiting writer.

I'd let it sit for days, but when she emailed, asking again, I sent what passed for my CV, which was really a list of publications with the Selden Award on top, Barth listed with no graduation date. She'd called an hour later. "Oh, thank God," she said, "the semester starts in *weeks*." She launched into an interview without pleasantries. I muddled through her questions about how my nonexistent teaching experience might apply to teenagers ("I've sat in on so many workshops," I said, "and I remember what it was like to be a teenager, so vulnerable . . ."), and when she asked if I had questions for her, I confirmed she understood I had no college degree. "Nathaniel told me about that," she said. "It's unconventional, but the book is the primary credential. And the Selden, of course. And your references, which are phenomenal." Reference. Her voice dropped to a new register. "Tell me," she said. "As his—someone who knows him well. Do you think what's happening to Nathaniel is fair? It all just feels a little . . . hysterical." They'd been classmates at Rosendale. He'd never mentioned her to me, but several times on the call she alluded to their long history. "Hysterical," I repeated, attempting neutrality. "Maybe." She hired me a few minutes later.

The sun was back, and I squinted into it, standing up to search for a shade. The phone cord trailed behind me, knocking a stack of books off the corner of the desk. The director was saying something, sotto voce, about the tutor I'd replaced. "His poor, poor family," she concluded as I pulled a string and a shade thundered down over the window, casting the room into darkness. "Actually. Are you free now? Come down to Warren and meet me for a coffee. I'll get you all caught up." Warren—the long, windowed cafeteria would be quiet at this hour, breakfast service over. It was unlikely I'd see my mother, who'd be well into lunch prep already, but the coffees would need to be finished before she came out to check the restock, clipboard in hand, her hair clenched in a plastic claw.

"I'll just grab my coat."

"Wonderful," the director said. Repeated, "We have much to discuss." His name pressed against the edge of her sentence. The morning prickle of his jaw against the curve of my neck, the fetid tang of his socked feet, nosing my legs on the couch.

I hung up.

Warren had gotten a makeover in the years since I'd seen it—new tile under the food stations, a creamy matte color, and they'd removed the window blinds, so the room appeared to be bobbing over the lake. Instead of round islands floating through the dining section and inviting students to self-select into cliques, there were homey rows of long wooden tables, benches. I wondered if my mother had made those choices, if, after poring over the student surveys she begged the kids to fill out every year, she'd lobbied her boss for the sparkling water tap at the drink station, right alongside the juices. How often she—a person who rolled her eyes at anyone who used anything other than whole milk—had to refill the carafes of almond and oat, replace their labels with fresh Sharpie. The director wasn't there yet. I had the urge I always did when surrounded by resources—to take as much as I could without anyone noticing. I drank a sparkling water cut with cranberry between bites of banana. I was still chewing when the director appeared.

"Wilhelmina," she said. "You knew just where to go."

I swallowed. "I guess that's true."

"We keep a coffee station out all day, every day, for impromptu meetings like this one and in case any hungry student wanders through," she said, as if she'd set it up herself. Her hair was witchy and long—dark brown with few grays, as if she'd dyed it that very morning. She was wearing, when she unzipped her coat, a dress that appeared to be made of boiled wool, stiff and mauve with visible golden stitches on the cuffs and neckline.

We moved together, each carrying a steaming mug, to a table in the center of the room, sliding onto opposite benches. I'd never sat at a table in Warren before. I'd wiped them, hid under them, dropped off, before events, tiny vases full of fake bluebells, arranging each dead center. But I'd never sat down. The view was different.

The director rustled around in her shoulder bag and pulled out a folder with my name on it. For a moment, I was afraid I was already being let go—the debt collectors had gotten in touch, or @fuxboi had sent some DM, or maybe it was Nathaniel, rescinding whatever good word he'd given, as I was still refusing to answer his calls and texts—but then the director began to go over a list of contacts in the administrative offices. She pulled out a patchily printed campus map, and I let her tell me where the library was, the various copy machines, the gym, drawing a little path in pen from my residence to each building of interest.

"Do you have everything you need for your first class?"

"I think so," I said. Sensing her real question, I recited my plan for the first weeks: writing prompts to break the ice and generate material for workshop, a beefy packet of poems including classics, contemporary work, and a couple of poets who'd recently gone viral, a listening "field trip" to the meadow behind the writing house, and an erasure exercise that involved cutting up newspapers. Leah, of all people, had helped me with the syllabus. She'd reached out a few times, less because of the Nathaniel fallout than her eagerness for proximity to a winner of the Selden Award, I suspected, but I would have been regurgitating Nathaniel's first-year MFA workshop if it hadn't been for her PDF of prompts, her sample syllabi, her notes in track changes asking if I really wanted to break down Shakespeare's sonnets with a bunch of fifteen-year-olds.

The director smiled. I'd passed. "How lucky for us that you're here," she said. "And on such short notice. Sometimes the stars do align." Maybe not in her office, but one nearby, there was a computer with an archive containing every application from the year I'd applied to Rosendale. My tortured portfolio of high school poems. When I'd sent the employment paperwork to HR, I'd worried they would pull some lever in the system, drag up that application and whatever rejection notes accompanied it—or even some record of my mother's, another Miles in the Rosendale machine. But nothing happened. It seemed that rejected girl; my mother; and me, the visiting artist, were, for Rosendale's purposes, entirely separate entities.

We'd gathered our things and were standing near the double doors leading out to the mall when my mother entered, carrying two large bags from Gordon Food Service. Something she needed for dinner must have gone missing or spoiled. She was trying to open the door with her shoulder, and I grabbed the handle, pulling it for her. "Thanks," she said. And then: "Oh. You're here."

I'd told my mother about the job, but I hadn't seen her yet. When she offered to pick me up from the airport, I told her Rosendale had already made arrangements—we had tentative plans to meet up that evening, after her shift, for dinner at a Tray-less location near campus. The position, I'd told her over email, was temporary. Just a semester. Long enough for me to get another project underway. The city was wearing me out. I wanted teaching experience. I left Nathaniel out of it, and the Selden, too. But my mother liked to click around on her computer at night, and it wouldn't have surprised me if she'd read Lili's piece, the dozens of responses it spawned, the long threads on Twitter. I knew she kept track of the reviews of my novel—in our fights about it, sometimes she referenced things people said in Amazon ratings.

"Yes—got in yesterday," I said.

"You two know each other?" the director said to my mother as she pulled her gloves from her coat pocket.

"We do," said my mother. She was still holding the bags, keeping them away from the slurry of snow and salt and mud on the floor. They were heavy—she kept adjusting them against her hips.

"Oh, goodness—that's right. I keep forgetting you grew up near here, Wilhelmina." The director had pulled her phone out with her gloves and was holding it with both hands, trying to pretend she wasn't looking at her notifications. Maybe that's why she didn't notice how alike my mother and I looked. "How nice to have contacts in town, especially in winter."

"Can I get one of those for you?" I said, gesturing to the grocery bags. The director looked at me with a glimmer of impatience—I was supposed to walk her to her next meeting.

"I don't need any help from you," my mother said, heaving the bags upward. "But I do have to get this stuff squared away," she added, her tone lighter. "Nice to see you both."

"Mary," the director said, reaching out with her phone and touching my mother's arm. "I must tell you—I just love the new baked eggs you're doing for breakfast." One of the bags was slipping, and my mother, sighing, let it slide down her body, keeping the toe of her boot underneath it so the paper didn't get entirely soaked.

"That's great," she said.

"Delicious. Better than anything you could order in town."

"I'm glad you think so."

"I tell everyone," the director continued, "we have the best food services staff around."

My mother smiled without warmth, nudging a wisp of hair that had escaped from her long braid back behind her ear. Around her nostrils and right eyelid, a patchy red rash looked flaky and inflamed. No makeup, but that was standard. A pair of earrings I'd never seen before, iridescent disks made of bone or shell, flashed when she shifted her body, passing the bag she still held from one side to the other. "That's nice of you."

"I'd rather do my meetings here! All my breakfast meetings. No need to drive off campus."

"But not dinner," my mother joked.

"Well. Not until it comes with wine."

Both women laughed.

"I'll work on that," my mother said. The bag by her feet had absorbed water up to the Gordon Food logo; when she lifted it, the heavy thing inside would probably fall out.

"Yes, let me know who to petition!"

"See you around, Will," my mother said as the director and I headed for the door. I heard something tumble softly to the floor as we left, my mother's irritated hiss, but I didn't turn to look.

The director and I shuffled along a path in the snow that cut, diagonally, from Warren across the campus mall to the administrative offices. The students, she said, were bright creatures, but they could be demanding. Boundaries would be necessary, she told me, and then pivoted to Rosendale's storied reputation as a home not just for artists, but for *teaching* artists, and her own early years as a tutor, when she served as the faculty adviser for two student publications, the student reading series, and an unofficial novel club. One of those students, she said, went on to write a bestselling fantasy series. I must have read a thousand pages that first winter alone! She also wanted me to remember that they were teenagers, away from home and often—they were writers, after all!—dealing with personal challenges. They could sometimes get confused about the tutor/student relationship. Imprinting, she said. A little is good, even helpful, pedagogically speaking. Too much, on the other hand! I'd gone with her into the hallway, a long corridor with admin offices on one side, math and science classrooms branching off the other. We stopped outside the door to a conference room.

"That reminds me," she said. "I forgot the main purpose of our chat!"

I thought I knew what was coming. She was going to bring up Lili's article, try to feel out whether we were, definitively, in alignment. Some story about Nathaniel as a caddish teen, scaling the amphitheater and reading Proust out loud to the ducks. Some comment about girls and boys, mixed signals, how some of this stuff—don't you think?—has been a little overblown.

"Forgive me if you already know, but I've just gotten the wonderful news. We've invited him for years, and I'd pretty much lost hope, but—stars, again!—our Nathaniel has agreed to be the visiting writer this term."

I looked at her. "I—"

"No, no, no," she said, misunderstanding the look on my face. "He's not dislodging you from your new role, of course not. For our *reading* series. Just a couple of days, an evening event and an afternoon workshop. March, the week after spring break. Marvelous, right? Of course, you'll do the introduction."

I remembered now—I'd turned down the invitation for him before. It paid five thousand dollars (one thousand less than my stipend for the semester), plus transportation, meals, and accommodations at the campus hotel. The invite came every couple of years. Nathaniel always said no without even thinking about it. He must be desperate. And in the wake of Lili's piece, the Selden Foundation was probably just the tip of the iceberg in terms of canceled speaking invites. Desperate, yes.

Plus, I was here.

Very carefully, I said: "How nice. But, forgive me for asking this, I do wonder—is it the best timing? Given the—optics."

"Optics? Wilhelmina, dear, look around. We don't deal with optics and Twitter fights of the month at Rosendale. We deal with *literature.*"

"But, the students—"

"It will be a teaching moment," she said. "We like to lean into complexity here."

2

It has been a long day, my mother texted. *And I still need to run a few errands. We will do dinner another night this week.*

I'd dipped into Warren for just a few minutes, filling a Tupperware I'd found in my residence with the same whitefish filets Rosendale had been serving once a week probably since its founding year. The tables were only half full—most of the students, it seemed, were arriving the day before classes. Benji and the girl I'd seen him with that afternoon were sitting in the corner with a large kid, his hair buzzed close to his skull and shaved entirely in swirling patterns above his ears. My mother appeared and disappeared every few minutes, moving in and out of the swinging doors that separated the kitchen from buffet lines. I grabbed some more fruit and filled a ziplock with hunks of tofu, stuffing all of it into my backpack.

Instead of my residence, I took the food to my office. The writing house was still unlocked, hulking in the winter dark, and cold inside. All the Rosendale writers eyed me from the walls—there was Nathaniel, surrounded by other white men, except for the gardener woman—as I climbed the stairs. In my office, I found a space heater in the corner left behind by the tutor who really worked here, and I turned it on high. I ate everything and then took two of the vitamins I'd purchased around the time of the Selden Awards.

My credit report was a confusing mess. I took a screenshot and sent it to Dev. Some of my medical debts—the oldest ones, it seemed—

had vanished, though Google assured me I still owed the money. My student loans were in default, but I had a plan for those. *Pretty sure they can't garnish your wages unless it goes through a court,* Dev texted. *Relax and try to enjoy having a normal job. This is good. This is growth.*

Northern Michigan University would take all but three of my credits from Barth, and everything from QCC—that left me two courses shy of a bachelor's in communication studies, and multiple online options would meet the degree requirements. I signed up, then and there, for New Media Literacy and Introduction to ASL, and registered for a payment plan. Classes would start at the end of January and were mostly asynchronous. Then I searched, as I had a million times, for information about abortions in Michigan. They were legal up to twenty-four weeks, though recovery was more complicated the further along I got. I'd have to miss class. I'd have to tell my mother. I didn't have any moral qualms about abortion—but the process made me uneasy, how the evolving cluster of cells would now require surgical removal. Why had I let things go so far?

Nathaniel's university email password didn't work. I tried a few important dates, mashups of old titles, exclamation points added to the original one. Nothing. I hadn't yet felt anything at all, except for sick, though I'd just crossed over into the second trimester. Even when I was throwing up, the pregnancy felt as unconnected to me as if it were happening to a stranger. I entered my conception date into an online calculator and looked at the date on the screen: June 26. Two months before Rosendale's fall semester. Six months from now. Almost July, my favorite month in Michigan. A summer baby, like my mother. Nathaniel's. I didn't think he would dispute paternity, but if he did, I could get tests. There would be child support. I couldn't imagine him wanting to be involved in any other way—he'd told me when he found out Maxwell's mother was pregnant, Nathaniel's first impulse was to change his name. And of course, he was old, and we both knew his memory was failing. He'd never leave his apartment and if I entered that place again, sat down on that cursed leather couch, I would dissolve, I knew, dissolve right into those worn leather cushions until I *became* the couch, a permanent fixture, something for him to sit on and fuck on and fart into, a few paragraphs of context in the closing chapters of the story about his life. I didn't want to do it with him either. Did I want to do it at all? I'd been so focused on writing, on Nathaniel, I'd hardly ever thought of children.

Of all the choices I could make, it was the one my teenage self, whom I could still see, skulking in hall just outside my office with her nose in some random chapbook, would find most unforgivable. A woman, not even thirty, without a partner or a stable job or a permanent place to live, without a college degree, in debt up to her ears. The oldest, most bogus cliché in the book: Baby as doorway to a new life. Or: Woman takes what she can get. Or: Woman, faced with unscripted independence, closes door to trap of her own making instead. Or, worst of all: Woman becomes her mother. It was like something Nathaniel would write. How horrified that girl would have been—the great poet wasn't her father, but her *baby's* father. And the great writer would represent something entirely different to the baby, who would go searching just as I had, find out all the things the man had done. Because the baby would know what I hadn't. I had done almost everything wrong, but I could start there, do that part right. Tell the truth.

Such a final, permanent connection to him, a map drawn in bold from this very building, decades earlier, to the person growing in my uterus. Fate, et cetera. Was it possible part of me didn't want to let that go? Proof, in its way, of all that was between us. Not very fair to the baby. And could I spend another eighteen years cashing his checks? I knew what I was supposed to want. What the kind of woman I admired would do. Lili, someone like her. Choose myself, with or without the baby, refuse Nathaniel's scraps, turn away from him forever.

But maybe there was another way to see it. Or maybe I was another kind of woman.

It was 5:49 P.M. Nathaniel would be eating dinner soon; thoughts like these were automatic. Quincy Women's Health was open until six. I called, spoke to a nurse, told her I need to make an appointment, that I was almost fourteen weeks. After we set the time, I texted my mother again. *I have an important doctor's appointment on Friday. Can you leave work early to take me?*

I can try, she texted back.

On my way out, I stopped by the library alcove where I'd first found Nathaniel's poems. The back issues of *The Rosendale Literary Review* were as I'd left them, fifteen years before. Nathaniel Fellow, 14. The poems were accomplished, especially for a kid, but within a few minutes they repelled my attention. Student work, as Nathaniel would say, the paint still wet. I'd been such a silly, vulnerable, open girl. How lovely, how disappointing, to be so transformed by something so mediocre.

If only there'd been more teenage girls in those pages. Maybe then I wouldn't be standing there in the dark, reading the same old books.

3

I taught two classes a day, four days a week, and was mostly done with prep and teaching and unofficial conferences by three-thirty or four. I'd inherited both classes from the tutor: a poetry workshop, and a seminar on writing about the environment (for that one, I had his syllabus).

On my first day, the students in my poetry workshop, all twelve of them, were already seated at the seminar table when I entered three minutes before class started. Even in their uniforms, they each had taken pains to stand out, and these little flourishes of expression endeared them to me immediately. Benji, a ribbon of inked hearts descending, now, from his tear ducts, was in the place immediately to the right of the empty chair at the table's head. My chair. Not in the back or corner, but right at the center. When I sat down, I half expected one of them to begin. "This is a special place," I offered, after realizing no one else was going to speak. "And I am very glad to be here with all of you." A surge of panic rippled through my bowels. When class was over—intros, mostly, Leah had called it a "freebie"—I darted to the bathroom on the second floor, turned on the faucet full blast, and prayed one of my students wouldn't come in. It would take almost the entire semester before I could teach without panic-shitting before or after class.

But the students! Even their intro prompts—I'd asked them to write, in whatever form they liked, about something they believed in wholeheartedly—were disarming and genuine and distinct. Though they were all eager for my enthusiasm, casting glances my way as I listened, waiting for my verdict before speaking, they didn't seem self-conscious in the slightest, and turned to their notebooks with a focus and excitement I hadn't felt while writing since my Saturdays with Lili. When I asked them what they liked to read, they named E. E. Cummings, a dystopian YA series I'd never heard of, Mary Oliver, the liner notes from Beyoncé and Taylor Swift albums, *Middlemarch*.

In the second week of class, the Wednesday before my appointment, I took them on a trek through the meadow and asked them not to speak for the entire thirty-five-minute walk, to pay attention, using all five senses, to the details offered up by the world around them. After, sitting in the gathering space in the writing house, Nathaniel's portrait as present in the circle as another student—I asked them what they'd observed.

Nathaniel wouldn't have liked the nature walk—fluff, not real work—but he would have appreciated the intent of the exercise, which was to emphasize attention as the first step to a poem. He'd taught me that, and as much as I wanted what I did here, with these students, to be different from everything I'd absorbed from Nathaniel, it was, in the end, the thing I loved most about writing: the turn from what you thought you saw to what you *really* saw, the act and art of looking, and looking again.

A girl with pink hair and gauges in her ear—Mel, I remembered, still learning everyone's names—spoke first. "There was a sock on the ground."

"Okay," I said. "Where on the ground?"

"In the snow? Right before we crossed the street to head into the woods."

I waited. Mel looked at me. "Anything else?" I prompted. I sort of knew what I was after, but also, I was making it all up as I went along—teaching, in my very limited experience, was wild like that, one person riffing while everyone waited for the point. "What kind of sock was it? Was it wet or dry? Buried or resting on top of the snow? Did you get closer to look? Was it there when we walked back?"

Mel tapped her pencil against her notebook. "It was one of those totally generic socks from the big packs you get at, like, Walmart. White with a long ankle part. If I picked it up it would have been the size of my whole forearm." She stuck out her arm to prove her point. Of all the ways Nathaniel would haunt me forever, this was the stupidest: via sock. "When I think about it, it was dry, and pretty clean, too, like someone had just dropped it, poof, out of the sky."

"Did anyone else notice that?"

"I noticed different things depending on where we were," said Lane, the quiet, serious girl I always saw walking around with Benji. "On the trees, when we got to them, the lichen on the bark reminded me of my mom's lace tablecloth, the one she never uses except for superspecial occasions. And in the meadow, the long grass poked up out of the snow in places like hair. Or, not real hair—but like a drawing of hair, a child's drawing. All stiff and spiky. And the further we went from the campus buildings, the more it smelled like woodsmoke."

"Lovely," I said. I could feel the room wondering, with me, what I was after with this. "What do you guys think I'm after with this? Can you feel a poem here, in the sock, maybe, or in any of these things you noticed? Some special resonance?"

"I noticed the sock," Benji said. "The toes were kind of dirty. Someone had definitely worn it." He was sitting with his legs over the armrest of his chair, and he began the complicated process of shifting until he was cross-legged and upright. This, somehow, indicated that he had more to say, and we watched him quietly until he was ready. "So I mean, yeah. I can. At first it just seems like details, details, details, but when you look close at each one, they are really a bunch of questions."

"Say more about that, Benji."

"In the kind of like—" He groped around for the word, making a gesture with his hands as if trying to tie something together.

"Intersection?" said Lane.

"Yes! The intersection!" I had no idea why she'd guessed that based on what he said and felt a bit awed by their connection. There was something about them—his pretty androgyny, her brainy confidence, the opacity of their friendship/romance—that reminded me of my first impressions of Reg and Lili. Or maybe I just missed them both. "Between the details, the concrete parts, and the questions—that's where the poem lives. Because, I mean, how did it get there?"

"I like that," I said. "Between the concrete details and the questions they inspire. What are some of those questions?" They chimed in as a group. Who took the sock off? Did they walk without their shoes through the snow? Hopping on one foot? Or did it fall from a bag? How could the person have missed it? Where is the other one? And why, I thought but did not say, was the sock they described exactly like the spare pairs Nathaniel kept in his office? Was I teaching them about poems, or stories? I didn't know, but they'd run out of questions and were staring at me. "Let's write. Take ten minutes. Pick up something you noticed on our walk and shake the poem out of it."

When the timer beeped, I asked them to share. Every single person except for Lane wrote about the sock. Scary, a little, how easy it was to get them to do what I wanted.

After class, Benji appeared in my office doorway. "Can I help you?" I asked, and he came right in, dropping a candy bar wrapped in fancy paper on my desk.

"I know you're into chocolate, and my mom sends me like nine hundred of these a month."

"How did you know I liked chocolate?"

Benji grinned at me like, silly Will. "You told us on Monday. Right before class started."

None of them had clocked any of the things from my own list—not the footprints near where the sock was found, not the ice cream wrapper right smack in the middle of the meadow, not the hawk that had plunged off the storage shed, disappearing into a snowy thicket. But they often seemed to be, in their distorting way, paying very close attention to me.

4

The appointment at Quincy Women's Health was at four forty-five P.M. on Thursday, an hour after my last conference, about three hours before the end of my mom's Thursday shift, but she told me she'd gotten cover for dinner service. She pulled up in front of the writing house, still wearing her uniform. I slid into the passenger seat and shut the door. The air was dense with air freshener, a psychotic vanilla odor that coated my throat. I rolled the window down, and my mother rolled it back up from her side.

"Too cold," she said.

"Mom, please. It *smells.*"

"Women's health, Will? Your first week here you urgently made an appointment for a pelvic exam?"

I didn't say anything. It was already almost fully dark, the streetlights on, and I was glad we couldn't see each other.

"It's not for a pelvic exam."

"I know," she said. Underneath the air freshener, stale deodorant, her sour work shoes, dinner leftovers—for Tray, probably—in the back seat, something tomatoey. I was one week more pregnant than when I'd made the appointment. Each week was a step, vanishing as soon as I took it, thirteen, fourteen, fifteen, until thirty-seven, thirty-eight, thirty-nine, forty, no easy way to head back down, begin, again, at zero, with all its possible futures. It wasn't my fault, or Nathaniel's fault, or even my body's. It was just time, pressing down.

In the parking lot, we sat for a minute in the car. "Do you want me to go in with you?" my mother asked, and though I'd anticipated this, planned, already, on telling her no, I said yes.

The doctor's office was the same as all doctors' offices, everywhere: fish wheeling through the tank, thank you notes taped to the walls, middle-aged lady behind the reception desk glass, typing away. In the windowless exam room, I took the patient's chair, my mother, a folding chair in the corner of the room beside the bin for hazardous waste. The doctor was a woman—a relief. I'd asked for first available, but I'd learned from my years of hospital visits that women were usually better. I was behind on certain recommended tests, given the father's age—when I said the number, my mother flinched, and even the doctor looked surprised—and needed blood work immediately. She asked about my medical history, and as I talked, I realized I hadn't had a single heart episode since arriving at Rosendale, my longest stretch for years. "That happens sometimes," the doctor said. "Pregnancy tends to make things like WPW much worse, or much better. I know a wonderful electro-cardiologist. When the time comes, I'll give you a referral." Abortions were legal in Michigan until twenty-four weeks, the doctor confirmed, but they didn't do second trimester abortions at their clinic. She handed me a printout with some phone numbers and addresses. Every clinic was downstate, the nearest a four-hour drive away. My mother didn't speak. The rash near her eye had migrated down along the right corner of her mouth, and every now and then she knuckled it. When the doctor rolled the fetal Doppler along my belly, we all listened together to the insistent whoosh, stronger than the sound I'd heard before. "One fifty-six," said the doctor. "Beautiful." That meant very little to me, but when I glanced at my mother, her eyes were wet.

We didn't talk when the doctor left the room, in those long minutes before the nurse arrived with a flu shot. We didn't talk in the car, the first twenty minutes or so of the drive, the darkness as thick between us as a wall. Finally, as we passed the gas station that marked the final stretch before campus, my mother said, "I'll drive you to the clinic. Just give me a week or so notice, so I can get the time off work. I have days saved up."

"Okay," I said. I tilted my head onto the icy glass, just as I had at eighteen, tired from wiping down toilets, heading home to my bedroom, where the laundry my mother still washed for me was always folded in a basket just inside my door. "Mom," I said when the Rosendale sign filled the windshield. "What if I don't go?"

"What do you mean?"

"To the clinic. What if I don't go."

"You want to keep it? What would you—"

"I know. It makes no sense."

"No, it doesn't." We were in front of my residence now. I'd left the dining room light on, and through the window I could see a snapshot of someone's small and peaceful life. Piles of student poems on the dining table, bananas hanging from the fruit basket, the book of Louise Glück's poems I'd left split open, right beside my crumby egg plate from breakfast. No baby, no partner, just a woman, alone. I longed for that life even as I raised my arm to throw a rock through the glass. "But you really don't need to explain it to me," my mother said, picking up my knit gloves from the storage compartment between us and balling them into each other. She tossed the soft bundle, warm from her hands, onto my lap. "I understand."

But I already knew that, didn't I? Of course she did.

His name was Albert Korhonen. He was thirteen years older than my mother. She'd been lying when she told me she'd forgotten his name. I was right, at least, about that.

She'd been new to the area, living in a spiderwebby studio above a sandwich shop in downtown Quincy, that smelled day and night of peppered beef. Twenty-two. She'd moved there from Grand Rapids, where she'd lived with her mother's sister after her parents died in a car crash when she was seven. For five years, before her aunt took her in, my mother had been in foster care; I knew about her parents, her aunt, but she'd never told me about foster care until that afternoon in Greening, the first Sunday in February. We met at home—at her house, that's how I thought of it.

It was smaller than I remembered, my mother's house. I hadn't been inside since the day I left for New York. When I came back for Janet's funeral, I hadn't even driven by. There was the gravel driveway, the cracking concrete steps to the door, where I'd once tried to wipe off my name in chalk; there was the doorknob, an object I'd never had any special reason to notice but was as familiar as my own hand; inside, the same coat organizer from Meijer, a new photograph of a field of lavender, the same faux suede love seat backed up against the front window. The same smell. The stairs up to the second floor, which consisted only of my mother's room, newly carpeted; and through the kitchen, my room, the door closed.

I sat with my mother at the dining room table, also the same, draped with a cloth that was white and crisp and new. The same smell; her smell. I didn't see anything of Tray's.

"Where's Tray?" I braced myself. I'd come there ready to sit next to him at her table, to make small talk, to eat and leave. I could do that one Sunday a month—for her, I could.

"Not here."

"Not here?"

"We split up," she said casually, as if she were talking about a TV show, her weekend plans, not the dissolution of a fifteen-year relationship. She hadn't told me; I don't know why I was surprised, since she so rarely shared anything personal, but I felt I somehow should have known, should have sensed it, such a big shift.

"Oh, Mom. I'm sorry."

"It had run its course. Should have done it a long time ago." Had she done it for me? Because I was coming back?

"When?"

"Right after Janet's funeral." Not for me, then, for herself. Maybe that was better.

"Are you okay?"

"I forgot about the cookies," she said, and then she was up, moving around the kitchen, pulling cookies out of the oven and plating them and getting me a napkin and refilling my tea and wiping up a spill on the counter and turning on the faucet. When she finally sat back down, a cookie in her hand, I asked her again.

"Will, you always want to talk about feelings," she said. "Yes, I'm okay. The hardest part is deciding what to do. What comes after is nothing." She bit her cookie, very neatly. "He took a lot from me. But I don't want to think about him anymore. The day he left, I cut him out of my brain."

I would never be able to cut Tray out of my brain. The cookie was awful, too sweet, baking never my mother's strong suit. I took another. "Mom," I said. "He used to—" I found I didn't know how to say it. "Watch me." Out loud, it sounded like such a small thing. "Did you know?"

She was brushing crumbs off the table onto her plate. "He only did it once," she said. "I caught him outside your room—I kept an eye on him after that. I didn't want to worry you."

"Even after the trash bags? You didn't think I knew?"

"The trash bags were so you could sleep in," she said, stacking my plate on top of hers. "Your room gets so much light." *Once.* Anger boiled up—if I let it, it would eat us both alive. She'd known. Of course she had. Did she really believe that: once? I could tell her about the pictures; I wanted to. She thought she was protecting me; really, she was protecting herself. But—my heart broke, for both of us—didn't I understand why she needed to believe it? The window in the kitchen revealed the sky, the abrupt, secretive blue of a robin's egg; a gift, that sky in February. I would never, ever have to see him again.

"Yeah, it is bright in there," I said finally.

It wasn't forgiveness, exactly, but the anger changed. It was still there, but it wasn't for her, and for the first time since I could remember, it wasn't for me, either.

When I asked about my father, she seemed surprised. "You still think about that?" And then, as if she would have been happy to tell me anytime, she released the story. She'd chosen Quincy because she'd visited once when her parents were alive, a camping trip that was one of her happiest memories. She'd liked the lake. But the apartment was lonely, her job in the coffee shop was terrible, and at night she went out and drank too much at the bars downtown. She'd seen Albert a few times. Handsome and very tall, she said, you couldn't miss him. They were drunk, so drunk they got kicked out of two different bars before going back to her place. She could barely remember the sex, but when her pregnancy test was positive he was the only possibility. A small town. She knew of him, Albert Korhonen, the guy who ran the UPS store in the old strip mall between Quincy and Greening. Married, with twin girls, five or six, who sometimes came with him to the coffee shop where my mother worked and for whom he'd order warm milk with a dash of cinnamon. When she saw him there in the days after their encounter, he looked at her so blankly she believed he didn't remember any of it, that he'd been fully gone, blacked out. She'd had an abortion when she was seventeen—this shocked me, from my Catholic mother, how matter-of-factly she said it—and she didn't want to go through that again. "I was very lonely," she said. "And a lot of my childhood I didn't have any parents at all. I thought one could be just fine."

He didn't know. Until she told me, nobody else did. Thirty years of silence; what had it felt like to hold all that in? She moved from the table back to the sink, holding our cookie plates, washing them and then the sink, rinsing the teapot and getting a towel on which to spread each dish. Setting everything right, in her way.

Before I left, I opened the door to my room. My twin bed, made up with the Goofy pillowcase I thought I'd lost in New York; my mother must have had another one. My desk, drawer filled with dozens of old poems. My window, where the sun streamed in, trash bags taken down. All these years, as if she expected me to visit any day.

The following Monday, after classes and tutorials, while my mother was still working dinner, I borrowed her car and drove to the old strip mall. It had experienced something of a revival since I'd been gone.

Before, the UPS store had been between abandoned storefronts, but now it was bookended by a smoothie place and a trendy workout studio. I didn't know what I was going to do, what I would say, if I would say anything at all. Unlike the last time I'd made this drive, I wasn't searching for a new life, a way out: I just wanted to see.

My father was standing behind a table taping up boxes, wearing a sunny blue polo with a cocked nameplate pinned to his breast. "Can I help you?" he asked, putting down his tape gun.

"Hi," I said. "Yes, thanks. I need to send a package to New York City, and I'm curious about what my options are." Face-to-face, he was a couple inches taller than me. Gray mustache, heavy eyebrows. His blue eyes were lively, the same shade as mine, maybe, under the fluorescent lights, a tick greener. I waited for it, recognition—biological or supernatural or whatever it is that might connect you to a person responsible for your existence—maybe even just the satisfaction of resolution. He picked up the tape gun, waved it at me.

"Well," he said. "That'll depend on a few factors. What you're mailing, how protected you want it to be, and how fast you need it to get there. If it's heavy. Box of sand, that's going to cost you." He laughed, as if he made that joke every day. And why not? I was a stranger, just like he was to me.

"Thank you," I said. "That's helpful for me to think about."

5

Two nights before spring break, just a week and a half until Nathaniel's Rosendale event, my doorbell rang. The woods were dark and quiet except for the intermittent slop of wet snow dropping in clumps off the trees, the skitter of squirrels bouncing from the roof to low-hanging branches. I kept my outside light off when I was home, and the nearest streetlamp was a hundred steps or so down the road, near where it branched off to campus proper. I closed the browser window—Lili's Twitter, still dormant, as it had been since the backlash to her article started—and put my laptop on the side table, moving from the couch to the door in a couple of steps. The bell rang again. Almost nine at night, and I was in leggings and a T-shirt, no bra. I grabbed a sweater from the coat rack, to hide my belly. The first person my mind went to was Tray. I cracked the door.

"Can I come in?" Benji asked. "It's really cold."

Without thinking, I opened it, and then he was inside, taking off his coat. He sat down on the couch, moving the pillow I'd used to elevate my laptop onto the floor. One of my bras was dangling off the back of a dining chair, and dirty clothes—the laundry was a long walk from the residence, and it *was* cold—were piled up and overflowing a plastic basket at the foot of the unmade bed. More dirty clothes were in the bathroom. On the floor, very near his feet, were the three poems for workshop the following day, not a mark on them. I liked to annotate them in the morning before class, but if he saw, would he think I phoned in my feedback last-minute? I swooped down and picked them up, holding the papers in front of my body like a shield.

"What are you doing here, Benji? Sign-in is in like thirty minutes, and it's at least a fifteen-minute walk back to the dorm."

He looked at the space next to him on the couch, as if suggesting I sit, but I backed away, choosing instead the dining chair with my bra. He pulled his legs up into his lap and buried his face between his knees. It took me a long second to recognize that he was crying. He wasn't in uniform, and there was a large rip in the back of his T-shirt, as if someone had cut it with a knife. His shoulder blade peeked out.

"Benji," I said again, gently. Alarm clanged through me. The baby fluttered in my stomach, trying out one of its brand-new limbs, the second time I'd ever felt it. "What's going on? Is there someone from campus I should I call? Maybe the director?"

He moved his head off his knees a few inches and told me no, emphatically, before crying harder. The right thing to do, human to human, would be to hug him. Or maybe pat his back? Would he curl into me on the couch? Would I have to *hold* him? I didn't move. "Benji?" If I said what I thought—that no matter what had happened, this was not the place he should be—he might not like me anymore, and Benji liking me had made class not only easier, but more fun. He was the beating heart of the clique of smart writer kids, and even when I said something dopey, if Benji nodded, or turned to his notebook to write something down, they all followed suit. He came to my Thursday tutorials every week, and sometimes dropped by other times, too. He tended to come at the end of my window, when he knew I wouldn't have another appointment, and often lingered, walking with me to the dining hall or to the library, talking about what he was reading or watching, things that felt class-adjacent, but weren't strictly connected to workshop. I liked him. He read everything I suggested, everything I mentioned, usually within days of it appearing in conversation. Probably, when all was said and done, he was my favorite, though I hadn't thought of it like that—but maybe I'd articulated it somehow. Not maybe. Obviously, I had. Why else would he be here, crying on the couch in what amounted to my bedroom?

His breathing quieted and he unfurled himself, putting both feet on the floor. They were bare. He'd worn boots, which were melting on the entry mat just inside the door, but still, it seemed troubling he'd walked the mile or so out here without socks. Something must be very wrong. He wiped his face with his forearm. "Do you have anything to drink? Tea or something?"

I didn't really see a way out of it. I got up, filled the electric kettle, dropped a bag of Sleepytime into the only clean mug I had left. When I brought it to Benji, it seemed cold to go back to the chair, now that he was sitting normally, so I wedged my body against the opposite end of the couch. He spent some time blowing on the tea. After testing it with a finger, he took a tiny sip. Sign-in was in twelve minutes. When a student didn't show within fifteen minutes of curfew, an alert was sounded, and a mechanism roared into place. Rosendale security sped off in their ATVs, scouring central campus and every spidering road. One would be by here, too, before long. Parents were notified, and eventually teachers. There'd been a brief footnote in my onboarding documents about students in private residences. It was off-limits, unless for a prearranged gathering that included the entire class. This, the director had told me, was a newish rule, due to some complaints. She'd put *complaints* in air quotes. But even if she didn't much care, it was hard to imagine a parent receiving a call about their missing child and then taking it in stride when he was found alone in the woods after dark with a teacher.

"It's my mother," Benji said, as if he'd heard my thoughts. "She's divorcing my stepfather, and—" His voice broke, and some of the tea sloshed from his mug. "Ow," he said, licking it off his hand.

"Forgive me for asking this, but isn't that not terribly bad?" Veiled comments in previous conversations had made it clear Benji did not like his stepfather. In his freewrites and poems about family, there were often suggestions of physical abuse—images of rough-knuckled hands, a bruise covered with thick concealer, a description of the first whistling breath after getting the wind knocked out of you. I'd made some assumptions—perhaps also because he related so to my novel—about why. I hadn't mentioned the violent images to the director. Every student in my class had written something with a red flag. I usually tried not to assume what they wrote was true. There was life, and then there was the thing you made out of it. But sometimes I was surprised by what I found in my brain, residing there as confidently as truth.

"It's a fucking catastrophe."

I waited.

"He pays my tuition. My mom says there's no way she can afford Rosendale next year. I'll be back in South Dakota. Right when it's time to apply to college. You know they only offer one creative writing class at my old school? If you want to write, you have to take it over and over. The teacher also teaches gym! There isn't even a club! A bookstore in town! I can't. I can't go back there."

"I'm so sorry, Benji," I said. Now that I knew he wasn't dying, he needed to go. But I could understand why the news was exploding his universe. Hadn't I cried for an entire night after my Rosendale rejection? Didn't I think of it sometimes, still? How different my life might have been? "Maybe there's something you can work out with the program, some special financial aid."

"I already have special financial aid. I have the max special financial aid. There's no more. My mom can't afford the difference. It's so selfish of her. Why couldn't she just wait until I was done with school like every other parent?"

"Your stepfather," I said. "I got the impression he's sort of a bad guy? Maybe it's good for her, for both of you. Things like that, the usual trajectory is bad to very very bad."

"It's not like he beats her! He's just a bully," Benji said, taking another gulp of tea.

Just a bully? I wondered what that word meant to Benji, and what it meant to his mother.

I tapped my phone, overtly checked the time. "I don't know your mother, but it's hard, the hardest thing in the world, to change everything. It's much easier to just let things go on as they are. I really doubt she'd do this without a very good reason." Seven minutes past sign-in. Campus security would be by soon. Should I flag a vehicle down? Would that be better than sending him out to dart through the snow, making him promise not to tell anyone where he'd been? "Benji, you need to leave. It's late, and both of us could get in trouble."

He put his mug on the ground. "Don't worry, I asked my roommate to sign in for me and we're on the ground floor. The windows aren't alarmed. Can I stay for a little bit? There's no one else I can talk to about this."

"No," I said. "I'm sorry. You have to go. We can talk about this tomorrow." I picked up his mug and took it over to my sink. "During school hours."

Surprise and then irritation moved across Benji's features. He walked barefoot to the door and dried the sole of each foot against the opposite calf before bending to slip on his boots. He stood, teary again. "Do you think I can be a writer? That I'm good enough? If I'm not here?" His face was splotchy, red patches crawling up his neck to his cheeks, his eyes pinned on me, desperate, real tears streaming from them. He'd asked the question so intensely I felt it in the room, a wild animal he wanted us to tame together.

"Oh, Benji," I said. He was sixteen; sometimes they seemed so smart, it was easy to forget. "You're the only person who gets to decide that." Was it true? I'd said it, but had I ever believed it for even a second? The animal disappeared. What would it have felt like to pick it up, give it something tiny to eat, right from the palm of my hand?

Benji shook his head, as if disagreeing, and stood lingeringly on the doorstep, half aglow in the snowy dark.

"Your coat," I said, handing it to him without making eye contact. I didn't watch him leave. As soon as he was down the steps, I bolted the door.

I got the biographer's email a few days later. I stared at it between classes. Opened it, closed it, opened it again. He'd included a PS. *I am trying to reach a woman named Geraldine Keene. If you have her contact information, might you put us in touch?* I searched her name in my inbox, and there she was: *Please delete this address from your contacts.*

I know who you are, I finally wrote to the biographer. I thought about sending just that. *We met at a party Nathaniel took me to about a year after I arrived in New York.* I deleted the sentence, replaced it with a single line: *I don't have anything to contribute to Nathaniel's authorized biography.*

I didn't give him Gerry's email. All this time, I'd felt her a few steps ahead. If anyone would understand the choices I'd made, wouldn't it be her? I could reach out. I felt almost entitled to her, as if, now that I'd finally left Nathaniel, I'd learn exactly how her story and mine mapped onto each other.

But in the end, I left her alone. Her story was hers to tell. She didn't owe it to me, or to anybody.

6

Early March, in Quincy, often meant snow, but the morning of Nathaniel's arrival was unseasonably warm, high fifties by nine A.M, when I walked through campus to the dining hall. The mall was flooded with Rosendale students in shorts and pleated skirts, coatless, their arms and legs pebbled with goosebumps as they roamed in groups from bench to blanket to picnic table, many of them seemingly skipping first period. "Morning, Will," shouted a girl I didn't recognize as first—Mel, in a minidress over a collared shirt, her pink hair in low pigtails. I raised my hand, and the girls she was with raised theirs, too, one of them giving me a funny salute.

I'd tried to get out of giving Nathaniel's intro, of seeing him at all. The second time the director brought it up, I said I'd forgotten she'd asked, what with all the onboarding details, and now couldn't possibly—how would I have time to do his work justice? That's great, she told me. You can just speak from the heart! I'd alluded to escalating stomach troubles—not exactly untrue—planning on some climactic catastrophe the evening before she collected him from the airport. But when I suggested the director do it—after all, they had a lifelong connection—she told me he'd requested me. She said it with gravity, as if it had been a condition of his visit. I knew there was no way out. In normal clothes, I was showing, so I'd taken to wearing extra-large sweaters from Meijer, blankety scarves I left unwound, hanging over my body. The baby was due in late June. The director had all but told me I'd be back next year—I'd even given her course descriptions, trying not to look at the box where I'd packed away the tutor's personal life, his misfortune my saving grace—but I hadn't signed any paperwork, and I wasn't going to tell her about the baby until the contract was submitted, even though I did not plan on taking leave. (My mother had put in for three months' family leave, and her request—after all, she'd been there forever—had just been approved.) I needed the job. Everything in my life depended on it. If I had to give Nathaniel's intro—yes, I knew I was a coward—I would. I'd read from his Wikipedia page. After, I would sit between him and the director at the restaurant, finish every bite of my free steak, and smile when I was talked to. One on one, I'd refuse to talk to him—this part was, admittedly, a little hard to imagine—and after forty-eight hours, he'd be gone. In June, his lawyer would receive a letter about the baby.

But in the end, the students saved me. I didn't assign any of Nathaniel's work in advance of his visit, but Lane, in her studious way, had checked out Nathaniel's first collection, his memoir, and one of his novels from the library before spring break, intending to read them all in preparation for his reading. Her mother, a Rosendale alum and a former copy editor at *The New Yorker,* saw the books on her daughter's bedside table and asked why she was reading that monster. When Lane told her he was coming to campus, her mother called the director's cell.

Lane got online. She read Lili's interview and then ordered her chapbook from the publisher. She searched "Nathaniel Fellow" on Twitter. She read every blog post, the write-up on the book websites, the long-form piece in *New York* magazine about toxic men in the literary world, among whom Nathaniel was just one of a handful named. She sent the articles to the writing students, and then to her friends in other majors. The last day of spring break, she emailed me, our entire poetry workshop on cc, asking if I was aware of Nathaniel's violence toward women, and if I would help them boycott the events. I told them, simply, that I was aware. But I had not—coward, again—felt myself in position to raise a fuss, given my tenuous employment status at Rosendale, and Nathaniel's long history with the program. And then, surprising myself, I asked them what they wanted me to do. After I sent the email, I wrote a note to the director, explaining that while I understood I was putting her in a difficult position, it was important to me—as a teaching artist—to support my students. I would not be giving the intro, for the reading or the workshop, and I would not attend any dinners or lunches with Nathaniel, or for him. She called me, breathing a little hard again. I imagined her charging down the main campus road, headed straight for me.

"I'm not rescinding the invitation," she said. "Can you believe, that's what they asked me to do? They offered a list of writers I could invite instead! The man hasn't been convicted of anything. I should have known when he told me about his job—"

"What about his job?"

She exhaled. "Are you two not in touch? Just yesterday he told me you're thriving here. They pushed him out. Forced retirement."

Forced retirement. For a man of his age, it was no tragedy, the least he deserved. But I couldn't imagine him without that place—his office off the secret annex, that whole thrumming world he'd built, a network of voices with himself at the center. All those years, all those books. Nathaniel, without students, sitting in the park with the birds, slowly forgetting how he got there. I wondered if the person who inherited his office would try to change the curtains, if they'd figure out how to unhook that infernal rod. Who would help him pack everything up, what they'd find in those boxes, all those letters and drafts, one loose, faded picture, my mother with her mouth forever open, ice cream inches away from her lips. How did this get here, they'd think, one of Nathaniel's girls, if they thought anything about it at all.

"I'm sorry to hear that."

"Yes. It's awful," she said. "He built that place. Anyway, I'm just calling to say I understand. The atmosphere in a workshop is important, and I don't want to put you in a bad spot. But I'll forward you his itinerary, so you two can find some off the books time to connect."

The itinerary was a Google Doc. The only people who had access were Nathaniel and the director, and now me. There was no arrangement for ground transportation from the city to the airport and back again—I usually did that for him and added it to the itineraries prepared by the programs that sent the invitations. I'd call up an old-fashioned car service, the same one he'd been using for decades. Most of the time, after adding the ground transport details for the program's reference (once he'd missed a flight, and after being chewed out by an admin person about his changed travel plans, I'd learned to share every piece of information), I made a separate copy in the font he liked (Times New Roman), printed out for him in sixteen-point font. He must not have a new assistant. It seemed very feasible, looking at the document, knowing he had to manage so many small details alone, that he might not make it at all.

But I underestimated him. Or, he'd probably say, I overestimated how much he'd needed my help. The morning of his event, as I filled my thermos with coffee, adding a few inches beyond the amount recommended for pregnant women, the director texted me:

Will! He's here!

All day, I hid in my office. I tried not to look at the window, even though I knew the director was keeping him off campus so he wouldn't bump into any students before the event. The students, led by Lane, intended to protest the reading; I was meeting them at five right outside the building. My door was open a crack and I could hear them in the lounge, laughing and shouting at each other as they sharpied cardboard signs. The director planned to take Nathaniel in the writing house the back way, walking from the parking lot to the meadow. Every time my phone vibrated, I picked it up in seconds, my hands trembling. The director, Mom, Dev, a meme, Mom again. Around three, a text, like a lightning bolt, from Lili.

Today completely out of nowhere
Ansel told me you are at the zoo

you probably don't want to talk to me
But Ansel says you're coming back right after you feed the penguins
so I guess I'll see you soon

I put the phone face down, as if it were Lili herself, looking at me. Asking, what are you going to do this time?

7

Benji's sign was the biggest. It said, in capital letters: NO MOLESTERS IN OUR BOOKS. Lane had printed out a black-and-white picture of Nathaniel's face—it was blown up from *Vanity Fair*, that shot in profile, his tense, irritated jaw—and taped it to her poster board, a red *X* drawn corner to corner. I stood with them, a little to the side. Instead of a chant, they'd decided not to say anything at all. Mel thought it would be more effective that way, their silence, their signs, their bodies spanning the entrance: silence, both in honor of the women who hadn't been able to, for whatever reason, speak up; and in condemnation of the institutions, like Rosendale, who perpetuated Nathaniel's decades of harm. I wasn't sure the silence could represent both things, but it was undeniably powerful to see them standing there, a group of thirty or so, writers and a spattering of kids from other majors, some faculty members, too. The students ranged in age from thirteen to eighteen. Eighteen; I'd been older than that, which had always meant something to me when I played our story back. No child. But the girls. They looked so young—a decade, at least, away from adult faces, adult lives. So much younger than me, and I still hadn't caught up to him yet, the age he was when I sat down with him on that leather couch.

I hadn't expected anyone to show up. Silly of me—Nathaniel, unlike every other writer I'd met, didn't have a single story of reading to an empty room. But the students had been so forceful in their anger; I'd believed in them, that they would win. The reading was at six. Ten minutes before, people started showing up. Men, mostly, roughly Nathaniel's age. When a teacher from the English department pushed by, a boy booed. A few administrators entered, too, and then a handful of fisherman-y guys from town, confused by the signs. Six came and went, and the students looked at each other, disappointed. They were waiting for Nathaniel himself. "I'm sorry," I said, wishing I'd told them. "I think he went in a different way. But I'm sure he got the message." A few sat down, backs against the big glass doors. It was freezing again, winter returning as if it had simply forgotten its keys, and they were still dressed in their outfits from the warm morning, bare knees raw and red. Lane rested her sign against the glass, picture facing inward. When Benji put his arm around her, she shrugged him off. The writing house glowed. From inside, faint applause.

I could feel him in there, behind me. I couldn't look. I had to. I didn't want to see him, to talk to him, to smell him, but I couldn't just walk away, disappear into the woods, knowing he was right there. I sent this explanation, somehow, to the baby as I drifted around the side of the building to the long, large patio with its double-wide windows. It was dark back there, under the overhang, and I pressed myself against the glass on the far side, where I knew I'd be able to see the podium. There he was. Nathaniel Fellow.

Behind the podium, he looked completely at ease. A faded denim shirt and jeans in a darker wash, Rosendale the exact right place for one of his outfits. He was reading from a book, not printed pages—maybe the new collection, those poems we'd found together, tucked in old notebooks, the ones I'd retyped for him, gotten back with his penned corrections, typed up again. When he read, he lifted it up, close to his face, straining to see. He put the book down, grinned, gesturing with one arm—a joke, to break up the poems. He always gave a countdown.

Don't worry, he'd say. *The rest of this will be quick. And painless, I hope. You see, I only have a few left to read.*

I moved my attention from Nathaniel to the audience. Because of my angle, the room appeared empty—no one had sat in the first three rows. On the wall, just above the empty seats, Nathaniel looked out from his portrait, almost thirty years younger, in that awful suit. When I stepped back, I could see both Nathaniels at the same time, the older one emphatic, moving both arms now, trying to say something very important to the other, something, maybe, only he would understand.

Nathaniel's Thursday workshop was canceled, but instead of filling my day with the usual tutorials, I told my students I had a doctor's appointment. On my way back to the writing house from an early breakfast, just as I crossed the mall, I saw Nathaniel and the director walking in my direction. The mall is a wide expanse, dotted with bushes and gnarled, shrubbish trees; there's nowhere to hide. I'd gone early so I wouldn't run into them, but there he was anyway, as, for me, he'd always been.

"There she is," the director shouted, waving. "We've been looking all over for you."

The director wanted to walk faster than he did, or could—maybe his knees were acting up, from the flight, or the long car ride, or the bad bed at the Rosendale Inn. She'd get a couple of steps ahead and then wait, hoveringly, for him to arrive at her side. He carried nothing, wore the blankety wool jacket he hadn't replaced in seven years. I think the director expected me to rush to them. He looked very small from far away, and, as the distance between us halved and halved again, very small from up close. On his right cheek, among the other creases, a fading imprint from last night's pillow.

"Wilhelmet," he said without any sadness or anger, but maybe some surprise. "You look so much like yourself."

"Helmet?" said the director. "That's a funny name."

"So do you," I said, though he didn't.

"She's doing a terrific job. A stroke of luck for us, your call last year."

"Of course she is," Nathaniel said.

"How did you ever find her?"

Nathaniel looked at the director like he had no idea how to answer the question. A small brown bird landed a few feet away, battering a seed in the dirt.

"It's an interesting story," I said. "When I was a girl, I thought Nathaniel was my father."

The director glanced between us, confused. "Oh," she said. "Like your literary father. We all have those!"

"No. My actual one." There. It changed nothing at all, but now he knew.

The director waited, unsure if I had more to say. Nathaniel's eyebrows knit together, the way they did when I was not being good. As the words lingered, his face changed. "Ha," he said, the syllable, not a laugh. The director ran with it, convincing herself I'd been telling a joke. The bird fluttered closer, after something near Nathaniel's foot.

"An old friend?" the director said.

Nathaniel pulled a crumbled bit of muffin from his coat pocket, watching the tiny brown blur with an attention that, for him, was interchangeable with love. I could have said anything next, and he wouldn't have heard it.

"You'll have breakfast with us," the director told me.

"I can't," I said. "I have a tutorial."

"This early? Cancel it! Send the email right now," the director said. "Say I made you."

"I'm sorry," I said. "It's about to start."

"It's all right," said Nathaniel, rejoining us. "If that's where she'd rather be." The bird wheeled off above our heads. Nathaniel reached for my hand, the one that wasn't clutching my thermos, and held it between two of his. They were very cold; I felt my warmth bleed into him. "What a joy," he told me, "to see you looking so well." And then he let me go.

I stopped by my office to pick up my students' revisions, tucked into the plastic folder nailed to the wall outside my door. I gathered them up and arranged myself at the tutor's desk, my desk, empty now except for a bouquet of dried thistles, the lamp, a notebook where I'd begun, very slowly, to add one sentence to another. I could tell from what my students wrote what they had been reading. Lane had inhaled Lili's chapbook, carrying it around with her like a talisman. I took a picture of it on the seminar table, texted it to Lili. I read Lane's newest draft once, straight through. There, in the curve of a line, a clever little enjambment, was my friend. I could hear her plain. I picked up my pencil. Early still, and gray outside, the same endless winter I'd known since my earliest memory, the warm weather just a trick. My daughter rippled underneath my sweater, and I pressed her movement with a palm.

I read Lane's poem again, my pencil moving along the lines. Stopped.

Here! I wrote. *Right here.* This part sounds like you.

Acknowledgments

When I was very young and lost, writing workshops saved my life. I never would have had the guts or skill to finish anything without many wonderful, patient teachers who treated my writing with care and steered me toward the books I so desperately needed. If any of your kind words or good lessons got chewed up by my imagination and channeled into Nathaniel, please forgive me—it wasn't intentional, and I hope it in no way undermines your work or my gratitude.

Famous Men would not exist if it weren't for the MacDowell Colony. I wrote its first pages in Star and a draft of the true ending in Van Zorn, watching a bobcat mother stalk through the snow outside my window. Thank you, thank you, thank you to the staff, board, and donors of that magical place.

Claudia Ballard, I am fully convinced there is not nor ever has been a better literary agent in the business. I am the luckiest; thank you for all of it, forever. TK WME.

Andrea Walker, your belief in me is the stuff of my wildest dreams. Thank you for encouraging early notes, the time and space to find my way, and a vote of confidence I'll never forget. Caitlin McKenna, getting to work with you has been another fortune-changing stroke of lightning. Thank you for rolling up your sleeves—you got me here. Naomi Goodheart, thanks for being a dream reader and for your precise, intuitive edits. Erin Richards, thank you for helping *Famous Men* meet the world. Thanks to Oliver Munday for the terrific cover and lots of patience throughout that process. Thanks to Evan Camfield and the rest of the production team; thank you to Andy Ward for welcoming me into the fold; thank you to TK MARKETING; thank you to every single human in the Random House universe who has helped this book along the way. I am so grateful.

For financial and material support that made writing this book possible, thank you to the Ellen Levine Fund for Writers Award from the New York Community Trust, and thank you to the University of Michigan.

Thank you to every reader who read, shared, and/or reached out to me about *Marlena*. You kept me writing.

As my friend Gina María Balibrera says: "Books are made of other books." This one exists because of so many others. TK REFERENCES. And thank you to independent bookstores—my first job in books, and my favorite places in the world.

Thank you to Halimah Marcus, first reader, best reader. You held my hand through the hardest parts; if I wrote for anyone, I wrote for you.

Thank you to Rebecca Dinerstein Knight, for welcoming me into your inspiration for *Notes to New Mothers*. The fun I had making a book with you rubbed off on this novel in so many ways.

For helpful feedback and words of support, many thanks to Julia Pierpont, Cecily Wong, Yelena Akhtiorskaya, Gina María Balibrera, Lillian Li, Alana DeRiggi, Ali Shapiro, Colin Drohan, Kiley Reid, Julia Philips, and Marie-Helene Bertino. For friendship, good advice, and a place to sleep and work, thank you to Laura Aull and Jenny Blackman. Thank you to Lynne Raughley for the special food. Thank you to Kathleen Carroll and Sarah Kurz for porch talks and nutty kid dinners, and to all the Ann Arbor friends who fed us during the summer of 2024.

My dedicated colleagues at the University of Michigan and in the Helen Zell Writers' Program have inspired and supported me. Thank you. And thank you to my brilliant students; it is an honor to be part of a long conversation about what literature can be with all of you.

Peter Ho Davies, thank you for all your work on my behalf and for always reminding me what it means to do this job the right way.

Thank you to Brittany and MaryEllen for taking care of my children while I wrote. Thank you to Paige, Alejandra, and Stacey from the Spring Peepers room at NCCC. Thank you to the entire staff at Towsley Children's House, and especially to Jess, Sheila, and Skyla from Birch; Allie, Derek, Heather, and Sam from Oak; and Angelique, Darius, Evie, and Molly from Magnolia.

Mom, I could not have finished this novel or taught my classes or raised my children or washed my hair on a regular basis, if it weren't for your stability and organizational know-how and endless creative play. Thank you. I suspect you wish I'd write something easier, happier, less twisted. Until I figure out how, I'm grateful to you for accepting my imagination in its lightness and dark.

Thank you to Jean Luczkowski and Stephen Habash for your steadfast support. Jean, thanks also for introducing me to the work of Jill Ciment at a crucial point.

Gabe, I've lost track of how many times you've read this book, how many boatloads of perfect notes you offered, how many afternoons and mornings and weekends you whisked the kids away so I could poke around in a Word document. Thank you. Thank you for all of it, for our whole lives. I love you.

I wrote most of this book while pregnant and/or nursing, and in that way had two quite influential collaborators. Thank you to my children. You are the reason, and you are the joy.